Recipe for Rivals

ALSO BY KASEY STOCKTON

Contemporary Romance

Cotswolds Holiday

I'm Not Charlotte Lucas

I'm Not His Style

Love on Deck

Falling in Line

Cabin Crush

His Stand-in Holiday Girlfriend

Snowed In on Main Street

Melodies and Mistletoe

Snowflake Wishes

Regency Romance

Properly Kissed

Sensibly Wed

Love in the Bargain

All is Mary and Bright

A Noble Inheritance

The Jewels of Halstead Manor

The Lady of Larkspur Vale

To Forge Her Fate

A Proper Governess

Recipe for Rivals

AN ARCADIA CREEK ROMANCE

KASEY STOCKTON

This is a work of fiction. Names, characters, places, and incidents either are the product of the author's imagination or are used fictitiously. Any resemblance to actual persons, living or dead, events, or locales is entirely coincidental.

Copyright © 2025 by Kasey Stockton
Cover design by Melody Jeffries Design
First print edition: January 2025

Library of Congress Control Number: 2024925316
ISBN 978-1-952429-57-6
Golden Owl Press
Boise, ID

All rights reserved. No part of this book may be reproduced or used in any manner without written permission of the copyright owner except for the use of quotations for the purpose of a book review.

*For Sarah—friends like you take the pain out of moving.
Thanks for welcoming me to Texas so well*

And for Grandpa—our original cowboy

CHAPTER ONE

NOVA

ARCADIA CREEK LOOKED like something out of a 1950s movie. Idyllic homes wrapped in porches lined the road leading to Main Street, which was emblazoned with red and gold flags bearing panthers mid-leap—obviously the high school mascot. All it was missing was a parade down the center of the road with the mayor waving from the back seat of a red convertible. One word popped into my mind when I saw this place for the first time yesterday: quaint.

Ironic, since that's the word my ex most frequently used to describe me, a born and bred New Yorker. If I was quaint, this place was primitive.

I'd only been in town for twenty-four hours and already felt out of my element. The slow northern Texas twang was soft here, lilting, and entirely the opposite of the brisk New Yorker speech I was used to.

It was like stepping back in time, which I still wasn't sure was a good thing. Certainly not for Ben and Alice, who had been removed from an elite private school in Manhattan. Yesterday, I peeked at the elementary school they would be enrolled at down the road, and it was—you guessed it—quaint.

"Mom, can we get ice cream?" eight-year-old Ben asked, hanging onto my cart with both hands, his round brown eyes peering up at me. We were walking the aisles of the small town market, the wheel swiveling like a spasm every few feet.

"I want root beer floats!" Alice said, joining her brother's campaign.

"Gigi probably has ice cream," I told them, pushing the grocery cart away from the frozen foods aisle and back toward the snacks. Carter had always been a stickler for organic foods and avoiding high fructose corn syrup. It was important, he'd said, to keep our bodies clean from toxins and our kids free of harmful dyes. I tossed a box of Fruit by the Foot into my cart alongside the Captain Crunch we picked out earlier.

Ben shifted his eyes to me suspiciously. "Does Gigi have root beer too?" He'd jumped on Alice's dessert train, apparently. It wasn't often my kids joined forces and agreed. Usually their bickering forced them to opposing sides, where they each dug trenches and held strong.

It almost made me want to fold on the ice cream. A quick calculation of what I had in the cart proved I'd already spent more than I could afford by hate-buying the junk food. Besides, now I had to balance those choices with something better. "Let's swing by the produce again," I said, earning scowls from both of my blond-haired little sprites. I didn't know why they were so short when I was a solid five-foot-ten. No, I knew. They got their height genes from their dad.

Ben groaned, dragging his feet like I was forcing him to the dentist, but Alice skipped along, holding on to my cart and clutching her pink monkey to her side. It was one of those long-limbed stuffies with the Velcro paws that could fasten around her neck, but she mostly carried it around like a toddler on her hip, arms flipping about.

The aisle with household necessities like toilet paper and

Hot Wheels caught Ben's eye, and I groaned inwardly. His gaze flashed to me. "Can I look at the cars?"

"Yes, but we aren't buying any today."

He agreed, though I knew he was already working on his pitch to change my mind.

"Me too!" Alice squealed, following him toward the Hot Wheels.

"I'll get the carrots and be right back."

Produce was two aisles away and we were almost the only ones in the shop. We'd passed a tall guy looking at cat food earlier, but otherwise the only sounds were the tinny country music from the overhead speakers and a woman stocking soup cans. I'd never have left them in another aisle in New York, but this place felt different.

How many vegetables did one need to eat to reduce the harm caused by Captain Crunch and Fruit by the Foot? I threw a bag of baby carrots into my cart and searched the fluorescent-lit shelves for something else my kids would reasonably eat, something that wouldn't end up as brown soup in the veggie drawer.

Cucumber, maybe? Broccoli if it was cooked and doused in teriyaki sauce. I chose both of those and threw in some celery for good measure. I could maybe persuade Alice to eat ants on a log.

The kids and I had gotten into the habit of eating on our own at least a year before Carter asked for a divorce. He usually left for work before the rest of us woke and didn't get home until the kids were preparing for bed. I had still kept our meals to his dietary specifications on the off-chance he might join us but, by the end, that wasn't even occasional.

The end. It was such a dramatic way to look at the death of a ten-year relationship, but so fitting. Occasionally, while I was packing our things in New York to vacate the apartment, I found memories of moments that panged my stone heart. Things that made me nostalgic for the way he used to be in college. That version of Carter had disappeared by the time Alice was born. My kids only experienced the overworked and impatient Carter, not the one who used to text me ridiculous haikus about my hands and went out of his way to bring me my favorite pad thai on his way home from work.

My blood heated anew, simultaneously angry and saddened that I'd been forced to leave my life behind—my home, my friends, my brother, my husband…my *ex*-husband—and go at life on my own.

Passing an endcap covered in Pringles, I tossed a few canisters on top of the broccoli. Forget my budget today. Rage-buying junk food Carter would never see was the lowest form of revenge, but it felt amazing.

If he wanted a say in our children's lives, he should have fought for more parental rights. How easily he'd given them up made me see red when I thought about it for too long. He was supposed to get the kids for two weeks during the summer, but I had a feeling if I never booked their tickets to New York, Carter wouldn't enforce it.

The idea of sending my babies to him for any length of time might make me break out in hives. It was a new thing my skin was doing. Super attractive, especially during legal proceedings with my ex and the lawyer he was seeing now.

I could hear my kids talking, so I knew I had another minute before they missed me. I rounded the aisle toward the ice cream, wholly committed to this new junky version of myself, and nearly collided with Cat Food Guy. "Sorry," I said perfunctorily, moving out of his way.

He gave me a once-over so quick I almost missed it, then his face broke out in a wide smile, catching me off guard. He was one of the types who knew exactly how attractive he was, with a square jawline so sharp you could peel a cucumber with it. He was much taller than me, which was a feat in itself, and his arms were muscled in a way that was visible beneath his navy blue Arcadia Fire Department shirt.

This guy was exactly the sort of man who would have made Carter puff up his chest and flash his five-thousand-dollar watch to assert his manliness.

My eyes dropped to Cat Food Guy's watch. Plain, black, and looked like it probably came from Walmart.

Of that, at least, I approved. Mostly because I knew Carter wouldn't.

His light brown eyes danced with interest as they raked over me.

That was where he lost me.

My current status was: mom. Not single, not looking for love, not content being on my own, just *mom*. My kids took my entire focus right now. Getting checked out in the market gave me the ick.

I pushed my cart further away from him and scanned the ice cream for a good, cheap brand.

He came to stand beside me. "Have we met?"

"No," I said and kept looking. The prices were so low here compared to what I was used to paying in New York. It surprised me what I could get for under five dollars.

"You sure?" he pressed. "I know your face."

I quickly glanced down at his hand—no ring, so it probably *was* a stupid pickup line. "Let me guess. You've seen it in your dreams?"

He chuckled, the sound rich and warm like a dark chocolate brownie. "If I wanted to flirt with you, I wouldn't have started with that."

Noted.

I opened the freezer and pulled out the cheapest vanilla ice cream.

"You didn't go to Arcadia High, did you?" he asked.

I glanced at him. So he was from here, a born and bred

Texan. It wasn't a surprise. He had that slow way of talking the rest of them had, like he felt around all the words instead of spitting them out at maximum efficiency.

"I'm not from here." I started to walk away. "And if I wanted to meet a guy, it wouldn't be in the ice cream aisle."

He didn't get a chance to respond when I kept walking right out of the aisle.

Oh, rice. I would need rice if I was going to make teriyaki chicken. I peeked at the kids, found them still looking at tiny cars, and went to find rice.

By the time I found the rice, I remembered more things I needed for dinner and went back to the produce section for green onions and garlic. A loud crash echoed through the store. I dropped the garlic and ran for the household necessities aisle.

Ben was on the floor surrounded by blue Hot Wheels packages, his face beet red, and Cat Food Guy kneeling beside him.

Alice stood behind them, clutching her pink monkey and biting her thumb with wide blue eyes. At six, she was too old for that. I was supposed to stop it when I caught her—which was seldom as it was—but all I saw now was a girl halfway across the country from home and stressed about getting in trouble.

Cat Food Guy picked up the long silver hooks that most of the cars had probably fallen from. "It's nothing to be embarrassed about," he said to Ben. "I pulled the wrong orange out of a pyramid a few weeks ago and oranges rolled everywhere. Mrs. Jefferson was fixin' to swat me with her broom."

What was he even doing in this aisle?

"Who's Mrs. Jefferson?" Ben asked, starting to gather the cars. The red stain on his cheeks was already beginning to fade.

"Did you see the lady with the glasses in the soup aisle?"

Ben nodded eagerly. Had they not noticed me join them? I was surprised Alice hadn't run to clutch my legs already.

"That's her." Cat Food Guy lowered his voice while he slid

the hooks back into their slats. "She's been working here since I was a kid, and she used to chase us out with her broom when she thought we were up to no good."

"But you're a grown up," Ben said with wide-eyed fascination.

"I am, but she still scares me. You better believe I picked up every one of those oranges before she could fetch her broom."

Ben started picking up the cars faster and Alice joined him.

Cat Food Guy met my eyes and winked.

The *gall* of it. I knelt down and started picking up cars.

"Sorry, Mom," Ben said.

"Don't worry about it, babe. Just clean up your mess."

"We need to hurry before Mrs. Jefferson gets her broom," Alice whispered, panicked.

Cat Food Guy cleared his throat. "She's a nice lady," he said, seeming to realize he'd put fear into my children.

"I've got this," I said to him in a subtle dismissal.

He reached for another car and slid it onto the hook. "Almost there."

"Are you a firefighter?" Ben asked, looking at his shirt. "I'm going to be a police officer when I grow up."

"Why would you want to do that? They don't get to climb ladders or fetch kittens from trees."

Was that why he had five different kinds of cat food in his basket?

Ben looked thoughtful. "No, but I'll get to catch bad guys."

Cat Food Guy lifted a police car from the pile on the floor and handed it to Ben. "Cops are pretty cool." I had a feeling he was lying for the sake of my kid, which was oddly sweet of him. But still, I didn't need his help. It wasn't his mess, after all.

"Really," I repeated. "I've got this."

He glanced up, leveling me with honey brown eyes. He seemed to realize I meant it and got to his feet, lifting his shopping basket.

Cat Food Guy ran a hand over his jaw and smiled. "Y'all have a pleasant day." Then he moved down the aisle and selected a roll of paper towels before leaving.

Alice shyly waved, but Ben was staring at the police car.

He held it to his chest. "Mom, can I get this?"

"Not today. Finish cleaning these up so we can get on our way."

Ben scowled, but he obeyed.

By the time the mess was picked up and we'd reached our cart, I was on a one-track to get out of there. This errand had already taken twice as long as it needed to and Gigi was expecting me before the dinner crowd rolled in. It was our deal —she let me live in the apartment behind the diner, and I cooked for her diner. She planned to get me on a daytime schedule while the kids were in school, but tonight I was going in to be trained.

We made our purchase and carried everything out. The market was only a block from the diner, so we'd walked.

"Oh, ma'am," the white-haired checker said, calling to me. "You left this." She was waving a blue Hot Wheels package.

"We didn't buy that," I said with a smile. Ben was going to get an earful when we got home about not sneaking things onto the conveyor belt.

"Dusty left it for you. I was supposed to slip it in your bag, but I plum forgot."

So Cat Food Man had a name. Dusty. Was that really on his birth certificate? "You must be mistaken."

Her white eyebrow shot up. "He paid for it, ma'am. You might as well take it."

"For me?" Ben asked, his voice all breathy and excited.

"Go on then," I said, resigned. "Take it so she can return to the store."

Ben ran the distance and accepted the Hot Wheels car. When

he reached my side again, I could see it wasn't the police car I had been expecting.

It was a firetruck.

The sound that left my mouth was somewhere between a laugh and a scoff.

"There was a message too," she said, chewing her lip. "Something about considering your options."

"Alright, thank you." I adjusted my grip on my reusable grocery bags and ruffled Ben's blond hair. "Come on, guys. Let's get back to Gigi's."

Ben beamed, sending a twinge of sadness through me. It didn't take much to make this kid feel like a million bucks. This stranger had already given Ben more joy and attention than his own dad had in the last year.

My blood simmered, and it took great care to chill my breathing.

We skirted the diner and slipped through the alley leading to our building. It was a squat fourplex behind the diner, with tall metal stairs leading up to our front door.

A memory of Dusty winking flashed through my mind. Had he done this out of a warped sense of flirtation, or just to tease Ben about his current career choice? Which one of us did he want to consider our options?

"Don't open that," I said, before Ben could ruin the package.

"Why not?"

"Do we accept gifts from strangers?"

He looked bewildered. It wasn't something we'd had to go over before. "Yes?"

"No. We don't." I was glad he didn't immediately throw Halloween in my face. "Keep it wrapped up, please."

"But Mom!"

"Ben, we don't know what kind of person that guy was."

"But you let me take it!"

I had, hadn't I? Where was the manual now when I needed

it? *Divorcee 101: How to Handle Your Children as the Sole Parent. Subsection: Enforcing Rules.*

Sighing, I dropped the bags on the kitchen counter and looked into Ben's eyes. "Let me talk to Aunt Gigi before you open it, please."

Ben grunted in frustration and went off to his room, closing the door with force. It wasn't quite a slam, so I let it slide.

Probably because I hadn't *quite* turned the firetruck down yet.

Alice climbed up on the counter stool and peeled off the lid to the Pringles. I was glad she didn't throw a fit about not getting a car, too. She put a chip in her mouth, grinning around her bite, and I didn't have the energy to tell her to put it away until she had a real dinner in her. I reached over and took a chip, popping it in my mouth.

I'd been solo parenting for years now, so why had it suddenly become so much more exhausting?

Crunching down, I sighed.

"What's for dinner?" Alice asked.

"Teriyaki chi—" Shoot. Guess it was Pringles for dinner tonight, because I forgot the chicken.

Story of my life.

CHAPTER TWO

DUSTY

MARCH in north Texas meant the beginning of spring flag football season and planning for summer training. I was only the assistant coach for the high school, so I sat in on planning meetings, but most of my free time was spent with my younger footballers and their short attention spans.

When I wasn't at my day job, that was.

Station 4 was my home every few days for long, slow, 48-hour shifts. I loved my job, but it was never my dream to become a firefighter. When I had to fill out those forms in elementary school asking what I wanted to be when I grew up, I always had the same answer: quarterback for the Dallas Cowboys.

But we can't all be Dak Prescott.

So here I was, keeping my small town of Arcadia Creek from burning down and teaching the next Prescott how to land a tackle in my spare time.

Henry Gable sat at his desk, across from mine, tossing a football in the air and catching it. He was the high school's head coach and uncle to my best friend, Tucker Fletcher. Almost everyone in this town was related in some way to Tucker, and since the Fletchers had taken me under their wing when I was young and nearly abandoned, I felt related to the entire town, too.

"We need funds." Henry put the football on his metal desk with a thud and rubbed a hand over his face, leaning back in his squeaky chair. We shared a small office right off the boys' locker rooms at Arcadia Creek High School, which smelled of stale sweat and rubber. "The car wash didn't bring in nearly enough money last fall. If we're going to take the kids to camp this summer, we need to get thinking."

I spun my pen on my desk. "Do we have cost breakdowns? Facility, transportation, food, all of that?"

Henry's lips pressed into a thin line. "Yeah. Even with the car wash funds, most of our kids can't afford this camp on their own."

I quit spinning the pen. I was one of those boys in high school who never would've stayed on the team if it wasn't for the robust efforts of my coach—the worried man at the desk across from mine—and our fundraisers. Those summer camps were so important for the team. Not just for the skills practice and keeping the boys primed for football season, but also for the camaraderie and brotherhood they developed.

"We have a chance at state this year," Henry whispered, almost reverently. "Brody can take us there. He has the team spirit and the talent to lead."

"He's also a bit of a hothead," I mumbled. Watching Brody sometimes felt like looking into a mirror of my past, which wasn't a good thing. Both of us raised by a grandparent, both of us abandoned by our parents as toddlers, both of us alone, poor, and quick to throw a punch.

I'd turned myself around. My parents were in and out through my earlier years, but I'd maintained a steady, healthy relationship with my grandpa, and he made me into the man I was today. Him and Coach Henry Gable.

Ten years later, Henry still wore a scowl and puzzled over how to help troubled youth on his team. The man deserved a trophy. Or, better yet, he deserved to coach a team that took him to state.

Brody had a chance. I shouldn't be so pessimistic. If I could turn things around, so could he.

"I'll be thinking," I promised.

Henry sat up a little taller. "That date fundraiser your firehouse did a few months ago, you made a lot of money off that?"

My stomach tightened. I'd been part of a date raffle to earn money for the fire station, and Henry's daughter had won my date. She'd been into me for a few years, but despite how honest I was about my lack of feelings, Gracie Mae hadn't been able to take the hint. Or she'd flat out ignored it, which was far more likely. I'd been fairly blunt about wanting to remain just friends.

"Not as much money as the silent auction we did a few years ago," I said. "What about a bake sale?"

"We need to think bigger." Henry stared at the wall, his mind working. "What about another raffle, but we'll keep you out of it."

"No dates?"

"No dates," he confirmed, then his gaze slid to me. "Unless you want to."

I didn't. Nothing against Gracie Mae, but taking her out was only fun when I forgot I was her date. She was a good friend. I just didn't feel the connection that made me want to make her a girlfriend. I'd given it a solid effort over the years, but that sizzling, popping magic, feeling like I couldn't wait to see her again once we left—I'd never had that with Gracie Mae. She was a wonderful person and a thoughtful friend, but that was all.

Not like the automatic zing I felt in my stomach when I saw the woman in the market. She'd looked so familiar, but maybe she just had one of those faces. She didn't dress, talk, or act like she was from around here. The way she shot me down so swiftly left no room for misinterpretation.

Generally speaking, it wasn't a habit of mine to flirt with a mom—which was exactly why I didn't try. In fact, I was trying *not* to go that direction since I'd heard her talking to her kids. No one wants to get picked up in the middle of a grocery trip with two little kids in tow.

Or I imagined not, at least.

A knock rattled the blinds hanging over the door window. Gracie Mae pushed it open, her eyes falling on me for a full moment before shifting to her dad. "I brought you lunch."

"Thanks, sugar." His face crinkled into a smile, and he rose to take the bag from her, leaning forward to kiss her cheek. It smelled of burgers and fries from Gigi's, making my mouth water. "You staying to eat with me?"

"Of course." Her gaze moved to me, and she pushed her blonde hair behind her ear. "As long as I'm not interrupting."

I stood, stretching my shoulders. "I need to get moving, anyway."

"Be thinking about that raffle," Henry said.

Gracie Mae's eyes lit up. "Another date raffle?"

"No." Henry dug around in the bag and pulled out a foil-covered burger and fries. "Just a raffle. Maybe we can convince Gigi to provide dinner at cost again."

"She has a lot on her plate already," Gracie Mae said, pilfering a fry from her dad's red and white plaid paper boat. She ate it slowly, watching me. "Her niece just moved in, brought kids with her."

My ears tuned in to this. This had to be the woman with the children I'd seen the other day. Suddenly, it clicked. I bet she looked familiar from the pictures Gigi tacks to her register.

"I heard something about that," Henry said, taking a bite of his burger.

Gracie Mae wrinkled her nose. "Nasty divorce, apparently."

Those words, *nasty divorce,* made my stomach hurt. That woman did not need men ogling her in the grocery store.

"She probably needs a lot of support right now," Gracie Mae continued. "You're better off getting someone else to do dinner. Or make it part of the fundraiser? People can pay for a meal."

Henry tilted his head to the side. "Something with little overhead."

I rubbed a hand over my eyes, which made both Gables look at me. "Pancakes?" I suggested. "Or tacos?"

"Let's think on it."

"I'll start working on a list of who we can talk to about donations. Maybe we should do a silent auction this time, let people drive prices up on their own." My brain was already working out our options—businesses, parents, schools, small companies. There were a lot of people we could tap for donations. We should start putting fliers up to get the event on peoples' calendars, maybe spread word as far as Beeler. "I can pick a day and get it on the school's schedule so we know we have the gym."

"Sure, auction it is." Henry's thoughts had already moved on to his lunch, but he raised his face. "I'll put the deposit on the camp, then, or we'll lose it. We need to flesh out a schedule, maybe get a few parents on board and form a camp committee."

It was a good thing my schedule worked the way it did; I'd have time to do all of these things. I started my next 48-hour shift in the morning, so I planned to work on the fundraiser when all my tasks were completed at the firehouse.

"Let me know what day you choose and I'll get Sharon on the flier for us." Henry always pulled his wife in for our creative needs because she was much better than either of us.

"Will do." I gave them a smile. "Y'all have a good day."

I left them behind with a thunk as the metal door swung closed. Gracie Mae's red car was parked directly next to my truck in the otherwise empty lot. I pulled out of the high school's parking lot, making my way into town. I should've gone home, but the smell of Gigi's burgers made me realize how hungry I was, so I made a pit stop for lunch.

I parked and pulled out my phone to text my buddy, Tucker.

DUSTY

Meet me for lunch at Gigi's?

TUCKER

Can't today. Out on Alburn with Grady.

I sent him a thumbs up before ambling inside and letting myself into a booth right in front of the window, sunlight streaming in. Tucker was a lineman for Arcadia Energy and Grady was his apprentice. If they were out near Alburn Road, they were too far, anyway. Since Tucker's high school girlfriend came back to town last year and managed to get a proposal out of him, I hadn't seen him as often. We still got together, but he was much busier in general.

Which was fine. I didn't love June's return. She'd hurt him so much in the past. I was a tough sell on their relationship, but I was getting over it.

I would. Really.

Eventually.

"What'll you have?" Gigi asked, coming over with a tall glass of ice water and setting it in front of me.

"Bacon cheeseburger with a Dr Pepper, ma'am."

She didn't bother writing it down. Gigi fed me lunch most days. "Fries?"

I remembered Gracie Mae eating the fry slowly in her dad's office and the way she'd looked at me. "Not today."

She nodded, but her mouth was tight.

"Is something wrong?" I asked. "Anything I can do?"

Her face flushed, but she shook her head. "Nothing, sweet pea. Your lunch will be right out."

Well, that was strange. Guess Gracie Mae wasn't far off when she said Gigi had a lot on her plate. I pulled out my phone and found my calendar. A month was plenty long to plan an auction, right? Drafting an email to the building scheduler, I chose a day, threw in some alternative options to be flexible, and sent it off. Once we had a date and Sharon made the fliers, the rest would fall into place.

The bell over the door chimed, bringing with it the sound of kids chattering and a woman on the phone.

"No, that's not necessary. I'll—" She stopped, then lowered her voice. "I'll call you back. Yes, I promise. I just need that birth cer—okay. Sure. Bye."

My grocery store gal was here, by the sound of it. I glanced over my shoulder to see her toss her phone into her purse, frowning.

"The fireman!" Well, the boy had noticed me.

I shot him a grin. "Hello, future police officer." Then I looked at his sister, once again clutching that pink animal and dipping her head shyly. I offered her a smile, and she hid behind her mom's legs.

Her mom's *long* legs, hidden under baggy pants. *Stop, Dusty.* This lady did not need me checking her out again.

"Come on," she said to her kids, walking toward the back and utterly ignoring me. "Let's get started on this paperwork."

I faced forward in my seat again, pretending to be absorbed in an email on my phone, but this little family had my attention. A newsletter for a sale on cat beds did not.

"I don't want to," the boy whined. "I'm hungry."

The mom sucked a breath through her nose, ostensibly for patience. "Let's go and—"

"Nova," Gigi said, coming out of the kitchen with my burger. "Let me feed them."

Her name took me by surprise. I was expecting a Jocelyn or Rebecca or something else equally dependable-sounding. Nova fit her, though.

"You really don't have to. I need to finish these registrations, so I'll just hop over to our apartment and get—"

"Nonsense. It'll only take a minute to whip up a few sandwiches. You do what you need to and I'll take care of these two."

"Okay." Nova sounded more resigned than grateful.

So she wasn't living with Gigi, after all. She was living in the building next door. Gigi's house was down the road, wrapped in a porch and painted green, but she also owned the fourplex across the alley.

Gigi put my plate down. "Whoops. Forgot your drink. Give me a sec."

"No worries, Gigi."

She hustled the kids toward the counter and got them settled on stools, then went behind the counter to fill a cup with ice and Dr Pepper.

I lifted my burger and took a huge bite. Nova hesitated at the back door before approaching me.

I'd never chewed so quickly in my life.

"Thanks for the firetruck," she said quietly, her eyes on mine. They were dark brown, tunneling through me. "I checked with my aunt to make sure you're not a psycho, and you passed her inspection. But I would appreciate it if you didn't do something like that again. I had to talk to my kids about accepting gifts from strangers."

"It wasn't a *gift*," I said quickly, then sipped my drink. Hopefully she wasn't getting a whiff of bacon beef breath. "I was just trying to influence the next generation. You know, stop your son from making a mistake."

Her eyes sharpened. "How altruistic of you."

"I don't know." I shrugged, stretching my arm across the back of the bench. "Just doing my bit for society."

Her arms folded over her chest. "Your *bit?*"

Gigi stepped around her and set my Dr Pepper on the table. She eyed her niece. "Everything okay here?"

"Dusty was just telling me how selfless he is."

Nova knew my name. Not really a surprise, since she'd had to describe me enough to get approval from Gigi. Or maybe Mrs. Jefferson had given me away at the market. Either way, something about it sent a flush of heat through me. But I needed to keep a strong wall between us. No recently divorced mother, no matter how hot she was, wanted a random stranger hitting on her.

I dropped my eyes to my burger and took another huge bite. Nothing was sure to signal I wasn't interested more than eating like a sloppy pig.

She took the message and walked away. When I looked up and caught her daughter watching me from the counter, I winked.

Gigi frowned at me. A blush spread over the girl's little cheeks, and she spun to face the counter. Apparently I had a knack for driving the women in their family away.

Maybe I needed to take a break from Gigi's lunches for a while.

CHAPTER THREE

NOVA

THE FIRST DAY of school arrived, and I was woefully unprepared to drop my kids off at a strange new place. We'd been in Arcadia Creek for over a week. They should have started days ago, but getting them registered took longer than it should have, no thanks to my irresponsibility in somehow leaving Alice's birth certificate behind in New York and Carter's snail pace in sending it to me. The extra few days did nothing to soothe my nervousness at leaving them with all new people and new rules and no one familiar to turn to if something went wrong.

The kids sat in our empty living room, bundling up in sweatshirts, scarves, and jackets to make the trek down the street to the elementary school. I stood at the kitchen counter in sweats and an oversized Neon Trees shirt that was more than a decade old, trying not to fret.

"PB&Js?" I asked, laying out the bread and spreading peanut butter over two slices.

"I want ham and cheese," Ben said.

My smile twitched. "Then I'll need to go back to the store.

Can you eat a PB&J today and I'll make sure we have what we need for ham and cheese tomorrow?"

He looked disappointed. "Can't we take ham from the diner? Aunt Gigi has a lot."

"No."

"Why not?"

"Boundaries. That's not our kitchen or our food. Gigi has to pay for all of it, and she makes her money back when people buy meals. It wouldn't be right." I picked up the jar of strawberry jam and tried to open the lid, but it wasn't budging.

"But she made me a ham and cheese yesterday."

I moved to the sink and ran the lid under hot water. "Which was nice of her, but we can't use the diner as our personal grocery store."

"If she *wants* us to, I don't understand why we can't," Ben muttered before bending his neck to fasten the buttons on his jacket.

The jam lid still wasn't budging. I hit it lightly on the counter a few times and tried again.

"I like PB&J," Alice said, her head popping out of her sweatshirt. Her blonde hair was staticky, strands sticking out every which way.

"How do you feel about just PB?" I asked, straining against the lid with no movement. Would my children consider me unhinged if I chucked the jar on the floor just to watch it break open? Probably. Better set it down gently on the counter.

"*Just* peanut butter?" Ben asked, affronted as if I had requested he disassemble his LEGO X-Wing and throw away all the black bricks.

"It's all we have." I gave the jam jar one last solid effort before returning it to the fridge in utter defeat. It needed to be out of my sight. I wasn't a weak person, but looking at the jar hurt my feelings in a weird way, like the strawberry jam inside had meant to be unreachable. "I can't get the jam open."

Ben sighed. "Fine."

My entire body slumped. It was unfair that I was half a country away, justified in my frustration with Carter—especially after it took him *three days* to send me Alice's birth certificate—and still wishing with the smallest part of me he was around to open the jar of jam. The man wasn't home much to open jars in the first place, which was why it felt so unfair to wish he was here. No, not him. Just his arms.

It'd been over a year since he'd come home from work and asked for the divorce, then promptly moved out. We'd signed the papers quickly, moved through the divorce proceedings while I was still trying to figure out what was going on. Even then, I knew I'd have to leave the apartment to him when it was all finalized—it was rent controlled and had been passed down to him from his grandmother.

Me? I couldn't afford to stay in the city. I used most of the settlement money to buy a car and get myself and the kids to Texas, where Aunt Gigi offered to take us in until I figured out what I wanted to do.

Carter would've paid for half of the kids' private school if we'd stayed, but that meant me coming up with the other half and I didn't even have a job. It was never going to happen.

Now here I was in an apartment that smelled faintly of diner food, screwing up my kids' lunches on a stressful day, and I couldn't even open one stupid fetching jar of strawberry jam.

Alice noticed my defeat. "I think peanut butter sounds good," she said.

"You're just saying that," Ben snapped.

"No, I'm not."

"Yes you are."

"No. I really think it. I *love* peanut butter."

"Not by itself you don't."

"Enough, please," I asked, and the sharpness in my tone

worked. I finished the sandwiches and cut up apples to go in their lunch bags.

"Can I have school lunch instead?" Ben asked, then stuck his tongue out at his younger sister.

It was the final straw. I put down the knife and looked at him. His blond hair stuck up a little in the back and his brown eyes were so defiant, I didn't want to find any other reasons to put him on edge. This kid was nervous. I could see it in his challenging stare and closed jaw.

"Yes. You can have school lunch. Alice?"

"I want the peanut butter sandwich," she said, sitting on the floor and looking through the keychains hanging on her backpack. A few of her friends in New York had given them to her as going away presents, and my stomach clenched in response. I wasn't going to think about the fact that we still didn't have a couch, let alone a kitchen table, chairs, or real beds. We had lunch and school registration and I had a job. In the triage of my life, I couldn't let myself think about what I was lacking right now.

"Great." I pasted on some semblance of a happy face, tossed Ben's lunch into the fridge for me to eat later, and Alice's in her backpack. "Let's go meet your teachers."

ARCADIA CREEK ELEMENTARY SCHOOL, home of the Panthers, had the friendliest front desk attendant I'd ever met. Her hair was highlighted and curled within an inch of its life, and I was fairly certain none of her perfect teeth were real, but her smile when she welcomed us gave me a warm, buzzy feeling.

"The Walker family, isn't it?" she thundered when we entered the office, coming out from behind her desk to greet us. She had the kind of voice that didn't need a megaphone to reach across a room. "Welcome to our little school. We are *overjoyed* to have you."

I could sense Ben trying to make up his mind about whether he liked this woman or not, since she was nothing like the staid attendants he was used to. Alice had already begun to soften, though. Her hand still held mine with ferocity, but she wasn't trying to hide behind my legs any longer.

"I'm Ms. Corbin," she said, then crouched to reach the kids' eye level. Her voice lowered in conspiracy. "You both are so lucky—you got the best first and third grade teachers we have. When I read your transcripts, I knew right where you needed to be."

I glowed a little at this. "That was kind of you."

She lifted her eyes to me as if just remembering I was in the room. "Oh, don't mention it, honey." Her attention returned to the kids. "We want you to have the best experience at Arcadia Creek Elementary. Go Panthers!"

"Isn't that the same mascot as the high school?" I asked, unable to help it.

"These kids are Panthers now, and they'll stay Panthers clear until they graduate." She returned to the computer. "Let me see your driver's license and I'll get you in our system, Mrs. Walker."

"Ms. Walker," I corrected, fishing in my purse for my wallet. I retrieved my New York license and handed it over.

She put it in a scanner and clicked around the computer for a bit before giving it back. "If you'll follow me."

Ben's teacher was a young woman with curly black hair and a faint drawl. She welcomed him eagerly and showed us around the classroom. She had me write my email address on a Post-It note so she could send me everything I needed to know later. It was seamless. Ben waved at me as his teacher took him by the hand and led him through her back door onto the playground.

Alice's teacher, Mrs. Vick, was precisely what I'd imagined

Mrs. Claus to look like, with white hair drawn back and a rosy-cheeked smile. She spoke softly, ushering Alice toward her desk. "I've put you between Lily and Kendall because they are both very kind girls, and they have agreed to help when you need extra guidance. Do you want to come to the playground with me now and we can see if they've arrived yet?"

Alice looked at me.

"Go," I ushered. "I'll be here to pick you up when school is over."

She crushed me in a desperate hug that made the back of my eyes prick with emotion.

"We'll have a lovely day, Ms. Walker. Don't you worry about us," Mrs. Vick said, taking Alice by the hand.

I left the school feeling like my world was imploding, and I didn't quite know why. Cold air stung my nose. I reached for my phone, finding Carter's number like a reflex. It was ringing and nestled against my ear before I could think better of it.

"Nova? Is something wrong?" He sounded out of breath.

"No." I left the parking lot and walked along the side of the road. It butted up against the backside of the buildings on Main Street, leading directly to the back door of the diner and the stairs leading up to our apartment. Houses lined the opposite side of the street, with wide yards separated by chain link fences. "I just took the kids in for their first day of school. Everyone seems great. Alice's teacher is like a nice old grandma, which is perfect for our little girl."

He was silent. I heard what I thought was him powering off a treadmill. "You take them out of one of the best schools in Manhattan, drop them in the middle of nowhere, and I'm supposed to be glad their new teachers are nice? Honestly, Nova, I don't know what you want from me."

"Nothing." My hand clenched into a fist, my stomach dropping. "I figured you'd appreciate the update, but I can see it's not a good time."

He gave a long-suffering sigh. "Not really, no."

"Goodbye, Carter."

"Wait."

I was tempted to pretend I didn't hear him and hang up anyway, but I waited a beat too long to make it believable. "What?"

"Will you have the kids FaceTime me after school?"

"Sure."

"Great. Bye, Nova."

He hung up before I could say any more.

It took a tremendous feat of self-control to refrain from chucking my phone against the cold concrete. That would only hurt me. I didn't have the money to replace it.

I was still grumbling inwardly about the conversation when I let myself into the diner. Why did I even bother? He didn't care, not really, or he would've overnighted Alice's birth certificate immediately instead of waiting days to do it. The man had a secretary. He hadn't had to do it himself. Anything that helped him feel better about abandoning his family was fair game, I guessed.

The kitchen was empty except for Dal manning the stove, his salt and pepper buzzcut tucked under a hairnet, and Lacey leaning against the counter sipping a cup of coffee.

"Good morning," I said to them. "Is Gigi in?"

Lacey gave me a sympathetic look. She was half my age—or somewhere around there. I was thirty-one, and nothing teens said these days made any sense to me. This girl, freshly out of high school, was a whole different class, making her pity all the more painful.

I'd reached that point. I was aged.

"She's brewing coffee," Lacey said. "Want me to send her over once you're dressed?"

I glanced down at my clothes. Skinny jeans—I'd thought to change out of my baggy sweatpants before taking the kids to school after Ben had given them a wary once-over—and an NYU crew neck I'd had longer than I've known Carter. My hair was in a messy bun, already falling to the side. No wonder the elementary school staff was extra nice to me. I looked like I needed charity.

My pride reared its messy head. "I'll go speak to her now, but thanks, Lacey."

She raised her Gen Z eyebrows at me. Why did every young girl have incredible eyebrows these days? Be a kid. You'll be plucking for the rest of your life.

I pushed the door open, letting myself into the main dining room and straight to Gigi's side. Her familiar helmet of white hair and rosy smile soothed me at once.

She peeked at me before returning her attention to fiddling with the coffee maker. "Good morning, honey. Are the kids off all right?"

"Got them settled in. It seems like a nice school."

Gigi's eyebrows went up.

"Okay, not *nice facilities*, but the people are."

"They are," she agreed, though she sounded distracted. "Stupid machine's busted again."

"Can I look at it? Carter had a fancy espresso machine that was always giving us grief. I might be able to do something with it."

"I want you in the kitchen. Dal plans to show you how to do the chicken today." She hit something and coffee started pouring into the pot. "Success. I better take this. I have a thirsty table over there."

I glanced in the direction where she'd gestured and my eyes landed on Dusty. I couldn't help but look at his arms, the width of them a product—no doubt—of free time in the firehouse gym. All firehouses had gyms, right? Because firefighters were notorious for using their time off to lift weights and build that people-carrying muscle so they could do their job in emergencies. All I could really see when I looked at his biceps, though, was the jar of jam that evaded me this morning.

Dusty could probably have popped the lid off with a flick of the wrist. He had such jar-opening arms.

But those arms were none of my business.

He was seated beside a blonde woman with a couple across from them. It very much looked like a double date. Weird. "Breakfast date?" I asked.

"Planning meeting. That couple is getting married soon."

Which couple? Dusty and the blonde or the people across from them? "Should I warn them it's not all it's cracked up to be?" I muttered.

Gigi turned a sharp eye on me. "Did he make you cynical?"

He could only be Carter. My cheeks burned. I wanted to complain about the phone call I'd made that morning, but it wasn't a good idea. Gigi was going to regret inviting me if I stayed bitter. "No."

She hovered, holding the full steaming pot of coffee. "Get me a hot chocolate, will you? Extra sugar."

"What does that mean? Like extra whipped cream?"

"Yes, ma'am. Tucker only drinks sugar on top of sugar. The boy is going to need a set of root canals one day."

I pulled down a mug and got to work. By the time I finished piling on a mountain of whipped cream, Gigi had disappeared. I glanced around the room, but she was nowhere to be seen, and the double-date wedding planners were deep in conversation.

So much for needing me in the kitchen with Dal. I put the mug on a small round tray and carried it to their table. "Hot chocolate?" I asked.

The brown-haired guy across from Dusty lifted his hand, sending me a polite smile. "Mine."

I set it in front of him before turning away, avoiding Dusty's eye.

"Excuse me?" a woman at another table asked, her helmet of

dark hair in a perfect, round fifties-grandmother style. "Would you mind refilling my coffee?"

"Not at all," I said pleasantly and went for the pot. When I returned to her side, I glanced at Dusty's table again and found him watching me. A weird flutter went through my stomach. Averting my eyes, I smiled at the woman and turned to hide behind the counter. Where was Gigi? Why had she left me alone? I was supposed to be learning something about chicken, not developing a schoolgirl crush on the hot firefighter.

That thought sent off a chain reaction of ick and disturbing feelings. Gigi or not, I did not need to remain out here any longer.

I moved toward the kitchen when a deep voice spoke behind me. "Nova?"

The hair stood up on my neck, proving I didn't need to turn around to know who it was. Dusty.

CHAPTER FOUR

DUSTY

NOVA FACED ME SLOWLY, a tight smile on her mouth. She was the classical type of beautiful, one that didn't need makeup and neat clothes to stand out. She was rumpled, in skinny jeans and a crew neck and not an ounce of makeup, but still wildly distracting, making me second-guess my objective in approaching her.

Why had I come to the counter again? I knew it had to do with the diner, and not the fact that I wanted to speak to Nova.

Especially with Gracie Mae watching. I wasn't that much of a jerk.

"Where is Gigi?" I finally asked, remembering my goal.

"Do you need something? I can get it for you."

"Just her."

Nova narrowed her brown eyes slightly. "Food? More coffee? The check?"

"I want to discuss a fundraiser with her."

"Oh." She looked over her shoulder.

The door pushed open and Lacey came through, blowing a bubble with her gum and popping it in her mouth. The girl was barely out of high school, but somehow not intimidated enough by Gigi to refrain from unprofessional gum smacking. Young people were a different breed. Or maybe I was becoming an old curmudgeon and would soon be telling my little footballers how things were done back in my day.

"Where's Gigi?" Nova asked.

"On the phone." Lacey walked past both of us and started fiddling with the register. I glanced at the photo on the side of the register and recognized a younger Nova with her arm around Gigi beside a Christmas tree. The picture next to it was of her two kids on a merry-go-round, Nova standing between their plastic horses.

Nova's eyes slid back to me. "If you want to leave her a message, I'll be sure she gets it."

That was one possibility. The other was hanging around until Gigi returned. My head was spinning with all the wedding talk. Colors and food and where to find enough chairs and who would host the bridal shower and so many things that had nothing to do with me. As the best man, it was my job to throw a memorable bachelor party and make a speech, but the rest of it was up to the ladies. Of course, I'd lend my muscle to help in whatever capacity they needed, but that wasn't the same as choosing themes and deciding between peonies and lilies. I still didn't fully understand why I had to be here.

"Just pretend to talk to me for a second."

Nova's eyes narrowed further. "Is this a backward attempt at flirting? I'm not interested in reenacting a 90s romcom scene where the guy pretends to use the girl as a cover instead of just saying what he actually wants to say."

There went the final tendril of any belief I might stand a chance with this woman. Not that I wanted to ask her out; she'd *just* moved here and she had kids, two major things I didn't mess with. The first because she'd recently upended her entire life, the second because it wasn't cool to mess with a mom. She didn't only have herself to worry about. I wasn't in the market to break three hearts when it inevitably didn't work out.

Swallowing my frustration, I met her gaze with equal zeal. "I'm not looking for a woman, Nova, so you don't need to keep throwing your guard up. Can't a fella just talk to a lady without everyone assuming he wants to get with her?"

Her cheeks went pink, but she didn't back down. "Pretty sure your signals haven't been entirely innocent."

"My signals?" I asked her, planting my hands on the counter that ran between us. "I've been nothing but friendly. Welcoming. Good. Neighborly."

She held my eyes for a beat, hers unblinking. "That's fair."

It took great effort not to reveal my surprise. I half-expected her to dig her heels in and insist that when I checked her out in the market, it was anything but friendly. She wouldn't have been wrong.

In my defense, I was a teaser by nature. Teasing didn't have to mean flirting.

"My focus in life is two-fold at present: disregarding women and acquiring currency." Which was true, in a sense. I didn't want a girlfriend just to have a girlfriend. I'd rather save my money, invest, and prepare for the future so I'll be ready when the right woman walks into my life.

"It's been a while since I was single," she said quietly, likely hoping not to be overheard by the hovering Lacey. "Sorry for jumping to the wrong conclusions. I can send Gigi to chat with you when she's off the phone."

"And force me to return to the table? I can't listen to the debate about butter yellow versus goldenrod for another minute or I'll throw up."

"That bad, huh?" She shook her head. "Gigi mentioned you guys are planning a wedding."

"Best man, at your service," I said, dipping my head in a

little bow. "My best friend is marrying his high school sweetheart."

The swinging door to the kitchen shoved open and Gigi came through, looking a little frazzled. Her white hair was a perfectly sprayed curly cotton ball, but her mouth was pinched in a frown. Maybe not the best time to ask for a donation. "Dal is ready for you," she said to Nova.

"Dusty needs to speak with you about a fundraiser," Nova said, then slid her gaze to me. "Goldenrod, all the way. Maybe with ivory flowers."

I nodded once before she looked away and left. It took maximum willpower not to watch her walk from the room.

Gigi's gaze was hard. "You leave her alone, Dusty Hayes. That girl doesn't need you badgering her."

I threw my hands up. "No badgering, Gigi. I swear."

"You better mean it. I asked if you'd leave my niece alone when I found out she was coming, and you agreed. Don't forget that."

Wait, what? "When was this?" I asked, hazy on the particulars. I wasn't really a drinker—I'd seen what it could do to people when I still lived with my parents—so I knew I had to have been fully aware during the conversation.

She wasn't backing down. "When you and Tucker came here after the rodeo."

Ah. It was ringing a bell. That was months ago, and I'd thought she was kidding. "Well, uh…I just want to chat with you about the fundraiser we're putting on to send our boys to football camp this summer."

Her face softened slightly. Bingo. "What do you need?"

"It's a silent auction. Most of the boys on the JV and varsity teams can't go to camp without assistance, and anything extra will help cover some of their uniform fees for the next school year. If you'd like to donate for the auction, we'd be grateful."

"You're thinking free meals?" she asked.

"We have no expectations, Gigi, we're just grateful for anything you can donate. I can give you time to think about it. The auction won't be until the end of the month."

She nodded slowly before her gaze came back to me. "You promise to leave my girl alone?"

It was a little hurtful that she disliked the idea of me dating her niece so heartily, but I couldn't really blame her. My reputation around this town hadn't been that good until recent years. My grandfather's influence had gone a long way in keeping me from following my parents' terrible examples, but it had been a rocky road from high school to the man I was today.

I'd been an upstanding citizen for some time. Some people just had long memories, and Gigi was apparently one of them.

"I'm not looking for a relationship," I told her, though it was really none of her business. "Nova has nothing to worry about from me. Trust me."

"Okay." She looked skeptical. "Put me down for a meal pass. Whoever wins the auction can eat here once a day for a month without paying."

I hesitated. "That's a lot of food. Want to make it a week?"

"I want it to be so enticing that someone pays a lot of money, Dusty. We can stand it. Don't you worry about us."

"Thank you, Gigi. I'll verify with you before printing the auction sheets, so don't feel like you can't change your mind."

"I won't change my mind, young man. Now you better return to your table. Gracie Mae is going to break her neck watching for you."

My eyes fell closed for a moment. When I opened them again, Gigi was looking at me with suspicion.

"What's wrong with the Gable girl?" she asked.

"Nothing," I said honestly. "I told you. I don't want a relationship. I'm not looking for a woman."

Gigi's eyes shifted to my table of friends before falling on me again, and I had the impression I'd just made it possible for her to believe me. If I could reject someone as beautiful, smart, and kind as Gracie Mae, maybe I truly didn't want to be with anyone right now.

Thank heavens for that. I didn't need Gigi chasing me around with a broom, too. One old woman with a penchant for treating me like a punk kid was enough in this town, and Mrs. Jefferson at the market had that covered. Whether Gigi wanted to admit it or not, she didn't force me into the box I'd created in my youth, not when she was willing to take me at my word. Or the box was translucent and a size bigger, because she was willing to believe I'd grown at least a little.

I dipped my head to her and returned to my table, but my brain snagged on the conversation.

"That took a while," Gracie Mae prodded, her expression stiff.

"Gigi is donating a month's worth of free meals for one lucky bidder."

"That's fantastic, man," Tucker said, finishing off his drink. He looked at his watch. "We better run. We're meeting Lauren at the inn next."

Lauren was Tucker's new sister-in-law, having married his brother Jack last month.

June slipped her hand around his arm. "I think she's going to love my indecision. Maybe she'll choose the color so I can stop going back and forth."

"Goldenrod," I said, repeating Nova's idea. "With ivory."

June looked up at me, her freckled nose wrinkling. "You don't care about color, Dusty."

"Nope, but I mentioned it to Gigi's niece and that's what she said she'd use."

"Hmm."

"Like a sunflower," Tucker said.

June beamed up at him. "Why didn't we think of that before?" Her eyes widened as the idea grew. "A whole theme with sunflowers. Goldenrod, green, ivory. Can you get sunflowers in June? You can, right?"

"That's a question for Lauren," Tucker said, getting out of the booth and taking June's hand. "She knows everything about events. She'll know this."

"Let me know what I can do to help," Gracie Mae said. "Dusty and I are at your disposal."

I'd be annoyed with her, but she wasn't wrong.

When we made it to our cars, all parked on Main Street, I waved at them and climbed in my truck before Gracie Mae could finagle anything more out of me. I had let that woman down so many times—gently and bluntly. I was shocked she kept trying. The direct way hadn't gotten me anywhere, so lately I'd settled for whatever I could think of. Last time she asked me to go see a movie with her, I told her no because I had to go home and feed my cat. It wasn't a lie, but it was also a thin excuse.

I hadn't foreseen the way she would try to get me to invite her to my house instead.

This time, however, I had a valid reason to be on my way. I pulled my truck onto the road and started toward Beeler, the next town over, and the closest assisted living facilities we had. Grandpa had raised me. When his mental state had reached a point where he needed round-the-clock supervision, I'd had no choice but to put him in Pleasant Gardens Assisted Living. I tried to visit as often as my schedule permitted. One of the things I appreciated about our 48-hours on, 96-hours off schedule was having four solid days of no work so I could see him every day. Those two days I couldn't get away from the station were tough. I tried to call in sometimes, but he didn't understand where he was half the time, and not seeing me in person only made Grandpa more confused.

My parents had met and had me in their mid-twenties, but neither of them were fit to care for themselves, let alone a baby. We made it until my fourth birthday before Grandpa stepped in and offered to take me, which had been a blessing all around. My parents, no longer tied to a child, took off for a compound they'd heard great things about in North Carolina. We didn't see them again for almost a decade. By then, I knew enough to understand I was better off in Grandpa's clean house with running water than going off to live in a tent with two addicts.

That didn't make it hurt less, especially when I was fourteen and they took off with my ceramic Darth Vader bank holding my entire savings. It had been a good chunk of money. I'd been squirreling cash away doing odd jobs around town the summer before ninth grade, and right before school started, it was gone.

I almost didn't make the football team that year, and not because Grandpa had a hard time affording the fees. I'd been angry at being abandoned and stolen from, and I took it out on the school equipment with spray paint and a far more rebellious attitude than my grandpa allowed. It didn't help that I'd been in and out of the principal's office for fighting, either. It was the last straw, so the school wanted me expelled or, at the least, suspended and kicked off the team.

Henry Gable had stepped in. To this day, I had no idea what he said to change anyone's mind. He vouched for me, and I worked that entire football season as his assistant to make up for some of the damage. I owed him a lot.

Running a hand through my hair, I pulled into the Pleasant Gardens parking lot and found a spot. Grandpa would be finishing his morning walk now, if his schedule could be relied on. I signed in and let myself out back to find him, waving at Patty, Brody's grandma, as I passed her in the hallway.

There Grandpa was, sitting on a wooden bench and checking his watch. When he looked up and saw me, he grinned. Lines wrinkled his face, but the twinkle in his blue eyes was familiar. He was fairly lucid today. "Ready, Dusty boy? I got us a brand-new puzzle. You're going to love it."

I helped him stand. "You know it. What's the picture?"

"Can't tell you." He pushed his walker as we made our way inside and toward the rec room at the end of the hall. A round table was waiting for us with a black reserved sign. I'd asked for this perk and offered to pay for it, but the nurses were happy to oblige so long as the table wasn't needed for anything else. It made it possible for us to keep our puzzles up for days at a time, until we finished and moved on to the next one. Sometimes we'd show up and a new section would be added for us, but that never bothered me.

Grandpa reached over and slid the box toward me, brandishing it with pride. It was a 1000-piece puzzle of cats lined up in western wear, complete with cowboy hats.

"This looks like a doozy," I said, noticing the use of repeat colors. Some puzzle makers were such tricksters.

Grandpa sat down with a sigh. "We can handle it, son."

I had to agree.

CHAPTER FIVE

NOVA

WAS it legal to strangle an ex-husband for failing to answer FaceTime calls six days in a row? Asking for a friend.

Okay, not true. I was the friend, and after watching my kids look crestfallen as their calls went unanswered day after day, I was ready for murder. Carter hadn't answered when the kids called after their first day of school, and he hadn't answered any evening since.

I typed that thought out in a text and sent it to Blair, my brother's wife and one of my closest friends. She had wanted us to move in with them after the divorce, but they had two kids and a two-bedroom four-floor walkup. I wasn't about to invade their lives like that.

I'd tried my best to keep the problems in my marriage to myself over the last few years. Gossip never helped anyone, and I wasn't about to complain about Carter's late nights and disinterest to my friends. Once he left me, Blair came to my aid. She saw me at my lowest, through multiple stages of grief, and never once batted an eye. She was one of my rocks.

My parents would have been there, too, had they not recently gone to the Philippines on a mission trip. Their

Brooklyn terraced house was leased out in an ironclad agreement for the duration of their trip; otherwise, I wouldn't have needed to come to Texas to live with my dad's sister. It was still hazily in the back of my mind that we could move home in nine months when my parents returned to New York. I needed to think harder on that later.

I finished blow-drying my hair, scraped it back into a ponytail, and swiped mascara on. I pulled on the closest clothes I could reach. Gigi didn't enforce a dress code in the diner—except the necessary closed-toed shoes—so I kept it casual. Blue T-shirt, jeans, and sneakers. Basically a mom wardrobe. No shame, since I was a mom.

My phone lit up with an incoming message. I picked it up off my bathroom counter.

> **BLAIR**
> According to my research, it's generally frowned upon. But I'll be your hitman. Just give me a time and a place and there will be blood

> **NOVA**
> Maybe you've been watching too many true crime documentaries? That got dark fast

> **BLAIR**
> Not possible. Plus, I've learned a lot

I picked up my keys and let myself out of the apartment, walking across the alley to the diner and sucking in a breath of frigid air.

> **NOVA**
> I've changed my mind. A good, solid cold-shoulder will suffice

> **BLAIR**
> We both know you aren't going to do that

She was right, as loath as I was to admit it. Annoying, really.

I could talk a big game, but if Carter put in any effort to speak to the kids, I would move mountains to make sure they answered the phone.

NOVA

I won't. But it has nothing to do with Carter

BLAIR

I know. It has everything to do with Tweedledee and Tweedledum. Where are my babies today? Can I FaceTime them?

NOVA

School. Same as yours

BLAIR

Are you in the kitchen? Have you been baking?

My stomach constricted. There wasn't a need for my specific baking skills here. Even if there was, it would probably feel weird and raw. My family had urged me to take the leap into starting a cookie company over the years, but Carter didn't like the idea of me peddling for change—his words—so I'd mostly kept it to school functions and friends' parties. I hadn't made any cookies since he'd left.

NOVA

Gigi has me cooking at the diner. I learned southern fried chicken last week and it wasn't half bad

BLAIR

I think we need a two-hour phone date tonight and a solid update. Your texts don't provide enough information

Make it FaceTime, because I want to see everything

NOVA

> It's a date

"Good morning, lovey," Gigi said when I let myself in through the back door of the diner. "You want to jump in and get the meatloaf going for lunch?"

"You spoil me," I said, squeezing Dal's shoulder on my way past him. Bacon sizzled and pancakes bubbled on the long flat cooktop.

But Gigi didn't laugh.

I put my things in the cupboard at the end of the kitchen and faced her. Purple circles lined her eyes and her smile was forced. "What's wrong?"

"I got bad news last night." She gave a wan smile. "Had trouble sleeping, is all. I'm a little tired."

She *looked* tired. I waited for her to continue, but she didn't, which made me wonder if it wasn't the right time or place to share her bad news. "Go home," I told her. "Dal and I have this covered. Who's coming in to waitress?"

She yawned. "Me."

"Go home," I repeated. "We can get Lacey in here."

"She's in at noon."

"Pat?"

"Nope. She helps at the school on her days off."

I wracked my brain, but the rest of the waiters were high school kids.

"I'll make the meatloaf," Dal said, freeing me up to waitress.

Gigi didn't look convinced.

"Between the two of us, we can handle the place until noon," I pressed. "Go home and rest. What's the point of having me here if you don't use me?"

She reached for her cup and knocked it over, flooding the counter and the floor with dark soda. "Fine," she relented, staring at the mess. "I'll go take a nap and return less clumsy."

I picked up a rag and got to work mopping up the drink. "Don't set an alarm. Just sleep."

Gigi grunted, but she opened the cupboard and took out her phone, keys, and jacket, so I still won. She paused, looking at the floor. "It's Phoebe, my old college roommate. Do you remember her?"

"Yes." I picked up ice cubes and tossed them in the sink.

"She just found out she has a brain tumor. They didn't give her long. And, you know, she never had children, and Bob has been gone for almost fifteen years."

"So she's alone," I said, realizing why this would deeply affect my aunt. Their situations were not so very different, to say nothing of how much she cared about Phoebe.

"She has friends. Her neighbors are wonderful."

I put the rag down and pulled Gigi in for a hug. "Go rest. We'll be fine here."

She gave a watery smile and sighed on her way out of the kitchen. My heart felt sore from the emotional roller coaster I'd been through over the last few years, but hearing about Phoebe's situation made me grateful for my health. Carter was a royal tool, but I still had my kids, a warm place to sleep, and bacon whenever I wanted it.

I reached over Dal's arm and snagged a piece of overdone bacon in the reject pile and chomped down. We couldn't send it out when it was too crispy, but that was just how I liked it. "Is anyone out there right now?"

"A few cops having breakfast. They might need a coffee refill, and their plates will be ready in about three minutes."

"Got it." I pulled a red apron from the wall and tied it around my waist, slipping an order pad and pencil in the pocket. I'd only been on the floor a handful of times to carry food out, and it had been years since I waitressed at a diner in college. It was probably like riding a bike, right? Either way, I'd been juggling children for over eight years, so I could handle a few hours of balancing tables.

I pushed through to the dining room and lifted the pot of coffee from the long Formica counter, carrying it to the booth against the window. Two uniformed officers sat across from each other, sipping at mugs. "More coffee?" I asked.

They looked up in unison. One of them was red-haired, freckled, and wore the curt smile so many cops adopted after years on the force. I would know, because it reminded me of my dad whenever he had been on duty. The other was blond, blue-eyed, and sharp jawed in a way that resembled my ex. He gave me a knowing smile, like he had a secret, and it unnerved me.

I raised my eyebrows.

"Yes, ma'am," the redhead finally said.

I focused on pouring coffee into his cup, then turned my attention to the blond. "You?"

"Not right now, thank you."

"Let me know if you need anything. Your breakfasts will be right out."

I turned to leave when the second cop stopped me. "You new in town?"

Obviously. Having personal conversations with men wasn't on my list of priorities, but I understood why police officers wanted to know more about me. It was their job to serve and protect, after all. "Yes, I'm here with Gigi for a bit."

"Only a bit?" Blondie asked.

I shrugged, my hand growing sweaty beneath the coffee pot handle. "I'm not sure. My kids are enrolled at the elementary school, and my aunt gave me a job, so for now, we're here."

"For now," he repeated, nodding, his mind working around something. Blondie put his hand out. "Officer Chad Lincoln, and this is Officer Travis Partridge. Pleasure to meet you, ma'am. Welcome to Arcadia Creek."

Maybe they weren't so bad after all. I shook both of their hands. "Thank you."

When I returned to their table a few minutes later with their plates of breakfast, the bell chimed above the door to admit two men and a woman in firefighter shirts and navy pants. Dusty caught my eye and my stomach swooped.

They walked past the table of cops but didn't bother looking in their direction as they chose a booth further away.

"Good morning, Miss Walker," Dusty said, sliding onto his bench. The woman sat beside him, and the other guy sat opposite.

I carried the pot of coffee over. "What can I get you to drink?"

"We just came off a 48-hour shift," the other guy said loudly, probably for the benefit of the police officers, given the way he eyed them afterward. "A vat of coffee would be great."

They all nodded, so I flipped their mugs and poured. "Are your shifts always so long? When do you sleep?"

"Two days on, four days off. The whole department does it this way," the woman said, sliding her full cup toward her and inhaling. "We sleep when we aren't needed."

"But we were needed last night," Dusty said, lifting his cup. "Structure fire out on Haddon Road."

"Is everyone okay?"

"It was a mostly empty warehouse, so yes, everyone but the owner's property is okay."

"I'm glad."

Dusty gave me a friendly smile. He looked tired, his eyes a little droopy. "As are we."

"Let me fetch some menus. I'll be back to take your order shortly."

"Don't need them," the other guy said.

"Great." I put the coffee pot down and pulled out my pad and pencil. "What can I get for you?"

They placed their orders, and Dusty introduced his coworkers, Randy and Jill, who were both tired but polite. Randy was older than me, with a receding hairline and jovial smile, but he wore no ring. Jill looked to be in her mid-thirties and like maybe life hadn't been too easy on her. Her brown hair was tied back in a knot, and her skin was free of makeup. She was small but looked strong. Although, I towered over most women, so she could be perfectly average.

"Do first responders often make a habit of breakfasting here?" I asked, my gaze drawing to the policemen and back.

Jill's nose wrinkled. "Shift work," she said with mild disgust.

"Don't tell me the rivalry is real." My dad had never been anything but appreciative of firefighters. He'd always been charitable—he was a missionary now that he'd retired, remember—so maybe that was a reflection on him more than his profession.

"It's good-natured," Randy said, as if that was enough of an explanation. I was beginning to think I'd fallen out of the real world and landed in a little Hallmark village.

"Dusty is rivals with everyone," Jill said. "Linemen, anyone who went to A&M, cops, the secretary at the elementary school—"

"Ms. Corbin?" I asked, slack-jawed. "She's so jolly."

"She won't let us spray the kids when we bring our trucks to the school," Dusty said in defense.

Randy took a drink of his coffee. "Safety hazard."

"So she says, but they love it. They all line up to get soaked every parade." He leaned back and drew his arm along the back of the bench seat, flopping it over Jill's shoulder. "They *love* it."

They probably did, but I imagined her disapproval had more to do with keeping all that water out of the school. "Maybe the safety hazard isn't about spraying the kids and more about the slick floors when they return to their classrooms all wet."

Dusty pulled his arm from the back of Jill's seat and sat up, frowning. "She didn't say that."

I shrugged. "Just a guess. I'll get your orders in now." I looked at the policemen. "How's your food?"

"Great," Chad said, winking at me.

Eww, weird.

"Careful making friends with the enemy," Randy called as I walked toward the kitchen, "or you might join Dusty's list of rivals."

I looked at him over my shoulder while I walked toward the kitchen. Dusty and I had started out on the wrong foot, and I didn't think it was going to right itself anytime soon. "Pretty sure I'm already on it."

Then I pushed through the door to give Dal the order, my stomach doing a weird leap. That wasn't flirting, right? Definitely not. I wasn't even ready to look at another man, not really. I could objectively notice how attractive Dusty was or the way my heart started beating a little faster when he walked in the diner, but it was too soon to act on teenage fluttering. My kids needed my full attention during this transition period, and that could be nine months long and followed by another transition if we returned to New York when my parents came home.

But none of that needed figuring out now.

No, now I just needed to make it until noon when reinforcements would show up.

I could do this. One minute at a time.

CHAPTER SIX

NOVA

"I WANT TO PLAY FOOTBALL," Ben said, tossing his backpack on the floor and climbing onto a stool. The apartment was small—we're talking a quarter of the size of our New York place—and it had no kitchen table, so we used stools at the counter Gigi had on hand. It worked for us. Alice went to the bedroom she shared with Ben, carrying her backpack, and closed the door.

I pulled an apple from the fridge to make an after-school snack and paused with the fruit over the sink. "Football," I repeated. "Do you know what it is?"

"We play at recess," he said defensively. "Pete's on a team where you get to pull flags from the other kids. It sounds fun."

"I bet the teams are already full, babe."

Ben shook his head, his eyes widening. "No, Pete said I can still join them. His dad is the coach, and they haven't started games yet."

I stared at him. Was this a Texas thing? Him wanting to fit in? In Ben's eight and a half years of life, he'd never once been interested in sports. I didn't know if he even had the hand-eye coordination for it. "Do you want to see if the school has a

LEGO club? Or maybe see if Pete wants to come over for a *Star Wars* movie night?"

On my laptop, since we still didn't have a couch or a TV.

Ben looked at his hands.

I immediately knew I'd said the wrong thing. "If you want to try football, I can speak to the adults in charge, but I'm not making any promises. I don't know what it will cost." My voice gentled. "You know our situation has changed."

Ben got down from the stool on a weary sigh that reached right through my ribcage and tore my heart in two.

I looked over his small frame, his sad brown eyes. Maybe flag football was a good way to introduce him to the game and make him realize it wasn't really his cup of apple juice. "Will you ask Pete for his dad's phone number tomorrow? Or give him mine?"

"I already did." He dug around in his backpack and pulled out a piece of paper with a phone number in messy, childish handwriting.

Cold calling a stranger wasn't on my list of comfortable situations, but Ben's pleading eyes had a magic of their own. It was amazing what I would do for my kid. I took the paper. "Eat your snack and get started on your homework. I'll look into this."

Ben's face lit up. He jumped like his body could not contain his excited energy, bouncing on his toes. "Thanks, Mom! You're the best!"

"I haven't made any promises," I reminded him. "Just eat your snack, and we'll see what Pete's dad says."

He grinned, diving into his sliced apples with peanut butter and ignoring his celery. I went to find Alice and pulled her from the Barbie wedding ceremony on her bedroom floor. The groom was a stuffed Minion, which was no surprise, since she'd been obsessed with them since I'd shown her the first *Despicable Me* at the age of three.

Alice made her way to the counter via a sequence of somersaults.

I watched her. "What are you doing?"

"Kendall taught me to roll, but I need more practice." She stopped when she reached the kitchen's linoleum floor and got to her feet.

"As long as you're on the carpet, I suppose there isn't anything wrong with it."

I put her plate in front of her on the counter when my phone started to ring. An unknown number flashed across the screen, but it was a Texas area code, so I swiped it to answer and started toward my bedroom. "Hello?"

"Is this Ben's mom?" a gruff male voice asked.

I closed the door. "It is. Can I ask who's calling?"

"Jake Hart, ma'am. I'm Pete's dad. He told me your son is interested in joining our flag football team."

"Well, to be honest, we just moved here, and I'm not sure Ben understands exactly what he's asking for. He's never even watched a football game."

There was a beat of silence before he asked, "Never?"

"His dad and I aren't really sports people," I told him. "Is there a way for Ben to watch a practice first and see what it's all about before committing to it?"

Jake sounded like he was sucking air through his teeth. "Problem is, Thursday's the last day to register, and our next practice is Friday. Pete told me they play at school."

Ben had said the same. Was I holding him back because I didn't think he would enjoy it or because I didn't want to add another thing to my plate? I sank onto the edge of my air mattress and wore a smile so my voice would sound happier. "True, Ben mentioned that."

"How about I send you the link to sign up? If I see your registration come through, I'll text you details for the practice."

My stomach felt unsettled. I pictured Ben running out on the field and having no idea what to do, feeling lost, getting embarrassed. "You don't mind him joining if he doesn't know much about the game?"

"Shoot, no." He laughed. "You're in Texas now, ma'am. Kid needs to learn, anyway, and we'll teach him."

This stereotype was turning out to be somewhat true—these people loved football—but they didn't seem to take it as seriously as I imagined if he was willing to let a novice on the team.

"Okay, I'll look into it. Thanks for calling."

"No problem. Reach out if you have any questions. I'll send you the game schedule, too."

"Great. Thanks."

When we got off the phone, I sighed and rubbed my eyes. I pulled up Instagram and swiped through the happy, unchanged lives of so many people I knew in New York. My kids' friends eating at our favorite deli or walking through the park now that spring was touching the trees. Perfect, beautiful Upper West Side homes curated specifically to look good on socials. My stomach panged, wishing to be back in the home where I'd brought two babies back from the hospital, cooking in the narrow kitchen with sunlight coming through the gauzy drapes, meeting friends at the park after school, bundled in scarves and hats with enough room for our eyes to peek through.

In all my memories, Carter wasn't present in the ones I longed to slip back into like nothing had changed. He hadn't been there a lot in our recent lives, which was why it hadn't been terribly surprising, in retrospect, when he didn't want to remain in our family unit any longer. Even then, when he'd said he wanted a divorce, it had surprised me. I didn't realize his ultra long days at the office were a precursor to ending a ten-year relationship. He was willing to throw it away without attempting counseling or making any effort to reconnect. His apathy might have been what hurt the most.

Losing my life, my home, my friends—all that hurt second.

Feeling like I wasn't worth fighting for was a blow I'd yet to recover from.

I sat up, shoving my phone into my pocket because I wasn't going to spend this time wallowing. My feet hurt and I smelled like greasy diner food, but I needed time with my kids and some fresh air.

"Who wants to go for a walk?" I asked, finding both of them chomping away on their apple slices.

Ben jumped down from his stool. "Can we go to the school playground? I want to show you the monkey bars."

"Sure thing. Layer up."

He abandoned his snack and went for his coat and gloves. Alice shoved her last apple slice along the inside of her lips and smiled before chewing her overly full bite. She somersaulted toward her bedroom again, and I had a feeling it was going to take much longer than usual to get out the door for the foreseeable future. I inhaled patience and went for my coat.

As expected, we were slow to get outside, but we made it. We walked down to the elementary school at the end of the road. Ben and Alice took off in a race across the lawn toward the play structure. I slid my hands into my pockets and followed them slowly, my sneakers tight after a full day on my feet. I wanted to sink onto the concrete edge of the playground, but a girl came out of the slide, surprising me.

"Kendall!" Alice squealed, jumping up and down with her in a giggly embrace. A woman stepped around the play structure and came into view, and I immediately regretted not changing out of my diner clothes. At the very least, I could have put mascara on.

"Hi!" she said loudly. She was dressed like she worked in an office, wearing slacks over boots and a long camel-colored coat. Her over-highlighted blonde hair was coiled into a perfect chignon and her smile was wide. She looked like she fit in with my New York friends more than the people I'd seen here.

Today, someone had come into the diner in a giant Bluey onesie and cowboy boots. He looked about seventeen, but still. No one had batted an eye. There were some strange people here.

I'd seen much stranger in the city, though. Like the woman who lived in the stairwell a block from the kids' school who offered to paint our nails every time we passed. She didn't seem to remember us specifically, so we just politely declined. Every day.

She also didn't appear to have nail polish.

Fine. I would reserve judgment on Arcadia Creek a little longer.

The woman flashed straight white teeth. "I'm Kendall's mom, Desi. You must be Alice's mom."

"Yes, Nova Walker," I told her, reaching to shake her hand. She had a firm grip, reminding me of the lawyers in Carter's firm. "We haven't been here long. I'm so glad Alice and Kendall have seemed to hit it off."

Desi looked at where our daughters were giggling together, practicing backbends on the grass. "Alice is sweet. I help out sometimes in class, so I've gotten to chat with her a few times."

My neck prickled with an odd sense of awareness. Desi was still watching the girls, but her words felt loaded. Had she grilled Alice about our situation? Or *my* situation? More people than I could count had bombarded me for information after Carter left. They cloaked their questions in sympathy, but really they just wanted the tea. Married people were especially eager to know how everything came to an end between us.

"Mom! Watch me!" Ben called. I gave him a thumbs up, and he started across the monkey bars.

"Is Kendall a gymnast?"

"Yes," Desi said with gravity. "She's on a small break right now, recovering from a sprained wrist, but she'll be back at it soon. In the meantime, we have cheer."

Kendall was now demonstrating how to twist from a backbend to facing the ground on her hands and feet, then back to a backbend. It was a feat of flexibility. Alice dropped to the ground, awed.

"Should she be doing that with an injured wrist?" I asked.

Desi made a clicking sound. "She knows her limits." Her gaze moved to me. "I hear you came from New York City."

"We did."

"I love it there. We try to go at least once a year. *Big* fan of Broadway," she explained.

My entire life had been spent between Brooklyn and the Upper West Side, yet I had only gone to one Broadway show ever. It was during a school field trip, and our seats were on the highest row furthest to the right, so we didn't have the best visibility. That was before Lasik, too, so I couldn't see as it was. "I've seen *Wicked*, but that's it."

"You haven't gone to *Hamilton*?" she asked, like I'd made an egregious sin.

"No, but I watched it on TV once Disney put it up." I could tell immediately this wasn't the right answer. "The music is great," I put in, hoping to appease her sense of disgruntledness.

Desi gave me a quick smile. "You can see them in Dallas sometimes, too."

If I wasn't going to take a twenty-minute subway ride to watch *Hamilton*, I wasn't going to drive over an hour to watch it here, but she didn't need to hear that. "Thanks for the tip."

"Are you planning to join the PTA?"

"Do I have a choice?" I asked, laughing. "There is no one more persistent than a PTA president with a quota to fill."

She blinked at me. "Well, I'm the president, but I promise not to pressure you too much."

I should have known. The camel coat was too posh for anything less than Arcadia Creek Elementary's It Mom. This whole conversation was just one strikeout after the next. I swallowed, my cheeks burning. "It would be kind of hard with my work schedule the way it is. I'm not sure I'd have the time."

"Everyone says that, but it's really not terribly involved. Let me know if you change your mind. We have a spring carnival coming up and we can always use parents to man the stations."

"Of course. If I'm not working, I'm happy to help."

In true PTA president fashion, she managed to get a commitment to commit out of me. How did that happen? Apparently PTA witch voodoo crossed state lines.

Desi checked her watch, one I couldn't help but notice kind of resembled Carter's—a smaller, feminine version, but equally expensive. As far as new friends went, I wasn't interested in pursuing anything with this woman. She'd done nothing but remind me of my ex, and I could tell I hadn't made a good impression on her either.

"We'd love to have Alice over for a playdate sometime."

I looked at my daughter and the sheer joy on her face while she tried to do a handstand beside Kendall and fell on the grass. Her giggles floated on the cold breeze and filled my heart. "I think she'd love that."

We exchanged phone numbers and watched the girls play for a few more minutes before Desi called Kendall over and they said their farewells. I convinced Ben to get off the monkey bars, where he'd climbed to the top and was trying to crawl across. "Let's go home and get started on your homework. Aunt Blair is going to call later, so we better finish up if you want to chat with your cousins before bed."

They obliged immediately. I put my hands in my pockets while my children skipped ahead, down the empty road toward our apartment. The air was cold and smelled fresh, the only sounds a car and some chatter on the other side of the row of buildings, where Main Street was, and a man watering his dead grass a few houses down.

After living amidst the hustle of the city that never sleeps, it was foreign to be surrounded by silence. The man watering his lawn waved, and I waved back. When was the last time a stranger had smiled at me on the sidewalk in the city? Probably a tourist, whenever it was.

This peaceful, slow way of living didn't seem sustainable in the long term, but for this moment, I breathed in deeply. It was good for now.

CHAPTER SEVEN

DUSTY

THE CREW HAD GONE to Gigi's for breakfast once our shift ended this morning, but I drove straight to Pleasant Gardens instead. I'd gotten a call last night that Grandpa had been trying to walk across the street to the McDonalds. He'd had it in his head that we were going to meet for lunch—at three in the morning. Waiting four hours until my shift ended to go see him was brutal, especially when we got a call about a man's arm getting stuck in a pipe only an hour before I was off duty.

But it all worked out, we got the guy's arm free, and I was on my way to see my grandpa.

By the time I reached his room, he was in the shower. I sat in the facility living room on a stiff armchair and waited for him to finish getting ready for the day, staring at the indistinctive painting of a bowl of fruit on the opposite wall. It was undoubtedly someone's attempt at creating a homey atmosphere. There were always a handful of residents hanging around here, and now was no exception.

Grandpa left his room using his walker, and I met up with him in the hallway on the way to breakfast. "Getting a late start?"

He glanced at me and, for the briefest moment, I thought he didn't know who I was. Then he pushed into the dining room and toward his regular table. "Did you bring me a new puzzle?"

Relief sluiced through me. "We haven't finished the cowboy cats yet, Gramps." I helped him sit and took a chair next to him. The thick smell of breakfast sausage and antiseptic filled the room.

He eyed the place setting in front of me. "That isn't yours."

"Should I wait for you in the rec room?"

"You'd better. I don't want John accusing us of dirtying his fork." Grandpa shook his balding head, the fluorescent lights shining off his scalp. "He's loony. Thinks everyone's out to get him."

This coming from a man who had been trying to get lunch in the middle of the night, but I swallowed my retort and pushed away from the table. I was just thrilled he didn't seem any worse than normal. Last night was a blip. "Take your time. I have all day."

My phone started ringing when I walked toward the rec room, so I let myself outside to answer it. "Hey, Tuck."

"You busy?"

"Just in Beeler."

"Pleasant Gardens?" he asked.

"Yep."

"How's your grandpa?"

I rubbed a hand over my jaw. "He had a bad night. Lots of confusion. But now he seems perfectly normal."

Tucker sighed. "I'm sorry, man. It's all those UT games. You've got to stop letting him watch the reruns."

A grin spread over my lips. I shook my head, even though he couldn't see me. "The Longhorns are probably the only thing keeping him sane."

"And the Cowboys?"

"You know he bleeds blue and silver." The air was cold out here, so I slipped my hand into my jacket pocket. "What's up?"

"Not trying to rope you into auctioning yourself off for a date or anything, don't worry."

I chuckled. I'd done that to him last year, but it had worked out all right for him.

"My dad had an idea for your auction," Tucker said. "He offered to bring Steve."

"His steer?"

"Yeah. He thought you could use him for a photo op. Let people sit on Steve for five bucks or something like that. You know they rake in money doing that in the Stockyards."

"We aren't the Stockyards, though. Anyone can go to your dad's house and he'd let them have a photo."

"Well, you don't have to do it. He didn't have anything to donate, so he came up with that."

As one of the town's school bus drivers, Tucker's dad knew most of the kids fairly well. He was also Henry's brother-in-law, so it was no surprise he wanted to do something to help the football team. "It's a good idea," I finally said. "I'll call him later, and we can work out the logistics. Think Jack would build us some steps or something to make mounting easier?"

"I can do that," Tucker said. "Jack's pretty busy with the inn right now. Have you asked him for anything? I bet he has something lying around." Jack had renovated the entire inn, flipping it and turning it into an amazing little bed and breakfast with his new wife. He also restored furniture on the side.

"He's donating a free night's stay," I said.

There was silence for a minute before Tucker responded. "You should stop in Baker Books sometime this week. June is happy to put together a gift basket."

My stomach tightened. "Your family has given us enough already."

"My family makes up half the town, so if you cut off Fletcher donations now, you won't get much else."

True. But I still felt awkward around June, and I didn't want to accept a basket from her. She knew I hadn't loved the idea of her returning to Tucker's life. It worried me. I didn't want to have to pick his shattered heart off the ground again if she decided to leave a second time. I kept those thoughts to myself instead of showing them on my face when I was around her.

My silence stretched, so Tucker filled it. "Let her help, man. You guys won't fix things if you stay weird around her."

"I know," I muttered. "I'm trying."

"Want to come over? It's been a while since we roped."

"I've got practice for my little flag footballers later. Maybe next week."

"Just let me know when you're free. And Dusty?"

"Yeah?"

"Just go to June's store and pick up the books, man," he said, slightly lowering his voice.

I swallowed a sigh. "Okay."

We hung up the phone and I leaned back, looking up at the golden arches across the street and imagining Grandpa following them like a yellow glowing beacon in the middle of a dark, quiet world.

I rubbed my tired eyes and turned to go back inside.

ONE OF MY favorite things in the world was watching eight- and nine-year-olds run for a ball with all their might, faces flopping in the wind like a dog with its head out a car window. It was part of the reason I helped coach in the flag football league. Really I would take any excuse to be involved with the sport that had given me my love of the game. As a new kid in town with parents who had left for a better, childless world, I had been kind of a punk, even at four years old. But Grandpa put me in flag football when I turned five and it gave me something to focus my energy on.

I was on my way to Heritage Park where our practices were held when I noticed a familiar teenager walking a beat-up bike down Main Street. I slowed my truck and rolled down the window, an idea forming in my head. "Brody."

The kid looked up at me, a nasty blue bruise spread over his cheekbone. My jaw tightened. I knew he ran with a tougher crowd, but I didn't like seeing bruises that couldn't be explained on the field.

"Yes, sir?" he asked.

"You busy?"

He was wary.

"My co-coach can't make it tonight, and I've got to wrangle a bunch of kids at practice. Want to help?"

He still didn't seem totally sold on the idea. "Will you pay me?"

"No, but I'll buy you dinner after."

This seemed good enough for him. He swung his leg over the bike.

"Heritage Park," I told him. "See you there."

The school had strict rules about driving kids around, and I didn't blame them. I just hoped Brody would come to the practice and not choose to blow it off.

I pulled into the park and hopped out of the truck, moving to get the bag of flags, cones, and footballs from the bed. We still used the Pee-Wee sized balls, but Jake wanted to start working with the regular balls toward the end of our season. Our boys were right on the cusp, so I could see why he wanted to introduce the larger balls before next year, when they'd be forced to move up.

It took a few minutes to set up for practice. Kids started arriving and playing on the field, racing each other to the trees and back. I liked them getting their wiggles out first thing, and it also counted as a sneaky warmup.

I checked the time on my phone and slid it back in my pocket, raising my gaze to see Nova Walker coming toward me, holding Ben's hand. My immediate reaction was more excited than it should have been, that eagerness when you see someone you want to talk to coming your way.

It didn't seem like Nova shared my excitement, given the way her steps slowed when she noticed me. Her ponytail swung as she walked, and she wore a thick sweatshirt over yoga pants and sneakers. There was something very cozy about everything she wore, whether it was in the diner or running around town.

She leaned down to say something to Ben, but he shrugged.

"Howdy," I called, giving them a wave. Immediately I regretted it. I should have tried something a city girl wouldn't find weird.

"There's Pete!" Ben said, trying to run away.

"Wait." Nova tugged on his hand. "We don't know if this—that is, where's his dad?"

"Jake couldn't make it tonight." Everything clicked into place. When Jake had mentioned a new kid was joining the team who would need direction and probably a lot of teaching, it didn't occur to me it would be Ben. "He told me about a newcomer. Have you signed all the waivers online?"

"Yes," she said, releasing her hold on her son. He took off like a rocket toward Pete and a few other kids who were trying to climb a tree on the far side of the field. The waivers here were important.

"Anything I need to do?" she asked.

"Be back to pick him up in an hour."

She looked past me, watching Ben nervously, then leveled an intense look at me with her dark brown eyes. "He doesn't know the first thing about football, Dusty. I tried to explain some of it, but I'm just as ignorant, so I don't know if I was helpful or made things worse."

Brody rolled in on his bike then, his wary eyes scanning the field. I let out a breath, relieved he'd chosen to show up. He started toward us, and I closed the distance with purposeful steps. "Don't worry, Ms. Walker. Brody here will be Ben's personal coach." I clapped him on the shoulder. He gave her a fleeting smile.

"Which one's he?" Brody asked.

"Red shirt climbing trees," I said, pointing.

Brody nodded. Nova looked uncertain.

I hoped to put her worries to rest. "It's just until Ben's comfortable in the game. Brody, round everyone up and start a stretch routine."

Brody looked equally uncertain, and I had to swallow the impulse to do it alongside him. I'd seen him lead the high school team. Judging by the bend in his shoulders, though, he needed the reminder that he was good at it. I lifted my eyebrows.

"Yes, coach." Brody jogged off.

"Am I allowed to stay and watch?" Nova asked.

"Of course. Most parents drop the kids and run, but a few will bring chairs and hang out, though it's a little cold for that right now. You're welcome at any of our practices."

She nodded, but that groove between her eyebrows remained.

I took a small step toward her, lowering my voice. "He won't get hurt in flag football, you know. The waiver is just to cover everyone's butts."

"I'm not worried about that." She chewed on her lip, her eyes scanning the group of boys now circled around Brody and doing their warmup stretch routine. "We've had a lot of changes lately, and I just think this is a lot for Ben. He'd be embarrassed if he knew I was telling you this, but he's never been interested in sports. He's a LEGO and *Star Wars* kid."

"He can be both," I said gently. LEGOs were never my thing, but I understood his appreciation for *Star Wars*. "Flag is fun. It's a good way to get kids outside playing a game and interacting with their peers, but it's also a solid introduction to teamwork and developing obedience and listening skills. It's not just football, Nova. I think he's going to like it."

She peered at me, the worry on her brow shifting to interest. "Okay. I'll let you do your job. Sorry for bringing all the anxiety to your doorstep. I've never really been a worrier, but it's all I seem to do these days."

"It's all good," I said, and I meant it. I flashed her a smile. "We'll see you after practice."

She walked back to her car, a very practical Toyota Highlander, and settled in the front seat. I noticed Alice sitting beside her with a tablet, the screen lighting up her face. I shot them a reassuring smile and crossed the field toward my team.

I had a feeling it was going to be incredibly difficult to focus for the next hour.

CHAPTER EIGHT

NOVA

MOM ANXIETY WAS a beast of its own. Logically, I understood flag football wouldn't make or break Ben's introduction to Texas, but I also remembered tearing him away from the friends he'd known his entire life and the amount of tears he'd shed on our three day drive to Arcadia Creek. This felt a little like a Band-aid over the real, raw pain he was facing. I worried it would only serve to make things worse if he didn't enjoy it but persevered because he thought it was the way to make friends.

At least with the practice looming and his new friend Pete, he hadn't asked to call his dad in the last few days. Watching him hold the phone so hopefully and the FaceTime ring going unanswered was like a knife to the kidneys every time.

I slid my gaze to Alice, watching her play Letterland on her Kindle in the front passenger seat. In the two weeks we'd been here, the kids talked to their dad once, and it was a quick phone call Sunday morning on our way out the door.

The kids in the practice looked like they were rounding up and about to finish. My eyes trailed to Dusty standing in front of them, his hands around a football, smiling at the boys as he talked. The man was everywhere. It didn't seem like I could get away from him—not that I wanted to. He was extremely respectful and, despite being crazy attractive, I hadn't felt any sort of predatory behavior directed my way. He was friendly and kind of a tease, but he wasn't a flirt.

Which made me like him, but it also made me wonder if I'd imagined him checking me out in the market that first day. It would make the most sense. I was constantly in some form of wrinkly clothing and hadn't worn my hair in anything but a ponytail in eight years.

Not literally, but it felt that way sometimes.

There was that phase where I'd chopped my hair to my chin to make it harder for Ben's pudgy baby hands to grab, but that only made it more difficult to get out of my face while I did chores or changed diapers or threw up thanks to my second pregnancy.

My phone lit up with a call from Trish, a woman who'd sat on the PTA board at my kids' school in Manhattan. She'd called four other times, but I hadn't bothered to listen to her voicemails. I knew I'd better answer so she'd leave me alone.

She'd been one of the moms eager to know how it had ended between Carter and me, and definitely didn't believe me when I'd told her we'd drifted apart. He had been distant the last few years, but so had I. Two people could take blame for the end of my marriage, and I was one of them. Carter certainly hadn't made it easy for me to try, but I *did* stop trying.

Though I will—privately—forever maintain that he checked out long before I did, he probably thinks the same about me. The difference was that I was busy trying to be a mom, and he was just bored. I didn't love watching him flirt with waitresses or people at office parties, but I never wanted to argue either.

"Hey, Trish," I said, infusing my voice with such false cheeriness that Alice looked up from her game for a moment in confusion.

"Nova! Hi! I didn't think I'd get a live version of you!" She trilled a laugh that made me clench my teeth.

"Just been busy, getting back into the workforce and all that."

"I've heard," she said, lowering her voice. "Things are different for you now. How *are* you?"

The inflection was meant to make it sound like she really cared, but I knew her. Our kids had started in preschool together, so we had five years of history. Trish was the queen of the parent association and the biggest gossip in the Upper West Side. She was good at shrouding it in enough empathy that I'd felt safe confiding in her, so I constantly had to remind myself that anything I told Trish would be around the entire school by the end of the next day.

"Great," I said. Okay, that was probably too much. I softened my voice. "Things are going well. The kids have found friends already, which is a relief."

"I can only imagine," she said, slowly and sadly. "I saw Carter the other night."

Everything went silent around me, except for the sudden strange ringing in my ears. "Oh?"

"At that new restaurant off Amsterdam. Pickle. Have you heard of it?"

"Yes, I have." It was in my planner, still, under the To Do List section as a possible date night when it opened. I had circled it because early critics had nothing but nice things to say and the ambiance looked romantic.

Which meant Carter probably hadn't gone to dinner alone. "He was with the blonde, I'm guessing."

"No, a redhead."

Oh. Had he left the lawyer, or was he dating around? It wasn't any of my business, but I felt a wave of umbrage that he had time for multiple women but couldn't seem to answer the phone when his kids called. I inhaled patience, tracking the team on the grass and watching the boys disperse to waiting parents in idling cars. It was the end of twilight and dark, the lights over the park glowing orange on the grass.

The silence extended, and I didn't know what Trish wanted from me. Crying? Raging? Dirt about the hot cowboys filling this town? My gaze flicked to Dusty, gathering cones with Brody, then fell to my lap. "Listen, I need to run—"

"Did you get my messages?" she asked.

My cheeks went hot. "I've been so busy, Trish. I haven't had a chance to listen to them yet."

"Well, we have the spring science fair coming up, and a few of the parents mentioned those adorable cookies you brought last year. We were hoping you could make them again."

I blinked. "I live in Texas now."

"I know. You can ship them, can't you? How much would you charge for five dozen?"

My mind spun. I couldn't ship her sixty cookies. I hadn't even made cookies since that science fair, so I was probably rusty. "They'll end up a box of crumbs."

Trish's laugh grated against me. "I researched it, Nova. I'll send you the article on how to pack them. But we'll pay you before they arrive anyway, so you don't need to worry about losing all that money if it doesn't work. Is three hundred enough?"

Dollars? I almost choked.

"That's for the cookies, shipping costs and postage fees," she said.

I could use three hundred dollars, easily. After paying the fees for this flag football endeavor, my bank account was dangerously low. But when would I have the time? After the kids were asleep?

"Nova?"

"Sorry, I was trying to figure out if I could fit it in. When do you need them by?"

"Next Friday. We can overnight them so they stay fresh. Let me know what the postage comes to, and I'll reimburse you if it's extra."

"Okay. I'll do it."

"Fantastic!" Trish made a kissy noise. "Lovely. Thanks, Nova. We'll chat later."

We hung up the phone right as my car lit up from Ben opening the door. "Who was that?" he asked.

"Trish. She wants cookies for the science fair. I'm going to make some and mail them to her."

"Rockets and astronauts like you did last year?" he asked, sounding excited.

"Maybe some beakers or DNA, too. What do you think?"

"I liked the rockets."

Of course he did. "Hop in the back," I said to Alice, who obeyed with a world-weary sigh.

"Everyone's going to Gigi's for milkshakes," Ben said quietly, buckling his seatbelt.

My hand hovered over the gear selector. "They do this every practice?"

"No, just on Fridays."

Mentally, I calculated how much money I'd already spent registering for the team and buying the necessary shoes, socks, and athletic shorts. Bring in milkshakes once a week, and whatever else they were going to throw at us, and I didn't know if my bank account would survive the rest of the season.

"I don't know, babe."

"We don't have to get ice cream," he said hurriedly. "Or we can all share one."

That sounded worse. The fact that he knew it was probably money keeping us away made my stomach hurt.

A knock on my window made me jump, screeching in surprise. When I rolled down the window to Dusty's laughing face, I tossed him a wry smile.

"We're all heading to Gigi's for milkshakes," he said, his voice rich and slow. "She does kid sizes for a dollar on weekends, but I'm guessing you already knew that."

I didn't, and it made a difference. I could manage two dollars. "She doesn't have me work evenings, so I wasn't aware. Thanks."

He waited a second before his attention shifted to Brody walking a bike past my car. "Toss that in my truck," he told Brody. "I'll drive you to Gigi's."

"That's okay."

"I owe you dinner, and it's getting too dark to ride that thing without a light."

Brody hesitated before turning his bike toward a black truck.

"We'll see you there?" Dusty asked, winking at my kids over my shoulder.

"Yeah, you'll see us there."

His gaze dropped to my face, a flash of something in his eyes I couldn't name. I held my breath, my eyes locked on his, before breaking the connection and looking down at my phone, ostensibly to check the time.

"Great," Dusty said, tapping the hood of my car before walking toward his truck.

I rolled up the window, letting out a shaky breath.

Yes, okay, so I could no longer deny the attraction I felt to Dusty, but that didn't change anything about my situation or priorities.

"That's mine!" Alice said, her shrill whine cutting through my thoughts.

"I just want to play one round. I'll give it right back."

"But you didn't ask," Alice cried. "You have to ask. *Mom*! Ben took my Kindle!"

"Give it back, Ben," I told him, putting the car in reverse and looking in my rearview mirror.

His face was lit by the screen. "After I finish this round."

"Mom! It's mine! He didn't ask!"

"Ben," I said, more sharply this time. "If you expect me to take you for milkshakes, your behavior needs to earn it."

He scowled, but it only took a second for him to toss the Kindle on the floor. "Fine."

Alice scoffed in outrage. "He threw my Kindle!"

"Ben," I repeated, more pleading this time.

He made a frustrated sound, but picked it up and put it in his sister's lap, then frowned out the window. I wanted to ask about practice, but that conversation would probably go better at bedtime, so I bit my tongue.

Gigi's was noisy when we let ourselves in the back door, having parked just outside the entrance to our apartment. Bonnie looked up from where she was manning the stove and gave us a wide grin. I hadn't gotten to work with the evening cook yet, but we'd met a handful of times.

"Gigi's out there." Bonnie's eyes dropped to Ben. "A crowd just came in that looks to be about your age, young man."

Ben grinned, his face lighting up and all contention with his sister forgotten. "It's my football team."

The ownership with which he said this made my heart sing. "We'd better join them. Good to see you, Bonnie."

The dining room overflowed with people. The boys had crammed themselves into two booths and parents were milling about, chatting and taking seats at different tables. I imagined waitressing and figuring out bills here was a nightmare in the evenings, and was glad Lacey was the one on shift. She seemed competent.

"Mom," Alice whispered, grabbing my hand.

I leaned down. "Is this overwhelming? We can leave and come back for Ben later. I bet Gigi would keep an eye on him."

"No, I see Kendall."

I looked where my shy girl was pointing and found Kendall at a table with Desi and a redheaded man in a blue button-down shirt, which accounted for Kendall's strawberry blonde hair.

"I think they're having a family dinner. We shouldn't interrupt."

Alice tugged on my arm. I didn't know why we had to run into people my kids knew everywhere we went, but it was a little exhausting.

Desi looked up and noticed me. She lifted her hand in a wave.

No choice but to speak to them now.

"Come on," I said to Alice, weaving our way through the people.

"Hey," Dusty said, pressing lightly on my arm. He immediately removed his hand. "Do y'all need a place to sit?"

"Maybe. We were going to say hi to Alice's friend first."

He pointed to the booth he and Brody had with another couple I had seen at the practice. "We can fit two more. I'll save you seats."

"Thank you."

"Not a problem, ma'am."

His slight Texas twang with those southern manners were going to give me weird cowboy dreams tonight. I could feel it in my blood.

"Sit with us!" Kendall said when Alice and I approached their table.

I glanced up to see Officer Partridge sitting with them, the one I'd met with the red hair. I hadn't realized Desi was married to him. Now that I thought about it, I don't think she ever provided her last name.

"We have a seat already," I told them, not in the mood to eat with their perfect little family. "We just wanted to say hi first."

"That's sweet of you," Desi said, leaning close to her husband. "I've heard y'all met already."

"We have." I smiled at him.

"Listen," Desi said. "We're having a little dinner at our house tomorrow night. Why don't you come? Bring the kids."

"I don't want to impose." Especially since we were clearly an afterthought. She'd said nothing about this the other day at the park.

"Nonsense. It's just a casual group of friends. Bring a side or a dessert and we'll throw it in."

Every part of my being wanted to turn down the invitation, but the pleading way Alice looked at me clinched it. "We'd love to," I said.

"Great." Desi flashed her perfect teeth. "I'll text you the details."

"Well, we'd better sit, Alice."

The noise was growing, energy in the room buzzing. Ben was sitting with his friends, beaming, which gave my heart a little shot of joy. We slid onto the bench beside Dusty, a little more relaxed.

He crossed his arms over his chest and leaned back, cushioning himself in the corner of the seat to face me. "Are we scaring you away with our Texas customs, or are you buying into our southern charms?"

Despite the overwhelming nature of the crowd, the fact that Gigi was so caught up talking to people she hadn't greeted us yet and the unending smell of diner grease that seemed to live on my skin, I couldn't deny the way this place was starting to grow on me. A little.

"Jury's still out," I told him.

His laugh was dynamic. It slipped under my skin, making me feel warm and glowy. He introduced me to the other parents at the table. I admired the easy way he had about him, like he wasn't conscious of his attraction or size or accent. He just occupied his space with nothing but the easy confidence of a man content with himself.

Brody folded his napkin into a triangle and tried to flick it into a goal post made from Dusty's fingers.

Alice watched them eagerly, but she was too shy to ask if she could join them.

I was about to ask on her behalf when Dusty seemed to notice. He reached over me to put the paper football in front of her on the table, narrowly missing a drop of chocolate milkshake. He angled the goal posts her way. "Get it in one," he challenged.

Alice took some coaching and about forty flicks, but she finally made it. The way Dusty and Brody cheered, you'd think she'd gotten it on her first try.

I didn't think I could smile any wider after watching her succeed.

"You've got a little admiration on your face," Dusty said softly, pointing to his lips like I had chocolate milkshake on my mouth. "I think that means you like it here."

My eyebrows shot up. "Awkward. Yours is covered in try-hard."

His eyes glittered. "Weird. I've never had to do that in my entire life."

That one I could believe.

CHAPTER NINE

DUSTY

IT WAS EARLY in the morning, almost time to leave for my shift at the firehouse. The sun had started to make an appearance, the hazy light sneaking through my farmhouse windows and softening the edges in my dark living room. I sat on the couch and leaned my head on the back of the cushion, closing my eyes.

My grandpa had left me his house when he'd moved into the retirement home, which felt uncomfortable for the first year. He'd still live with me if I had the ability to pay for someone to be here with him at all times. When he'd reached a place where he needed more help than I could provide, he was the one who selected his assisted living facility, met with the lawyers to move the house to my name, and made me an executor with the power to manage his finances.

It was necessary, because we didn't have anyone else left. The last time we'd heard from my parents was almost fifteen years ago, when they visited the summer before I started high school and took my Darth Vader bank when they left. It had been radio silence ever since. They could be living in Kentucky for all we knew. Or Mexico. Or a compound in Oregon.

Or maybe they were still in North Carolina.

I stopped googling them about five years ago. It wasn't that I'd given up, exactly, but Grandpa had made me realize that at some point it was healthier to let go.

A soft furry head pushed itself down my arm, and I opened my eyes to see my orange striped cat climb onto my lap. "There you go, Leia," I said, rubbing my hand down her back. She always seemed to sense when I needed a companion and slipped out of nowhere to fill the empty space. It felt good to be chosen for a moment. Cats were picky little things, so I never took it for granted.

Tucker had thought he was playing a prank on me when he'd left the kitten on my doorstep last year, but he was really providing me with exactly what I'd needed. He'd also christened her with the name of the A&M mascot, but I quickly corrected that misdeed.

"I need to go to work," I told her, running my hands through her soft fur over and over again while she nestled in. "I should have left already."

She purred, completely ignoring me. Typical.

Mustering the strength to stand, I lifted her with me and carried her to the window, dragging my hand along her back like the villain in a kid's show. Some days were easier than others, and today, for whatever reason, was one of the harder ones. I put Leia in the middle level of her climbing gym and fetched my things before letting myself outside. Cold air hit me like a wall. The old farmhouse was much too big for one person, but it was solidly built, keeping in the warmth in like an oven.

The drive into Arcadia Creek was quick, and station 4 was busy when I arrived with people leaving for the day and the new shift taking over.

"You making breakfast, Chef?" Randy asked, stashing his things in his locker.

My smile went wide. "You know it." I wasn't formally trained or anything, but living with Grandpa had meant a lot of meat and potatoes until I learned my way around the kitchen. My secret Pinterest board of recipes and techniques was still one of my most opened apps, and Tucker's mom, Jan, had filled in the gaps in my cooking knowledge where the internet couldn't.

"Please tell me its quiche again. I woke up drooling just thinking about it."

"That's disgusting," Jill said, passing us to get to her locker. "But I'll put a second in for that quiche if you have all the ingredients."

I'd been thinking waffles, but quiche was fine, too. So long as the fridge was stocked with what I needed and the spinach hadn't gone bad yet.

"Hayes," Captain Bowman called, his voice clipped. "Come to my office."

"Yes, sir." I finished putting my things away and closed my locker, exchanging a glance with Randy, who shrugged.

"We'll start the chores," he said.

Jill lifted her hand. "I'm folding hoses."

Great. I'd be stuck cleaning the toilets, thanks to this meeting.

Captain Bowman was a middle-aged man with a rounded belly and a shiny forehead, but I will undoubtedly be jealous of his thick head of dark hair someday when mine thinned like Grandpa's.

"Take a seat," he said gruffly.

I closed the door to his office and sat on the other side of his metal desk. He looked tired, so I kept my mouth shut and refrained from teasing. Was I in trouble? I was generally well liked and kept my nose clean.

"Battle of the Badges is coming up. Stephanie has been working with the police officers to plan an event that will bring in a good crowd."

"Boxing always—"

"We're not boxing this year." He scrubbed a hand over his

face. "Some people were saying that the violence of it isn't a great way to show camaraderie."

My mouth fell open. "It's a tradition as old as this town."

Captain Bowman shrugged. "I'm not opposed. I look forward to it every year. It's been nixed this time in favor of flag football."

"Flag?" I asked, shocked. "We can't even tackle each other?"

His lips pressed into a thin line. "There was some concern about injury, particularly among the older set."

I clenched my jaw to keep from responding. Captain Bowman didn't seem to agree with the directive either, and it would do no good to complain together. "What do you need from me, Cap?"

He rubbed his jaw again, looking at me like he was trying to figure out how to word it.

I swore internally. If he wanted me to coach the firefighters, that was going to be worse than wrangling cats.

"It's a multi-layered event," he finally said. "We're going up against the cops in every way to find the ultimate winner—who has the most ticket sales, who wins the game, who makes the better strawberry shortcake."

"Strawberry shortcake?" There was no way I'd heard him right.

He looked frustrated, like he didn't support the decisions. Grooves lined his forehead between his eyebrows. "We'll provide lunch after the game—burgers, chips, dessert. The people will vote for a winner after sampling both meals. The way they've designed the points, we have the ability to win if we pull in a landslide on the meal, even if we lose the game and the ticket sales."

Which mattered, because there were more solid football players on the police force by a wide margin. There was no guessing necessary to figure out who chose football as the game.

"Can you lead the kitchen for us, Hayes?" Captain Bowman

asked, holding my gaze like he'd asked me to head the charge into battle.

I supposed he had, in a less literal sense. Obviously I had no choice but to accept. "What does that entail?"

"Plan the menu, bring in a team to help you cook if necessary, and execute on the day of. I'll have numbers for you, but they recommend we size our burgers like sliders so everyone has a chance to eat from both teams. Since the community is voting, the more people who sample your food, the better."

"And dessert needs to be strawberry shortcake?"

"Yes, or some variation. The meal has to be generally the same for both teams so it's easier to judge." He looked at me long and hard. "Will you do it?"

"You know I will," I said, leaning back and linking my fingers across my stomach. My head was already spinning with ideas. "The cops won't stand a chance."

I'D BEEN SITTING on one of the recliners in front of the TV while Randy watched a game, doodling possible menu plans in my notebook, when a call came in through our overhead speakers for a possible fire in the elementary school. Randy had kids at the school, and I'd never seen him jump up so quickly. To be fair, he was always appropriately urgent, but these were his kids.

We drove to the school and parked in front, meeting the principal before the doors. "Smoke in the teachers' lounge," he said.

It took a few minutes to discover that the microwave was on fire, and only a few seconds to put the fire out with the extinguisher. Randy opened the microwave and pulled a blackened bag of popcorn out, raising his eyebrows at me.

"At least it wasn't a real crisis," I said.

"It's gonna stink in here for weeks."

I chuckled, moving past him to open the windows. Given how much paper was on the bulletin board behind the microwave, it was a miracle the entire building hadn't ended up in flames.

"They need newer appliances here," Randy said, looking around the teachers' lounge.

"Mention it to the principal," I told him.

Within an hour, we were able to deem the building safe for re-entry. Fans were blowing air out the windows and the area was closed to the teachers for the time being. Aside from a little smoke clinging to the walls, everything was fine.

Randy spoke with the principal and took down statements for our report, then we stepped back so the teachers could return to the building with the kids. I stood near the door, resting my thumb in my belt loop and high fiving the kids as they walked back inside. I lifted my hand a few times to make some of them jump, and the grins were worth it. Ms. Corbin, the secretary, gave me a tight smile when she walked by, so I didn't offer a high five. She didn't have to like me, but it was a little ridiculous when my biggest crime was trying to make it fun when we attended school festivals.

When Alice Walker passed me, I offered her my fist and she bumped it with a bashful smile. The girl was shy, and I was determined to win her approval.

"Hayes," Randy called, jerking his chin to indicate he needed me.

I reached over to a little black-haired boy and ruffled his hair on my way out of the school line.

"Bet you didn't expect to have such an adventure today," I said, approaching Randy and Principal Hurst.

Neither of them looked very pleased.

"Parents are going to be a nightmare after this," Principal

Hurst muttered, looking at the parents lined up on the sidewalk waving goodbye to their kids.

I scanned the moms until my sight fell on Nova giving Ben a wave. She pulled her sweatshirt tighter around her waist and grinned. Her smile was so pretty, less guarded, when she was looking at her kids.

She glanced over and caught me watching her. I felt like I had a split second to decide how I wanted to play the moment out. I sent her a big, wide smile. I *was* looking at her, so there was no sense in pretending otherwise.

Nova seemed to chuckle lightly, shaking her head and pulling her attention away. I finished speaking to Randy and Mr. Hurst about the situation, and when I looked back at Nova, she was chatting with Chad Lincoln.

Hold on. I threw up inside my mouth a little.

"Don't go over there," Randy said in warning when he followed my gaze. "There are kids around."

"They'll be gone soon," I muttered.

"It ain't worth it, man."

My stomach was already clenching, as if preparing for a fight. Which happened to be the case most of the time when I saw Chad.

If there was a bigger tool in this town, I didn't know him.

There were textbook, good-natured rivalries all over town. My beef with anyone who went to Texas A&M, my university's rival. Or people who didn't hand out candy to kids on Halloween. Or my best friend and his fellow electrical linemen. We all engaged in good-natured ribbing.

But Chad Lincoln? The man was actually a jerk. I tried not to engage when possible, but his smug little face made it hard to walk away sometimes.

It was going to feel so great to beat his department in Battle of the Badges.

Because I was going to win. In most things, I just faked my cockiness and it usually turned out all right. There were few things I was legitimately confident in, but cooking was one of them.

Watching him flirt with Nova, though, made my blood run cold. It sent me flashes of high school, when Chad had always tried to steal whatever girl I was into at the time. He wasn't successful every time, but the fact that he constantly tried made me hate him back then. I didn't feel much differently now. He'd been jealous of my relationship with Coach Gable, and since I worked with the man on the high school football coaching team, that hadn't gone away.

I started toward them and heard Randy muttering behind me, but I ignored him. Pasting a wide smile on my face, I kept my gaze entirely on Nova. "This guy bugging you?"

Her eyebrows shot up, and I realized immediately I'd made an error in judgment. She wasn't going to appreciate me riding in on my trusty red engine and trying to save her.

But, because I'm an idiot, I kept talking. "I've heard the cops around these parts can get mighty pushy. It's better to be firm when dealing with them. Know your rights."

"Hello, Dusty," Chad said tightly, like he deserved sainthood for putting up with me. "Can we help you?"

My blood simmered with jealousy, which was exactly what he wanted, given his use of the word 'we'. My reaction was entirely unwarranted, so I tried to suppress it. I widened my grin and clapped him on the back. "You know I'm just messing with you, man."

We both knew how strongly I disliked him, because the aversion was mutual. I dropped my hand.

Nova peered at me with bemusement. "I need to get back to the diner. Is everything okay in the school?"

"Microwave caught on fire in the teachers' lounge, but it didn't spread. There will be some smoke damage, but it was contained. The students shouldn't be affected."

"Even the ones with asthma?"

"Even them," I confirmed. "We've aired it out and are leaving the fans for a few hours."

She nodded. "Thanks for keeping our kids safe."

It took everything in me not to send a smug look to Chad. "Just doing my job, ma'am."

"I better run," she said again and turned to go, sliding her hands into her sweatshirt pockets.

"See you tonight," Chad called after her.

She shot him a smile over her shoulder before her eyes flicked to me.

When she walked away, I wanted to hit something, so I started back toward Randy just to get out of swinging reach of Chad. I hadn't thought Nova was interested in dating. It was disappointing to hear she was entertaining the idea and *Chad* was the waste of space she'd accepted.

I really, *really* hoped I'd misunderstood that interaction.

CHAPTER TEN

NOVA

WHEN DESI HAD TOLD me to bring a side or a dessert to her house for dinner, I'd gone into panic mode. What did people bring to group dinners in Texas? What would go with the main dish? What was unlikely to be a repeat? At home, my friends would at least tell me what the main entree was so I could make sure I'd chosen something that went with it.

I'd settled on berry crumble bars. Dessert doesn't have to match a theme. Then, because I was worried my kids wouldn't have anything to eat, I also made macaroni and cheese in a small crockpot.

Ben asked to carry the plate of treats when we arrived, so I handed it to him and followed him up the walkway to a large white house with blue shutters. Alice shuffled behind me.

Ben knocked on the door. I balanced the slow cooker on my hip and reached around my leg for Alice's hand, giving it a little squeeze.

"Welcome!" Desi said, flashing a bright smile when she opened the door. "Come on in. You can put those in the kitchen," she said to Ben, then looked at the crockpot in my hands. It was old and a little worn. Carter and I had gotten it for our wedding and it was one of the things I'd packed in the car when we left. I used it constantly and Carter probably didn't even know how it worked.

There wasn't much room on the counter, so I had to shuffle a few things over. I set the crockpot in the opening I'd made and stirred the mac and cheese. Alice took my other hand and held on tight. She'd left her pink monkey in the car, which meant her hands probably felt empty.

"That looks great," Desi said. She eyed Alice. "The kids are playing in the backyard."

Alice didn't let go of my hand. I'd have to walk her out there, which was fine. Her shyness ran on a sliding scale, with varying degrees of depth that had to do with who we were around, how long we'd known them, and how familiar the location was. A new place with new people and one new friend from school meant she was likely to hover at my side for most of the night.

This wasn't like seeing Kendall on the school playground—a familiar place with no one else around. I spied Kendall through the back window, running around the exterior of a large blow-up jump house with a group of girls.

"Is it someone's birthday?" I asked.

"No." Desi waved the question away. "Just a little dinner for Travis and his work friends. We do this from time to time."

With jump houses and a spread fit to feed half the town? She and I had very different ideas of what *a little dinner* entailed. Gigi had filled me in on some of the townspeople last week, and she'd told me Desi didn't work outside the home. It was obvious she'd made a career out of showing up for people, though—the school, her daughter, her husband, his work friends. And now me. I couldn't help but be grateful for her kindness to us, even if I was feeling ten levels of uncomfortable.

"Drinks are in the coolers out back," she said.

"Thanks." Ben had already spotted the bounce house and

went in the backyard, so I pulled Alice along with me. "Let's find your friends."

My phone buzzed with a message from Blair, telling me to call her later with an update. I liked her message and shoved my phone into my pocket, assessing the current social war Alice and I were waging. We stood on the edge of the back porch, just out of the shade and in the sun's warming rays. The group of girls ran by us but didn't stop or seem to notice Alice. Sometimes it was hard not to try and influence my daughter in these social situations—the girl was so painfully shy it was difficult to stand by and throw her to the wolves. But I wasn't at school with her. She needed to learn how to manage these things herself.

Her little fingers tightened on mine and her feet remained unmoving. Where was the elated girl who ran across the school field when she saw Kendall the other day? I could help her wade out, surely.

"You want to join Ben in the bounce house?" I asked.

She shook her head.

"Kendall is over there." I pointed.

Alice said nothing.

I wanted to physically pry her away from me and toss her toward other kids, to watch her happily run away with them to play. But that wasn't my girl. That was Ben—no tossing required. Inhaling, I lowered myself to her level, peering into her wary blue eyes. "Should I walk you over to them? It looks like they're about to climb into that tree house."

Alice chewed on her lip. "I want to go home."

My stomach constricted. New York home, or our apartment on the other side of town home? It took her so long to warm up to people, but she'd had years to grow used to her New York friends. "You were so excited to see Kendall."

She lowered her voice. "Penny is here, Mom. She's not nice."

My body froze while my brain sped up, flashing through bits of conversations and moments with Alice, trying to figure out if

I'd heard of this girl before. I came up empty, but a warning bell flashed in my head. "What do you mean?"

Alice closed down. "Can we go home?"

She meant our Texas apartment, at least. That was something of a relief.

The back door swung open behind us, chatter snaking outside.

I straightened reluctantly and tugged her down the steps. "Let's see if we can find Ben in the bounce house. We can make faces at him through those mesh windows."

We did that, standing outside the bounce house for what felt like ages. I held Alice's hand, and we waved at Ben doing somersaults and high jumps inside. He could meld with any group of kids. He'd always been good at that.

I couldn't wait anymore. I crouched to Alice's level and tucked a loose lock of blonde hair behind her ear. "What did Penny say that made you think she isn't nice?"

Alice's wide blue eyes met mine. "She's Kendall's BFF. You can't have two BFFs, Mom."

"Why not? Don't we try to collect friends?"

"A BFF isn't just a friend," she said with gravity. "It's a *best* friend."

"Well, maybe she needs a reminder that Kendall can be both her friend and yours. Should we go try—"

"Dinner is served!" Travis Partridge called from the porch. Even off duty, in a gray T-shirt and jeans, he looked like a police officer.

I glanced down at Alice. "We'll talk about this later?"

She frowned.

"Let's go eat," I finally said.

We went inside where people were dishing up plates and chatting with each other, the smell of smoked chicken and grilled vegetables wafting through the kitchen. People milled about, the essence of this party both familiar and wildly foreign.

The presence of a police family was so comfortable and recognizable, this group made me feel like I fit in even if they were all strangers. The door blew open behind us and Kendall barged in with a group of girls. She noticed Alice. I found myself holding my breath, hoping on repeat she would invite my baby to eat with her.

"Alice!" she said, her face lighting up. "You're here!"

Alice said nothing. I nudged her in the back. "Do you want to go eat with Kendall and the other girls?"

Kendall didn't give her a chance to refuse. She took her hand. "Come on! My mom put cupcakes in the back. Let's get some before they're gone."

Alice looked at me over her shoulder, wide-eyed and nervous. She could eat cupcakes for lunch for all I cared. Carter wasn't here to enforce veggies and I was just glad she was socializing.

Which one of the pesky girls following her was Penny, though?

I smiled encouragingly at Alice until she disappeared around the corner.

"How is everyone settling in?" Chad asked, startling me. I hadn't seen him approach, my attention was so heavily on my daughter. Ben was in line, holding a paper plate, so I wasn't worried about him.

"We're getting there." I smiled to soften my vague response. He didn't want the real answer anyway. Most people didn't. It was just a way to start a conversation. Besides, my nerves were a little frayed. I didn't want to talk about myself. "Do you work with everyone here?"

"Almost everyone." He stepped a little closer, lowering his voice. "That one by the corn is our station secretary, and the man talking to her is our captain." He continued, giving me a rundown of each adult in the room and their position in the police station or who they were related to. I had the sense Chad was leaning closer with each explanation, given how I could smell his aftershave stronger than the chicken.

"Thanks," I told him, shifting away like I was going to join the line. "Are you going to get a plate?"

"Yes, ma'am." He followed me.

We loaded up our plates with an assortment of food—smoked chicken and corn and salads and rolls. When we reached the desserts, Chad whistled, picking up one of my berry crumble bars. "These look amazing."

I didn't say anything. He'd probably seen Ben carry them in.

Only, he wasn't here when we arrived, was he?

We took our plates outside so I could watch the kids—mostly Alice—and sat on wicker chairs on the back porch. Chad told me about growing up in Arcadia Creek and how he and Travis had gone to high school together. He asked questions about me and New York, but I tried to be brief in my responses and turn the conversation back to him. To Chad's credit, it sounded like he wanted to get to know us and not like he was vetting me for a date, or I wouldn't have stuck around. The moment things seemed more romantically-minded, I was out.

He finished off his berry crumble bar and moaned. "I need another one of those. Want me to grab you one?" he offered. His blue eyes searched mine, and I looked away.

"No. I had one earlier, thanks."

He took my empty plate and walked back inside, probably to throw it away, and returned shortly with a napkin and two more bars. Both were for him.

"A bird in there told me you made these."

I glanced at him, but he seemed amused more than anything. "Guilty," I said.

"I guess that's why Gigi has you in the kitchen, huh? You must be a great cook."

"Mostly just the skills most moms have, but I get by. Dal is a major help."

"Dal has been cooking in that kitchen my entire life."

"So I've heard."

He took another bite and leaned back a little, appraising me. "Hey, what are you doing on the nineteenth?"

"Probably working."

"It's a Saturday. Do you work weekends?"

I glanced at the tree house, where Alice was sitting inside with the other girls. I couldn't see her, but I hoped things were going well. "I'm not sure. Sometimes I help at the diner, but when the kids are home from school I try to be with them."

"You can bring them," Chad said.

There was a slow coiling of unease through me. I held his blue eyes, thinking again how he resembled Carter in some ways. Not just physically, but something about his mannerisms made me think of my ex. That wasn't a point in his favor, to say nothing of the way I was still emotionally reeling from the recent changes in my life. "Listen, I was recently divorced and then dragged my kids halfway across the country. I'm not in a position to think about anything but them for a while."

He looked confused, but then his face cleared. "I'm not asking you out, Nova."

My cheeks warmed. "Then what are you asking?"

Chad shoved the last bite of his bar into his mouth and chewed. He took his time swallowing and chasing it with a swig of his drink, probably to form how best to put me in my place. "We have a Battle of the Badges coming up. It's a competition thing, and I need someone on my team to make a killer lunch. We have to make sliders and a strawberry shortcake style dessert, and I was hoping you'd be able to help. I'm in charge, but I'm hopeless at this sort of thing." He lifted the crinkled, berry-streaked napkin in his hand. "Clearly you're great at it."

"I don't know. My calendar is pretty full." We'd only just moved here but flag football, the diner, the kids' schooling, the cookies for Trish back in New York, the management of the kids' relationship with Carter—there was already a lot on my plate. The thought of adding one more thing made me itchy with pre-imagined hives.

"You don't need to do much," he promised. "Just help me plan a winning menu and tell me how to execute it."

"You don't have anyone more qualified on your team?"

"No, and I don't want to lose again." He gave a self-deprecating smile. "Please?"

He got me with that pleading expression, his blue eyes so hopeful. I could help him plan a menu. That wouldn't be too hard, would it? "I can't commit to much, but I can help you figure out what to make."

"Life saver," he breathed, grinning. "Mark the nineteenth on your calendar. The whole day should be pretty fun for the kids, so if you don't have to work, we'd love to have you."

I didn't commit to that, but I nodded, sweeping the yard again looking for my kids. The sound of familiar giggling came from the tree house, and it made my shoulders relax.

"Can I give you my number?" Chad asked. "You can text me later to figure out a good time to meet and plan out the menu."

My hesitation was slight, but it was there, and he seemed to notice. I was grateful he didn't say anything about it. "Sure." We exchanged phone numbers, then Desi brought her friend Annie to meet me, a short blonde woman who looked a little younger than me, holding a little baby wrapped in a muslin blanket.

She smiled widely. "My friend told me about you. He said your son joined his football team recently."

"Oh, yeah, he did. Jake?"

"No, Dusty. He said your son joined with no experience, but picked it up before the first practice was over." She laughed, the sound friendly and pleasant. "I'd say he must have some Texas blood in him somewhere."

She was so likable I couldn't help but return a bit of her smile. "Maybe. He's trying his best to fit in."

She blew a raspberry and started rocking when her baby began to fuss. "We don't care much about that. I hope he has fun. He's got great coaches."

Chad had gone silent, which wasn't a surprise. There was definitely some weird tension between him and Dusty both the times I'd seen them together.

"Are you planning to put Alice into cheer?" Desi asked.

"Oh. I hadn't thought about it." My little quiet girl? I didn't think she'd enjoy standing in front of a crowd of parents shouting encouragement to the boys, but maybe I was wrong.

"Too late now," she said, cringing. "You could get her in tumbling so she's ready for the fall season."

Goodness, this was a lot to absorb. Who knew if we'd even be here for the entire fall season. And *why* did a six-year-old need tumbling lessons to throw pom poms around and chant at six-year-old boys? I still needed to talk to my parents about options, but it was difficult to find time to chat with the twelve-hour time zone difference while they were in the Philippines. My skin started to itch, and I worried this conversation was bringing on my friendly companion: hives.

I gave them a bright—probably too bright—smile. "Right now, I think we're just going to get through the rest of this school year and see how we feel."

Motto of my life right now. Get through today. Survive today. Squeeze my kids extra tightly when I read them bedtime stories.

Then, tomorrow, do the same thing.

CHAPTER ELEVEN

NOVA

GIGI HAD PUSHED me into a corner. Literally. Then she settled her hands on her hips and raised her white eyebrows. She was like a garrison leader burdened with the personal conviction that I needed protecting at all costs. It hardly mattered that I'd lived in Texas for weeks now and was finding my own routine.

The kids were growing used to their new school and making friends. Ben's flag football practices took place three days a week in the evenings, sometimes shifting—I learned recently—with Dusty's schedule. The boys had two coaches, so they maintained a steady routine, but things changed sometimes.

Like now. It was Tuesday, not a regular practice day, but a text had gone out saying Jake had been called to Dallas for a work thing and Dusty started his next shift at the firehouse in the morning, so practice was tonight. They'd get the next two days off.

Gigi, watching me read the text in the diner's kitchen, pressed her lips together and positioned herself as commander of my protective forces. "I will take Ben to practice. You go home and finish those cookies for your New York friend."

Friend was a loose term when it came to Trish. I was one hundred percent doing this for the money.

Gigi knew my deadlines, she knew my schedule, and she'd known I was overwhelmed merely from whatever my face did when I read Dusty's text. It was hard for me to accept help. Aside from being a woman and a mother—there was nothing like female determination to prove we can do it on our own—I had come to Texas because it was the only way I could maintain a semblance of independence while trying to get back on my feet.

But my choices were to stay up all night with the cookies for Trish or make Ben miss his practice.

"You aren't needed here?" I asked, glancing at the swinging door that led into the diner's dining room.

Triumph shone in her eyes. She knew I was weakening. "It's my diner, love. I can leave if I want."

"Which isn't actually answering the question."

"Vicky will be here soon. Between her and Tyler, they have the floor covered. Bonnie will take over for Dal."

"Who's washing dishes?"

"I'm trying to hire someone for that. Phyllis can't do evenings anymore."

"I'll come back tonight and help, then," I said.

Gigi shook her head, making a disgusted noise. "You'll run yourself ragged." Taking me by the shoulders, my short little aunt forced me to look down into her eyes. "Let me help you, Nova. Your mama would if she was here, but she isn't. She's trusting me to do what I can."

When she said it like that, it made me want to sink into her arms and let her hold me. But I was a grown woman with too much to do today, so instead I nodded. I couldn't open my mouth or the burgeoning, threatening emotion would take control.

Sagging, I nodded. "Okay. Thank you."

"Have the kids ready to go, and I'll be by to pick them up in an hour."

"Practice isn't until seven," I reminded her. It was just after three, and I was about to head out to walk them home from school now.

Gigi's eyes twinkled in that way aunts had, knowing they were slipping Hershey's Kisses to the children while the parents remained unaware. "I know. Have them ready."

The door swung closed behind me as I walked into the crisp sunlight. I missed my mother right now more than I had for the duration of this whole ordeal. She'd always been a stalwart support, to the point of offering to cancel the mission trip to remain behind and take care of me. But I wasn't going to stand in the way of something my parents had worked for and sacrificed for and looked forward to for so many years.

I pulled out my phone and sent a text to the group chat with my mom and dad.

NOVA

Love and miss you.

I found my kids on the far side of the lawn at what we'd dubbed our "pickup tree"—very original—and started walking back to the apartment.

"How are things going with Penny and Kendall?" I asked carefully. It was hard being the new girl and trying to find her place on the playground.

"We're all BFFs now," Alice said simply.

Well, that didn't sound like a good idea. Penny was clearly a volatile component here. "I'm glad you're getting along."

"Sarah wants to invite all of us to her birthday party, so we're going to go together. Can we, Mom?"

"When is the party?"

She wrinkled her nose. "July, I think."

Months away. There was time for all of them to find new

BFFs. I wouldn't be surprised if they did. "We'll chat about it when the invitation comes in, okay?"

My phone buzzed with a text from Dusty, which was a first. He only had my number in the group chat for the flag football team.

DUSTY

> Heads up, you put that in the wrong chat. Unless you meant for it to go out to all the parents on the team

I swore, swiping out of the message and into our group chat. There it was, my blasted text to my parents. I pressed and held it, but the chat was a mix between iPhones and Androids so it wouldn't let me unsend. I typed out a quick message.

NOVA

> Sorry, all! Wrong chat

"Mom, why is your face so red?" Ben asked, peering up at me.

I reached over and ruffled his hair. "Just told your whole team how much I love and miss them."

His mouth dropped open. "Mom!"

Wow. Was he old enough to be embarrassed now? This was kind of a first, and it cracked a hairline fracture in my heart. "I didn't mean to," I said, defending myself. "I thought I was texting my parents."

Alice wrinkled her little, round nose. "How can you mix those people up?"

"With extreme skill." Honestly, I didn't know how I'd done it either. It seemed like sometimes my brain was so full, keeping up with the important things, that trivial details fell by the wayside, like checking the top of the chat to make sure my finger had hit the proper thread. "I corrected it though, so don't worry. They know it was an accident."

Ben huffed, then ran ahead of us.

Alice slid her little hand around mine, and suddenly my mistake really didn't seem like a big deal. Her small fingers squeezed. I would do anything for this girl.

I texted Dusty separately with my free hand.

> NOVA
>
> Thanks

> DUSTY
>
> I would say anytime, but I'm guessing you don't want it to happen again

> NOVA
>
> Preferably not, but it wasn't the first, and it probably won't be the last

> DUSTY
>
> I've got your back

My stomach did a weird leap. I shoved the phone in my pocket and tugged Alice closer. "Tell me about your day, little sprite."

When we reached the apartment, I helped the kids empty their folders and sort their homework. Ben beamed over the perfect score on his spelling test and munched on pretzels. I laid out his clothes and rubber cleats for practice, then filled his bottle with ice water.

He went into the room he shared with Alice, and I sat beside her at the table, helping her finish her math page.

"Alice!" he called. "Where's my Chewbacca?"

"I don't have it," she yelled back.

"It was on my bed and now it's gone."

"Quit yelling," I yelled at them both. "Ben, come out here if you want to talk to your sister."

He stomped from the room, his brow furrowed. "I told you he couldn't marry your Barbies. Where did you put him?"

She looked outraged. "I didn't want him to marry my Barbies. I was using him as Bob's *brother*." Bob, her Minion.

"What about Stuart?" Ben asked.

She kept a straight face. "He's in the hospital. He had an accident."

Good grief. "Did you take Chewbacca?" I asked her.

She focused on the bumblebee she was supposed to be filling in on the page, different colors coordinating to different math problems.

"Alice," I said sternly.

"No."

"Can you help Ben look for it?"

"Fine." Alice hopped up and ran into their bedroom. Ben let out a long-suffering groan before following her.

When she came back to the table a while later, it was after a series of somersaults, one of which landed her back against the wall. "Can I do tumbling with Kendall?"

"Maybe," I said, my whole body tightening. How much did it cost? Those classes could be pricey. "I can ask her mom where she goes and look into it. For now, let's worry about your math. Gigi will be here soon to pick you up."

And then I had cookies to decorate.

Once the homework was finished, Ben was in his uniform with his shoes and water in a bag, Alice had packed exactly three toys—one Barbie and two Minions, one of which was mercilessly covered in Band-aids—Gigi arrived. It only took a few minutes to get the tornado of children and their belongings out the door. Gigi didn't look the least overwhelmed. Was it her unflappable nature that lent itself to running a diner for so many years, or had the diner given her this unruffled calm?

It was no matter. Closing the door and faced with a mess left behind by the kids, I breathed out my relief. The house was quiet and they wouldn't be back for hours. Time to decorate some cookies.

BENT OVER THE COUNTER, holding a large piping bag of dark gray royal icing, I squeezed shadow outlines on a few of the moon's craters. I'd opted to avoid buying new cookie cutters and did the same planets, astronauts, and rocket ships we had last year. All of them were now outlined and flooded, and I'd moved onto the details I was able to do before the first layer of icing hardened.

The door swung open and Alice raced inside holding her pink monkey, her eyes wide. "Ben's hurt."

"What?" I dropped the bag of icing on the counter and hurried toward the door in time to jump out of the way, avoiding a collision with Dusty, who held my son in his arms. My stomach turned over.

Together, they filled the doorway. Dusty must have seen the panic covering my face, because he was quick to speak. "Twisted his ankle in a hole in the grass." He shook his head. "This is why I prefer to practice at the school."

Ben's face was pinched, his brown eyes squinting.

"Where should I put him?" Dusty asked.

Since we didn't have a sofa yet, or any other furniture really, I motioned to the bedroom he shared with Alice. "His mattress is in there."

Gigi came through the door and closed it behind herself. "He's dirty, Nova. Maybe put him on the kitchen chair—" She looked around and grimaced at the lack of kitchen chairs. "Maybe a bar stool?"

"Bring him to the bathroom," I decided. "I can change his clothes in there." I walked ahead and put the toilet seat down, picking up a towel from the floor and kicking aside Alice's discarded pajamas. I didn't love Dusty being in here and seeing the mess, but he followed me in and lowered Ben slowly to the toilet seat.

Looking at the bathroom through his eyes, though, all I could see was evidence of children and a tired mom. Blue toothpaste dotted the sink bowl and water spots covered the mirror. Toys littered the tub floor and the bathmat was bunched up against the wall.

It took everything in me not to straighten the room more.

Dusty looked from Ben to me, then jerked his head to the side a little like he wanted to speak to me in the hall.

I crouched in front of my son first. "I'll grab PJs and a bag of ice. Just sit tight for a minute."

"Okay." His blond hair was darkened with sweat and sticking out on top. His eyes were red and his cheeks were streaked with dried tears. "Mom, it hurts."

I pulled his shoulders in for a squeeze and felt his arms tighten around me. "I'll be quick," I said, kissing the top of his head.

Dusty was waiting right outside the door. "I don't think it's a bad sprain. Probably just rolled it."

"Are you a paramedic too?" I asked, hoping he had medical training.

He gave me a half smile. "No, just a basic EMT. Billy's dad is a doctor, and I asked him to take a look before we left practice. He told me to let you know you don't need to bring Ben in for an X-Ray unless he can't walk on it in the morning."

My shoulders deflated, carrying a heavy breath. That was money I didn't want to spend and an injury I didn't want Ben to suffer. "Thank you."

"Don't mention it." He hesitated, then a glint flashed in his eyes. It felt like the moment he chose to forge ahead. "Gigi was going to carry him home, but I thought I might as well show Ben exactly what firemen are good for."

My eyebrows lifted of their own accord. "You're never going to change his mind about that, you know."

His head fell a little to the side, a curious line forming above his eyebrows. "Why not?"

I started toward the bedroom to get Ben's pajamas and tossed over my shoulder, "Because Ben's hero is a cop."

"Oh yeah? Who's that?"

I smirked, walking away. "My dad."

CHAPTER TWELVE

DUSTY

OF ALL THE things to say to fully stuff my foot in my mouth, maligning police officers to a cop's kid was one of the stupidest. They bred some loyal people, which I could understand. My cheeks warmed, but I decided not to let Nova win so easily. I followed her down the short hallway and leaned against the door jamb, watching her pull some Yoda-themed pajamas from the top drawer of a cedar dresser.

"I can forgive you for that," I said.

Her laugh was somewhere between surprised and amused. She opened another drawer, rooting around for something, her ponytail moving as she looked. She was on the taller side for a woman, her legs long and lithe. I forced myself to look away before I was caught staring.

The room clearly belonged to the kids, evidenced by the bins on each side holding toys. Two mattresses sat on the floor, one covered in a yellow bedspread with Minions, teddy bears, and bananas on it, the other with a classic *Star Wars* blanket boasting different droids ranging from R2-D2 to BB-8. There was no other furniture except the toy bins and a dresser they probably shared.

Nova shut the drawer and looked at me. "We're Team Blue in this house."

I grinned. "I wear blue most of the time."

She rolled her eyes, passing me to go back to the kitchen. "We all know who the real heroes are."

"The ones who pull kittens out of trees and people from burning buildings?"

She lifted an eyebrow. "The ones who put murderers in jail."

Okay, that was a hard one to argue with. "Your dad is a pretty big deal, I take it."

"The biggest," Gigi said from the kitchen. "That's my brother you're talking about, so watch your tongue, young man."

My arms went up. "I've said nothing."

Nova opened a Ziploc bag and filled it with ice cubes from a freezer tray. "He was pretty well liked," she said casually, in a way that made me think he was extremely well respected.

"Who?" Alice asked quietly before her eyes darted to me and her cheeks pinked.

"Grandpa. I was just telling Dusty how much we like police officers in this family."

"I miss Grandpa," Alice said, before ducking her head. She climbed down from the kitchen stool and ran toward her room.

"She's shy," Gigi said.

Nova lifted the bag of ice and pajamas. "I'm going to take care of this."

"Okay, I'll clean this up." Gigi motioned towards the cookies spread out on the counter. They were everywhere. How did I miss them before?

"I'm not fin—*shoot*." Nova dropped everything in her hands and moved to Gigi's side, peeling a large icing bag from a section of cookies. "I dropped it when you guys arrived."

The bag had ruined at least five circles. No...they were moons.

"Mom?" Ben called, clearly feeling forlorn and forgotten on the toilet.

Nova tossed the icing bag in the sink and picked up the pajamas and ice. "I'll deal with it later." She disappeared immediately.

The moons weren't alone. There were planets, rockets, and astronauts littering the counter, too. "These are amazing," I breathed.

"Just wait until she's added the details." Gigi picked up a rag and rinsed it out, then wiped the spilled icing on the counter. "She has a gift."

I couldn't imagine the cookies looking even better than they did right now.

Gigi peered down the darkened hallway before settling her gaze on me. It made me want to run, like the time she'd caught me fighting behind her diner in high school, or when she had seen me and Tucker stealing the Gables' cows and leading them to the football field. It was a harmless senior prank, but she'd put a stop to it. That look said better than words how she expected more from me.

I didn't know why I was being silently reprimanded this time.

"You promised, Dusty," she said softly. "That girl has been hurt. The last thing she needs right now is an entanglement."

Nova had been hurt. I could only imagine. She put on a brave face and seemed like a tough woman, but if Gracie Mae was correct and she'd just had a nasty divorce, then there were many layers to the pain she'd endured. I wanted to take it away, but knew it wasn't my place or my right to take that on.

I swallowed. "I'm just Ben's coach."

Gigi's eyes narrowed. "I know you're a good guy. You can't help some of these things you do. But I don't think it's a good idea for her to go falling in love with a local boy."

Falling in love was a bit of a jump. The text she'd accidentally sent to the parent group today ran through my head. *Love and miss you.* My stomach hurt, thinking she might have meant to send that to her ex-husband.

"I'm flattered you think it's even possible," I said, grinning to hide all the other things I was feeling. "You don't need to worry, ma'am. I'm not looking to get in the middle of whatever is going on in her life. But I'm going to level with you."

She gave me a hardened stare.

"I really like her kids, and I'm going to keep being Ben's coach. I do promise I have respect for her situation. I'm not trying any funny business."

Gigi seemed to lean closer. For such a short woman, she sure could be formidable. Apparently, she believed me, because she gave a quick, distinct nod. "Like I said, you're a good man, Dusty. I'm only looking out for my girl."

I could respect that.

There was a flash of movement in the hallway. Nova carried Ben from the bathroom into his room and laid him on the mattress.

I rubbed a hand over my face, wondering if my next question was going to break the boundaries I'd *just* said I intended to keep. I decided to ask it anyway, but leaned forward and lowered my voice. "Do the kids not have beds?"

"She wouldn't let me buy her anything," Gigi whispered. "I should have furnished the place before she arrived, but I wanted her to help me choose things. I didn't know she'd refuse. Most of what she has are things I made her believe I could spare. I didn't want to push her too much."

"I have a bunk bed coming in the mail," Nova said from the mouth of the hallway, hands on her hips.

Gigi and I sprang apart, caught with our hands in the proverbial cookie jar.

"And I don't need you guys discussing me."

I put up a hand in surrender. "I was wondering because I have a spare bed frame—"

"I don't need charity, either."

"—that I was going to let you *borrow*."

She clamped her mouth shut.

"If you have beds coming for the kids, then do you want to borrow a kitchen table and a few chairs instead?" I asked.

"The counter works fine for us." She passed me to find a cup in the cabinet and fill it with water from the tap.

"It's been gathering dust," I continued. "It's nothing glamorous, but it works well enough."

Gigi looked at Nova, eyebrows up.

I thought maybe I had her there, because the kitchen stayed silent for a beat longer than I'd expected.

Nova gave me a tight smile. "Thanks for helping Gigi get Ben home."

Dismissed. I wasn't about to hang around if I wasn't wanted, so I nodded at her. "Anytime. Good night, ladies."

"We'll see you later, Dusty," Gigi said.

"Yes'm." I was reaching for the knob when Nova's voice stopped me.

"Can Ben sit with the team Saturday, even if he can't play?"

"Of course."

She nodded, her mouth pressing into a line. Did the woman ever *not* look like she was carrying the weight of both of her children on her shoulders? They were small, but that would still be a lot to bear. She was clearly overwhelmed and determined not to look like it, so I did what any chivalrous guy would do. I let myself outside and closed the door behind me, taking the stairs down to the street.

I understood Nova's determination not to accept charity, so I needed to get creative. One way or another, she was getting my kitchen table.

I FINISHED GRILLING the last of the sliders out behind the station firehouse and slid them onto the buns. Cooking at work was always something of a gamble, because it was impossible to know when a call would come in and put a kibosh on the meal. Today was working in my favor and lunch was ready.

"Be brutal," I said, putting the tray on the table in our station kitchen. "These have to go up against the cops and win."

Randy walked toward me, munching on a glazed donut.

"Seriously?" I asked, gesturing to the tray of sliders I just carried inside. They all knew I was making lunch.

He shrugged, shoving the last of it in his mouth. "The elementary school brought them by."

"They wanted to thank us for helping," Dan added.

"So you both ate them?" Dan hadn't even been on that call.

Jill pulled a chair out and sat, reaching for a slider. She took a bite and nodded. "These will win."

Her confidence was inspiring, but it wasn't until Randy and Dan agreed with her that I felt a modicum of relief. They liked my cooking, generally speaking, but none of them were afraid to tell me what they really thought. Dan was the youngest by a few years, but even he wouldn't hesitate to share his opinions. He did it all the time, whether or not we asked.

I sat next to Randy and pulled a slider over, sinking my teeth into it. I didn't tell the guys I'd made the buns myself. I'd done it last night when I'd gotten home from Nova's because I couldn't sleep. It was a new recipe but they were dang good, all soft and pillowy, and probably half the reason these sliders were a success.

Which was good and bad. Now I had to make hundreds of buns for the Battle of the Badges, too.

It would be worth it if it meant seeing a win. There was nothing more insufferable than police officers during the entire year after they won the Battle of the Badges. We beat them last year, and I wanted that relief to continue.

I picked up another slider and took a bite before sending a text to Nova.

> **DUSTY**
> How is Ben's ankle doing?

The little bubble ellipses popped up, and I paused with the slider before it reached my mouth. I set it down on my plate and waited, holding my phone with both hands.

> **NOVA**
> Much better. He could walk this morning, so I'm sure he just rolled it. I don't think it's a good idea for him to run, though

> **DUSTY**
> He can sit the game out this weekend if you're both more comfortable with that
>
> It's early in the week. You don't need to decide today

> **NOVA**
> We'll see how he feels Friday

> **DUSTY**
> Good plan. So, about that table

> **NOVA**
> You know tables aren't necessary, right? There are so many more important things out there

> **DUSTY**
> Totally. Like waffle makers. Did you bring one of those with you or should I lend you my extra?

The bubble ellipses popped up and went away so many times, I set my phone down and pinched a bite of meat from my slider. Hmm. A little heavy on the paprika and not enough onion.

My phone buzzed.

> **NOVA**
> We're a pancake family

> **DUSTY**
> Apparently, no one has taught you how to make a good waffle. How sad for Ben and Alice

> **NOVA**
> But not sad for me?

> **DUSTY**
> I definitely pity you, but you're old enough to know better.

> **NOVA**
> You're flattering today

> **DUSTY**
> You want flattering? Say the word.

Heart pounding, I reached for another slider, vaguely aware of the conversation going on around me and the dwindling pile of little burgers on the table. That wasn't flirting. It was tactful teasing. I teased everyone. There were no exceptions in this town.

Well, except for Ms. Corbin and Chad Lincoln. Mrs. Jefferson at the corner market terrified me, but I still teased her.

Was I trying to convince myself I hadn't flirted? Maybe.

Gigi would slap my wrist.

> **NOVA**
> My pancakes would win against your waffles any day

> **DUSTY**
> Bring it on.

A call came in for an accident on the highway. We abandoned

the meal and left immediately, my phone going into my pocket. Regretfully.

I did my best to keep my attention on the matter at hand and off the phone sitting in my pocket for the duration of the call. I was usually pretty good at compartmentalizing, and when I was at work—especially out on a call—I tried to keep my life out of my head so it was clear enough to do my job. But Nova was different. She had gotten in my mind and taken her shoes off, stretching out on the sofa to stay a while.

A *sofa*. She didn't have one, did she? Or a TV, now that I thought about it. Where did she wind down after a long day? Where did she put her feet up after being on them at the diner for hours? Forget a kitchen table. I needed to bring her a couch. Something weird sizzled in my chest, thinking about the dirtbag who let her drive across the country with so little. Did he even know the kind of place his kids were living in? It was clean but barren.

On further thought, Nova had a point—none of these things were necessities. That didn't make me want to help her any less.

The only problem was getting her to accept it.

When we finished with the call, I pulled out my phone, gratified to find a message from her.

NOVA

I wouldn't want to shame you. I'm a professional, remember? Unfair fight

DUSTY

Fine. Table that for now, because I have something better. Are you free Saturday after the game?

NOVA

I'm not dating right now

DUSTY

Cool. Not relevant, but cool

> **NOVA**
> Then you'll have to explain

> **DUSTY**
> I have a way to get you all the furniture you want, and it won't cost you more than a couple hundred dollars

> **NOVA**
> I'm listening

> **DUSTY**
> Are you and your kids free after the game? I'll need a few hours of your time

I didn't realize I'd started holding my breath until Nova's next message came in, and I let out a massive exhale.

> **NOVA**
> Yes

CHAPTER THIRTEEN

NOVA

I HAD a feeling Dusty would have an aneurysm if he saw the air mattress I'd been sleeping on, so I was glad my bedroom door had been closed when he'd come over the other night. Why the man had taken it upon himself to become the advocate for our furniture situation, I didn't know. He saved people by trade, which made me think he was one of those types who didn't like to stand by when someone needed help.

It didn't mean he had any sort of preference for us or ideas about dating, apparently. He'd been extremely clear about that. It meant he saw a problem and felt it was his duty to fix it.

Admittedly, not my favorite trait, but if he knew of some warehouse selling cheap furniture, I wouldn't turn down a real bed. I might even be tempted to dip into my savings.

I filled our bottles with ice water while the kids got dressed. Ben insisted he was well enough to play in the game today, so I took a page from Desi's book when I'd asked about Kendall's injured wrist—I was going to trust his body and let him make that call. He knew how he was feeling better than I did, for sure.

My phone rang, so I answered it. "Hey, Blair. Just about to head out. Ben has a flag football game this morning."

"Does he still wear that Kylo Ren helmet everywhere? I'd love to see him take down another kid in that thing."

"I think it would be frowned upon. They just take flags off each other—there's no tackling." I hunted through the cupboards until I found Alice's yellow bottle. "What's up?"

"Just checking in. Are you feeling more settled?"

"Still sleeping on the floor, if that's what you mean. We might remedy that today."

"I wish I could go shopping with you," she whined. The kids were growing louder in the background, and I missed my nephews. Blair seemed to go into a room and close the door, because the sound grew muffled. "Maybe we should come out and visit."

"In the middle of March?"

"It's almost April."

I raised my eyebrows.

She couldn't see me, but I sensed she understood my question. "Or maybe you'll move back. Have you talked to your parents?"

"Blair," I said, drawing out the word and taking her off speaker. "I can't think about that yet."

"We miss you."

"I know. I miss you too—not just you, but home, all of it. But it's been good for all of us to get out of there. You know how people talk. Trish called me up last week and told me Carter was out with some redhead." I swallowed, lowering my voice. A quick glance proved the kids were still in their room, but it was better to be careful. "It's been hard coming here. Maybe if I'd had a better option, I would have stayed. But I think the distraction of a new home has been good, too. I wouldn't want to hear about Carter's new girlfriends every time I went to a PTA meeting."

Blair swore. "I can't believe she called to tell you that. Stupid cow."

"She also paid me three hundred bucks for a bunch of cookies, so I don't hate her." Five dozen cookies that arrived in New York yesterday mostly in good order. There were only a few casualties, according to Trish.

"Okay, fine. I half-hate her."

"Blair."

"I'm allowed to," she said. "There is literally no reason to tell you who Carter is seeing unless she wants gossip or she's trying to hurt you."

Something unsettling nestled in my gut, but I was afraid to voice it aloud.

Blair remained silent.

"What do you know?" I asked.

"Nothing," she said firmly. "Absolutely nothing, except I really don't like Trish."

"You've never liked Trish."

"Now I feel justified in that." She blew static into the phone. "I'm Team Nova, okay? Whatever you need, I'm here for it. Want me to light Carter's building on fire? Done. Key his car? Done."

"He doesn't have a car."

"Want me to leave a flaming pile of—"

"No," I said, laughing. "I need to go."

"Please send me pictures of that boy playing football. I need to see this for myself."

"You got it. Give my brother a hug and squeeze my nephews."

"Done." She blew a kiss and we both hung up.

Ben appeared in the kitchen, his brown eyes eager and his blond hair—like always—in disarray.

"Ready?" I asked, my love for him swelling in my chest.

He nodded.

"Let's go."

THEY LOST THE GAME, but you wouldn't know it by looking at Ben's face. He beamed, his cheeks flushed and brown eyes glimmering. Alice and I were bundled in sweaters and coats and wrapped in flannel blankets. We were sitting on the cold metal risers on the side of the football field when Ben found us, a blue Gatorade in one hand and a bag of goldfish in the other.

"Did you see me?" he asked, looking for confirmation.

I pulled him tightly against me, enveloping his cold nose in my swath of layers. "You were amazing."

"I pulled a kid's flags," he said proudly, his voice muffled.

"You were so fast, too," I added with an extra squeeze. "How's your ankle?"

"Feels fine." He looked up at me, eyes bright and cheeks ruddy from the cold. "Can I go to Pete's house? His dad said it was okay."

"We planned to go furniture shopping, remember?"

He wrinkled his nose. "Do I have to come?"

If this had been a year ago, I wouldn't have batted an eye at the request. Something about the turmoil I'd put my kids through made me want to hold them closer and not let them out of my sight. Maybe the divorce and the move had culminated in sending me over the edge into proper helicopter mama bear territory. I wanted to protect my babies, and I couldn't protect them if they were off on their own.

Even as I thought these things, I understood how ridiculous I sounded. Pete seemed like a good kid, and his dad had proven he could handle a group of rowdy boys during their practices.

"Please," Ben pleaded. There was dirt smudged on his cheek, so I reached to rub it off with my thumb.

"You can go. Let me talk to his parents, though."

"Yes!" Ben said, jumping up and down. We were immediately forgotten as he ran to find Pete.

I reached for Alice's hand. "Guess it's just us today. I'm relying on you to help me make decisions."

She looked up at me, hugging her pink monkey close under her arm. "I want a pink couch."

"Or I guess maybe I'll make the decisions on my own," I said with a long-suffering sigh.

"Mom," Alice said, laughing. "Pink would look good in our house."

"Sure it would," I teased.

"*Mom,*" she repeated, smiling so wide she revealed the wonky teeth on the bottom where her adult teeth hadn't grown in yet to close the gaps. Her laughing expression immediately fell to stone, and she pushed close to my side. Alice was like a light switch with how quickly she could turn herself off or on.

Dusty's shadow fell over her. He wore a zip-up jacket over Wranglers, but it didn't seem to hide the shape of his arms very well. They were folded over his chest, that perpetual smile playing over his lips. "Y'all ready to go?"

"Almost. I need to speak to Jake first." I turned away from him, pulling Alice's arm. It wasn't that I was running away…but I was running away a little. His jar-opening arms were none of my concern. They were just hard not to notice when he was shoving them in my face.

Okay, that was unkind. He couldn't help being so attractive. Apparently I couldn't help being attracted to him. At least I had the wherewithal to recognize that this little crush was probably a result of him being kind, which made me want to shut it down even faster. One guy is nice to me and I melt? No, that's not me. I'm strong, resilient, and independent. I don't need him.

Jake and his wife Ashley were standing by the Gatorade cooler talking to other parents when I found them. They confirmed the invitation to their house had been approved.

"I'm heading out to go furniture shopping, and I don't know how long we'll be gone," I said.

Ashley bounced a baby on her hip while he tried to reach for her dangling earrings. "Are you kidding? These boys would play all day and night if we let them." She flashed a smile. "Don't you worry about it. Just pick him up on your way home."

I recognized her tone. She meant it the same way I used to mean it when I'd take my friends' kids or my nephews to the park or to check out the giant LEGO creations on Fifth Avenue. There was no child better distracted than a kid with a friend over.

"Thanks. Call me if I need to pick him up earlier."

"I will." She smiled, then looked down at Alice clutching my hand like a lifeline. "You can leave your little girl, too."

Alice's hands tightened. "That's okay. She wants to help me shop." Which was probably mostly true. I'd learned the hard way that Alice didn't like me telling people she was shy. It brought her too much attention.

Dusty was leaning against his truck when I finished kissing Ben goodbye and reminding him to be on his best behavior.

"Want a ride?" he asked.

And be stuck without an escape route? "No, thank you."

He chewed his lip. "It would be easier, considering I know where we're going."

"I have maps on my phone."

"I don't have an address."

It was on the tip of my tongue to make a serial killer joke, teasing him about how hard he was trying to get us in his truck, but Alice's little ears were tuned in. Besides, I trusted Dusty. Or rather, Gigi trusted him and I trusted her judgment. That first day we'd met in the market, I had gone straight home and called to ask her about him so I could decide whether or not to let Ben keep the Hot Wheels. She had told me in no uncertain terms he was a flirt and to stay away, but that he was a good man and him giving Ben a fire truck wasn't worrisome in the least.

"Besides, it would be easier to put your stuff in my truck." His light brown eyes were almost golden in the sunlight. "Your call, Nova."

"Fine, you can drive."

He looked so triumphant, my stomach did a weird leap. I fetched Alice's booster seat before opening the back door of Dusty's truck to help Alice in.

"You okay, babe?" I asked her.

She nodded, letting me buckle her seatbelt. "Can I buckle Peaches too?"

"Of course." I helped her get her monkey situated in the middle seat, then climbed into the front.

Dusty glanced over his shoulder and noticed Peaches, then winked at Alice. Her little giggle from the back seat froze my entire body. Holy stomach-melting man. I didn't know if my crush would hold off much longer if he made my daughter emit sounds of joy like that. There had been so little of it lately, her giggle was like a sudden shot straight to my heart.

Dusty pulled onto the road and started driving slowly through town. "Do you have a list of what you need?"

"It's so long. I'm mostly just planning on seeing what they have and going from there."

"Good plan. It's best to be flexible."

My phone buzzed, so I pulled it out to find a message from Chad. He'd been sending me recipes and ideas for his competition dinner the last few days, but I hadn't nailed down anything concrete.

> **CHAD**
> Want to meet tonight to go over menu options for Battle of the Badges?

I glanced at the time. We had all day before dinner, but even if we got home in the early afternoon, that didn't leave me much time to finish planning some menu ideas.

> **NOVA**
> Can't today. Maybe tomorrow? Gigi's for lunch?

CHAD
Perfect.

Dusty turned the radio on low, letting soft country music fill the cab. He fiddled with the heater, then dropped his elbow casually on the center console. His phone started ringing and the name Tucker popped up on his Bluetooth screen. "Mind if I answer this?"

"Not at all."

"What's up?" Dusty asked.

Tucker's deep voice filled the truck. "You coming to Gigi's tomorrow after church? June wants to plan the rehearsal dinner."

What were the chances?

"You don't really need me there for these things," Dusty said.

"June doesn't," Tucker agreed. "But you seriously can't leave me alone with them and the wedding notebook. It's a level of misery I don't wish on anyone."

"Elope." Dusty sent me a grin I promptly ignored.

"Nah, I want her to have this wedding. She's planning most of it with my mom anyway. I think these meetings are just a way to involve us."

"Why?" Dusty asked.

"Who knows. You coming?"

"Yeah, man. I'll be there."

"Sweet. How was your game? Sorry I couldn't make it. Jack bought like sixty armoires and I had to help him get them to the workshop."

"Sixty?"

"Probably more like eight."

"The game was good. Listen, I've got Nova Walker and her daughter Alice in the truck, so I better run."

Tucker was silent. "Cool. Hi, y'all. I'll let you go."

"Bye," Dusty said, then reached forward to hang up and switch the music back on. He glanced at me. "Will I see you there tomorrow?"

"Maybe," I said, looking out the window as we passed a farm and turned onto the highway. If my internal compass was correct, we were heading toward Beeler. I'd only been there once, but I'd heard it spoken about regularly. Really, I didn't know what time their church ended anyway, so I had no idea if we'd run into each other in the diner.

"I thought you didn't work on the weekends."

"I'm not." How much to tell him? He clearly didn't like Chad, and I didn't want him thinking this was a date. But he was likely to jump to conclusions if he saw us there together tomorrow. "I'm meeting with Chad Lincoln. Just helping him out with a menu thing."

"Menu thing," he repeated, shooting a side eye glance at me. "You aren't helping him with the Battle of the Badges, are you?"

"How do you know about that?"

Dusty laughed, rubbing his hand over his face. "You are, aren't you?"

"Maybe."

"Hey, Alice," Dusty said, looking in the rearview mirror. "Is your mom cooking for the cops?"

I wanted to jump in and tell her she didn't need to answer, then smack Dusty for trying to bring her into the conversation. She hated being called on.

"Yes," she said quietly.

I whipped my head around to look back at her, more surprised that she'd answered than anything else.

"What?" she asked, giving me her little impish smile. Her cheeks were scarlet. "You were talking to Aunt Gigi about it yesterday."

I hadn't realized she'd overheard. "It's nothing. I'm just helping because Chad doesn't want to lose again."

"He's going to be disappointed."

I scoffed. "Ouch."

"It's nothing on you, Nova. I just happen to know the competition."

"Then it's completely on me. Who am I up against?"

He flashed his white teeth in a perfect smile. "Me."

CHAPTER FOURTEEN
DUSTY

KNOWING Chad Lincoln had his nasty little claws in Nova made me want to hurl a football at his face. The guy was not good news. When he'd been talking to her before, I hadn't been too worried because Nova seemed smart enough to sniff out danger like him. I could see, plain as day, he was playing the long game with her. It was smart. She was super clear about not wanting to date, so he didn't date her. He just found other ways to spend time with her.

Which sounded like what I was doing right now, but it was different. Completely different. Not even close to the same thing. Chad was lowlife scum, and I really just wanted to fill Nova's apartment with furniture. Well, and see how many times I could get Alice to smile today. My tally was already at one, which was a solid start.

Neither of those things made me a creep. Right?

"You're cooking for the other—" Nova stopped herself and turned on the seat to face me more fully. "Hold on. Battle of the *Badges*. Like, cops against firefighters?"

"Yeah. What did you think it meant?"

"One squad against another." She rubbed her eyes and

groaned. "Is this a huge town event or something? I thought it was all in good fun. Like a police family party kind of thing."

I swallowed, careful about how I worded it. "None of our town events are really huge, but this fundraiser brings in a good chunk of money and we usually have a decent showing."

"Which means yes, it's huge."

"I'm surprised Chad didn't talk it up more." Translation: I was shocked he hadn't talked *down* about the firefighters more.

"He just wanted help figuring out a menu because he didn't want to lose again this year," she muttered. "I don't think I'll actually be cooking."

"You afraid to lose?"

"Against you? No." Nova sat up straighter. "Do you even cook?"

"Not professionally." I was what *The Great British Bake-Off* called a home cook and would undoubtedly be sent home the first week if I ever made it on a show like that. But I enjoyed my time in the kitchen and figuring things out. What had started as a necessity—feeding Grandpa and myself so he would stop buying frozen TV dinners—had morphed into a hobby over the years. "Just for fun, and mostly at the firehouse. Do you?"

"Before coming to Gigi's? No. I mean, I made dinner for my family, but I never had ambitions of cooking for other people. It's just a job for me right now." She settled into her seat, seeming to grow more comfortable. "Chad only asked for my help because he ate one of my dessert bars at a dinner thing and loved them. He thinks more highly of my abilities than he should."

Green envy snaked through my stomach. I didn't like the idea of Chad hanging out with her or enjoying her dessert bars. "So, you bake," I said thoughtfully, like I was only interested in the competition. "Which means I need to step up my dessert game."

Nova shrugged.

"Did we just become enemies?" I asked her, hoping she could hear the teasing in my tone.

"That's a strong word. What did your fireman friend say at the diner? You have a lot of rivals in this town. I guess you can officially add me to the list."

"It was only a matter of time."

"Pretty much inevitable," she agreed.

"It's basic math, like all baking."

She gave me a look. "How?"

"Take a heaping spoonful of cop blood and a dash of city girl. Mix them together and throw in a partnership with the devil. Boom, you'll get a rival."

Nova let out a laugh. "Fair enough." She looked out the window, watching fields and farms pass by. "Where are we going, anyway? You've been cagey about this whole thing."

"Not cagey. I'm nothing if not upfront."

I could feel her roll her eyes, and I liked that she seemed more comfortable around me. "We're garage-sale-ing."

"I don't think that's a real verb."

"We're making it one today."

Nova was quiet for a minute, making me wonder if I'd made an error in judgment. Was she a germaphobe? Unable to fathom owning someone else's cast-offs? Too high and mighty for used sofas?

"That's such a brilliant idea, Dusty. I don't know why I didn't think of it myself."

Relief flooded me. "You couldn't have known that the first Saturday in April is Beeler's annual spring-cleaning weekend. There will be so many garage sales, you'll have your pick of things."

Or so I hoped. We were getting a late start because of the game, but given how these Spring Clean Saturdays went in Beeler, I was pretty positive there would be plenty left. As long as Jack was the only furniture restorer who swept in and took all the good things, like the eight armoires Tucker had to move.

"Should we narrow down the list a little, talk priorities?"

"Honestly?" she breathed, looking at me. Her brown eyes were relaxed, and she tucked loose hair behind both ears. "A couch would be ideal. A kitchen table and chairs would be nice too—and I don't want to hear anything about what I said about the counter, okay?"

I put up one hand in surrender, keeping the other on the wheel. "I won't say anything about being right."

She shook her head, but her smile was beautiful. "What do you think, Alice? Anything else?"

"A pink couch."

"Well, you can't be picky at garage sales, babe. We'll see what they have."

"Would you settle for purple?" I asked. "Or maroon?"

"Pink," Alice whispered.

I looked at the monkey carefully buckled into the seatbelt beside her through my rearview mirror. "If we can't find pink, can I convince you to approve of a red couch?"

"Red?" Nova asked. Her tastes seemed to run neutral and plain. I'd seen her in nothing but jeans and plain T-shirts since she'd moved here. Always the same sneakers, always her hair in a ponytail. This was the first time I'd seen her hair down, falling around her shoulders, and it softened her in a way. "I would be very surprised if we find a red couch."

"You never know what you're going to get at garage sales. Don't count anything out yet."

Nova glanced at me briefly before turning her attention back to Alice. "Maybe we'll get lucky and find a yellow couch covered in Minions with banana pillows."

I glanced in my rearview mirror in time to see Alice's face scrunch in a giggle, her eyes lighting up. "I changed my mind. I don't want a pink couch. I want a Minion one."

"Never say never, I guess."

THERE WERE no Minion-themed couches to be seen, but as we drove down Manning Street, there were certainly a number of colored sofa options. I'd chosen this particular neighborhood because it ran higher-middle class—there was no one willing to let go of well-used furniture for cheap like a housewife trying to upgrade her living room. We were the ones doing them the favor by getting the bulky things off their hands.

"Remember," I said to Nova as we parked. "Appear ready to walk away, even if you love it."

"You're a haggler, aren't you?" she asked.

"I've been garage-sale-ing my whole life. There's a science to getting a good deal."

She looked at me, then nodded. "Should we come up with a code so we can communicate around the sellers without giving away what we think?"

I pulled a stick of gum from the center console and popped it in my mouth, trying to gauge if she was serious or not, then offered her one. She refused. "How about the Cowboys? We can discuss going to a game. If you like the couch, you want to go. If you don't like it, you want to get rid of the tickets."

"That would work if it was football season."

Well, she had me there. "Dinner, then?" I asked. Her face tightened, so I hurried to reassure her. "There's a new pizza place in town called Stone. We can debate whether you want to eat there. You can communicate how *hungry* you are for the couch."

"That works."

"If you hate it, just say you want to eat Chad's burgers."

Nova laughed, the sound sudden and sharp like she had surprised herself. "You don't play fair."

I looked at her. "I'm always fair."

She held my gaze for a beat before hopping out of the truck and going to help Alice. They walked hand in hand to meet me on the sidewalk, Alice holding her pink monkey under her arm.

I offered Alice a piece of gum, which she took, her cheeks blooming with color.

"What do you say?" Nova prompted.

"Thank you."

"No problem, little lady. Now let's go find us a couch."

Our search proved to be more difficult than I'd expected. Nova, Alice, and I walked up and down Manning Street, then turned onto the next road and walked that one. Most of the good couches had been sold already, and none of the kitchen tables were small enough to fit in Nova's little dining area. There was a bed she lingered over, but then she told me pizza didn't sound great and we walked on.

"I'm tired," Alice whined softly. The last hour had loosened her up around me a little. I'd wondered if she was always this quiet, or if her shyness stopped once they reached the safety of their own space.

"We can call it a day," Nova said, sounding just as done as her daughter.

"And give up? How about one more street, then we'll try another neighborhood. Deal?"

It took a beat too long for Nova to agree, but she said, "Deal."

I started walking past the next house because there was no furniture to be seen, when Alice tugged on her mom's hand and pulled her toward a shallow table holding knickknacks. She picked up a pink jewelry box with a ballerina that popped up when she opened the lid.

"I think you need to wind it," Nova said.

Alice turned it over and knew exactly what to do. "Lily has one just like this."

A pained expression crossed Nova's face. Her eyes cut to me. "Friend from New York," she whispered, then turned back to Alice. "Can I see it?"

A small Post-it note on the side labeled it two dollars.

"Can I have it?" Alice asked, her little blue eyes pleading.

"Yes." Nova dug around her purse when her eyes shot up to me. "Cash. Dusty, I didn't bring any cash."

I'd thought of this already, which was why I'd stopped at the ATM that morning and loaded up on twenties, just in case. "I have it, but you could ask if they take Venmo first?"

She looked relieved. "Good idea."

Nova walked to the top of the driveway and spoke to the lady there. They both had phones out, so I imagined they'd found an app to pay with.

I crouched beside Alice. "Do you dance?"

"Not like this," she said, watching the ballerina twirl. "My friend does."

"So can I," I said.

Alice looked up sharply, a delighted expression on her face. "You can't dance like a ballerina."

"Oh, I bet I can. It can't be that hard."

She giggled. Make that two tallies, now.

"Do you think they make these in my size?" I asked, flicking the frilly pink tutu on the porcelain dancer.

Alice giggled again, shaking her head. "No."

"Hey, Dusty," Nova called, "Should we get that, uh, pizza now?"

I looked past her to the woman she was chatting with, a puzzled expression falling over the homeowner's face.

"It looks like your mama might have found herself a couch," I whispered to Alice. "You coming?"

Alice nodded, closing the jewelry box lid.

"Are you hungry?" I asked, climbing the driveway to reach her side. There was a navy blue sofa tucked in the shade of the garage that I hadn't seen earlier. Soft lines on the cushions made it look like it might be fuzzy or fake velvet or something.

"Pretty hungry, yeah."

"It can wait a bit." I turned to the gray-haired homeowner. She had a young face for silver hair, but was probably old enough to be my mother. "Good afternoon, ma'am. Is that couch for sale?"

She gave a pained smile. "My husband wants it to be. I'm having a hard time parting with it."

Ah, so it had sentimental value. "You have any kids?"

"Four," the woman said. "All out of the house now."

I wondered briefly if I'd played any of them in school. Beeler was our rival, but I wouldn't mention that now. "It's hard when family moves away." I nodded to Nova and Alice, who stood beside her mother, gripping the pink monkey under one arm and the jewelry box under the other. "These two just moved to Arcadia Creek from New York, along with her little boy."

"Did you leave family behind?" the woman asked.

"My brother and his family," Nova said. "My parents live there too, but they're missionaries in the Philippines right now."

Great. Her father was a cop *and* a saint. No wonder Ben wanted to be the man when he grew up.

"Oh, bless their hearts," the woman said. "It must be hard to be so far away."

"My aunt lives in Arcadia Creek, so we aren't totally alone," Nova said. "She's letting us use her apartment for a while."

It was left unsaid that her situation wasn't ideal, and even a stranger could pick up on the fact that Nova had run away from something. The woman looked down at Nova's hand, where the wedding ring was absent, and her eyes softened. Then she looked at me. "You two been together long?"

Nova and I tried to set her straight at the same time.

"Oh, we aren't—"

"We're just friends," I told her. "I'm the guy with the truck, and we're fixin' to get some basic furniture for their apartment."

"Well, if you want the couch, it's yours."

Nova's face brightened. "How much?"

The woman shook her head. "Free."

"Oh, I couldn't possibly—"

"It's the sofa we had in our loft, and my kids spent many years on it with their friends. There were a lot of movie nights and morning cartoons on this thing." She glanced at it with affection. "It's old but in decent condition, and I just wanted to see it go to a good home."

Nova's eyes looked suspiciously bright. "I'm happy to pay for it."

The woman squeezed Nova's shoulder. "Don't worry about it, darlin'."

"I'm parked over on Manning, but we'll fetch the truck and be back in a minute."

"Take your time. We aren't going anywhere."

Nova practically bounced beside me, holding Alice's jewelry box in one arm and her hand in the other. "Can you believe that?"

I could. "Welcome to Texas, where good people live. I don't know if it's your smile or the fact that your parents are missionaries, but something you said won that lady over."

Nova scowled at me. "I wasn't trying to win over anyone."

How did she not see it herself?

"That's the point. You don't have to try."

CHAPTER FIFTEEN

NOVA

CHRISTINE, the woman with the sofa, offered to sell me a queen-sized bed with a mattress if I was interested, so we went into her house and looked at the guest bed she had been thinking of replacing for some time.

Two hundred dollars later, I walked out of that house a whole sofa and bed richer. She had obviously charged me so I wouldn't have to accept charity, but I wasn't blind to her kindness. She had been trying to help. She'd even offered to get her husband to follow us home in her truck with the bed, but Dusty turned her down. "My buddy is already on his way," he told her.

I shot him a glance.

"Tucker," he said. "I texted him while y'all were haggling. Gotta tell you, ma'am, it's been a while since I've seen the buyer trying to pay more and the seller talking her down."

Christine grinned at me. "That's how we do things here in Beeler."

Not true for everyone. There had been two other couches I'd liked today and neither of them were willing to go under a thousand dollars, which was outside of my budget by a long shot.

By the time we'd finished loading the couch into the back of

Dusty's truck and tying it down, Tucker showed up in his black truck with another guy in the front seat. They both hopped out, and though the second guy was shorter and leaner than Tucker, the resemblance was high.

"Jack, come meet Nova," Dusty said, then introduced me to Tucker's brother.

"You caught us delivering one of Jack's pieces to the homestead, so your timing was good," Tucker said.

"Jack refinishes furniture," Dusty reminded me. "They call their parents' house the homestead."

"Thanks for the translation."

Dusty winked. He leaned down to Alice's level. "You want to climb in the back of my truck and wait there?"

Her eyes brightened and she looked up at me. "Can I?"

"Just don't crawl under that couch. I don't want it falling on you."

Alice and her pink monkey ran off.

Dusty lowered his voice, his caramel eyes on me. "You can wait out here if you want to watch her. I'll get you if we need another set of hands."

Looking at the three pairs of arms in front of me, I knew my puny muscles were unnecessary. I bet they could open any jar in the world, especially with the three of them together. Dusty, Tucker, and Jack followed Christine inside, and minutes later they were carrying out the mattress and the headboard. The bed had been taken apart and carried out in pieces. It took twenty minutes for the guys to load everything and tie it down. I'd tried to help, but they were clearly used to working together. They were more efficient without my meddling.

I stood on the lawn, the sun warming my face, while they finished up. Carter would never have done this. Never. He would have paid guys like these men to help us move things, but he wouldn't have called a buddy and gotten it done.

I knew the comparison wasn't smart. Maybe this wasn't

Carter's style, but he still had plenty of good qualities—things that had made me fall in love with him in the beginning.

But, after being the person in charge for so long, I'd be lying if I pretended not to love how they were taking care of me right now, even just a little.

Dusty patted his truck twice when he passed it. "Let's get these ladies home."

My heart squeezed a little.

He stopped near Alice. "Want to fly down?"

She looked uncertain but nodded.

He put his hands up and she stepped into them. Dusty flew her like an airplane in a circle down to the ground, plane noises and all. Alice beamed.

My heart, in that moment, might have fallen just a little bit in love with the Texan firefighter. He opened the back door for Alice to scramble into the truck, and I slipped past him before he could do something crazy like open mine as well. My pulse was racing. I was probably high on the excitement of having a real bed to sleep in tonight, but I didn't even care.

For the first time in a really long time, I felt happy.

THE FEELING LASTED LONG into the afternoon. The men carried our new-to-us sofa upstairs and put it in the small living room. When they went back for the bed, Alice followed them down. She stayed out of the way while they untied the frame, but she wanted to watch them, and I let her. I snuck into my room and let the air out of the mattress, rolling it up quickly so I could shove it in a closet before the guys got up here.

"I thought you'd still be out shopping the garage sales." Dusty's voice carried into my room. I balled up the air mattress and tossed it into the closet, pushing the accordion door closed.

It popped out a little, so I pushed harder and stood back. It stayed.

Jack grunted. "Didn't want to be too greedy. I went first thing this morning. Had to make three trips to get everything I bought, but Tucker doesn't mind."

"You need your own truck," Tucker shot back gruffly.

Apparently, by the sound of their struggling, the bed frame was heavy. Made sense, since it was solid wood. I glanced around the room, trying to see it through Dusty's eyes, and felt the merest hint of shame at my fall in life. It wasn't overwhelming, so I snuffed it like a birthday candle flame, pinching it away between two fingers. The sparse room was temporary. It was a fresh start, with white walls and fresh carpet—I was convinced Gigi had it redone when I accepted her offer to move in, even though she'd insisted otherwise—and a few boxes of my things. The kids and I had stuffed my Highlander with as much as we could when we moved, and it was brimming full, but once we arrived and spread everything out, it was clear how much we didn't have.

Little things, like a toaster. Bigger things, like dressers. It was lucky Gigi had a spare one, but her offer to outfit this whole apartment with furniture was too much, especially when I wasn't sure if we'd even be here next year.

"Knock, knock," Dusty said, backing into the room. He had one side of the headboard and Tucker had the other. Jack followed them in with some other pieces and I got out of their way.

"Which wall do you want it on?" Jack asked.

I pointed to the place my air mattress had been. "That one is fine. Are there more pieces in the truck?"

"Yes, ma'am."

I helped them bring everything in. My phone started ringing when they went back for the mattress. It was Ashley, Pete's mom, so I answered. "Hello?"

"Hi, Nova. It's Ashley."

"Is everything okay?"

"Yes! Yes, of course. Sorry, I should have led with that."

Relieved, I leaned against the kitchen counter. "Should I come get Ben now?"

"That's why I'm calling. There's this new pizza place in Beeler the boys wanted to try—mostly Jake, but you know what I mean." She laughed. "Anyway, do you mind if we take them? We can drop him off on the way home."

"Has he been good for you?"

"Are you kidding? Ben is a dream. Pete hasn't been bugging us all day. Jake actually made progress on the mudroom he's making for me, thanks to the distraction."

"I'm glad to hear it." And a little jealous that her husband seemed to be such a great guy—building her things, wanting to go to dinner with the family, coaching their son's flag football team. It was so ridiculous, I could recognize that, but it didn't stop the tendril of jealousy from making its way through me.

I wanted to be strong and happy with my new direction, but sometimes I also wanted to curl up on the couch in someone's strong arms and complain about the PTA president bugging me for cookies again. But not Carter's arms. I wanted the scenario, but I didn't want him anymore.

The revelation felt like a weird punch to the gut. My body was weightless.

"Do you mind?" Ashley asked, dragging me back to earth. "You're welcome to join us."

It was probably a good idea if I ever wanted to make friends in this town, but I didn't want to spend the money after buying that bed today. "We have dinner plans, but you can take Ben. I can Venmo you."

"It's on us. Thanks, Nova."

"Thank you," I countered, and we both hung up.

"All set in here," Dusty said, coming out of my bedroom. He

noticed Alice peeking over the counter, her fingers gripping the edge. "You want to jump on it a few times, little lady? Give it a good test for your mom."

He didn't even ask me first. I guessed if the bed broke, he'd fix it.

"Mom?" Alice asked, her blue eyes round and excited. I was glad she still remembered the proper order of things.

"Sure," I said, resigned. "But grab Peaches. You know she won't want to miss it."

"I'll supervise," Dusty said, following her back. "It's a solid bed."

How much of my phone conversation had Alice heard? I glanced at the clock. The outing had taken all afternoon, and I needed to start our dinner now. I pulled my pan out of the cupboard and threw on a pound of ground beef.

Alice's giggles came from my room, and my chest squeezed. I turned the burner on low and went to check on them. All three tall, muscular men were standing around the bed like a set of bodyguards, arms crossed over their chests, heads bouncing along with Alice's movement.

Alice was *delighted*. She jumped like the bed was a trampoline, holding both of her monkey's overly long arms and flinging her around, her blonde hair lifting with every jump. I hadn't seen so much joy on her little face in what felt like months, yet Dusty had made her light up repeatedly today. I didn't even have the space to be jealous that he'd accomplished what I couldn't, because I was so glad to see my baby happy like this.

"Look, Mom! Peaches is flying!"

I laughed, drawing Dusty's attention. He gave me a look that sank to the bottom of my stomach. When was the last time a man had looked at me that way? I tore my gaze away. "She's a natural," I said to Alice.

"We'll get out of your hair," Tucker said, slapping his brother on the back.

"Thanks, guys," I said. "I owe you."

"I wouldn't say no to those cookie bars I've been hearing about," Jack said.

"From who?" Dusty asked, sounding offended.

Jack shrugged. "Annie, I think?"

I'd met her at the Partridges' barbeque. "Berry crumble bars? I'll make you some," I promised, then looked at the other two men. "All of you."

They grinned. Tucker and Jack went for the front door and I hurried back to the kitchen to stir my beef. "Off the bed now, Alice. That was a one-time thing."

She muttered, but she listened. "Can Peaches still jump?"

"Only if she's jumping alone."

Dusty walked his friends out as I went back to the stove. I wondered for a brief second if he wasn't coming back, but I heard the tread of his shoes on the exterior staircase and something like relief filled me.

I busied myself fetching an onion, knife, and cutting board while he let himself into my apartment and crossed the living room, stopping on the other side of the counter. "Listen, Nova, I know you don't want charity, so I'm going to be straight with you."

I lowered the knife.

He looked at the cutting board. "Do you want to finish that first so we both don't start crying?"

I glanced at the half-chopped onion. "We won't cry. It's a sweet onion."

"That's a thing?" He looked thrilled.

"Yes. Yellows are the worst. Stay away from those."

"Noted." Dusty's expression was so earnest, his pale brown eyes soft. "So, I live in a big farmhouse alone with my cat."

That explained all the cat food he had been buying when we met the first time.

"When I tell you I have things sitting around, I mean it. My grandpa left me two rooms full of furniture that aren't being used."

I opened my mouth to protest, but he put his hand up to stop me.

"Listen, Nova. I'm not offering you charity. I won't ask you to take them for free. You can give them back when you don't need them anymore. But let me bring you a few things."

My hand rested on the cutting board beside the onion, the other gripping the knife. Sweet onion and garlic and sizzling beef filled my nose, but all I could think about was Dusty facing off with me on the other side of the counter. For a rival, he pretty much seemed to be on my side most of the time.

It had been so long since someone was truly on my side. Other than Gigi, of course.

"Okay," I said quietly.

He lifted his eyebrows. "Okay?"

"Okay," I repeated.

A grin slashed over his face, so wide you'd think I offered to take him to a Cowboys game.

"Tucker is taking Jack home, but he's going to help me pick it all up now. We'll be back in an hour or so."

"Now?"

"Yeah. You free tonight?"

He could see me making dinner, so I obviously didn't have plans for the next bit. "Yes. If you're sure."

"I'm sure." He looked at me for another beat. This close, with only a counter between us, I could see the rough stubble on his jaw and the shadowed curve between his bottom lip and his chin. I wanted to reach across the counter and touch him.

It was an impulse I hadn't felt for anyone but Carter in over a decade, and it shocked me with both its speed and ferocity.

This was treading dangerous water. Swallowing against a dry throat, I searched for something to say.

My phone rang with the sound of an incoming FaceTime call,

cutting into the silence with tinny, jaunty music and slashing through the spell. I flipped it over and Carter's smile filled the screen.

I really needed to change that old picture out for something less attractive. Maybe even a snapshot of a dog's butt—something that fit my mood better when I saw who was calling. The briefest temptation to reject the call slid over me, but he'd missed the kids' calls all week. I knew Alice would want to speak to him.

When I raised my gaze to Dusty, his expression was guarded. "I better take this."

"Of course. I'll see you in an hour."

I nodded, moving toward the kids' room while he made his way out. I slid my finger on the screen to answer. "Alice, Dad's on the phone."

I heard the quick movement of little feet as she jumped up from whatever she was doing and ran toward me.

"Hey, Nova," Carter said, his face filling the screen.

There were things we needed to talk about, like money for the kids' school lunches and health insurance now that we were in Texas. Things that would best be handled without little listening ears, though, and besides, I had hamburger on the stove.

The front door closed with a snap behind Dusty.

"Ben's at a friend's house, but here's Alice," I said to Carter. For the first time, it was easy to shove the list of things we needed to discuss into a folder and hide it somewhere in a dark corner. I didn't want to chat with Carter. I wanted to make sure this lasagna made it into the oven without burnt filling.

I handed off the phone and went back to the kitchen. It took thirty minutes to get the rest of the lasagna compiled and into the oven, but Alice had brought me my phone at least twenty minutes ago. I slid open my messages and found Dusty's number.

> **NOVA**
> Want to stay for a thank you dinner? I made lasagna.

> **DUSTY**
> Anything to size up the competition

I chuckled, shaking my head.

> **NOVA**
> Tucker's invited too

> **DUSTY**
> Okay. I'll let him know. See you soon, Rival

He seemed like the kind of man who meant what he said. I closed my eyes, listening to Alice sing to herself in her room, and breathed.

CHAPTER SIXTEEN

DUSTY

"NOVA MADE LASAGNA." I slid my phone into my pocket and looked at my best friend. "She invited both of us to eat with her. It's a thank you dinner."

Tucker threw back the rest of his Coke and tossed the can in my recycling bin. "The same woman you're giving your kitchen table to?"

"I don't need it, Tuck," I said defensively. "I live here alone."

"What about poker?"

"I have a card table in the garage somewhere. I'll pull it out when it's my turn to host."

Tucker's eyes narrowed. "What's going on with you two?"

"Nothing."

He didn't wipe the suspicion from his face. "I've known you too long to be fooled, Dusty."

My cat slinked from behind the counter and rubbed her back on my calf. I leaned down and picked her up, letting her relax in the crook of my arm.

"Reveille seems to be adjusting well," Tucker said, crossing his arms with a smirk. He'd left her on my porch as a kitten. Lame prank, if you ask me. I got a cat out of it.

"Don't swear in my house."

"Reveille is a perfectly appropriate name," he argued.

"For an evil mascot, maybe. I told you—her name is Leia."

"Did your voice just soften?" he asked, his smile widening.

"No." I put Leia down and watched her scamper to her deluxe cat climbing mansion in the corner of the living room. Yes, maybe I spoiled her. The poor girl was alone here for two days out of every six, and she needed things to occupy herself so she didn't scratch up my entire house. My grandpa's old armchair had learned that the hard way. "Let's get this table outside."

I moved to one end, ready to lift, but Tucker wasn't budging from where he'd perched at the edge of the kitchen. "You can't distract me that easily."

I dropped my head back and sighed. "She just got divorced, and she has two kids. I'm not messing with her."

"Of course you aren't. You're better than that."

"Can we move the table now?"

"If you don't want to date her, what *do* you want?"

My stomach dipped. "Nothing. I'm just being a good neighbor. She's new in town and needs things. I have too many things. It's basic math."

Tucker watched me another moment before moving to the other end of the table. Before he lifted, though, he gave me a searching gaze. "We both know you've never been very good at math."

Translation: I'd never been good at staying away from women. That had been true in the past; my string of girlfriends since high school proved it. But things had been different since I'd sent Grandpa to live at Pleasant Gardens. Hadn't my consistent rejection of Gracie Mae proved I'd changed? If I was the same old Dusty, I would be taking advantage of her interest in me.

Instead, I didn't see things going anywhere with Gracie Mae, so I didn't string her along. She was stringing herself along behind me, and I didn't quite know how to get across to her that she was wasting her time. I'd tried to no avail.

Tucker and I got the table and chairs and Grandpa's old dresser—it was the nicest of the three I had—into the back of our trucks, then drove to Nova's apartment. I'd snagged the rest of the bread I'd made yesterday before we left, hoping it was okay that it had a few slices cut off one end.

Her place smelled rich and heavenly, the air full of garlic and onion and tomatoes. Tucker helped me carry the furniture into her room and the dining area, then we all brought up the chairs. It was amazing how the few small additions made the place less sterile and more livable. Having a place to sit was a game changer.

How many weeks had she lived here now? Way too many to be sitting on stools and mattresses only.

"June's waiting for me with my parents at the homestead," Tucker said. "But thanks for the invitation."

"Anytime. I'll bake you something instead. What do you like?"

"Sugar," I told her. "Tuck will eat anything with sugar."

"I remember now," she said, smiling. "Hot chocolate. You're the one with the sweet tooth."

Did she remember everyone by their diner orders? If so, what had she pegged me as? Burger Man? Bacon Boy? Coffee Kid?

"Yeah, guilty," Tucker said, rubbing the back of his neck. "Anyway, you don't have to worry about it. I'm happy to help."

She shot him a grateful look. "Thank you."

Tucker nodded, then let himself out, leaving us with heavy silence. Until the bed creaked, like a little monkey was jumping on the mattress.

"Alice," Nova called. "Get off that."

"Two more minutes!"

"Alice," she repeated, sternly. "Now. Dinner's ready." Nova picked up a hot pad and carried the lasagna to the table.

Alice ran from the bedroom, but stopped when she noticed me, her eyes growing wide and her motions drawing inward.

"Set the table, please," Nova said to her.

"Can I help you, Alice?" I asked. "I need something to do."

She nodded.

We worked together to set the table while Nova mixed a salad and sliced the bread I'd brought. By the time we all sat at the table, my mouth was salivating from the smell alone.

Alice ran her finger along the ridge of the table, her eyes wide. "It's like the one we had at home," she said softly.

Nova nodded, her eyes rising to meet mine. "Same shape, but that's about the only similarity. This is such a great table."

I ran my finger over the well creased ridges of letters overlapping math problems. "I did homework on this thing for many years, so it's a little worn in."

"That's the best kind of furniture though. The lived-in kind." She dished lasagna onto Alice's plate, then mine. "Our place back in New York was mostly filled with things I'd thrifted and painted or reupholstered."

My eyebrows shot up.

She was quick to straighten my perception with a self-deprecating laugh while she cut Alice's lasagna into bites, steam rising from the plate. "Don't be impressed. They were very obviously done by an amateur, but I loved each piece because it had been made to my specifications. I got to choose the color or the fabric or the hardware."

No wonder she loved her blue velvet couch. Nova valued connection, and that couch came with a story and a stranger's kindness. I was suddenly dying to see the furniture she had put such great care into. "Are you planning to bring your things out here eventually?"

Nova glanced up sharply. "No. I can't. None of it is mine anymore."

We finished making our plates before I ate a bite of lasagna and died, traveling straight to the Italian heavens. It was fantastic. I prided myself on being a good cook, but I didn't think I'd ever made anything so flavorful and rich and saucy, with the perfect balance of cheesiness.

"This is amazing."

Nova blushed. "It's just lasagna."

"It's the best lasagna I've ever had. So creamy."

"That's my secret ingredient."

"New York magic?"

"Cottage cheese."

"My mom is the best cook," Alice said quietly.

Nova's attention snapped to her daughter, her surprise evident.

"So far, I have to agree," I told her, taking another bite. "Did you know that all the firefighters in town think I'm the best cook?"

Alice shook her head, her fork hovering above a plate of lasagna cut into bites.

I shrugged. "They might be wrong though. I guess we'll have to wait until the Battle of the Badges to know once and for all."

"Sure. Because we both know people will be voting for the food and not the organizations," Nova said, her voice dripping in sarcasm.

"My grandpa voted for the police a few years ago, back before I was cooking."

"Were you a firefighter then?"

"Yes, and it brought me great shame," I said gravely. "People take it seriously. That's all I'm saying."

"This bread is delicious," she said, taking another bite. "Did you get it at the market?"

"No, I made it." Did that sound smug? I felt a little smug.

She tried to fight her smile, but I saw it playing on her lips. "You mentioned your grandpa left you two rooms of furniture. Is he the same traitor who voted for the cops?"

"The very one."

"Maybe I shouldn't have called him a traitor."

"He was. I think I probably used that same word on him for weeks after he did that."

Her cheeks were rosy, bringing out the depth of her brown eyes. She brushed loose hair behind her ears. "Do you have other family around?"

"No, just me and Gramps. He's in Beeler now at an assisted living facility, but he signed his house and everything over to me before he went. We don't have anyone else."

Nova put her fork down. Her eyes shot to Alice, who wasn't eating anymore. "You can clear your plate," she told her.

Alice hopped up, carrying her half-empty plate to the garbage to scrape it clean. What a disgrace. None of this lasagna deserved to make it into the trash.

"Sorry," Nova said more quietly while Alice rinsed her plate and ran off to her room. "I shouldn't have pried."

"It's no secret, Rival. My parents are long gone, and there wasn't anyone else, so my grandpa took me in and raised me. When his mind started to go, it wasn't safe for him to be at the house without me during my 48-hour shifts, so he picked a facility and started preparing to move."

"He chose it?" she asked.

"Yeah. He visited all the assisted living facilities in the area when they threw their recruitment BBQs and chose the one with the best food."

Nova laughed. "Is he the one who taught you to cook?"

"No." I took a swig of water and raised my gaze again. "He can't cook at all. He can pop a TV dinner in the microwave or fry eggs, but that's about it."

She stared at me, her deep brown eyes peering across the

table and into my soul. "Which is why you learned, I'm guessing?"

"Bingo." Usually talking about these things made me slightly uncomfortable, like I needed to defend Grandpa for his poor health choices, like I owed him so much it didn't matter that we didn't eat healthily for the first half of my life because at least I was eating. People could be so judgmental, and I always wanted to jump to his defense when he had been doing me the massive favor by feeding me at all. But Nova didn't give me the urge to say anything like that. She didn't judge me or my story. "He did his best, but I got tired of microwavable food."

"You know, one thing my doctor drilled into me when I had Ben was the phrase 'fed is best.' Have you heard it?"

"No."

"It just means that it doesn't matter whether you nurse your baby or feed them formula, as long as the baby is eating and growing. Fed is best." She pushed her plate away and leaned her arms on the table. "I thought about that a lot when my kids were toddlers. They picked at their plates or fought me on vegetables and would eat nothing but graham crackers and Go-gurt. As long as they were eating, I considered my job done. I think it's incredible you learned such a valuable skill on your own, but as far as your grandpa is concerned, he wasn't doing anything wrong."

My chest glowed in appreciation. "Thanks for saying that. He put up with a lot from me, so the least I could do was put hot dinners on his table. I'm pretty sure he missed the food more than me when I went off to college."

Nova lifted an eyebrow.

"Okay, maybe not," I conceded. "It was probably a tie."

"Have you always been such a tease?" she asked, rising and taking my empty plate over to the sink. I was going to go for seconds, but I didn't want to be greedy, so I sadly watched my plate disappear.

If she was starting to sense that humor was a coping mechanism for me, I wouldn't be surprised. Nova was one of those rare people who seemed to understand me on a deeper level. Like when everyone else saw the funny, charming guy, she could peel back the layer of charm and see the regular man underneath.

This was getting dangerous.

"I only tease people I like."

"Since we're rivals, I guess that disqualifies me, huh?"

I got up and started carrying things over to the kitchen, helping her put everything away. "No, because I know you like it."

I didn't know, actually, but I *hoped* that was the case.

The bed in her room started creaking again, and Nova rolled her eyes. "I blame you entirely for that, by the way." She went back to her room and told Alice to quit jumping on the bed. I heard her threaten to take Peaches away next time she caught either of them disobeying, and Alice squealed and ran to her own room, shutting the door hard behind her.

Staring at the door to Nova's room, I narrowed my eyes. We'd brought furniture into the apartment today, but we hadn't taken anything *out*. I waited for her to return. "Hey, there was no mattress already when I brought the bed."

She froze, putting the rest of the salad in the fridge, then closed it and turned to face me. "No, there wasn't. I cleared out the room."

She couldn't have hidden a mattress under the rug. "Nova, what have you been sleeping on?"

"Well, a few nights ago I shared Alice's twin with her because I fell asleep reading to her."

"And all the other nights?" She didn't even have a sofa.

She sighed, putting the salt and pepper in the cupboard with a snap. "Air mattress. Don't judge me, Dusty. Slept is best."

"Yeah, if you *can* sleep on an air mattress that long." I

considered the two twin mattresses in her kids' room and the rest of the barren apartment. To know she'd been coming home and crashing on a blow-up mattress made me want to strangle her ex-husband. He was an idiot for ever letting her go in the first place, but to allow her to come so far with so little? That was low.

"I slept well enough," she muttered.

"Well, I expect you want me out of your hair so you can go starfish on that bed for a while, then. It's gonna feel like the Ritz after weeks on a rubber ice cube."

She flashed me a hesitant smile. "I am looking forward to being warm tonight."

My stomach clenched in a weird way. I wanted to cross the room and promise she'd never have to sleep cold again, that she could have my entire farmhouse and I'd take this barren apartment. But I didn't know her well enough to offer her the world, and the impulse was inappropriate.

That didn't stop me from wanting to say something though.

My phone buzzed, and I pulled it out.

> COACH GABLE
>
> We've got a problem. Can you meet me in the locker room? It's Brody.

I swore. My head whipped toward Alice's door. "Sorry."

"What's wrong?" Nova asked, concerned.

"It's Brody."

"The kid who helps you coach?"

I nodded, firing off a text saying I would be there soon.

"Can I do anything?" she asked.

My impulse was to refuse her, but then I had an idea. "Can you wrap up a plate of dinner to go?"

She gave me one quick, searching nod. "Of course."

CHAPTER SEVENTEEN

DUSTY

BRODY HAD GOTTEN into another fight. Henry had found him trying to wash the blood from his nose and puffy lip in the locker room late in the evening. How he'd gotten in when all the doors were locked was anyone's guess, and nothing would induce him to explain. He sat in the coach's office, wearing his P.E. clothes and a heavy scowl. Water dripped from grown-out hair onto his heathered gray shoulder, but his arms didn't move from their stiff position on the armrests.

I'd put the plate of Nova's lasagna in front of him and he eyed it greedily but wouldn't budge. Something was definitely going on with this boy.

When he was with the team, he was a born leader. Alone like this, he was just a sulking kid waiting to find out how much trouble he was in.

Henry stepped out to call Brody's grandma. I was sitting on the edge of my desk, my arms crossed over my chest. "If you tell us what happened, we can help you. You know the school has a low tolerance for fighting."

As in *zero* tolerance. I was hoping the fact that it was a

Saturday night and the fight didn't appear to happen on campus were going to work in his favor.

He said nothing, so I continued, "They won't be happy about breaking and entering, either."

"Then don't tell them."

That was my impulse, too. But at some point Brody needed to learn his actions had consequences. If we coddled him through school, he'd make the same mistakes when he left us, but the consequences would grow tenfold.

The little voice in the back of my head reminded me that maybe all Brody needed was a little coddling. No, not that. Maybe just someone in his corner. I'd hoped helping me out with the kids on the flag football team would be a good distraction for him, but was that my attempt at recreating history? I'd quit fighting and straightened out after Henry had made me his assistant and forced me to work with him to pay off my idiocy in tagging the school with spray paint.

Brody hadn't done anything destructive like that. At least not to anything but his own face. And maybe someone else's too.

A million little things floated through my mind. *You need to step up. You can't act this childish when you're eighteen in a few months. The team is relying on you to make it to state your senior year, so don't screw it up. Care about your standing and your future enough to quit jeopardizing both.* None of those words left my lips. When I looked at the deep grooves on his forehead and the defiance in his posture, I deflated.

Brody didn't need another lecture. He needed to feel like he mattered enough to try.

I scrubbed a hand over my face. "Who's giving you trouble?"

He kept his mouth sealed shut.

"Are you the one starting it? Because I have a hard time believing that."

"It's stupid," Brody said.

That wasn't much, but hey, at least we were making

progress. "The fight, or the reasons for it?" Both, obviously, but I wanted to know what he meant.

Brody sulked lower in the chair. "It didn't mean anything."

So, both. Like I'd thought. "Were these the same kids as last time?"

Brody looked away, making me think they were. At least that meant he wasn't going around fighting anyone he could. There was a reason for it.

"Listen, I get it. You don't want to tell me anything, and you don't have to." I pleaded with Teenage Me to send me the right words. "I'm not judging your choices, though. That would make me a hypocrite. I've been in your shoes so many times, I can't hold the fighting against you. Just know I'm here if you need someone, okay, B? If you need help, you can come to me. I'm not going anywhere."

He looked up, some of the tension leaving his rigid posture. We sat in silence for a minute, Brody watching me as if imagining me getting in fights and being a punk kid. Or maybe he was debating whether to trust me. We were so close, I could taste it. He had opened his mouth to speak when the door opened with a metal clang, the blinds crashing against the little window, and Henry came back in.

Brody promptly closed his mouth again.

I swore under my breath.

"Your grandma's on her way," Henry said. "What do you plan to tell her?"

Did she have to leave work for this? I saw her at Pleasant Gardens most evenings I was there. It wasn't often she was on the morning shift and had the night off.

"Sorry," he muttered.

"That's a start." Henry seemed as lost as I was. We'd found Brody in the locker room, but he hadn't really done anything we could directly punish. The whole situation felt oddly out of our hands. There was no proof of forced entry and nothing broken. Just a kid using the facilities to recuperate after a fight.

An idea came to me, and I forged ahead. Henry had been quiet so long I didn't think he was about to dole out punishments, anyway. "Do you have an after-school job?"

"No, sir," Brody muttered.

"Do you want to go to camp this summer with the team?"

Brody's eyes snapped up at that. I took it as a yes.

"Then you can help with the fundraiser."

"The auction?" he asked. We'd had the boys put fliers up around the school and post it to the parent groups on social media.

"If we don't get the money we need, no one is going to camp. If you help us with the auction, we'll forget that you ever broke in here."

He looked interested. "What do I have to do?"

"Be my assistant," I said. I wasn't looking away, because I wanted to make him agree with my eyes. I was afraid of pushing too hard, but I sat firm.

Henry's gaze snapped to me. If he saw what I was doing here, he kept his mouth closed. We'd never directly talked about the influence he'd had over my life, and now that we worked together, we'd become friends on a different level. He was more than a mentor to me. But we didn't have to speak about these things to understand each other.

"I don't have a car," Brody said.

"You don't need one. I'll give you assignments when I have them, and you can help me get them done. It won't take much time."

"Do I have to?" Brody asked.

"No."

We were all quiet for a minute before he nodded. "Okay. I'll do it."

"Great." I tried not to sound too relieved. Now to come up

with tasks. "Stop by the office Monday after school and I'll have your first job ready."

"Yes, coach." Brody returned to sulking.

I pushed the plate and plastic fork closer. "Eat something before your grandma gets here."

He picked up the fork. I'd microwaved it, but it probably wasn't hot anymore. He dug in, making my body heave a quiet sigh of relief.

Henry gave me a subtle nod of approval when Brody wasn't looking at us. If he thought it was a good idea, then it probably wouldn't be a total disaster. Now I just had to see it through.

LACEY BROUGHT our food on a round black tray and set the plates in front of us. We were sitting in Gigi's like we were on a double date again—me and Gracie Mae opposite Tucker and June. I was beginning to think the girls were having these meetings more to get me and Gracie Mae together than out of any wedding-planning need. It wasn't like I had anything valuable to add to the conversations about flowers and music and cake.

This wasn't normal, right? I didn't think it was. Not that I had any experience with weddings. Jack and Lauren's was the last one I'd gone to, and all I'd had to do was show up.

"How's the fundraiser coming along?" June asked before taking a bite from her burger. I'd never gotten around to stopping by the store to ask her for a donation, and I hoped she hadn't taken it personally.

"We're getting there. I could use more donations, but I have a man on the job."

"Man?" Tucker asked around his fried chicken. He was all caught up on the Brody debacle and my intention of using the kid to get donations from the shops along Main Street.

"Brody McAllister is going to use his charm and his football jersey to get us more donations. These boys need a lot of money if they're going to make it to camp."

"I can donate some books," June said hesitantly. "Or a gift card to the store."

We used to be such good friends. I knew I was the one standing in the way of that by making things awkward, but I couldn't help feeling the residual dregs of her abandonment. It was stupid and unfair. She was back, she'd apologized, she was sticking around. But I'd been abandoned by too many people not to take it hard and, for some reason, my mind was having a hard time forgiving her entirely.

But I could try harder. "Books would be great, June. You can choose from whatever stock you want to move so it benefits you, too."

"Okay, great." She pushed back her curly blonde hair. "I'll get a few bundles put together."

"I'll send Brody by the store to pick them up next week. He's supposed to be my assistant for this thing. I need to come up with more jobs for him to do."

"Great. They'll be ready."

That wasn't so bad. Maybe a few more of those conversations and we'd be back to being real friends. I needed to reach that point before the wedding, at least. I couldn't stand up with Tucker while I still felt hurt over June's betrayal. If Tuck could forgive her, I really had no excuse.

The bell rang above the door, and I looked up to see Chad Lincoln come in with Nova and her kids. The lunch date.

Every muscle in my body constricted. I'd seen enough of his crappy relationships over the years that my gut clenched at the thought of him being with anyone I cared about.

I must have stared too long, because Tucker and June looked over their shoulders to see who had walked in.

"Don't let him bother you," Tucker said, taking the attention off Nova. Good man.

Gracie Mae took a sip of her Coke. "Did you see he's dating Hannah now?"

Another girl we'd all gone to school with who had returned to Arcadia Creek after college. I had never known her really well, but she was obsessed with Tucker's brother, Jack.

"I think they broke up," June said. "Hannah took some of their photos together off Instagram."

"I don't blame her," Gracie Mae muttered when Chad sat in the booth beside ours. Nova slid into the side facing my table—if I leaned a little to the side I could look right at her.

"Coach!" Ben said, jumping up from his seat and coming to our table. "I've been working on catching!"

"Nice, buddy," I said, leaning over Gracie Mae and offering my fist.

He bumped it. "My mom isn't good at throwing though, so it makes it hard to catch them."

"Hey," Nova called, "I heard that."

"It's not her fault she's a Yankee," I whisper-yelled.

"Heard that, too," Nova said.

"She doesn't play baseball," Ben said, scrunching his face in confusion. His blond hair stuck up in the back.

I tried to subdue my grin, sliding my arm along the back of the bench. "It's also a term for a person from the East Co—from New York."

"Then I'm a Yankee too."

"Nah," I said, settling in. "You're a Texan now."

Ben's grin spread over his whole face. "Yes, sir," he said. Clearly he'd picked up on how the other boys responded to an adult.

The reality that everyone at my table was watching this interaction closely should have alarmed me, but it didn't. I glanced at Gracie Mae and noticed she was settling in under my arm. I hadn't even realized I'd practically thrown my arm over her shoulders when I'd rested it along the back of the bench. I pulled it away. "Enjoy your lunch, Ben."

"Yes, sir," he said, hopping back to squeeze onto the bench beside Alice and his mom. Neither of the kids had chosen to sit by Chad, which made me happier than it should have. I looked at Nova between Tucker and June's heads and caught a smile on her lips while she looked down at her son. Then Chad scooted over, hiding her from view and making my chest go stiff.

The rest of the lunch was an exercise in extreme patience. Chad made Nova laugh a few times, which made me want to reach across my table and smack the back of his head. Obviously, I didn't. He'd probably arrest me for assault, to say nothing of the fact that making a woman laugh was not a head-slapping offense.

There was also the whole violence thing. I'd utterly avoided it since high school; I didn't want to break my record now.

But I was in one of those moods where everything Chad did made me want to hit something. Yes, I could see how unreasonable I was being.

We made it through the rest of our meal and paid our check without incident. I gave Ben a fist bump on my way out and winked at Alice, not looking up to see what Nova thought.

"See y'all," Gracie Mae called when we got outside. She gave me a wide smile and I returned it, then walked toward my truck.

"Hey, Dusty, wait," she called.

My body tightened. I was forming an excuse about heading out to see my Grandpa so Gracie Mae wouldn't rope me into doing something with her. But when I saw Nova hurrying my way, I realized she had called my name.

I instantly relaxed. It was time to talk to Gracie Mae again, I knew that. But, honestly, a guy could only say he wasn't interested so many times before it was on her to understand and move on.

"What's up?"

"I didn't hear from you last night," she said, a little breathless from hurrying after me. "Is Brody okay?"

"Oh, yeah, he's fine. A little scraped up."

She nodded. "Good. I was worried. Must be the mom in me."

Or just goodness, plain and simple. Not all moms worried about their kids. Mine certainly never had. "He's been fighting with some other kids. I'm trying to keep him from getting in trouble with the school, so I've brought him on to help with the auction we're having at the end of the month."

"That's good of you."

"I like the kid. It's not a trial."

She nodded. "Well, thanks for all you do for these boys."

"One more point for me?" I asked.

"Who's keeping track?"

"I am, obviously. Since we've met, I've been racking them up. I'm going to win."

She gave an incredulous laugh. "Win what?"

Her, hopefully. I swallowed the thought, shoving it to the furthest recesses of my brain. I didn't even know where it had come from, since I was actively trying not to think of her that way. I wasn't playing the long game here. I wasn't playing *any* games.

She turned and started walking back to the diner, probably sensing I had no ready response. "See you later, Dusty."

"See ya," I called, feeling like a total idiot.

Fine, I'd admit it, but only to myself. I was starting to fall for Nova.

CHAPTER EIGHTEEN

NOVA

"WE WATCHED *MATILDA* TODAY," Ben said while we were walking home from school. "The class read it together before we got here."

"Did you like it?" I asked, smoothing my hand over his messy blond hair.

"Yeah."

"Well, we can read it together," I offered.

Ben looked up, making my hand fall. "Really?"

"I want to read it!" Alice said.

I glanced down at her. She would probably love it too. "There's a book shop on Main Street. Do you guys want to go check it out and see if they carry *Matilda*?"

My kids chorused a resounding yes, so we slipped down an alley to get to the right side of the buildings and walked toward Baker Books. Tucker's fiancée, June, was sitting behind the counter, working at a laptop. Her blonde frizzy hair was wild and long. She lifted her gaze to us and smiled widely. "Welcome! This is a treat."

"Hi, June," I said. "We're looking for a book today. Do you carry *Matilda*?"

"Of course I do!" She hopped down from her stool and came around the counter, leading us to a corner strung with twinkle lights over a beanbag chair and an array of children's book characters in stuffed animal form. "It's a classic."

"Ben's class just finished reading it, so they watched the movie today. We're doing things a little backwards."

"That's how it goes sometimes." She pulled the book from the shelf and presented it to me. I was taking it when the bell jangled above the door again, and Brody walked in.

"Coach said you have books for the fundraiser," he said.

"Can you give me a minute?" June asked me. "Don't go anywhere."

I nodded, and she hurried toward the front door. "Come with me, Brody. I have a few bundles for you."

"Mom," Alice whispered, dragging me closer to the bookshelf. "Can we look at the other books?"

"There's a deal," Ben added, pointing at a sign taped to the shelf. "Twenty percent discount if you buy three books! That's perfect. *Matilda* and one more for each of us."

"I don't know, bud." Mental math wasn't my forte, but I tried to do some to see how much money I'd have to part with.

"There's a deal," he reiterated, pointing to the sign like I hadn't seen it.

"Right, but you still have to buy three books."

Both of them looked up at me with round pleading eyes, and I was having a hard time reasoning my way out of this one. I mean, we were talking about *books*.

"Okay, fine. But they have to be under ten dollars each."

They cheered. Ben dropped his backpack at my feet and started browsing small chapter books, and Alice went straight for the pink section.

I took both backpacks to the wall and set them out of the way, then sat on a small armchair near the beanbag, *Matilda* on my knees. I didn't want to browse the books or I'd end up spending even more money, so I pulled out my phone instead. Trish had sent me a text, so I opened it.

TRISH

Heard the news. Sending my love. 🩶

If she wanted me to ask her what the news was, she was going to be disappointed. Probably. I opened Instagram instead and went straight to Carter's page, but his photos were all pretty typical. Black and white, him at events, leaning on bars, holding drinks, looking for all the world like he wasn't a dad or a husband.

Well, he wasn't a husband anymore, but he was still a dad.

The ring around his profile photo was colored in, indicating he'd posted a story—a photo that would disappear in twenty-four hours. I was tempted to look at it, but he would be able to see that I'd seen it. Oh, gosh. This was childish. Who cared if he knew that I watched his story? I'd muted his account when he left because I found myself watching it for updates to an unhealthy degree. Now I didn't see his posts unless I sought them out, and he was none the wiser.

Trish's text left me uneasy, though, so I pressed the button. The first photo was almost expired, Carter holding a drink beside another lawyer from his firm. Total East Coast bros. Then the second one popped up and my stomach fell clear to the floor. It was a selfie of Carter with a red-headed woman. No, girl? Could she be considered a woman when she hardly looked old enough to be in college? She was sitting on his lap and the dancing words in the corner of the screen said *moving day*.

Oh, no. I was gonna hurl.

I dropped my phone like it was made of lava and sat back, my breaths coming rapidly.

Carter was living with someone else already. Another woman —yes, I believed she was at least eighteen—was going to live in my home, cook with my things, sit on my reupholstered armchair. I could see the rust-colored brocade of the chair they were sitting in, and that seemed like the worst thing of all.

Maybe my brain was snagging on that detail because I needed something to focus my confusing whirl of feelings on, but it felt really important to me. I didn't even know this person, and now she was living with my things.

No, not *my* things, not anymore. The settlement stating all those things were now his had happened so fast. We'd managed it out of court with a mediator and our own lawyers. My brother's friend had stepped up for me and I'd thought he got me a good chunk of money. Now I wondered if going through the courts would have gotten me more. Now I didn't care as much about being amicable and wished I would've fought a little more.

Now I wanted to throw this book at Carter's face.

"Coach!" Ben said, jumping up and running across the room.

I looked for Dusty, but it was just Brody looking ready to leave with a bag of books in his hand. His posture was a little bent and a yellowing bruise was spreading across his cheekbone. "Hey, little man." Brody put out a fist for a bump. "You been working on catching?"

"My mom tries to help me." Translation: my mom does her best, but it's not very good.

"Right on. We can work on it more at practice tomorrow, too."

Ben beamed at him. "Thanks, Coach."

Brody's shoulders straightened a little, his smile growing. He ruffled Ben's hair and left.

Would anyone notice if I dropped my head between my knees just to help me breathe evenly? My chest was rising erratically. I leaned over to pick up the kids' backpacks and focused on slowing my thundering heart rate. "Let's go, guys," I said softly.

The bell rang again, and a short older woman walked in, her

eyes scanning the bookstore before landing on me. "Nova Walker!" she called, like she'd come here just for me.

I'd never met this woman in my life.

"Flora, you're back," June said. "I thought you were moving to Florida."

Flora shot her a disgusted look. "I'm back, and I need to welcome our newest residents." She bustled toward us and put her wrinkled hand on my arm. "Your aunt is one of my most favorite people in the world. You are lucky to have her."

"We are," I agreed, a little startled by her vehemence and her cloud of overbearing perfume.

"Now, my salon is just across the road there." She pointed through the window to the pink door on the other side of the street. "You come on by and see me, okay? First haircut is free." She glanced at Ben and Alice. "All of you. I'd love to have a chat."

Well, that was weird. I didn't know how to respond—or identify if I was feeling off about what I'd just learned about Carter. Was the ickiness bleeding into my other interactions, or was this interaction organically weird on its own? Either way, it was probably better to get more information from Gigi before making any commitments. "That is so kind. Thank you."

Flora blinked a few times before smiling at all of us. She squeezed my arm again, then bustled to the door. "Have a blessed day, June," she said as she let herself out.

I felt like we had gone through a low-key tornado. Not that I knew what tornados felt like.

"Sorry about her." June cringed as I made my way up to the front desk. "Her salon is straight across the street, and sometimes I think she sits at the window and watches my store to see who is coming by, just so she can ambush them."

I glanced out the window at the short woman bustling across the road.

June gave a little laugh. "She means well, I think, but the free haircuts are a scam."

"What's a scam?" Alice whispered, putting the fairy book she'd chosen on the counter. Ben slid a book with a dragon on it beside hers.

I honestly didn't know what she could mean by a haircut being a scam, so I had no answer ready.

June started ringing up the books. "She expects an enormous tip, so you still pay for it. I'd be careful what you say around her, because it'll end up making its rounds by dinnertime."

"I got that impression," I said. Why else would Flora want to chat? She'd blown in here knowing my full name already and, apparently, what I looked like.

June rang up our purchases, then slid the bag over and pushed her long hair behind her shoulders. "Hey, I heard you make pretty cookies."

How? Who would have told her?

"Dusty might have mentioned it," she said apologetically, like she'd read the confusion on my face and wanted to explain. "I'm supposed to have a bridal shower this weekend, so I was wondering if you make them for events. It's totally fine if you don't. It's super last minute."

"Oh, I used to," I told her. "Mostly for friends or family. They aren't professional, but I can do most shapes."

"What about sunflowers?"

"I could definitely do those." I actually had a set of flower cookie cutters that had come with a sunflower. I'd never done it before, but it shouldn't be too hard. "What are the colors? Would you want anything else? Like a badge that says 'bride' across it?"

"Oh, cute! Yes, something like that would be fun. How much do you charge for…like…two dozen cookies?"

I had no earthly idea. Trish had overpaid, or so I imagined, so I wasn't going to charge June the same rate.

"Three dollars per cookie? Four?" she asked.

"Forty dollars per dozen," I said, feeling a little like I was overpricing, but also they took so much time to decorate. Days of layers to get the right detail.

"Done. Two dozen then? For Saturday morning. I'd love to have you stay, too."

"That's not necessary." There was nothing worse than a pity invite.

"No, I mean it. It's a great way to meet more people in town. You don't have to bring anything—except the cookies, of course."

"I don't know."

"Here. Give me your number, and I'll text you the details." She opened her phone and slid it across the counter.

I liked June. We hadn't been around each other much, but she seemed down to earth. Part of me wanted to spite Carter and allow myself to fall fully under the small-town spell of Arcadia Creek, making friends and building a life that didn't make me miss my home so much. The other part of me wanted to go home and let the kids play on their devices while I curled up in a ball and cried.

I put my number in her phone, took our bag of books, and ushered my kids outside.

"She's nice," Alice said when we left.

"I agree." I pulled her to me while we crossed the street and made our way down to our apartment. Ben was reciting the Texas pledge he'd been learning in school as we went. When we reached our place, there was a large, heavy rectangular box leaning against the door. I tried to move it aside, but it wouldn't budge.

"Guys, I think your bunk bed arrived."

They hollered and cheered, but I groaned. We were blocked. At least the delivery guys had brought it up the stairs.

Five minutes and some sad attempts at shoving later, I got

the bed to move enough for us to unlock the door and slip inside.

"Will you set it up now?" Alice asked.

Fresh on the heels of learning how fully and quickly Carter had moved on, I was determined to do this on my own. This wasn't going to be like the jar of unopened jam sitting in my fridge—a sign of my defeat. I was going to be champion. I sucked in a breath and looked at the heavy box. "Yes. I've got this."

Ben didn't look convinced. We'd see who was right.

CHAPTER NINETEEN

NOVA

BEN. Ben and his misgivings were entirely correct, and I was wrong. Just like the picture at the front of the instruction pamphlet said—and the picture on the side of the enormous box, and my quiet instincts—this bunk bed was a two-person job. I'd figured out how to get all the many pieces into Ben and Alice's room by opening the box where it was, leaning it against my door, and carrying in the planks of wood one at a time.

Stubborn? Me? No, the word was *resourceful*.

Now I realized why all the pictures showed two people lifting things. To lift one bed frame onto the other and screw them into place, you needed a second person. I'd bought a very inexpensive bed, which meant it didn't come apart and form two different beds, but I hadn't thought it would matter. This way they'd have more floor space to play. It also meant asking someone to help lift and hold it in place while I screwed it together. My kids were too small, and I wasn't about to ask Gigi.

Which left me with a glaring, obvious answer I didn't want to use. Mostly because I'd already used him multiple times.

There was also Chad, I supposed, but it felt a little weird and personal asking him to come help me. We hadn't reached that level of friendship. If I was being entirely honest, I didn't want to reach it with him either. Dusty, on the other hand, had already been in every room in my tiny home. He was intimately familiar with my failings as a mother, and he liked helping others.

I mean, the man was a firefighter.

My kids had gotten bored with this project and were snuggled on my bed watching *Despicable Me* on my laptop. I slunk down to the floor and pulled out my phone to send Dusty a message. Instead of doing that, I opened Instagram for the fortieth time since this afternoon and navigated to Carter's page, finding his stories. He hadn't updated them, and the picture of him and the redhead had one hour left before it would expire.

I wasn't ready to move on yet. I toggled over to Safari and asked Google if Carter would know if I screenshot his story. I'd never felt my thirty-one years more than I did in that moment. A few years ago, that was the type of thing I'd know offhand. Thankfully, I got the answer I was hoping for. I went back to Instagram and captured the image to live in my phone forever. Or at least for as long as it took to come to terms with this change in my life.

Would my kids have to be around this woman if they went to stay with Carter for any length of time over the summer? What kind of person was she? Did my friends—Trish, at least—know she'd moved in with Carter because of Instagram or from seeing them together around the city? Did he take her out every night? Did he make time for this woman the way he couldn't make time to call his own children consistently?

My eyes went hot when tears spilled over the edges, but I'd cried enough tonight for him. I dashed them away angrily and groaned. Sucking in a cool, long breath, I let it out and focused on exhaling, closing my eyes and commanding myself to put it aside for now. It could be managed later.

Right now, I needed to get this bed put together so my kids would have somewhere to sleep that wasn't littered with screws and spare pieces of wood and those weird round things cheap furniture came with. I typed out a message to Dusty, but my finger hovered over the send button. Once I did this, there would be no going back. Defeat edged into my body. I wanted to be enough for my kids on my own. I couldn't finish the bed alone, though, so I swallowed my pride, shoved away my failure with tired arms, and sent the text.

NOVA

Hey there, Rival

DUSTY

Why do I have a feeling you're about to ask me for something? I don't know how to say this, but you can't have my cat

I laughed despite myself and wiped my eyes again.

NOVA

Your instincts aren't too off, but I'm not a cat person

DUSTY

Wow. How disappointing. I was hoping we could be friends

NOVA

It's been a good run

DUSTY

Nice to know you

I took a steadying breath.

NOVA

Are you busy?

> **DUSTY**
>
> Just about to leave Beeler. What's up? Want me to show you what lasagna's really supposed to taste like?

> **NOVA**
>
> I thought you said mine was the best you'd ever had

> **DUSTY**
>
> It was. I was just trying to get you to make it again

I laughed again, the sound watery. It was a good thing he wasn't here to witness the mess on my face.

My phone started buzzing and I stared at it, sucking in a slightly panicked breath between my teeth. Dusty was calling. I cleared my throat and hummed a little to make sure it sounded mostly normal, then swiped to answer. "Hey."

"Hey," he said, sounding a little distanced from the phone. "I'm driving now, so I thought this was safer. Is everything okay?"

"Yeah, we're fine. I have this bunk bed to put together, but I've reached a point where I need a second person to hold things in place and I..." Drawing in a shaky breath, I fought the emotion clouding my throat. "I was hoping you had five minutes to come hold it for me." My voice went too high while I was trying to cover my sudden bout of fresh tears. This was stupid. I shouldn't be crying over this, and I *really* hoped he couldn't tell.

He was silent for a moment. "What's going on, Nova?" he asked, his voice low and steady.

Great, so he *could* totally tell.

"It's really just this stupid bed. It doesn't have to be done right now. But sometime when you have a minute—"

"Give me twenty minutes, and I'll be there."

"I thought you just left Beeler," I said, remembering it had taken more than twenty minutes to get there last time.

"I'll be there soon. Did you guys eat dinner?"

I glanced at the time. It was almost seven, and I hadn't even thought of what to make. It was looking like a Kraft night. "Not yet."

"Don't cook. I have dinner with me, and it's more than enough for all of us. Will your kids eat tacos?"

"They love tacos." My emotions were rising again, but this time I knew why. On top of everything else, I didn't have to cook.

"Okay. See you soon." He seemed to hesitate.

I didn't say anything. Honestly, I would have been fine sitting against my kids' wall, listening to him on the phone all night just to not feel so alone. Wow, could I be more depressing? *Pathetic, Nova.*

"Nova?"

"Yeah?"

"I'm really glad you called."

My heart flew to my throat. "Actually, you're the one who called."

Dusty laughed, a deep, hearty sound. "Okay, fine. I'm glad you texted me. I meant it when I told you I'm happy to help."

"I know." Truly, I did. It was abundantly clear. He was the man I called because I knew he would be authentically happy to come over and help me get this done—no strings, no expectations, no assertions of his manliness. I really wanted to be independent and handle things on my own. It was important to feel like I could after being codependent to some degree for ten years. With Dusty, it didn't feel like codependency. It didn't feel like each of us doing what we had to in order to survive. It felt like *true* charity, giving of oneself with sincerity and genuine kindness. There were no ulterior motives here.

At least I didn't think there were.

"Thanks," I finally said when the silence had stretched too long. The poor guy was probably waiting for me to break down, but somehow talking to him had a calming effect on me. "I'll see you soon."

We hung up, and I went into the bathroom to splash cool water on my face. Twenty minutes later, Dusty showed up on my porch. He wore a long-sleeve black shirt with Arcadia Energy written down the side of his arm that he must have gotten from Tucker. His muscles strained under the sleeves, his honey eyes shining against my porchlight and a shadow of beard growth on his jaw.

I didn't think anyone had ever looked so good. "Hi," I said softly.

He gave me a smile that wasn't overly large, but felt like it was just for me, then lifted a big dish of meat and a bag of corn tortillas and fixings. "Hi. Why don't we eat first and worry about the bed after?"

I released a sigh. "Sounds perfect to me."

Dusty preheated my oven, ostensibly to warm the meat, and got to work setting everything up.

"Do you always carry around emergency tacos?"

He laughed, which felt like a win. "I tried to take them to my grandpa tonight, but he was asleep when I got there and the facility won't keep the food on hand for tomorrow."

"Won't he be disappointed?"

"Nah, he won't even know. He forgets most things from day to day." Dusty shrugged, but I sensed it mattered to him more than he made it sound.

He'd told me his parents weren't in the picture and his grandpa had raised him. If the man who'd raised me was suffering from dementia in this way, I don't know how I'd cope. It would feel so *lonely*. Did he have anyone else? Anyone at all?

Dusty set out dinner while I retrieved plates and silverware. We worked around each other effortlessly. I filled glasses with ice water and Dusty searched my fridge.

"Salsa?" he asked, looking through the few condiments I had in the door.

"In the pantry. We haven't opened it yet."

He found the jar and popped the lid effortlessly before putting it on the table. My eyes rose to his arms. If I asked, I bet he'd open the strawberry jam for me. I couldn't bring myself to do it. Instead, I'd bought a squeeze canister of grape jam—my kids' second favorite flavor—and was determined to open the strawberry jar on my own. Once I'd built up more strength, maybe? In all honesty, I had only tried one other time after that first day of school, and it still didn't budge. I was half-convinced someone at the market had superglued the thing shut as an old April Fool's joke and forgot about it.

"Ready," Dusty said, pulling the meat from the oven. The aroma filled my small kitchen like a warm, billowing cloud of cumin and garlic.

Ben popped around the corner. "What's that smell?"

"Tacos," I told him. "Courtesy of Coach Hayes."

His eyes brightened when he noticed Dusty near the table. It did a weird, dangerous thing to my stomach.

"Will you get your sister, please?" I asked.

Ben ran into my room, calling for Alice as he went. I watched him hurry to the table and eagerly sit in the chair closest to where Dusty hovered. Alice rolled into the room in a long series of somersaults before climbing onto her seat across from Ben, her pink monkey on her lap.

Dusty said nothing, like it was totally normal to roll into the dining room, but I caught the glint of amusement in his eyes while he stood beside his chair. I fetched sour cream and a spoon before sitting, and he waited until I was in my chair before lowering himself into his. Sometimes the country boy manners were a bit much, but other times they were just sweet. Right now, while the reality that Carter had fully and completely moved on hovered in the back of my mind, I was leaning toward the sweetness.

Was it unhealthy to appreciate Dusty right now? I didn't have to marry the guy to like how he treated me or my children. Maybe I was leaning a little too easily into enjoying the way he seemed interested while Alice quietly told him the history of her pink monkey—how she'd gotten it on a trip to the zoo. I was tired of resisting, of being strong for three people instead of just one, and I let my walls down the littlest bit. Only for this dinner, I would let myself enjoy a moment where my kids felt heard by an adult who wasn't me, where I didn't have to cook after working all day and mom-ing all afternoon, and where the man at the other end of the table wasn't leaving me alone so he could move in with his new upgraded girlfriend.

Okay, I clearly wasn't over it. Carter's life change still bothered me. The weirdness of it more than anything else. Maybe that's why I couldn't shake it—he wasn't the type of guy to jump into a commitment in general. He'd asked for the divorce and left me over a year ago, and if Trish could be believed, he'd been dating around. Then *bam*, full on live-in girlfriend.

That was probably what bugged me about the situation. Not how quickly he'd moved on from me, but how fast he'd committed to this girl when they couldn't have been serious for very long. It was out of character.

I needed to stop thinking about Carter, so I bit into my taco and moaned with appreciation. "Okay, you win. Your tacos trump my lasagna."

Dusty shoved the last bite of a taco in his mouth, shaking his head. "You can't compare Italian to Mexican. That's unfair to both parties. They're different."

"I stand by what I said."

"Let's take it to a vote." Dusty looked Ben and Alice in the eye one at a time. "The kids can decide. What did you like better? Your mom's amazing, mouth-watering, rich lasagna or these frumpy tacos?"

I couldn't help but laugh.

"Raise your hand for lasagna," he said, shooting his arm in the air. Alice giggled, raising her hand. "Now tacos."

Ben put both arms in the air, wiggling them around, and I joined him.

"Shoot, it's a tie." I scratched an itch on my arm, then reached for another taco.

Dusty looked at me with a smile that melted my insides just a bit. "Guess we'll need a rematch."

CHAPTER TWENTY

DUSTY

STOP FLIRTING. Stop. It. If I commanded myself enough times, would it work? In an effort to be myself, I kept saying things that could be misconstrued. Really, it was no surprise Nova thought I was coming on to her when we'd first met last month.

I wasn't trying to. I just liked her and her kids and wanted to make them smile.

Okay, so maybe I was flirting a little. But I was trying my darndest not to.

By the time we finished eating, it was getting late. Way past the kids' bedtimes, I was guessing. Alice had chatted through dinner—well, she spoke a few times, which I thought was the equivalent to her being a chatterbox—and now her eyes were getting droopy.

"Let's get that bed assembled, then worry about putting this away," I suggested, rising from the table.

Nova looked from me to her kids. I could tell she didn't like the idea of leaving a mess. She glanced at the clock and seemed to like delaying her kids' bedtime even less. "That would be great."

The kids' room was cluttered with screws and washers and

pieces of wood. Their mattresses were shoved vertically along the wall, with a pine structure mostly put together in the center of the room. A second bed frame was on the floor, taking up the remaining space. We oriented ourselves with the final few steps of the bed, then took our positions and prepared to lift.

It wasn't very heavy by itself, but the size and shape made it impossible for one person to lift and hold it in place. I was impressed with how much Nova had done on her own before she'd reached the desperation point, especially when I imagined how difficult it was for her to ask anyone for anything. If she couldn't let her own aunt buy her a sofa, she was the worst kind of stubborn.

"Do you have it?" she asked, her arms lifted to hold her side in place.

The bed felt secure. "Yeah. You can let go."

Nova did so slowly, then hurried to retrieve the screws and washers and things she needed to fasten the rest of the bed together. It took less than fifteen minutes. She worked fast and knew exactly what to do. We each took different ends of the mattresses and slid them into place, then Nova bent and made the beds with what looked like clean sheets.

Once the whole room was finished, we stood near the doorway, shoulder to shoulder, and looked at the sturdy pine bunk bed.

"Well done, Nova."

There was a hitch in her breathing. "I didn't do it by myself."

"No, but you did most of it." She was silent, so I looked at her. She was tall enough that I didn't have to crane my neck down to hold her gaze, which I loved. "You do know there are no special gold stars for people who get it done alone, right? No one hands out awards for running yourself into the ground."

She looked up at me, her brown eyes surprised and wide.

"I know from experience," I explained. "It's not worth trying to win that race."

"Your metaphors are mixing."

"You still know what I mean," I challenged.

I took Nova's lack of response to mean that she knew exactly what I meant. When I'd called earlier, her voice had sounded so high and strange, I'd wondered if she'd been crying. Now, noting the tired red rim to her eyes and the weariness to her mouth, I was positive. It made me want to pull her in for a long, tight hug, but I knew my limits. That was definitely pushing boundaries.

"My kids need to get to bed."

"Say no more. I'll just get my taco stuff together and get out of your hair."

Nova gave me a tired smile. "Dinner and construction help. I owe you triple now."

"You owe me nothing, Nova," I said, and it came out so serious, she grew still. "This is what friends do for each other. Sheesh," I added, trying to lighten the tone. "It makes me wonder what kind of people come out of New York."

"There are plenty of excellent people from New York." She started toward the hallway. "Like me."

I laughed, not expecting that.

Nova disappeared into her room. "Who wants to see your new bed?"

Squeals and shouts preceded the stampede as the kids ran to their room. They were utterly delighted, which warmed my chest. If I was happy about it, their mom was likely ecstatic. I heard her telling them to get ready for bed, so I started clearing the table and bagging up the food I'd brought in foil dishes. Nova helped Alice brush her teeth, then got both kids squared away in their pajamas and tucked into bed while I put away the condiments. I could hear Nova reading to them, so I started the dishes. She didn't have a dishwasher, but I'd grown up without one, so I was pretty good at cleaning dishes.

"You don't need to do that," Nova said from the hallway.

I looked up from where my arms were plunging into sudsy water, scrubbing at a plate. "It's really not a problem."

She looked like she wanted to say more, but instead, she walked toward me. My heart rate increased, but Nova only picked up a clean dish towel and started to dry the ones I'd already washed, then put them away.

"We saw Brody at the bookstore today picking up things for the auction," she said. "Do you have a good amount of donations?"

"Quite a few. I won't turn down another one, if you have something in mind."

Her eyes flashed to me. "I don't have anything to donate."

"You're kidding, right?" I lifted my eyebrows but kept my attention on the dishes. "People would pay a pretty penny for a plate of those berry bars you made. I've heard about them from a handful of different people."

"Seriously?" She looked suspicious.

"Or your cookies. June mentioned you're making them for her party. I bet you'll have a lot of interest after that."

"I don't know if I really have time for more orders, but I'm happy to help June out."

"It was nice of you to agree to it."

We were silent for a minute before she spoke again. "I could do a dozen for the auction, but I don't expect they'll bring much money in."

"You don't have to," I said, handing her the last plate. I pulled the plug to let the water drain.

"I know." She dried it and stacked it with the rest of her plates. "I really don't mind. The cookies freeze well, so I'll just make a few more when I do June's."

"If you're sure."

"Consider it repayment."

Something about that felt a little weird to me. I picked up my bag of food and walked toward the door. She must have sensed my reaction because she followed me, holding the handle when I stepped outside. "You really don't owe me anything, Nova. You don't have to repay me. If you feel like you *have* to do this, then I don't want the cookies. I'm not trying to guilt anyone into helping."

She cringed. "I shouldn't have said it like that. I really am happy to help."

My eyebrows shot up. "So you can feel that way, but I can't?"

Nova chewed on her bottom lip, watching me. She glanced over her shoulder before following me out onto the porch. Testing the handle, she made sure it was unlocked before pulling the door closed, likely so the kids wouldn't overhear whatever she was about to say.

"I'm kind of in a weird position." She looked at me, the orange porch light from one of the houses across the street glowing in her eyes. "I've been acting like a single parent for the last few years, even though I had a husband. But he was still there, and when I had things come up like this bed or the stupid jar I can't get open, I could wait until he'd come home and help me out. Now that I'm actually a single parent and I don't have a husband around, it just feels…I don't know, like I'm supposed to be able to do it on my own? That if I can't, it proves I still need Carter?"

This was the most personal Nova had become with me, and I really didn't want to say anything stupid and mess it up. "You don't want him to win," I guessed. It made sense, and it explained why she thought everything needed to be tit for tat. Why she would only agree to make the cookies if she thought she was paying me back for all I'd done for her. She couldn't see how strong and resilient she looked from the outside.

Nova's shoulders relaxed. "Something like that. Right now, he's totally winning."

My stomach tightened. That didn't sound good. Did this

have something to do with why she had been crying earlier? "Right." I nodded slowly. "He got all the furniture."

She gave a watery chuckle.

"The way I see it, you're way ahead. You got the kids, and they're both pretty rad."

She peered at me. "Do people even say *rad* anymore?"

"I just did. You also got all this open space and clear air." I gestured to the world around us. "And, not to brag, but it seems like you got a pretty great sofa, too."

She leaned back against the door and looked out at the dark sky. "It is pretty out here. You don't see this many stars in Manhattan." Her gaze slid to me. "I know you're just being nice, but thank you. Ben really loves being on the football team. I think it's giving him a place to be included, to get involved. Alice never talks to anyone, so you're clearly a hit with both of them."

My chest warmed at this praise. Hearing from Nova that her kids liked me was almost as good as gaining the respect and admiration of a cat—hard won. "Like I said, they're pretty rad. I can't believe Alice willingly told me all about Peaches at dinner."

Nova looked at the stars as she talked. "She got that monkey on a day out with Carter. He took the kids so I could go to the hospital when my sister-in-law went into labor. My brother was out of town and the baby was early and…anyway, long story, but Alice got the monkey that day. It was probably the only time Carter had the kids without me for a twenty-four hour period, and they soaked it up to their bones. That monkey is a bonafide member of the family now, it's so important to her."

"I can see why. She probably connects it to her dad, whether it's subconscious or deliberate."

"Probably," she agreed lightly. "And he's so…I could just wring his neck. There is nothing so painful as watching your kids wait while the phone rings or the call gets rejected day after day. He's supposed to get them for two weeks in the summer as part of our divorce agreement, but I'm scared to send them. Especially not now that—" She pulled up short, her eyes darting to me and away.

Curiosity burned in my gut. "You don't have to tell me anything you don't want to share."

She groaned, sitting on the top step of the staircase leading down to the street.

I moved to sit beside her, putting the paper bag of food behind me.

Her head in her hands, her voice came out muffled. "His girlfriend just moved in with him. I think it's a girlfriend. I don't actually know anything."

My body froze. "I'm sorry, Nova."

She looked up. "I don't really care. I shouldn't, at least, but it feels weird. This strange girl is in my house, sitting on my chair, using my pots and pans to cook for my husb—*ex*. My ex-husband. Until a few days ago, the only thing I had to sit on were bar stools or a blow up mattress. I shouldn't be angry at him, but I am. And I don't even know how to navigate introducing my children to this woman I've never met or trust them in a house with her at some point in the future."

Wow. I couldn't even begin to understand the difficulty she faced. I wanted to pull her into my arms and soothe her stress, but that wouldn't make the situation go away or help her figure out what needed to be done.

"Then there's part of me that knows Carter has way more money than he needs, and he should be paying much higher child support since I have the kids ninety-five percent of the time. Now that I'm out of the divorce haze, I can see he swindled me in the proceedings somehow. He's a lawyer. I thought keeping it out of the courts and settling on our own would be healthier for all involved. I feel like an idiot."

"You aren't, so you can put that thought away." My blood

hummed angrily, but I shoved the fury down. It wasn't what she needed. "He preyed on your grief."

"He did," she agreed, turning her head to look at me, though it still rested in her hands. She gave me a self-deprecating smile. "It's no wonder I'm so screwed up."

"That's not how I'd describe you," I said, pushing down the urge to drive straight to Manhattan, find Carter Walker, and punch him in the face three times—once for each of them. "I see a reliable, steady mom who's working hard to put together a home for her kids, who has provided them with a safe place and a lot of love. When it comes to basic needs—the things we actually *need*—you have it covered, Nova. Your kids are loved. They aren't suffering."

The orange porch lights from across the street shone on the tears rolling down her cheeks. "You don't know how much I needed to hear that."

My entire body clenched, my muscles tight, struggling as I refrained from pulling her close. "I'll remind you anytime you want."

"Thanks," she breathed, dashing away the tears. She reached to scratch her arm, then glanced down and groaned.

"What is it?"

"My hives are back. I think I need to delete social media."

"Then do it."

She laughed. "And miss all the pictures of my nephews? No, thanks."

Okay, that was a fair point.

"I should probably go take some medication before it gets worse," she said, but she didn't stand. She sat there looking at me, and the line of connection running between us felt as taut as my clenched fists.

I relaxed my hands, with great effort. "You mentioned a jar you can't get open. Do you want me to try?"

"No, that's okay." She smiled. "It's just jam, so I bought a squeeze tube to use instead."

I laughed. "See what I mean? Resourceful."

Her face softened while she peered at me. "Did Gigi put you up to this?" she asked, rising to her feet. "Place you in my path to make me forget about Carter?"

My chest hummed. I made her forget about her ex? That seemed huge, so I did my best not to let her see how it affected me. "The opposite. When she heard you were coming a few months ago, she made me promise to stay away."

"Why?"

I shrugged. "Because I'm trouble, I guess."

Nova laughed, shaking her head. "You're a flirt, anyone can see you're harmless."

"Harmless?" I very much wanted to prove her wrong. I took a half step closer, making her step back until she was flush with the siding on the apartment building. I held her gaze, watching her eyes widen, her throat working a swallow. I kept some distance between us. She could turn and walk away if she wanted. A slow smile spread over my lips.

"Yes." Her tongue darted out to lick her lips. "I stand by what I said."

Tension filled the space between us. My chest rose and fell rapidly, my gaze glued to her lips. She could see through me, and I didn't know how I felt about that. But I could sense her breathing hastening too, and it was a relief to know I wasn't alone in how I felt. Which meant I needed to leave.

My mouth flicked up in a smile. "Have a good night, Nova." Then I turned and walked away. When I got to my truck, she was still standing next to her door, watching me. I waited until she went inside before driving away.

Man, I was such a goner for this girl.

CHAPTER TWENTY-ONE

NOVA

CARTER HAD BEEN TRYING to call me for two days, but since the kids hadn't been nearby any of the times he called, I hadn't answered the phone. Until I knew, without a shadow of doubt, I could speak to him without letting my emotions get the better of me, I didn't think it was wise to answer. If Ben or Alice had been around, I would have handed the phone off to them. Even then, I was tired of jumping to attention every time he deigned to reach out, only for their conversations to last five minutes or less. He always had some excuse, some reason he needed to run, that got him off the phone fairly quickly.

So now, when I was carrying two dozen bridal shower cookies up the porch steps of the Fletcher Homestead—Tucker's parents' house—and my phone rang, I ignored it without hesitation. My kids were at the diner with Gigi. She'd offered to pay them in ice cream to help her roll silverware in napkins and secure it with the paper sticker things, and they had eagerly accepted. I was sure she only came up with the plan to give me a free morning for the shower. I didn't intend to remain long.

"Hi!" June said, opening the door for me. Her cheeks were

flushed and her blonde hair long and wild, the corkscrew curls bouncing over her shoulders. "Thanks for coming early."

"It's no problem." I stepped into a stunning, worn-in farmhouse that made me want to consider a cowboy someday when I remarried. *If* I ever remarried. I wasn't sure there was a man out there I would trust to help raise my children. They already had one absent dad.

Dusty flashed through my mind. I hadn't seen him all week, since he'd had work and missed Ben's practices, but we had texted a few times. He was becoming the person who made my stomach flutter when I saw his name pop up on my screen, which felt all sorts of dangerous.

"You can bring those into the kitchen," June said.

I lifted the gift bag in my other hand. "This is from Gigi. She had to work, but she sends her love."

June smiled. "That was kind of her." She showed me to the table for refreshments and the tiered tray she'd set aside for cookies. I opened the lid on the large Tupperware and started placing them on her tray. June stood beside me and clapped her hands together. "I love them so much! The flowers are *perfect*. You did all this detail yourself?"

"I've always liked drawing, so it wasn't hard," I said, brushing the praise away. Inside I was glowing. Carter's voice in the back of my head was loud, calling my cookies quaint, with that edge of superiority proving how little he thought of my efforts. It was hard not to notice that they were finally being appreciated by someone in a tiny town in a flipping farmhouse. Didn't that scream quaint? Was Carter right all along?

An older woman—old enough to be June's mom—bustled into the kitchen. Her short blonde hair was styled perfectly and sprayed into submission, and her smile was kind.

"This is Jan, my soon-to-be mother-in-law," June said, then gestured to me. "Nova Walker, Gigi's niece. I told you about the cookies."

Jan smiled widely, the lines on the sides of her mouth well-creased from being so happy, or so she appeared. "Welcome, Nova. We're so glad—oh my lanta, you made these?" She leaned over my arm to inspect the cookies—sunflowers and badges that said *bride* in cursive with two rings linked together. She squeezed my arm, sucking in a gasp. "These are incredible."

"Thank you." My cheeks warmed from the praise. I shouldn't love it, but it felt nice to be appreciated.

The back door swung shut and Tucker appeared, carrying a small table. "Howdy, Nova," he said, dipping his head to me. He looked at his mom. "Where do you want this?"

"Next to the fireplace. We're putting gifts on it."

He left to deliver the table.

The front door shut loudly and a woman walked in the kitchen a moment later with a computer under one arm. She wore a collared shirt beneath her blue sweater and wide-legged chinos, her mid-length brown hair brushing her shoulders.

June rushed over to give her a hug. "Lauren! Have you met Nova? She just moved here with her two kids from New York."

"Another transplant," Lauren said, offering me a hand to shake. Her smile was wide. "You're Gigi's niece, right? We love her."

"She's pretty great," I agreed.

"Lauren is married to Jack," June explained.

The pieces were fitting together now. "Oh, he's helped move furniture for me."

"He's pretty great, too," Lauren said. "How are you settling in? I grew up in Dallas, but even that's a world apart from small town Texas. This is a very unique place."

"By unique, she's calling us quaint," Jan said from the stove, where she leaned down to peer into the oven.

"Which isn't a bad word," Lauren said defensively. "I don't know why everyone thinks it's bad."

I certainly did, but I could tell by the affectionate banter between Lauren and Jan that it was a well-meant tease and not a slight. Carter used to brandish the word like a sword meant to put me in my place. Here, it was an appreciation of the vibe.

I missed my apartment in New York and the little things I had done to make it feel homey. But this house? It was homey without even trying. It was comfortable and organized. Everything had character. I could see myself loving a place like this, lining up the kids' lunchboxes on the counter with muddy rain boots waiting by the back door and a smattering of homework papers on the table. I could see a Christmas tree looking content next to the fireplace or watching the sunset from the porch swing.

It was a strange moment to grow a dream, but I felt one plant a seed and sprout as I looked around the house.

Of course, on my salary, even with Carter's measly assistance, I could never afford a house like this. That didn't mean I had to settle, either. It was good having something to dream about.

My phone rang, and I pulled it out to see Carter calling again. A wave of weariness blew through me, and I wanted more than anything for him to stop. Which meant I needed to see what was so urgent that he couldn't just text me. "I'm sorry. I need to take this."

June brushed away my apology, and I let myself out the back door in the kitchen before I accepted the call.

"Hello?"

"I've been trying to get a hold of you." The expectation in his tone set me on edge, but I put aside my frustrations and breathed, waiting for him to continue. "I need to speak to the kids."

"They aren't with me right now."

"Why not?"

"I'm at a bridal shower, so they're hanging out with Gigi at the diner." Did I need to explain myself? No. Were they his children, so he had a right to know who was watching them? Yes.

"Is that a good idea?" he asked, taking me by surprise.

"Obviously, I didn't think it was a bad one."

There was silence while Carter digested this. It wasn't like me to snap at him, and I needed to rein it in. Fighting over the phone helped no one.

I tried for a calmer tone. "You called a few times, which felt kind of urgent, Carter. Is everything okay?"

"Yes," he said curtly. "We need to discuss which two weeks I can take the kids over the summer."

My stomach clenched. "Can we get through the rest of the school year first? We just got here."

He made a sound like he was going to argue with me. I was proud we'd made it this long on the phone without me mentioning the woman who had moved in with him. I was almost certain that was why he'd called anyway. He'd checked his stories, knew I'd seen the picture of her moving in, and wanted to really drive it home—pat himself on the back for being the first to move on.

The man's a lawyer. Everything with him was a trophy to be won.

Carter sighed. "Listen, Nova. We need to ta—"

"Well, isn't that a sight for sore eyes," a male voice boomed behind me.

I swiveled to see Dusty coming my way on the porch, holding a five-gallon bucket full of sunflowers. His honey-colored eyes sparkled in the mid-morning sun. A lock of his dark hair fell over his forehead, making me want to brush it back, my fingers dragging along his scalp. He lowered the bucket onto the deck before realizing I was on the phone.

"Who is that?" Carter asked, a tinny quality to his voice.

Dusty mouthed, "Sorry," cringing.

I shook my head. Someone lived with Carter. He didn't have

a right to ask questions about my life, anyway. "I'm at a bridal shower, remember?"

"It's the groom?"

"No." I opened my mouth to tell him it was the groom's best friend, but something stopped me. I didn't want to share anything with him about this. He didn't deserve to have a window into my life. I would tell him what was going on with the kids and we could talk every day about their schedules and homework and tummy aches or whatever else was going on, but he'd forfeited the right to know anything about me when he left me.

"Nova—"

"I need to get back inside," I said.

Carter huffed. I could hear the pacing, visualize him running his hand through his dark gold hair like he did when he was missing something in a case and might possibly lose. He wasn't used to this—the Nova he knew would relent, give in, tell him what he wanted to hear to keep the peace. "What's going on with you? I don't think I like what Texas is doing to you."

I swallowed a scoff, suppressing it deep down. I wanted to snap back, to remind him I was here because he didn't love me anymore. That I'd had to pick up and move halfway across the country because I had nowhere else to live. That he had inadvertently forced me into this. But instead, I tried for a pleasant smile so he wouldn't be able to hear how angry I was. "You lost the right to ask me anything like that when you walked out, Carter. I need to get back inside. If you want to talk to the kids, I can have them call you later tonight."

"I won't be home," he snapped, likely hoping to hurt me. The reason he'd go out on a Saturday night was to take out a woman, right? Or so he wanted me to assume.

"Okay, another time then. Let me know when you're free and we'll try to accommodate your schedule."

"Fine."

I hung up the phone without saying anything more, my one act of rebellion. But when silence hung around me, filling the cracks, an acute sense of loneliness swept over me. I could hear the muffled voices inside and tires crunching gravel in front of the house, probably more guests arriving. I dropped my face into my hands and breathed.

"You okay?" Dusty asked behind me.

I dropped my hands. "I thought you'd left."

He was standing in the same place, the bucket of flowers still at his feet. His mouth bent into a lopsided smile. "I wanted to make sure you were all right."

Warmth spread slowly through me, and I found myself smiling. "Why are you here, anyway?"

"Just got off work this morning and came to help set up." He shrugged. "I'm heading to Tucker's place with him to practice roping once y'all get this party started."

"Roping?"

"Don't tell me you're unfamiliar with it." He tilted his head to the side. "You ever been to a rodeo?"

"Can't say they have many of those in the East."

Dusty grinned widely. "You're in for a treat, little lady. I have a feeling Alice is going to like watching cowboys try to ride bulls."

"Alice? Why?"

"It's basically an acrobatic demonstration. Sometimes we get a local girl to trick ride the horse while she brings in the American flag. It's pretty good fun."

"Sounds like an adventure."

"Just wait until this summer." He walked closer, taking slow steps and stopping right in front of me. "We're going to sweat buckets, get us some stale nachos, and have the time of our lives."

How could he make that sound utterly divine?

"I'd like that," I said, and found I meant it.

Dusty bent his neck, his thumb brushing my chin. His eyes lingered there, his finger swiping over the curve of my bottom lip before his hand dropped to his side. "I like it much better when you smile."

My skin tingled where he'd touched, and a flush stemming from awareness creeped up my cheeks. I wanted him to do it again, which was terrifying. I couldn't pursue a relationship. Not this soon out of a ten-year marriage.

No, that excuse no longer held. But my kids hadn't changed, and I wasn't going to bring another man into their life so soon on a romantic level. He was amazing, but committing to me wasn't the same thing as committing to all three of us. Hanging out and teasing them was the easy part. It would take a long time for me to feel ready to take that leap. We could remain friends, but that was the extent of it. Anything else was too risky.

Only, the way he looked down at me now, the glitter in his gaze as it darted between my eyes and my lips, made molten lava pool in my belly. I remembered what it felt like to be wanted, back when Carter only had eyes for me.

It had been a few years since then. Now I was the Sahara Desert. Dusty was either a cold glass of water or a mirage. Probably the former, but it was too soon to know.

"I better get back inside," I said, but my voice sounded raspy.

He nodded. "Can I see you later tonight?"

"I'm making spaghetti with the kids."

Dusty's eyes narrowed. "That sounds like an excuse."

"It's not. Well—it is, but it's not a lie. I've been promising them all week. Alice plans to make hers purple."

"You sure? When I want to get out of something, I tell people I need to go home and feed my cat. She has a self-feeder though, and anyone who knows me understands it's a gentle way to let someone down."

My heart started racing. "I'm not trying to let you down. We make spaghetti occasionally, and Alice has been begging me all week. I would invite you, but we're doing it at Gigi's."

"Say no more." He gave me a lopsided smile. "I want proof of that purple pasta later or I'm going to assume this is a gentle let down."

"Have I been gentle yet?" I asked, raising an eyebrow.

"No." He gave my face a quick sweep. "You haven't."

Something about our conversation had shifted. The feeling between us in general was different. It was warm and comfortable, like fresh spring sunlight, and I wanted to stretch out in front of it and soak in the rays.

"I'll let you go," he said quietly, but he made no move to leave.

"Okay. Have fun playing with rope."

Dusty rolled his eyes, but his smile stretched so wide, it only made the action look boyish.

I turned towards the door to go back to the kitchen and found a woman watching us through the window. Gracie Mae, if I was correct. She leaned against the wall inside, chatting with June, but her eyes were on us.

Dusty swore.

"Your girlfriend?" I asked. She didn't look happy.

"She tried to be," he muttered. "I don't know how to be more blunt than I've been, but she's pretty persistent."

I felt bad for them. It sounded like an all around uncomfortable situation. "She's June's maid of honor, right?" I'd seen them having wedding meetings more than once.

"Yeah, they've been good friends for a long time. She's Tucker's cousin, too."

I nodded. Gracie Mae didn't feel like competition—I wasn't *competing* for Dusty, first off—but I still couldn't help but compare myself to her. She looked younger than me, her skin perfect, her smile flawless. I dragged my gaze to Dusty. "How old are you?"

"Twenty-eight."

Wow. I was crushing on a baby. This would go a long way towards dousing the flame of my inappropriate feelings for him.

"What?" he asked, narrowing his eyes. "You didn't like that answer."

"It doesn't matter. It just made me feel ancient."

"Why? You can't be more than..." He looked like he was doing math. "Actually, my grandpa taught me never to guess a woman's age. I'm assuming you were pretty young when you had Ben."

"I turned thirty-one at the beginning of the year. So yes, I'm ancient."

"Hey, we still would have gone to high school at the same time."

I laughed, moving toward the door and wanting to end this conversation. I caught Gracie Mae's eye through the window and looked away quickly, actively choosing not to compare her luscious blonde hair to my own. I was four or five years and two babies older than her, after all.

Let's be real. I was a mom. I was frumpy. My hair was almost never down because I couldn't be bothered to style it. I loved my crew neck sweaters and worn-in jeans more than anything else, and my feet just couldn't handle shoes without support for extended periods of time anymore.

He was young and handsome and a hometown hero. He could have anyone. Dusty definitely wasn't looking at me the same way I was looking at him. I shot him a bright smile. "See you around!" I disappeared inside.

CHAPTER TWENTY-TWO

DUSTY

MY CAT WAS my best friend, but Tucker was a close second. The man had been there for me since the fifth grade when we'd joined up for a science project and realized how much we both loved space. While he'd grown out of the obsession, mine evolved into a love of science fiction movies and books about different planets and saving up for my entire junior year to buy a telescope while everyone else traveled to Florida for spring break. Hence my cat's name: Leia. Also, hence why Leia and I were watching *Star Wars: The Force Awakens* while I ate sliders from another of my herb mixture tests. I kept trying new things, tweaking the recipe, and I was fairly confident in my final product. Next Saturday, it would be me against Nova and we'd have a winner.

Though, honestly, I'd be surprised if Chad let her do any of the cooking. The guy obviously asked for her help so he could spend time with her.

Rain pounded against my house, hitting it like little pebbles. I glanced at the window. We were on a tornado watch, which didn't mean anything, really. A tornado warning hadn't been issued yet.

But still, I didn't want to deal with broken windshields if the hail arrived in earnest. Had anyone explained the tornado vocabulary to Nova? I hadn't talked to her in a few days—since Saturday night, when she'd sent me a picture of funky looking purple spaghetti. She'd seemed a little weirded out that I was younger than her which, honestly, served to give me more confidence. Our ages were only relevant if she was starting to like me. No one cared how old the guy with a truck was when you only called him to help you move crap around.

But if you wanted a relationship with the guy with a truck, then age had some bearing. Not a lot, though. At least not to me. Why should it matter? I was a reasonable, mature adult. Those three years meant nothing.

My phone buzzed. I smiled when I picked it up.

> NOVA
> Where is the safest place to ride out a tornado in my apartment? Do we go outside so we can be under the steps? I read that under the stairs is the safest place, but our only stairs are outside

It felt a little rewarding that she'd asked me and not Gigi.

> DUSTY
> An interior room with no windows is ideal. In your place, I'd choose the bathroom

> NOVA
> Ben is freaking out

My stomach tightened. I could picture that tiny kid panicking at the thought of an enormous tornado ripping through his little apartment. That was extremely unlikely to happen, but they didn't know that.

> DUSTY
> Want me to come over? It's just a watch, so we really don't have anything to worry about

> NOVA
> What does that mean? When do we start worrying?

I debated texting more, but just dialed instead. It was difficult to determine tone through messages, but she seemed pretty nervous.

"Hey," she said, answering quickly. She sounded breathless.

"So a watch just means the weather is right for a tornado. We get watches all the time, and they don't usually turn into anything. When it changes to a warning, then you need to turn on the news."

"Why?"

"To see where the tornados are, what the trajectory is, if they're hitting down. A warning means the storm is in your area and possibly creating a tornado. You don't need to wait out the whole thing in your bathroom, though. The news will keep you pretty educated."

"Okay," she said, still breathless. "This is new for us."

I paused my movie. "I'll come over."

"You don't need to do that."

"I want to. If it's not a bother, at least." I went still, an idea growing in my head. What this family needed was a distraction. If they panicked every single time we got a tornado watch, they would spend the spring and fall rainstorms in a constant state of worry. "Are any of you allergic to cats?"

Nova was silent for a minute. "No. Why?"

"Um, you'll see." I'd planned on an early night since I started my next shift in the morning, but it was only seven-thirty. I had plenty of time to see the Walkers and still get a full night's rest. "I'll be there in ten."

We got off the phone, and I went to brush my teeth and gather Leia before heading out. Ten minutes later I was on their porch, holding my cat against my chest and knocking on the door. Nova swung it open. Her hair was back in a French braid, and she wore a cozy looking pullover.

Her eyes dropped to my orange striped cat, her eyebrow lifting. "You brought an animal." She smiled. "Hello, gorgeous."

I stroked the back of Leia's head to keep her calm. "I thought you weren't a cat person."

Nova shrugged, opening the door wider. "This one looks pretty cute. It also explains why you were buying so much cat food when we met."

"I like to give her a treat when I get off work sometimes, and she loves wet cat food. You know, bribe her to love me despite leaving her alone during my long shifts."

"I don't think she needs much bribing," Nova said, eyeing how content my cat looked in my arms.

Alice stood against the wall, watching me eagerly. Nova's computer sat on the counter, the news playing loudly.

"We moved to a warning," she said, her brown eyes wide.

I'd gotten the alert on my phone while I was driving. "Don't worry," I said quietly. "It's going to be okay." I turned my attention to Alice. "Should I sit on the couch so you can come meet this lady? Her name is Princess Leia, but I just call her Leia."

Alice nodded. It took about ten minutes of coaxing to get Leia to allow Alice to hold her, then she jumped to the floor and slinked away to explore the house. Ben and Alice followed her around at a distance while Nova sat beside me on the rich blue cushions, her laptop perched on her legs and the news playing loudly, the weatherman constantly repeating himself.

Ben giggled from behind the chair where he and Alice were bent, trying to see where Leia had hidden under the table.

"I'm gonna be honest," Nova whispered. "I'm almost as terrified as Ben."

We looked at him laughing with Alice, not a hint of concern on his face.

Nova leaned closer, her shoulder brushing mine. "Okay, he's distracted now, but he was—wait." She turned her head sharply to face me. "Is that why you brought the cat over?"

I shrugged, trying not to feel like an excited teen boy over the fact that the girl I liked was sitting so close. "I figured the kids could use a distraction."

Her eyes went all shimmery. Then her phone started ringing, so she pulled it out and looked at it. Her mouth turned down. I saw Carter's name on the screen and a photo of a dark blond man smiling with blue eyes and perfect teeth. It was clear where Alice had gotten her blue eyes. But something about his face looked extremely punchable.

"Guys, your dad is calling," Nova called. "Who wants to take it first?"

Neither of them responded.

"Alice?" Nova asked, rising from the couch and leaving her computer behind. "You want to go first?"

"Okay, Mommy." Alice took the phone and swiped it to answer, then walked toward her bedroom. "Hi, Daddy," she said, her voice disappearing when she closed the door.

Nova took her seat again. "Gigi went to Dallas to see a friend of hers who's having health problems. Will she have to stay there, do you think?"

Okay, so she didn't want to talk about Carter anymore. At least not while the kids were around. Her words the other night about how he was winning the divorce had weaseled their way into my mind, and it was hard not to press for more information. Why anyone would leave Nova was beyond my comprehension. The guy was clearly an idiot.

She watched me expectantly. What had she asked? Oh, yeah. Gigi.

"I don't know. It'll depend on the weather. She might want

to stay with her friend, just to be safe. I wouldn't want my aunt driving in this weather."

"You have an aunt?"

"No. But—well, Tucker's mom, Jan, is the closest thing. If she was in Dallas, I wouldn't want her driving home right now."

We watched the news for a bit, the weather guy going over the location of the storm and its projected path. "When do we take cover?"

"I think you're the one who needs a distraction now," I said, reaching over and hitting the volume button on the computer to turn it down.

She cringed. "That's probably true. What do you have in mind?"

Things we could not do, obviously. But I was a gentleman, so I pushed those thoughts aside and tried to think of anything but sliding her onto my lap. My mind traveled to Beeler and Grandpa. If anything was going to kill a sudden wave of attraction, it was thinking of my favorite old man. "Do you guys have any puzzles? Board games? We could play charades."

Nova glanced at Ben lying on his stomach on the dining room floor, trying to entice Leia from her hiding place. "I don't think the kids will want to do anything else but play with your cat."

"Okay. You and me, then." The thoughts came back, the images so clear in my head of what it would be like to kiss her, I couldn't help but look at her lips. I immediately snapped back to her eyes and swallowed. It was becoming increasingly harder to ignore my attraction, but I was doing my best. I would be a gold medalist in restraint by the time summer rolled around.

"I have a few puzzles, actually. Or Clue, if you feel like solving a murder."

"As much as I love murder, I'm a sucker for a good puzzle."

Nova hopped up from the couch and headed toward her room. "Okay, I have the perfect one."

I brought the laptop to the table, because I figured we could keep an eye on the storm while we were distracted. "Want me to pull her out, Ben?" I asked, crouching beside him. Leia was curled into a comfortable ball on the floor, looking at us. The legs of the chairs all formed bars around her, protecting her. I wondered if she'd gravitated here because it smelled familiar—it was our table after all.

"I want her to want to come to me," Ben muttered, still lying on his stomach, his arm stretched beneath the chair so his fingers rested near her.

I understood him exactly.

"Ben!" Alice called, running down the short hallway to join us in the dining room. "Dad's on the phone."

"I'm busy," Ben said, wiggling his fingers and not taking his eyes off Leia.

Alice turned the phone toward us. "See, Daddy? He's trying to get the kitty out from under the table."

The phone was pointing at me more than Ben, with Alice's arm moving so much it wouldn't remain steady. Carter sat up taller, his gaze narrowing. "Who is that?"

"She's Dusty's kitty," Alice said, getting down on the floor beside Ben and pushing the phone under the chair so her dad could see Leia.

"I meant the man," Carter said, and he didn't sound happy.

"Found it," Nova said, coming out of her room. She shook the box to rattle the pieces. "It's America, but every state is covered in its state flower. The ocean is impossible. Just solid blue."

I rose to my feet and took the puzzle, discomfort edging along my body.

"What?" she asked, her brow furrowing. "You look—"

"Nova," Carter snapped through the phone. "Alice, I want to talk to Mommy."

Nova took a step away, like she didn't want to deal with this right now, and I wondered if she realized she'd done that.

Alice crawled out from under the chair and lifted the phone.

Nova took it, pasting a smile on her face. "We're in the middle of something. Can this wait?"

"No."

She glanced at me apologetically.

I waved her away. "I'll get started on Texas." It felt weird talking, knowing her ex could hear me, but he already knew I was here.

Nova pressed the phone to her chest, blocking the camera. "I promise I'll be quick. He's probably worried about the tornado."

That was extremely unlikely and we both knew it.

She looked at me for a moment longer before the phone's speaker blew to life again. "Nova!"

She flinched. "Coming." Then she lifted her eyebrows. "Don't go anywhere."

My mouth curved into a gentle smile. "I'm not planning on it."

CHAPTER TWENTY-THREE

NOVA

I WENT into my room and closed the door. "The tornado isn't even close to us yet, and the trajectory doesn't look like it'll come our way, so you don't need to worry."

His eyes bulged. He sat on the edge of our bed—*his* bed—and loosened his tie. "What tornado?"

"Isn't that why you needed to talk to me?" I asked, feigning ignorance. "The kids were pretty freaked out, but they've calmed down." I wasn't about to tell him I was just as worried as the kids.

"Who's the man?" His face didn't give anything away, but his tone did. He wasn't happy. I wasn't going to pretend to imagine he was jealous. I imagine he didn't like the sense of control slipping away. Carter didn't like being in the dark. He wanted to know everything—to be the guy to tell you things for the first time. This was new territory for us.

There were a multitude of ways I could handle this situation. The petty side of me wanted to hang up. I hadn't called, begging him to tell me about the woman moving into his apartment. But the peacemaking side of me, who didn't want conflict and recognized that he was well and truly out of my life, wanted to end the conversation as quickly as possible so I could return to Alice, Ben, Dusty, and the cat.

Besides, there wasn't anything between Dusty and me but friendship, which meant I didn't have to broach the subject of romantic relationships anyway.

"He's a friend," I said lightly. "Gigi knows him well and vouched for him. He's a good man, but I didn't bring him around the kids until I felt the same way. Don't worry. I'm not being reckless."

Carter stared at the camera, his jaw working. "I don't like the idea of men I haven't approved of being around my kids."

"You don't trust me?" I asked simply, though my stomach was roiling. Between the two of us, I was the one who always put the kids first. He couldn't even manage a ten-minute conversation with them more than once a week.

"Of course I trust you."

"Then I don't see what more we have to talk about. I need to go, Carter."

He looked ready to argue.

I didn't let him. "I need to get back and check the news for tornado locations."

That seemed to work. He shook his head, but I could see how angry he was. When I hung up the phone, I dropped my head back and breathed out.

Ben and Alice were gone when I returned.

"They followed Leia into their room. They think she's playing hide-and-seek, but I think she's just not used to a couple kids chasing her around."

"Will she be traumatized?" I pulled out the chair kitty-corner from his and sat down.

"No, I think she likes it. She was being coy, watching to see if they were following."

I couldn't help but laugh. Dusty's eyes held mine. He seemed hesitant, like he wanted to ask if I was okay but didn't want to pry. The last thing I wanted to talk about was Carter. We had done that enough.

Surveying the puzzle piles, I lifted my eyebrows. "There's a lot of blue. I can see you didn't put Texas together."

"This puzzle is ridiculous," he answered quickly, starting to put the pieces into piles again—corners, edges, color and pattern schemes. The man was clearly not a novice. "The whole surrounding ocean is one solid color. How are we supposed to use cunning and smarts to figure out where each piece goes?"

"I think it'll have to be more of a *try each piece to see if it fits* kind of situation."

"Like I said. Ridiculous," he muttered.

We spent the next hour working on the puzzle, getting each state put together and starting on the surrounding water. We were interrupted twice when Ben wanted to bring out his Star Wars toys and show them off—all except Chewbacca, who was still suspiciously missing—and then to show Dusty his Kylo Ren costume.

"Alice took Chewie," Ben said, swiping his lightsaber around the small living room.

"I did not!" she argued.

"Did, too."

"I don't even like your dumb toys."

"Yes you do. You wanted him to marry your Barbie."

"Barbie doesn't need—"

"Okay, bedtime," I said, rising and clapping my hands. I hazarded a glance at Dusty, but he looked amused, bending over the table to fit blue pieces into the ocean until one fit, then moving to the next. We'd become methodical about it, and I think both of us just wanted to see the puzzle finished so we could burn it.

"Can Leia have a sleepover?" Alice asked.

Dusty looked up, giving her a sweet smile. "Not tonight. As much as she'd love that, we don't have her litter box or her Yoda."

Ben ran over, sheathing his lightsaber. "She has a Yoda?"

Dusty jerked his chin slightly toward Alice's pink monkey stuffed beneath her arm. "Leia sleeps with a stuffed Yoda, and I left him at home. She loves it as much as you love Peaches, so you can probably guess how hard it would be for her to sleep without it."

Alice shook her head, eyes wide. "She couldn't."

"So I'd better take her home, right?"

Alice was in full agreement. Ben, who didn't have affection for a stuffy, didn't understand. I held Dusty's eye while I ushered my kids toward the bathroom to brush their teeth. "I'll be right out, but if you want to leave, don't worry about waiting."

He glanced to where Leia had curled up on the sofa, then back to me. "I can't leave until this ocean is finished."

Weird, sweet relief sluiced through me.

It only took about twenty minutes to get the kids in bed, read them a few stories, and kiss them good night. When I finished, I went to the kitchen and filled a glass with water, guzzling it down.

"You made that look delicious," Dusty said from the table. His cat was curled against his chest, and he stroked her back like a villain.

Heat curled in my chest, but I tried to keep my feelings in the friendzone. I nodded toward Leia. "You make that look creepy."

Dusty's face split into a grin.

"You could be Lady Tremaine for Halloween."

"Who?"

"The evil stepmother in *Cinderella*."

"Ah," he said, nodding slowly like he understood and possibly agreed. "Should we finish the puzzle?"

"I'd love to. Want me to bring you some water? It's either that or chocolate milk."

"Water, please."

I filled a glass and brought it to the table. I should have had something else to offer him—I mean, all I was doing with that water glass was waving both of my flags, the poor one and the mom one. But, honestly, Dusty was well aware of both of those things, and it hadn't stopped us from becoming friends. I grabbed the plate of oatmeal chocolate fudge bars I'd made yesterday and put it on the table.

We sat together, working through the blue ocean pieces and snacking on cookie bars. Dusty told me about the small farm he grew up on and how he didn't keep animals on it anymore except his horse. Though half the time, even his horse stayed with Tucker, so they could practice roping for the local rodeo.

"Do you want to have animals again someday?" I asked, leaning back in my chair and watching him do everything with one hand while the other petted his sleeping cat.

"Maybe. It's impossible with my job schedule now. Eventually, when I have kids to boss around, I can think about getting some. You know, people I can command to feed animals and muck stalls."

"Kids are great for bossing around," I said, nodding sagely. "They always do exactly what they're told and never miss a single chore."

He seemed to sense I was kidding. "Hopefully I'll have a wife who likes animals too, and it'll be a joint effort."

A wife. So he did want one, then? When a guy was almost thirty and didn't have a girlfriend, it was hard to know what his priorities were, if marriage was even something he wanted. I itched to ask him why he wasn't married yet, but I couldn't breach the personal nature of that conversation. It felt like too much, somehow.

"I wish you luck in finding her," I said, pouring all my attention into the little blue puzzle piece that didn't fit anywhere. I could sense Dusty's eyes on me, but instead of looking up, I picked up a second piece and fitted it in place.

We were almost finished. The next ten minutes went by easily, our conversation shifting to what we had both been interested in during high school. Him, football of course. Me, choir and culinary arts.

"I did cross country for a while too, and I wasn't too shabby at it," I said.

"We have a few great places nearby to go running, if you want trails."

"Oh, it's been too long. I don't think I have it in me anymore."

He looked at me suspiciously. "What do you do for you, Nova?"

"Eat," I said, pinching another corner from a fudgy oat bar and popping it in my mouth.

"What else?"

"I have too many things on my plate to worry about hobbies."

"Okay, before, when you didn't have so many things on your plate. What did you do for you then?"

Nothing. That was the truth. I cleaned, cooked, got the kids everywhere they needed to be. When I had a minute to myself, I usually was trying a new recipe or meeting a friend for lunch. I did workouts in my living room to stay in shape and make it possible to eat all the things, but I hadn't run in quite a few years. Not since getting pregnant with Alice. But my life didn't seem lacking because of it, either.

"Honestly, I'm okay being in one of those stages where I'm always a little frazzled and don't worry about wearing makeup or getting me time. I don't think there's anything wrong with my kids being my focus, especially while they're going through this huge change."

He nodded, but his mouth pressed into a thin line, considering. "I'm not a dad, so I really can't give an opinion. But I have gone through a lot of first responder training, and I can't help but think about oxygen. We need it to breathe, right? It's important. When you're on an airplane and the oxygen masks drop, what do the flight attendants want you to do?"

"Put my mask on first. I know where you're going with this."

"Perfect. That makes my point easier to get across." He shot me a teasing grin, then sobered, his honey eyes glued to me. "You get to decide what your mask is, Nova. If it's baking, great. Running? Great. Trips to Disney World? Expensive, but great. You get to decide what you need to keep your oxygen levels healthy."

"Ben is dying to go to Disney World for the Star Wars rides. We haven't taken him yet."

"Him and me both," Dusty muttered, sending me a boyish smile.

"You've always been a Star Wars nerd, haven't you?"

"Maybe. I'm not ashamed."

"You shouldn't be."

"My parents promised to take me to Disney World when I was fourteen," he said lightly. "Not for the Star Wars, but because they were really good at promising things they had no way to follow through on."

"I thought you lived with your grandpa by then?"

"Oh, yeah. My parents had disappeared for years, but they showed up the summer before I went to high school and pretended to be interested. I haven't seen them since. They were heading to a compound in North Carolina last I heard, but since they took my piggy bank with them, I decided it was okay for me to stop caring."

My hand stilled before reaching for the final piece, then I dropped it in my lap, leaving the last piece on the table. "Have you considered looking them up?"

Dusty stared at the final piece. "I thought about it when I moved my grandpa into Pleasant Gardens, but decided not to. It took years to make up my mind about them. First I was bitter and hurt. Now, it still hurts—I won't try to pretend it doesn't—but the bitterness is gone. Instead, I just don't care. They chose drugs over me, so I choose to live a happy life without wondering why I wasn't good enough for them."

"Sounds healthy," I said, and altogether impossible—but I didn't add that part out loud.

"It wasn't always." He said no more than that. "Should we do the final piece together?"

"Sure."

Dusty picked it up, and I awkwardly took the other side. We shoved it into place in the wide expanse of blue and pushed it down together. "That was satisfying," he said.

I grinned, running my hands over the finished picture to smooth it out. "It's the best part of the puzzle."

Dusty stood. "I better get this girl home."

"Thanks for coming over."

He gave me a flat look. "I wasn't doing you a favor, Nova. I really like your kids."

"I know," I said, surprised to realize I meant it. Dusty had a way of providing service to me without making me feel like a chore. It was one of the things I liked most about him. Whether he meant to or not, he made me feel like he wanted to be here. "I won't even offend you by trying to tell you how I plan to pay you back."

He rolled his eyes. "At some point, you'll have to accept that getting to hang out with you guys is paying me back. If I hadn't come over tonight, it would have just been me, Leia, and an early night with Kylo Ren."

What did it say about us that I'd followed that sentence exactly? I walked him to the door but didn't open it yet. "You're a good guy, Dusty."

His smile was self-effacing.

Without thinking too much about what I was doing, I leaned toward him, my arms going around his neck in an awkward hug where I tried my best not to squish—or wake—the sleeping cat. His free arm went around my waist, applying pressure, and I pressed my forehead to his shoulder briefly, inhaling the scent of laundry detergent and a faint hint of manly soap. His fingers splayed on my back, increasing my pulse into dangerous territory.

It would be a downright lie to tell myself I wasn't falling for this guy, pointless to try and convince my pulse to calm down. It knew when I was being held by someone worth kissing, and all I wanted right now was to move the cat out of the way and do just that. But my kids were on the other side of the wall and his baby was literally between us, and I wondered if those were two reasons not to push it.

Besides, what if I was just another Gracie Mae, not getting the hints he was dropping in front of me? Maybe I'd been out of the game so long I didn't know the difference between teasing and flirting anymore.

No, that was silly. There was no way he would be this overt with someone he didn't have an interest in. That didn't make the situation easier. He might think he wanted to date a single mom, but it was a lot of commitment. For my kids' sakes, I couldn't just jump into anything yet.

Reluctantly, I pulled away. His hand dragged around my waist as I stepped back.

We stood there, looking at each other. He didn't move to leave, and I didn't turn away.

My phone rang. I wanted to ignore it, but it had ruined the silence and broken the spell between us. I pulled it from my pocket and saw my mom. I showed him the screen. "I'd better take this."

He nodded, giving me one last searching gaze before opening the door. "See you Saturday. And bring your A-game."

"Oh, don't worry, Dusty. I plan to," I said, then closed the door behind him.

CHAPTER TWENTY-FOUR

DUSTY

I WAS NOT a sophomore in high school, fresh off my first date to a homecoming dance and reeling from the awkward peck I'd gotten after dropping my date off. I had kissed *loads* of girls and women since that night. But, somehow, two days after my puzzle night with Nova, I was sitting in the firehouse with Randy putting together lunch, and I still couldn't stop thinking about that hug.

I was a grown man. It had only been a hug. It wasn't even a *peck*. But man, my body had been on fire. It had taken everything in me not to toss Leia aside and wrap my arms around Nova. Cats always landed on their feet, right?

Well, I hadn't done that. I should be inordinately proud of myself. Really, I just regretted letting the moment pass and was eager for it to happen again.

I finished grilling chicken with vegetables and had taken the rice off the stove when a call came in through the overhead speakers for a possible kitchen fire on Main Street.

"Isn't that the diner?" Randy asked, suiting up beside me and jumping into the truck.

Jill was there a second after us. "I don't think so," she said. "But it's probably close."

The nearer the truck drew to the address on Main Street, the harder my heart pounded. Most of these buildings were places of business. The only kitchen I knew near the diner was Nova's apartment building. But it couldn't be her. There were three other apartments in her building, and she was at work since her kids were in school.

When we pulled up to the street, I swore.

Nova stood outside, frowning, in a white T-shirt with a yellow apron tied around her waist.

I hopped from the truck before it came to a complete stop and ran to her side.

"I don't know what happened," she said. "I started the oven to preheat and left to get something from my car. When I got back inside, smoke was pouring from the oven. Something was inside, but I couldn't tell what it was. It smelled awful."

"Did you turn off the oven?"

"Yes, and I opened the windows."

"Stay outside while we investigate," I told her. Randy joined me on the stairs. "Left something in the oven. Probably not food."

"Got it."

It only took a few minutes to discover that the item melting in her oven was plastic and no longer on fire, but definitely melted on the rack. We pulled the rack out and I bent over it, peering close enough to recognize the remains of what was once a toy. Jill set up a large fan while Randy opened another window to air out the smoke. It was going to cling to the apartment for at least a few days.

It could have been so much worse.

"You want to talk to Ms. Walker?" Randy asked, looking at me.

"Sure." I let myself outside. Nova stood on the street with

her arms folded, her thumbnail in her teeth while she chewed worriedly. Her hair was back in a ponytail that trailed down between her shoulder blades.

When she noticed me, she started up the stairs, her hand dropping from her mouth.

"It was a toy in the oven," I told her. "Looks like it could have been a gorilla. About eight inches long."

Nova stopped on the step below me, her eyes narrowing before realization hit her. "No, not a gorilla. That was probably Chewie."

"Oh."

She leaned back against the railing, her head in her hands. "Ben is going to be crushed." She looked up at me. "Oh, gosh. Alice."

"You think she put it in there?"

"She hides things when she's mad at him, and he's been missing Chewbacca for a while. I don't know why she moved it to the oven, though. It wasn't there yesterday when I made dinner."

I grimaced. "We did our best to scrape the rack, but you'll want to clean it fully before using it. Melted plastic can be dangerous. We have the fan airing out the place, so give us another twenty minutes and we'll get out of your hair."

"Okay." Her smile slipped past me to where Jill stood in the doorway now. "Thank you guys for helping."

"No problem," Jill said before walking past us down the steps.

After we got the place aired out and squared everything away, the ride back to the firehouse was quiet. Jill and Randy chatted, but I was too distracted to pay attention. By the time we got back, I knew exactly what I needed to do.

I WAITED until after I got off work the following morning, went home, and showered before letting myself into the attic to search the boxes for my old toys. Dust particles flew around the air, disturbed by my motion and dancing in the orange glow of sunlight streaming through the dirty window. The box was a treasure trove. Old figurines of Han Solo, Chewbacca, Darth Vader, and Obi Wan Kenobi were littered among Teenage Mutant Ninja Turtles and Jurassic Park dinosaurs. We'd gotten most of my toys secondhand at the Goodwill, so they were usually a season behind and already well-loved, but I had never cared.

I took care of my things, which meant they were still in excellent condition.

My Chewbacca was smaller and probably not as cool as whatever newfangled thing Ben had, but maybe it would take some of the sting of loss away.

I sat on a plastic tote full of Christmas lights and sent Nova a text.

DUSTY

Can I stop by tonight? I have something for Ben.

I took a picture of the toy and sent it to her so she could decide if it was a good idea or not.

NOVA

Are you lending him this like you're lending the table? Because I can't ask you to part with that. I'm guessing it's vintage

DUSTY

Sure. Let's go with lending. He can take care of it for me

NOVA

Then come by anytime.

My phone started ringing, so I picked up Chewbacca and headed for the ladder. "Hello?"

"This is Maurice with Pleasant Gardens. Can I speak to Dusty Hayes?"

"Speaking."

"Hello, Mr. Hayes. I wanted to inform you of an incident we had this morning with your grandfather."

My steps stilled on the ladder. "Is everything okay?"

"His health is in good order," Maurice said. "It's of a different nature. Do you have a minute?"

"I do."

"Great. Well, when Mr. Hayes was walking to breakfast this morning, his...uh, pants fell down."

I took the last step so both my feet were on the hallway carpet and blinked. "His pants fell down?"

"Yes. We quickly helped him correct the situation, but it would seem he has a reputation now. Some of the women who witnessed the incident have taken to calling him Pants."

I leaned down to lift the ladder back into the ceiling. "Pants," I repeated. It wasn't very original, but I couldn't help laughing. Given the serious way Maurice was explaining the situation, I tried my best to stifle it.

"Indeed. Mr. Hayes seems unperturbed, but we thought it best to inform you. If he mentions discomfort from the nickname, would you please keep me informed? And perhaps you could bring him a belt."

"I will do that straight away. Thanks for letting me know."

"Of course."

I giggled like a child all the way down the hall and outside to my truck, imagining Grandpa standing in the entrance to the dining room, his pants around his ankles and his hands on his walker. Those women with the front row seats were teasers after my own heart. Of course my grandpa didn't mind the jokes. The man had lived with *me* for years.

Tossing Chewbacca on the passenger seat, I reversed out of my driveway. "Come on, Chewie, let's go get Pants a belt."

WHEN I REACHED Pleasant Gardens that afternoon, Grandpa didn't seem the least concerned with his new infamy. I stood in the doorway to his bedroom and held up a belt, grinning. "Hey there, Pants."

"Not you, too," he grumbled, his bushy eyebrows drawing together. "I tell you, the women in this place need better entertainment."

"You seem to be providing plenty." I closed the door behind me, dropped the belt on the edge of his bed, and took the second armchair that faced the TV, playing the sports channel. "Hey, what do you think about getting out of here this weekend?"

He didn't tear his frown from the TV. "Do I have a dentist appointment?"

"No. Arcadia Creek is putting on the Battle of the Badges, and we're having burgers and a flag football game." I had told him about it a few times, and every time I mentioned it, he wanted to go. He would forget by the next time I visited. "Thought you might enjoy seeing some old friends."

Grandpa eyed me. "Will they let me leave this place?"

"Yes. I checked with the front desk." That was weeks ago, but I didn't see why the answer would be different now. "What do you say?"

He looked at the belt I'd put on his bed, then back to the football reruns being analyzed on screen. "Sure."

"Great." I stared at the screen too, but my vision wasn't clear enough to recognize what I was seeing. Nerves shimmied through me. I drew in a steadying breath and tried to sound nonchalant. "There's someone I want you to meet."

Grandpa picked up the remote and hit the power button. He immediately turned in his leather chair to face me. "Who is she? The Gable girl?"

Sheesh. Why did *everyone* connect me to Gracie Mae? "No, not her. It's someone new. Gigi's niece, actually. She just moved here from New York City." I swallowed. "Brought two little kids with her. I coach one of them."

Great. I was rambling and he was seeing through me.

Grandpa looked at me through clear, narrowed eyes. "She must be special."

"She is." This conversation was so uncomfortable. Maybe because we both knew I wouldn't tell him about a woman unless I cared a lot for her. I had never brought anyone home before, not since high school—even then, I'd never had a steady girlfriend.

"You said she's Gigi's daughter?"

My stomach dropped. Gigi didn't have kids. "No, her niece. We aren't actually—things are very slow-moving. I'm not sure she's even ready to date. But I like her, and I want you to meet her." I wasn't sure he'd remember her—or even this conversation—but getting his opinion mattered to me.

"I'd love to," Grandpa said, a suspicious twinkle in his eyes.

"Just do your best not to embarrass me," I teased. "Can't have the woman running away before I get her to agree to a date."

He turned the TV back on. "Then it's a good thing you got me a belt, son."

CHAPTER TWENTY-FIVE

NOVA

IF YOU HAD TOLD me last year I would become a football mom, I would have laughed. The sport was so outside of what my family was interested in. I didn't know the first thing about the game myself, but I loved watching Ben snag a flag and search for me in the stands with triumph during his games and his practices. He was succeeding at something with a team of supportive friends at his back. It gave him a group to fit in with, something to put his focus on. Somewhere to belong.

The moment we reached the big park where the Battle of the Badges was being held, I loved that Ben noticed a group of boys from his football team and ran off to join them. He was fitting in. He seemed happy. Yes, he hadn't wanted to talk to Carter the last time we'd gotten him on the phone, but aside from that, everything seemed good.

I would proudly be a football mom forever now because of what it had given to my son during this hard period in his life.

That, and a forever supporter of firemen. When Dusty stopped by the other day to give Ben his old Chewbacca, my son's face had brightened like he'd been offered a trip to NASA.

Dusty played it off like it wasn't a big deal, but we both knew Ben felt differently. He took the Chewie toy everywhere he went now, but I'd asked him to leave it in the car when we'd arrived at the park.

Alice hopped around to the back of the SUV with me, clutching Peaches under her arm.

"Do you want me to help you find Kendall?" I asked. "Her mom told me they would be here today."

Alice looked unsure.

"Or you could help me take our things to the dessert table and prepare to assemble the plates?" Chad had decided to take over the burgers, and I was in charge of putting out the dessert. I was glad my oven had quit smelling like burned plastic when I had to make one hundred little angel food cakes, because I'd ended up making them late into the night while my kids were asleep.

It hadn't been a trial. I had sent pictures to Dusty so he would know what he was up against, but cutting out most of the important components with a peace sign or a shaka in front of the camera.

He'd replied with a picture of himself, frowning, in front of a table covered in some sort of bread item I couldn't quite identify.

This morning's text:

DUSTY

Today's the day! You're going down, Walker

Yeah, I hadn't minded when Chad had asked me to come to the event and help out. I wanted to win. I needed those bragging rights, because Dusty didn't seem like the type of guy to let things go easily, and I would never hear the end of it if I lost.

"I'll help you," Alice said. I could already see her growing uncomfortable at the crowd gathered around the football field, camp chairs lined up on the perimeter to watch the men start

RECIPE FOR RIVALS

their football game. The police team wore blue and the firefighters red, to make it easy to tell them apart.

My dad would be disappointed, but I was definitely Team Red today. Since I was cooking for blue, though, I would take that secret to my grave. Red could win the football game so long as Blue won the cook off.

Desi was standing at the tables when I got there. "The game has already started. Kendall is over there if you want to go find her, honey," she added to Alice.

Alice clutched the bottom of my shirt, pulling hard. I put my things on the table before reaching down to pry her fingers from my hem. "I'll walk over with you in a minute," I told her.

Desi looked between us. She poured more lemonade powder into a giant cooler and mixed it with a wooden spoon, ice clinking together as she stirred.

"Are you doing the drinks for everyone?" I asked.

"Yes. The firehouse is covering chips. The people can go down both lines and get a slider and a dessert from each side. Voting boxes are up by the picnic tables."

"It's so organized."

Desi preened. "Thank you."

I hadn't known she'd taken over the set up, but the woman was head of the PTA and dressed like a lawyer. She clearly meant business.

I finished setting out plates and shoved my coolers under the table, nestled in the grass. The sun had come out, shining down with steady, comfortable warmth. We had an hour before lunch, so I didn't need to come back here and set up for at least forty minutes. I tapped the top of the foil pans holding the little angel food cakes and considered how warm they'd get in the sun. They were better off waiting beneath the table, too.

After getting everything nestled on the grass, I reached for Alice's hand. "Let's go find Kendall."

"Okay, Mommy." She clutched Peaches tightly under her arm, squeezing my fingers with her free hand.

"See you over there!" Desi called.

Kendall was at the play structure on the other side of the field, hanging upside down on a gymnastics bar, when we found her. Last I'd heard, Penny had moved on to a different BFF, leaving Kendall and Alice to themselves. Neither of them seemed too sad about it, but if this was a preview of their teen years, we were in for some headaches and tears.

When Kendall noticed us, she flipped to her feet, landing on the bark, and ran our way. "My mom says you're going to be Chad's new girlfriend," Kendall said, then turned to face Alice with utter joy on her face. "If he's your new daddy, then we can be neighbors. He's my dad's BFF, but he isn't married yet, so my mom doesn't have a BFF. But *now* your mom can be my mom's best friend!"

My stomach somersaulted, following the reasoning behind her excitement with growing trepidation. Did Desi think this because Chad said something, or did she jokingly mention it in passing to her husband and was accidentally overheard by the six-year-old?

Alice looked horrified.

"I don't have a boyfriend," I told them both. "And no one is getting a new daddy, okay?" My stomach still felt sick. The more I thought about it, the more I could see Desi had only been chatting to her husband about me and Chad in the way happily married couples talked about their friends getting together. In a perfect world, I would marry Chad and we could have couples' dinners and go on cruises together and our kids could play all the time and we'd have houses next door.

I knew this, because it was the life I thought I'd have when my friend Blair had married my brother Jason. The only problem was that Carter and Jason never really saw eye to eye. There had been no couples cruises or double dates. It had been a lot of me hanging out with my family while Carter worked late and dropped in for a minute occasionally before we all went home.

Desi should have known better than to say anything like this around Kendall. Six-year-old girls didn't know how to keep secrets.

Well, except for Alice and the wretched Chewbacca situation. Ben still wasn't talking to her—most of the time, when he remembered he was mad.

"Will you be okay here?" I asked.

Alice nodded.

I leaned down to speak in her ear. "You know I'm not dating anyone, right?"

"Not even Dusty?" she asked quietly.

My body froze. It was on the tip of my tongue to ask her if it would be okay with her if I did date Dusty, or how she would feel about it, but this wasn't the time or the place. I didn't have a chance to refute the question at all though, because Kendall took her arm.

"Come on! Let's go practice our dance."

Alice let herself be dragged away. I hovered for a few more minutes before heading back toward the game. Desi and I needed to have a chat.

When I reached the game, she was nowhere to be seen. I waved at June and Lauren, sitting with Tucker, Jack, Gracie Mae, and a smattering of their parents. It was Dusty's little cheer section, which was the only reason I didn't join them. Until I understood exactly how Alice felt about Dusty, I wasn't going to do anything to put myself out there as his particular friend.

Not that anyone else thought there was something between us. But if Alice did, then Ben might too, and I couldn't have that. My kids deserved to be number one, which meant my top priority had just become figuring out where their heads were at.

I pulled out my phone and texted my sister-in-law.

> **NOVA**
> My kids might think I have a boyfriend. Or maybe just Alice does? I don't know how I feel about this. Do I want them to approve? Or will I be happier if they don't? Please tell me how to feel

> **BLAIR**
> I NEED DETAILS
>
> Who is it? Full legal name? I want to stalk him on Instagram

> **NOVA**
> No! I'm dying here. I don't even think I want a relationship, B.

She sent me a picture of the mound of laundry on her couch and my nephew in the background throwing it all over the floor with blurry, waving arms.

> **BLAIR**
> Can you not entertain me better than this, please?
>
> Okay, kidding. I know you're in a major panic, but obvs you are the only one who can know how you feel. If you're asking for permission to move on, you got it when Carter walked out

That was fair. What was I waiting for? Whose permission did I need to determine I'd waited long enough?

It hit me with a fresh wave—it was, again, all about my kids.

> **NOVA**
> You know I've wrecked Ben's and Alice's lives by tearing them away from home and family and bringing them to the middle of nowhere. I think it's less about moving on and more about whether it's too soon for them. I don't want to give my babies whiplash

My fingers typed furiously as I poured my stress into messages to my closest friend.

> **NOVA**
> Besides, what if it doesn't work out? What if he seems perfect, but he's really a scumbag?

I didn't actually think that, but I hadn't known Dusty terribly long.

> **NOVA**
> He's winning me over with his charm, but there's always a reason when a perfect man is almost thirty and still single.

> **BLAIR**
> Have you checked his basement for jars of eyeballs?

> **NOVA**
> Gross

> **BLAIR**
> I don't know what else you're worried about

> **NOVA**
> I haven't seen his house yet

> **BLAIR**
> We both know this isn't really about the house. You need to decide what you want. Definitely talk to the kids, but this is about you, too. It's not just about them

> NOVA
> Hardest balancing act ever

> BLAIR
> I'm still waiting on that name

> NOVA
> I'll try to get a picture for you

There was no way I was giving her direct access to stalk him online. I loved Blair, but I was also a little worried about what she might possibly do with that kind of access.

Maybe I'd snag a picture of him running across the field with a football. I folded my arms across my chest and searched the players, a smile tugging at my lips when I found Dusty. Man, he was hot. Sweat darkened the back of his shirt and made his forehead shine. He jogged with perfect form across the field and tossed a football to someone on the cops' team. When his gaze swept across the line of spectators, he pointed directly at someone sitting in a camp chair and clapping—an older man with a baseball hat and a red firefighter's T-shirt next to Tucker's dad. He had Dusty's same nose and identical laughing eyes, set within a mountain of wrinkles.

Had Dusty brought his grandfather? That was adorable.

He glanced my way next, and a grin spread over his face so wide it made me smile in answer.

I wasn't entirely sure, because I hadn't been watching Dusty before he noticed me, but I was pretty sure his performance went up. The man was a powerhouse. His muscles strained against his T-shirt sleeves, his back shifting while he caught and threw the ball. It was almost a shame they weren't playing tackle, because I wouldn't have minded seeing what that looked like.

Chad jogged by a minute later and winked at me. I flushed awkwardly, my cheeks growing hot.

"So which side are you on?" Gigi asked, approaching me at

the worst possible moment. "Because I just noticed you getting ogled by men from both teams."

"Which means both teams are on *my* side?" I asked, hoping to reroute the question. I slid my phone into my pocket. Photo evidence for Blair would have to wait.

I should have known Gigi couldn't be so easily persuaded. "I've been warning men away from you since the moment you told me you'd be coming to Texas, but it doesn't seem to have done much good. They still won't leave you alone."

She meant well, but it was still a little embarrassing when she acted like all these guys would want to date a tired mom of two. Not when my priority would always be Ben and Alice. I hip-checked my aunt. "Dusty told me about that."

"Chad didn't, though? I was a little more forceful with him," she said, raising an eyebrow. "Proof that he isn't good news. He does his job well enough, but I wouldn't trust him with your heart."

"I'm not trusting anyone with my heart, Gigi." Something about the way she said that nettled me.

"Not even Dusty?" she asked.

"No, not even him. I'm still…I just moved here. The kids are getting settled. I don't know if we'll stay in Texas forever."

She drew her arm around my shoulders and squeezed. "I sure hope you do, kiddo. It's been such a treat having you three around."

Time for a subject change. "How is Phoebe doing?"

"Her neighbor has really stepped up, but she might have to move into a facility soon. Her motor skills will be deteriorating quickly."

"That's terrible. Do you need to go out and see her again?"

"Maybe next week," Gigi said. "I need to look at the schedule. Her long-term memory hasn't been affected yet, so she still knows me."

"Don't worry about the schedule. I'm here, Gigi. Use me."

She gave me a smile but didn't say anything more. We watched the rest of the game until it was almost time for lunch, and Gigi walked back to the tables with me to start plating the desserts. A few older police officers and firefighters were manning the oversized grills and heating coals while women set up the burger fixings and table of potluck sides.

"I put everything under the table to keep it out of the sun." I reached down to pull out the foil tins holding all the cakes and shrieked, dropping them back on the ground. They were teeming with ants, the little bugs crawling all over the foil inside and outside, covering my cakes.

"Oh, no," Gigi breathed behind me, noticing at the same time.

I pulled out the plastic tote box and cooler holding the plates, forks, whipped cream and berry compote, and they were blessedly untouched. But the cakes were ruined. All one hundred of my mini angel food cakes were spoiled. I wanted to lie down on the grass and cry.

No, not the grass, because ants were everywhere.

"Don't pick them up," Gigi said, slapping the tin out of my hands when I bent over it again. "Those will bite, and it hurts."

I trusted her, so I left my cakes on the ground. "Garbage bag?"

"Good idea. I'll find one. You figure out how to salvage this."

Salvage it? How? Give everyone a scoop of berries and top it with whipped cream? I wasn't sure I had another option. By the time Gigi returned with an oversized black garbage bag and we managed to get all the cakes into it without getting bitten, the game was over and people were breaking up, taking down their camp chairs and moving to the picnic tables.

Dusty waved at me while he crossed the grass toward his side of the tables. The man was going to win now, no competition. He pointed at me with both hands and then dragged his thumb across his neck in the universal symbol of *you're going down*.

I put my hands on my hips, and shook my head, unable to dampen my smile. Yes, I was going down. Yes, he would win. *Ugh*.

A large hand slid over my lower back, and I jumped, turning to see Chad leaning close, his hand dragging to rest on my waist. "Are you ready?"

Those little ants felt like they were crawling all over my body now. My gaze sought Dusty, whose jaw was hardening, obvious even from here. I stepped back until Chad's hand fell and indicated the black garbage bag. "Well, we've had a bit of a setback."

He folded his arms across his chest and nodded along like he was listening. He didn't seem offended by my placing boundaries, but maybe he was just good at putting on a stone face. Cop skills.

"Ants got into the angel food cakes," I continued. "They're gone. We only have berries and cream."

"Okay, well…I guess we serve berries and cream," he said easily. I didn't know why that was such a relief to me. This was a silly fundraiser contest and the outcome wasn't going to make or break my friendships in this town—or so I hoped. All the same, it was a relief to know he wasn't angry.

"It's a plan," I said.

"I'll get started on the sliders." He nodded toward the older gentleman standing at the grill. "People will start picking up plates in about twenty minutes. They're going to make announcements about the winner of the ticket sales and the game and all that. I think the chiefs are going to rib each other a bit, too. We have time."

My smile grew. I loved being around a police family, and the firefighter family wasn't too bad, either.

He smiled softly, tipping his chin down like we were sharing a secret. "Don't worry too much about ruining the dessert. We won the football game, at least, so hopefully this doesn't lose the whole thing for us."

My whole body tensed as Chad walked away. Guess I'd mistaken his attitude earlier. Hopefully this doesn't lose the whole thing for *us*? He was riding high on the endorphins of winning the flag football game, but that didn't give him a license to be condescending. Like if we lose, it's because of me, and not because Dusty could possibly make better burgers?

It almost made me want to trash the rest of my dessert and guarantee him a loss. I glanced up and caught Dusty watching me again. A smile curved over my lips.

Or maybe not.

CHAPTER TWENTY-SIX

DUSTY

THE POLICE MIGHT HAVE WON the football game, but only because Chad was cheating scum. It didn't help that they had more younger guys willing to play. It certainly didn't help our chances at winning this year's Battle of the Badges. In direct man-against-man boxing rounds, the firefighters won every time. In flag football? You could do things to make it harder to pull flags, and I was fairly certain Chad had done that. But how would I prove it, short of finding his flags and testing them? I wasn't going to let Chad's childishness ruin this day for me.

There was still a chance we could take home the trophy.

I stood beside Brody at the grill after everyone had gotten their plates, doing my best to keep my eyes from straying Nova's way. Alice and Ben were sitting with Gigi at the picnic tables eating, and Nova was alone, plating her dessert. I'd done a strawberry shortcake bar so I wouldn't have to plate anything after the football game, and they'd turned out pretty good. You couldn't go wrong with a shortbread crust.

"These are delicious," Tucker's dad, Roy, said, coming through my line a second time.

"Did my grandpa get enough to eat?" I asked, sliding a hot burger onto his prepared bun.

"He ate," Roy said. "Not much, but some."

"Okay. Thanks for taking care of him. I'll try to join you soon."

Roy held my gaze. "You say that like I'm doing you a favor. I love that man."

My chest constricted.

He reached over the table and clapped me on the shoulder. "You're doing great, son. You got my vote, and not just because you're like one of my kids."

"Glad to hear it." My cheeks flushed, overjoyed at the praise and the kindness. "Don't forget dessert from both tables."

"You didn't hear?" Roy's face crinkled, the lines deepening. "Ants got into the police's dessert. They're just serving berries and cream. It's good, but I don't think it's quite the same."

My stomach fell. "Shoot."

"Don't worry. You would have won either way. These burgers are cooked perfectly."

I nodded, but it felt hollow.

"Gonna join us?" Roy asked.

"Yeah, in a minute."

He walked away, and I let out a quiet groan. Brody moved the finished sliders to the warming rack while I stewed.

"Girlfriend drama?" Brody asked.

That comment did not deserve a reply. "Grab a plate and eat while they're hot."

Brody looked out over the tables full of Arcadia Creek constituents, then back at the grill. "Nah, I'm good."

When I tried to see the groups of people through his eyes, I found plenty of his friends eating with their families. For one of the popular kids in school, he didn't seem to have a place. Or maybe he did, but he was getting in his own way about it. He needed a Tucker and Roy to pull him to their table.

Or maybe what he had was me.

"Come on. Let's get food, and you can meet my grandpa." It was a thin excuse, but it was the only way I could invite him to eat with me without embarrassing the kid or making him bolt. Some days he felt solid, steady, like he was the king of Arcadia High and knew it. Other days, he was more like a rabbit in the forest with a coyote lurking somewhere in the trees.

Today was definitely a rabbit day.

I didn't wait for him to agree. I grabbed two plates and handed him one, then started filling mine with sliders, chips, and fruit.

"Are you gonna try the cops' food too?" Brody asked.

"We have to or we can't vote. And we are voting."

Chad wasn't at the grill anymore, so I took a slider from the table and moved on to dessert. "Heard about your ant problem," I said when we reached Nova.

She stood at the table, folding her arms over her chest. "Here to gloat?"

"Don't try to blame the ants when y'all lose," I said. "My burgers beat Chad's fair and square." I hadn't had a bite yet, but they were obviously dry just from looking at them.

Nova tucked her chin. She didn't have time to reply when a voice boomed behind me.

"What are you trying to say?" Chad asked, his voice in my ear. Where had he even come from? "You calling me a cheater?"

I mean, he *was* one, but I wasn't about to start something. This was a family event and I would swallow my pride.

"No," Brody said, coming to my side. "He's saying your burgers are burned, so ours are better."

Chad looked ready to deck me, but his gaze fell to Brody's defiant stare and seemed to think better of it. "I got you a plate, Nova."

"Oh." She looked from Chad to the picnic tables. "My aunt got one for me already, but thank you."

Chad hovered. He didn't seem to want to walk away while I remained. My little yappy guard dog was giving him the evil eye, though, so he relented and retreated.

Nova stepped around the table, keeping her arms crossed. "Did he really burn the sliders?" she asked Brody.

"Yeah, they aren't very good. Wanna try?" He lifted his plate toward her.

"That's okay. I'll grab a fresh one from your table."

"What about the plate Gigi made you?" I teased.

She shot me a look. "I need to learn how to let people down firmly, I guess. That wasn't even gentle—it was a straight up lie."

My face screwed into incredulity. "You've let me down firmly many times, and I have only known you for a few months."

Nova's face split into a grin. "True."

"I want to eat," Brody said, walking away.

"Coming." I turned back and lowered my voice. "Hey, my grandpa is here. I'd love to introduce you if you get a minute. Just come find us."

She looked at me for a beat longer than usual. "Okay."

"Okay," I repeated, somehow feeling like I'd scored a major win today that had nothing to do with the Battle of the Badges.

MY WIN slowly deflated as the event petered to a close and Nova didn't come to our table. Had it been too forward to tell her to come meet the last member of my family? No, my parents didn't count. I had no idea if they were even alive. Nova had seemed to consider my invitation, so I knew she'd given it some thought. She hadn't answered blindly.

Great, now I was overthinking. That wasn't normal for me.

Someone had given Captain Bowman a mic, which everyone

knew was a bad idea. Our fire chief was a man of few words, but Cap never knew when to stop talking.

"Police won the football game," Mayor Dunmore said into the mic as he wrested it from Cap's hand. "Fire won the ticket sales. We've tallied the votes on food and are pleased to announce that, when added to other wins, the Battle of the Badge trophy this year goes to…drumroll, please."

People pounded on their tables, including Grandpa across from me, his wrinkled eyes twinkling. Great, had he voted for the cops again?

Randy sat hard on the bench beside me and scoffed. "They're gonna take it."

"We don't know that," I said, but I had a feeling he was right.

"The winners are the police crew!" Mayor Dunmore said. Cheering and shouting went up all over the picnic tables, but our section stayed silent. Grandpa frowned, which was something of a relief. Guess he'd voted for us after all.

I looked where Nova was sitting with Gigi. They were clapping, but a line formed between Nova's eyebrows. She was just as confused as I was. Yes, her berry compote and cream were delicious, but their burgers weren't. Not to be cocky, but no part of our meal had been messed up.

"Looks like we were destined to lose anyway," Randy muttered. "Hard to beat a cheater."

"Watch it," I said softly. "It won't do any good if you're overheard."

Randy lifted his eyebrows. "You know it's true."

"He's right," Grandpa called across the table, his voice carrying over the cheers. "Those flags weren't coming off during the game. Must've glued them on or something."

Glue was a bit dramatic. Time to get Gramps out of here before he landed me in trouble. "I'll clean up really quick and then we can go. Come on, Randy."

He groaned. "I knew I should have sat with Jill. She doesn't need to be the first one up and cleaning."

He was kidding. Or so I hoped. He followed me to the grill, where we passed Chad and his buddy Travis. "Maybe next year," Chad said in a way that made me think he was already planning a way to guarantee another win.

"In the ring?" I called back. "Can't wait."

"To wipe the floor with them," Randy muttered, finishing my sentence.

Man, he had a mouth on him today.

"What was that?" Chad asked, following us.

I stopped walking immediately and put my hands up. Clearly, emotions were riding high. It was just a little town function. It didn't matter who won. If they wanted it badly enough to cheat, they could take it.

"Nothing," I said, hoping my tone would de-escalate the situation. "We just like boxing."

"I could take you, Dusty," Chad said, his blue eyes gleaming. He was looking for a fight. Maybe he just wanted to prove he deserved the win he'd somehow schemed for. Either way, he must have been forgetting how quickly I had taken him down last year.

"I guess we'll find out next year," I said, shooting him a smile.

"Why wait?" he asked.

I turned to leave right as he stepped forward and clocked me across the jaw. Pain reverberated through my face, stars sparkling the edge of my vision. I looked back at him, anger pulsing through me at his cheap shot.

"Not cool, man," Randy said. His face was thunderous.

I had to agree.

Chad shook out his hand, bouncing on his toes. "Let's finish this."

"It's not the time or the place," I reminded him, waiting for the pain to ebb. I had taken a step back to get to cleaning up our tables when he rounded on me again. His fist was poised to strike, coming at my nose, so I lifted my arm to block the blow. My forearm took the brunt of his hit. I shoved him back. "Stop, Chad."

"Why? You're just going to let me win?"

"We already have twice today," I snapped. "What's once more?"

Anger flashed in his eyes, and he advanced again. I put my arms out and shoved him hard. He fell back into the table of Nova's berry and cream remnants, sliding off the other side and falling in a heap, covered in dessert and wrapped in the cheap tablecloth.

I stepped back in utter silence. The crowd had noticed, watching us with wide eyes. I swore. Nova and her kids had a front-row seat next to their aunt. Gigi's disapproving expression hit me in the gut, fed by the concerns she'd had months ago when she told me to keep away from Nova. Even worse, though, was Grandpa standing in the row behind them, gripping his walker and frowning at me. I felt sixteen all over again, getting in fights because I had a hole in my sneakers or I kissed the wrong girl at a party. His disappointment felt layered in years of stupid mistakes.

I wanted to take the mic from wherever Mayor Dunmore hid it and explain I'd been acting in self defense, but that wouldn't exonerate me. Grandpa pressed his mouth into a firm line.

Anger pulsated through me. I turned to the table and started cleaning up the dessert mess. Chad was on his feet, wiping whipped cream from his clothes. He seemed to have noticed the audience too, which cooled him off enough that I didn't think the other half of my face was in danger of getting a matching bruise.

"Leave it," Nova said behind me, reaching for some plates of dessert that had flown on the grass. "I'll take care of this."

"It's my mess," I said sharply.

She grew still, holding three stacked dessert plates and a fork.

Great. Could this get any worse?

Nova glanced at Chad's retreating back. "Dusty, we both know this wasn't your fault. I'll handle it. You go take care of your family."

By family, she meant my grandpa.

Was it pathetic that I wanted to cry? Nova immediately trusted that I hadn't asked for the fight. Her kindness bowled into me like sunlight in the early morning, blinding me with gratitude and an overwhelming surge of appreciation.

Nova seemed to sense my thoughts, because she took a step closer. "Go. I have this."

I nodded, at a total loss for words. Grandpa was quiet when I reached him. Together we weaved through the crowd to head back to my truck. Once I got him situated and his walker tucked safely in the back, I climbed in and rested my hands on the wheels. "Want to grab a Frosty before we take you back?"

"I'm a little tired," he said.

I glanced at him before pulling onto the road and noticed that he looked weary. I turned up his favorite country radio station and leaned into my seat. I'd disappointed him, and he didn't want to discuss it.

Well, upon further consideration, neither did I.

CHAPTER TWENTY-SEVEN

NOVA

MONDAY NIGHT, I counted eight days in a row that Carter had called to talk to the kids and Ben had refused to come to the phone. Eight days of ignoring his dad.

"What have you said to him?" Carter asked, disbelief marring his words.

I had just gotten Alice out of the bath and wrapped in a towel while Carter spoke on speakerphone from the counter. "Careful," I said. "The kids can hear you."

Well, Alice could as she dripped on the bath rug in front of me. As soon as I mentioned that their dad was calling, Ben jumped up from the tub and ran out of the bathroom, trailing water along the linoleum floor and out to the carpet. I'd grabbed a towel and chucked it toward him, which he came back for, but the carpet was going to take a while to dry. I could've used one of those giant fans the firefighters had.

I had finally answered the third time he called and held the phone out so Alice could chat with him while she played with the bubbles and her Barbies.

"Then take the phone to another room," he snapped.

Okay. Wow. There were two options here. First, I could hang

up on Carter. He didn't have a right to speak to me like that. Or second, I *could* go in the other room and try to get to the bottom of it with him. Were our roles reversed, my heart would be broken if Ben didn't want to talk to me for over a week.

Then again, that wouldn't happen. I always paid attention to my kids.

I took him off speakerphone and put it to my ear, nodding at Alice to go on and get her pajamas on. I waited until she left the bathroom, sank onto the closed toilet seat, and clenched my teeth. "Let's chat when you've had time to find a better mood."

"Nova—"

"No, Chad, seriously. It'll give me a chance to talk with Ben and—"

"Who's Chad?"

"What?"

"You called me Chad. Who is Chad?"

My stomach fluttered anxiously. Had I? I must have, or how else would Carter know his name? "Just a friend."

"The guy who was at your house last week with the cat?"

"No."

He was silent for a second. "So...what? Are you dating two guys?"

"I'm not dating anyone." Again, not that it was any of his business. "We aren't going to talk about this. Let me speak to Ben. He's probably going through something, and we need to get to the bottom of it. I don't know why—"

"I have an idea why he won't to talk to me. It must be your new boyfriends."

"What?" I asked, exasperated and surprised by the insane leaps he could make. "That doesn't even make sense."

"Sure it does. Why would Ben want to talk to his dad if he has other men poisoning him against me? What are you saying about me to all the hicks out there?"

"Nothing." Which was almost true. Dusty wasn't a hick.

"Why would I talk about you, Carter, to people I'm not even dating?" This entire conversation had spiraled out of control so quickly, I was losing my place. It felt like someone had tossed me into the center of a tilt-a-whirl at the pier and I had to find the car holding my family, but the floor was moving and everything kept spinning away.

Besides, if that was the first thing he jumped to, it stood to reason he was talking about me to other people.

I wanted to hang up, block his number, and lose myself in *White Collar* reruns. But that wasn't even a legal option.

"The kids need me," I said. "Can we try again tomorrow?"

Carter was quiet for a minute. "I don't like this."

Inhaling for patience, I waited for him to continue. The man loved to hear himself talk, so it was only a matter of time.

"I don't like the kids being so far away and having no way to see them regularly. It's going to strain our relationship."

Answering the phone regularly would help with that. Carter had only started calling every day after he'd FaceTimed during the tornado warning and Ben hadn't wanted to speak to him. It was a classic Carter move. Everyone wasn't worshiping him, so he would pester the kids until balance was restored. I had the sick feeling that as soon as Ben went back to wanting to hear from Carter, things would go back to the way they were pre-tornado night. We'd get him on the phone once a week if we were lucky.

There had to be a better way. It wasn't fair to send my kids on emotional roller coasters without breaks.

"Honestly," Carter said. "I didn't want it to have to come to this, but we might have to discuss location—"

An ear-splitting scream rent the air, curdling my stomach. I didn't think. My feet were up and racing to the kids bedroom. I flung the door open, frantically searching—I *knew* the bunk bed was going to cause one of them to break their arm—until I found Alice crumpled on the floor in her hot pink Barbie nightgown, clutching Peaches to her chest while sobs racked her tiny shoulders.

I dropped to my knees. "What happened?"

She shook her head, tears streaming down her reddened cheeks.

"Alice," I said firmly. "What happened?"

Her little arms peeled away from her body, separating her pink monkey into three pieces—the body in one hand, two arms dangling from the other. Clean slices went through the fuzzy pink appendages. This act of brutality was clearly done with scissors.

"Ben!" Alice wailed, like he had stolen her firstborn child. "He did this!"

Yeah, I had jumped to the very same conclusion. But innocent until proven guilty and all that. "We don't know for sure until we ask him," I said gently.

"I did it," Ben said from the doorway behind me, his arms crossed over his chest and his mouth flipped into a frown.

Oh, that little punk. "Honestly? Why, Ben?"

"She shouldn't have ruined my Chewie."

"Agreed, but she didn't try to ruin it on purpose," I said, exasperated. "She didn't know it would melt."

His frown was unrelenting.

Alice's sobs keened through the air.

No one was going to get to sleep anytime soon.

Alice started yelling at Ben, and his response was to yell back. The animosity grew in the room until my arms began to itch. Great, add a wave of hives to the mix.

"Okay," I shouted. "Everyone, *enough*." I pointed one hand at each kid. "You both messed up. You both made bad choices. You both owe the other an apology."

"But Peaches is *dead*!" Alice screamed. "She'll never live again!"

An idea hit me. "She'll live just fine. I can sew."

"Unlike Chewbacca, who I had to bury in the grass!"

What? When did he do that? "Where?"

"Not telling," he said, still glaring at his sister.

Oh, good grief. Emotions were high, it was past bedtime, and Alice would never go to sleep with a broken monkey. "Come on, both of you. Shoes on. We're going out."

"Where?" Ben asked.

"The monkey hospital. But not until you both apologize."

I was pretty sure I'd intrigued them, because while I went searching for the phone I'd flung on my run to the room, I heard them mutter half-hearted apologies to each other. Carter had tried to call six times since our conversation had been interrupted, but my first call was to Gigi.

"Hey, sugar," she said when she answered.

"We're having a sibling war over here and Ben cut Peaches' arms off. Any chance you have some pink thread? And a needle? I left my sewing kit in New York."

"Of course. Come on over. I might not have pink, but I know I have white."

"Great. That works too. We'll see you in a minute."

We hung up, and I dialed Carter to update him. He must've been out of his mind after hearing his daughter scream like that.

It rang once before a woman answered. "Hello?"

I looked down at my phone, but it was still Carter's face. Putting the phone back to my ear, I heard her speak again. "Hello?"

Okay. So this was really happening. "Is Carter there?" I asked.

"He's busy right now."

Silence. Why had she answered his phone if he couldn't come to it? This had to be his new girlfriend, and it suddenly felt ridiculous that I didn't have my sewing kit, but she could pull it from the closet right now if she wanted to hem a pair of pants.

"Do you need something?" she asked. Her voice was higher than mine, silkier too.

"I just needed to talk to Carter. I'll call back another time."

"I can take a message," she said.

So could his voicemail. It was an icky situation, and I didn't like how it felt to have my conversation hijacked like this, then made to feel like I was the weird one for not telling her why I wanted to talk to her boyfriend. We shared *children*, for heaven's sake. It didn't take rocket science to figure out that I probably wanted to discuss them, and not with a stranger.

"Mom, can we go?" Alice asked tearfully behind me.

"Yeah, babe. Just a sec." I cleared my throat to speak into the phone again. "If you'll have Car—"

"Was that Alice?" the woman asked.

"Okay, who is this?" I asked, my patience *gone*. If she knew my child's name, I could learn hers.

"Kristen," she said, and if I wasn't mistaken, she sounded a little hurt.

"What are you do—hello?" Carter said into the phone. "Nova? What happened?"

"Peaches' arms are broken. I need to run so I have time to sew them back on so Alice can sleep. Just wanted to let you know why it sounded like our child was dying. She's fine. Or she will be."

"Okay." He sounded slightly mystified.

"Bye, Carter." I didn't wait for him to say anything more. I was shaking, overwhelmed, itchy, and in need of a good, long scream into a pillow. I turned my phone to Do Not Disturb mode, slid it in my pocket, and went in search of my shoes. And maybe some Benadryl anti-itch cream.

GIGI HAD water boiling in her kettle when we arrived at the house. She ushered both kids into the kitchen to assemble their hot chocolate and make some toast to dunk in it. "Sewing box is on the sofa," she called before they disappeared.

I got thirty blissful, quiet minutes on Gigi's plush floral sofa, hearing my kids put aside their feud and giggle together while I stitched Peaches' arms back on with white thread that didn't quite blend in but wasn't too obvious either. Once the second arm was firmly in place, I leaned my head against the back of the couch and breathed. Everything felt so much worse in the moment, but time helped soothe each of the awful bits I'd endured this evening. All of them but one.

Kristen.

"Mom!" Alice said, rushing into the room in her Ugg-style Target boots and Barbie nightgown. She had chocolate smeared and dried on her upper lip. "Gigi said we can have a sleepover!"

"On a school night?"

"No, she said it has to be Friday or Saturday. She said it was up to you."

Gigi came through to the living room and sat on the sofa beside me with a sigh. "What do you think, lovey?"

I thought it sounded absolutely marvelous. "The fundraiser is this weekend, but we can do Friday."

"Let's do Saturday," Gigi said. "You can go to the fundraiser and take yourself out for an ice cream afterward."

"I think it's a family event."

Gigi looked at me. "I know."

"I want ice cream," Ben said, joining us.

"We'll have our own fun," Gigi said.

Why did it feel a little like scheming? I eyed her. "Don't you want to go to the fundraiser?"

"No. I've been to plenty, and I'll go to plenty more." She smiled at me. "But I know you won't want to miss it."

There was a hidden message there. I tried to figure out what she was trying to say.

Gigi leaned down and lowered her voice, looking at the kids. "Will you both go upstairs and see if I have enough pillows in the guest room? Then you'll know if you need to bring your own. Count the blankets folded on the cedar chest, too."

"What's a cedar chest?" Ben asked.

"It's the wooden box at the end of the bed. Work together, okay?"

"Okay!" they said in unison and ran up the stairs.

I cut the final thread and lowered Peaches onto my lap. We didn't have much time and I didn't want to waste it. "What are you trying to say?"

"The kids told me about Carter."

"That Ben won't talk to him?" I asked.

"No. Alice told me Carter doesn't want to talk to them very much, and today you fought on the phone."

I had a hard time seeing how what we did could be misconstrued as fighting, but the reality was that kids could often read emotions better than adults did. They were intuitive. "Apparently he has a girlfriend, and she just moved in with him. I haven't told the kids yet."

Gigi's face hardened. "How are you?"

"Not hurting, I promise. He can move on. But the woman answered his phone tonight, which threw me off. I left so many of my things there. I just…I don't like the idea of someone else having them. You know we couldn't fit everything in my car."

"Then go back and get them."

I laughed.

"I'm serious. I'll take the kids for a week if that's what it takes. Go back and get your things."

"Not possible. Our settlement is signed and everything I left in the apartment belongs to him now. I really am okay with him moving on. It was kind of nice when I learned all of it and wasn't jealous."

"It's also okay to grieve, sugar. Don't force yourself to be strong all the time. Take some time to feel what you need to feel. If Dusty is part of that"—she shrugged—"then so be it."

"Aunt Gigi," I said with mock shock. "You're the one who warned him away from me."

"Because I didn't want you to be bombarded when you arrived, and that man is a flirt. But even I can see that the feelings go both ways here."

Both ways? She thought Dusty might like me, too. I wanted to believe that. I longed to believe it.

"He might have been a punk kid," Gigi continued, "but I admit he's a changed man."

"Even after that altercation with Chad?"

"That wasn't Dusty's fault, which I think you already know. That was Chad being the idiot he is."

Little footsteps ran down the stairs while the kids shouted numbers at Gigi. She squeezed both of them in hugs and saw us to the door so we could get home.

"Think about it," Gigi said, waving from her porch. "It's okay for you to move on, too."

I took my kids' hands, Alice clutching a repaired Peaches to her chest, and walked away, Gigi's words floating in and out of my head for the rest of the night.

CHAPTER TWENTY-EIGHT

DUSTY

THURSDAY MORNING, I got off my shift at the firehouse feeling like someone had held my eyelids open and poured fine sand into them. I needed a tub of eye drops and forty hours of sleep. But Grandpa was waiting to see me, so I settled for breakfast at Gigi's and some extra strong coffee. I could practically taste her buttery eggs and crisp bacon as I pulled my truck into a spot on Main Street.

The bell jangled above the door as I pushed it open. Gigi stood behind the counter, holding a coffee pot and chatting with Flora. The only other tables were a group of older women having brunch in the center of the dining room and a booth in the corner holding Chad and Travis in their police gear. Was it too late to spin around and leave the way I'd come?

No. I would show no fear. Travis had glanced up and noticed me, but quickly went back to eating. Chad hadn't even looked my way, thank heavens. My jaw ached at the sight of him, the skin still tender. The bruise was already fading to an unattractive yellow color, but at least it was going away.

"Get that shirt out of here," Gigi said, lifting her eyebrows.

I glanced down. The burnt orange UT Austin shirt I wore

had nothing but a white longhorn symbol in the center. Sometimes I liked to wear my old alumni gear just to get on Gigi's nerves—mostly because it meant some sparring, naturally—but today I hadn't even thought about it. I had thrown on some clothes because I was going straight to Pleasant Gardens after this.

My mouth curved into a grin. "What, you mean the best team in the state? I can take it off, but that would be breaking the no shirt, no service rule, and I would *kill* for a stack of pancakes right now."

Gigi fought a smile. I could see it hidden there beneath her fake grumpy frown. "For you, I'd make an exception. I don't want to see that color in my establishment."

Was she serious? It was sometimes hard to tell.

There was really only one way to find out.

I reached down and pulled my shirt off by the hem. When the fabric cleared my face, I found myself staring at Nova. She stood frozen with a tray of mugs, the kitchen door swinging shut behind her. My whole cocky bravado thing was mostly an act, because now I sort of wanted to pull my shirt back on and hide in a corner booth with a plate of hot breakfast. But I did what I do best and sent her a dazzling smile instead.

She wasn't looking at my face, though. Too bad there wasn't a box for me to lift right now. If I flexed, she'd notice, because her eyes were running all over my chest. When she lifted her brown eyes, they were full of some emotion I couldn't place. Something full and heavy.

"Put that away," Gigi said, laughing and gesturing to my chest. "It's indecent. I have customers."

I flashed her a smile and tossed my shirt over my shoulder. "I wouldn't want to offend anyone with my longhorns, though."

"It's okay," she said, hand on her hip. "I'll just charge you double today. Longhorns tax."

I laughed, shaking out my shirt to put it back on. When I

moved to a booth near the window, I found Chad glaring at me. Well, let him.

"Can you take over for a minute, sugar?" Gigi was saying to Nova. "I need to check in with Phoebe."

"Of course." Nova followed her aunt into the kitchen and came out a minute later with a notepad and pencil. She worked her way around the tables, refilling coffees and taking orders, checking in with Chad and Travis and bringing them a side of syrup before she made it all the way to me and my grumbling stomach.

Which, as it happened, decided to growl the moment she approached.

Pink spots appeared on her cheeks. She posed the pencil on her notepad. "What can I get for you?"

"Coffee with the pancake breakfast. Sausage and bacon both, please."

She nodded, writing. "How do you want your eggs?"

"Over-easy."

"Toast?"

"Wheat."

She scribbled it down, the redness growing on her face. When Nova finished writing her notes, she turned away. "I'll have it right out."

Was she…embarrassed? The woman wouldn't meet my eye. I hadn't taken my shirt off for her—how would I have known she was here? It was only a joke.

By the time Nova returned with the pot of coffee and a clean mug, I was at a total loss. I leaned back in the booth, running my arm along the bench. "Have I done something to offend you?"

Her eyes dipped to my shirt. "Besides your obscene little show back there?"

"My *obscene*—wow, Nova."

She put the coffee pot on the table with a thud and leaned

forward on both hands, lowering her voice. "You're going to send that table of grandmas to the hospital with heart attacks. Don't you think about anyone but yourself?"

"I was thinking of you, actually."

She saw right through that little tease. "Oh? Not something stupid like football rivalries?"

"No, of course not." I grinned, loving how easily she could see through me. "I was wishing you were here, and then bam: wish granted."

"You're ridiculous."

"Heart attacks?" I asked, eyebrows up, my gaze flicking to the older women. "*That* was ridiculous."

"Do you own a mirror? I'm not the one exaggerating here."

A slow smile curved over my lips. She'd leaned so close, our faces were only inches apart. I wasn't even hungry anymore. I could live off banter with Nova. The rich aroma of coffee wafted up from the hot mug in front of me, making my stomach rumble again.

Comfort between us had been restored. I hadn't seen her since the Battle of the Badges. I'd backed off, leaving the ball in her court. I didn't know how she felt about violence or if seeing me and Chad fighting was a dealbreaker. She hadn't blamed me at the time, but she had kids, so I wouldn't fault her for being cautious.

"Do they not feed you over there?" she asked.

"At work? I'm the one who does the feeding. We had back-to-back calls all night, so I didn't have time to grab anything."

"I'll bring out your food as soon as it's ready." She hesitated, and I liked that she didn't seem to want to leave right away. "You doing anything fun today?"

"Puzzle shopping."

"Huh." She nodded. "That sounds like a fake excuse you'd use to let someone down gently. On par with cat feeding."

"Are you asking to hang out with me? Because the puzzles can definitely wait." I cringed. "But my grandpa can't."

"Why don't you take him that one we did of the States? It'll keep you both occupied for a while."

"Until he throws the whole thing off the table."

"Has he done that before?"

"No, but I almost did when we were putting it together at your house."

She threw her head back and laughed, pouring the sound into me like a funnel directly into my heart. "If you want the puzzle, it's yours."

"Maybe I do." I smiled at her. It wasn't really the puzzle I wanted.

At some point, I needed to figure out where she was at. At some point, I could ask her on a date. My pulse increased at the thought. "Are your cookies ready for Saturday?"

"No. I won't finish them until tomorrow. But they're almost there."

"What shapes did you choose?"

"You'll have to wait and see." She flashed me a smile, then looked over her shoulder, ostensibly to check the other tables.

"Are you planning to stick around for the auction Saturday night?" I asked lightly, rotating my coffee cup slowly.

Nova's eyes fell on my face and held. They seemed a darker brown than usual, more direct and questioning. She nodded. "I thought about it. Gigi is taking my kids for a sleepover so I can have a night off. She spoils me, but I couldn't help accepting her offer." She rolled her eyes. "Ben cut the arms off Alice's pink monkey the other day as payback for the melted Chewbacca, and it's been World War Three in our home ever since. But they seem to get along great when Gigi's in charge. Her house is Switzerland."

"Poor Peaches," I said, pulling a tired smile from her lips.

"Nova, dear," Flora called from the counter, her greedy eyes soaking us both in. "Can I get a refill?"

"Of course." She shot me a smile before leaving.

Nova had the night off on Saturday. She had a babysitter already and was considering staying at the fundraiser. I didn't know if she'd told me that as a hint or just to make conversation, but if ever there was a time to ask her on a real date, this was it.

I would need to set up and take down in the school gym, but that didn't mean I couldn't bring a date.

Chad and Travis got up to leave the diner, making my entire body tense and my jaw throb from muscle memory. Chad didn't scare me, but I'd been sucker punched once already, and I wouldn't put it past him to do it again.

"Keep walking," Travis muttered when Chad slowed at my table.

"I'm good," Chad said, his hand up. "Just wondered if you've had any jaw pain this week?" He gave me a falsely sympathetic look, like we were twelve in the cafeteria at school.

"I feel great," I said, sipping my coffee and offering him a wide grin. The yellow bruise blended into my skin okay, but I guessed the fluorescent lighting made it look worse. "Might want to practice fair fighting for our rematch, though. You can't steal a win in a boxing ring."

"Let's go," Travis said, forcefully pushing Chad toward the door before he had time to react.

Chad looked furious.

I didn't feel any better, though.

Nova watched them leave, approaching with my plate of steaming food. "Everything good here?"

"He's just a sore loser," I muttered. I really should have kept my mouth shut.

"Didn't he win?" she asked.

"Not really, and he knows it." A cheater wouldn't ever be

truly satisfied with his trophy. Maybe he'd fake it around town, but when it was me and him, I could see how it rankled. I breathed in bacon and eggs and syrup. "Smells amazing."

"You should be glad Dal is back there this morning," she muttered. "I'm not really cut out for this whole diner cook thing."

"I thought you liked to cook?"

"Baking is different," she said, looking at me like she expected me to understand. I did, sort of. Baking and decorating desserts wasn't the same as cooking eggs and fried chicken on command. Diner cooking was probably even more monotonous.

"Hey," I said, gathering her attention right before she turned away. It was all or nothing now. She wasn't immune to me, obviously—which didn't mean she wanted to date me, of course, but I wouldn't know for sure until I tried.

"Yeah?" She tilted her head to the side, her ponytail swishing with the movement. I wanted to run my hands through her silky hair.

Focus, man. "Want to go to the fundraiser with me Saturday?"

Nova went still, her body straightening like a soldier and holding there.

Which meant, for some stupid reason, I felt the need to keep talking. "Low key, I promise. We can grab dinner and go to the fundraiser as friends. It doesn't have to mean anything."

But it would mean something to me, and I was pretty sure she could sense that.

"Can I...actually..." She drew in a breath and let it out. "Sure."

My body exploded, fireworks going off in my head, but I tried to look cool and nodded. "Great. I'll text you later and we can work out the details."

"Sounds good." She hovered for a second, turning the wrong way and then spinning back the right direction, a smile playing on her lips and her cheeks going rosy.

I felt like I'd scored a million bucks. I shoved a bite of pancakes in my mouth to hide my grin, but when I looked up and found Gigi watching me, the food turned to sludge. Her mouth was in a flat line, her worried eyes shifting to her niece, and I tried to give her a reassuring nod.

To my utter surprise, she returned it with a subtle nod of her own. Did I have Gigi's approval? It sure seemed like it.

My chest glowed with warmth and anticipation, and I had a hard time finishing my meal because of the excessive smiling. This was a huge step for Nova and a turning point for us. I'd never lacked for dates when I wanted them, but I also never kept one girlfriend for long. It was hard to commit when I battled the reality that some people left for good without a backwards glance. With Nova, I knew it could be different.

After I paid my check and made it back to my truck to head to Pleasant Gardens, I found the puzzle of the United States leaning against my windshield with a note taped to the box.

I'm going to assume the puzzle shopping wasn't a gentle letdown and save you the trouble of shopping for a new one. Looking forward to Saturday.

—N

I drove to Beeler with a sappy grin. Pretty sure I was going to marry this woman.

CHAPTER TWENTY-NINE

NOVA

THE LAST TIME I had gone on a first date, Carter had taken me to a seedy little dive bar in Queens where a buddy of his was playing a gig. He'd started law school when I was beginning my sophomore year of college at NYU—we had been introduced by my roommate's older brother. At the time, I'd been so starry-eyed, I didn't care how long it took to get to the bar because he was holding my hand, or how dirty the bar was because he'd bought my drink, or how terrible the music was because we weren't really listening to the music anyway. I'd been so sunk for Carter, nothing else mattered.

Now, more than a decade later, the entire contents of my measly closet were strewn all over my bed, and nothing seemed good enough for an adult first date with a full-grown man who had his own house and career and opinions. The stakes for dating had risen exponentially in all the ways—my kids, my life, my baggage. *His* life and baggage. Just agreeing to this date was a step I hadn't known I was ready for until it was presented to me. My kids hadn't told me how they felt about Dusty yet, but I wanted to go out with him first and see how it felt before bringing it to them.

If I went on this date. I was pretty sure it wasn't going to happen, because nothing in my closet sent the message *more than friends*. Everything pretty much just shouted *I'm a tired mom!!!*

I sat on a pile of various colored T-shirts and held my phone up to my mouth, where my sister-in-law was standing by on speakerphone to approve my clothing choice. "I didn't bother bringing date clothes, Blair. I have *nothing*."

"You aren't really freaking out because of the clothes. You know that, right?" she asked, her voice filling the room. Kids were playing in the background and something was beeping—probably a microwave.

"Honestly, Noves," Jason said way too loudly. I could imagine my brother leaning over his wife and shouting to be heard, which made a smile tug at my lips. "It doesn't really sound like this guy will care what you're wearing. Wear that Neon Trees shirt you won't get rid of. Then you'll at least be comfortable."

"Terrible advice," Blair said, her feet stomping across the room. "Don't wear that shirt."

I glanced down. I was wearing the shirt right now—it *was* the most comfortable thing I owned.

Also, how did my brother know anything about Dusty? "What have you told him?" I asked Blair.

"I don't know enough to tell him anything." Blair closed a door and it grew much quieter. "He called Gigi."

"He *what?*"

"I told him about the date yesterday when you called me, and he wanted to vet the guy."

"Kind of a weird time for him to jump in as a protective brother. I'm an old lady and a mother. Does he seriously think some guy is going to take advantage of me? Or that Gigi, of all people, would let that happen?"

Blair was silent for a moment. "He cares about you."

Okay, fine. That excuse was fair.

"Honestly," Blair continued, "Gigi made it sound like you could show up in a paper bag and the guy would be thrilled you showed up at all. He's not desperate, is he?"

"No. She's exaggerating. He's a catch, which is why I don't think this will go anywhere, B. I'm not holding my breath."

"I'll hold it for you." She groaned, then moved the phone away and shouted. "Jason, just open the microwave so it stops beeping!" Then her voice returned to normal. "Okay, I'm back. Listen, there is wisdom to Jason's advice. Dress comfortably, and definitely let him kiss you."

My stomach somersaulted. Imagining Dusty's arms around me sent my blood into hyperdrive.

"You aren't an old lady," Blair continued. "You're young and hot, and you deserve someone who puts you first."

Tears sprang to my eyes. Thank heavens we weren't on FaceTime, because I didn't want her to know how her words affected me. "He's three years younger than me, B. Maybe more. I don't actually know."

"Does it really matter? The older we get, the smaller those gaps are anyway. Besides, from what I've heard, he's twice the man Carter is, and your stupid ex has like six years on Dusty."

Those were all valid points. "You know, Carter has been calling twice a day since Ben stopped wanting to speak to him, then yesterday he just stopped. I haven't heard from him in over twenty-four hours, which is not the relief you'd think it is."

"You think he's going to quit talking to you altogether? Because that doesn't sound like a bad thing."

"The kids deserve to have their dad, even if I don't like him."

She made an irritated noise. "Stop being a saint and block him for good."

"I'm not, and you know I can't. First off, it's the law. Second, what kind of person would I be if I got in the way of my kids having a relationship with their dad?"

"Like I said, *saint*. Honestly, I'm over him. Can we keep talking about the fireman, please? I can't believe I'm the one who has to say this to you," she continued, "but being a mom isn't a point against you, like you said it was. That man would be *lucky* to have Ben and Alice in his life."

"I know." I was unable to stop the tears now. "It's not a reflection on them—"

"It isn't one on you, either. Have you forgotten how hot you are? There's a reason you've got all these guys fighting over you."

"No one is fighting—"

"You mean the cop didn't deck Dusty last weekend? Gigi told us about that, too."

"She's such a gossip."

"We're family. Gossip doesn't count when it's family."

Not sure that was true, but okay.

"I need to finish making dinner," Blair said. "Remember to layer your mascara. You want those suckers to be nice and thick. Send me a picture when you're dressed."

"I will."

"Love you. Bye."

"Love you." I hung up and exhaled. Blair was an incredible one-person cheer team. Ten minutes on the phone, a few tears later, and I thought maybe I could do this after all. I knew Dusty wanted this date, that he wanted me. The hard part was accepting it. I'd spent ten years married to a guy who didn't want me, not after he had me. It was a lot to unlearn.

And Dusty looked like he stepped off the April page of the shirtless firefighters calendar. It had taken gargantuan effort not to drop my jaw when I had entered the diner the other day to see his bare chest on exhibition. The man's arms were probably thicker than my head. But he wasn't the kind of bro who wore tight shirts to make sure his muscles were on everyone's mind or displayed in their face. Not that I hadn't noticed before, of course, but I was doing my best not to notice.

On full display like that, though, it was impossible not to.

He was picking me up in forty-five minutes, and I still wasn't wearing pants. Time to suck it up and choose something.

A half-hour and six more outfits later, I settled on a black T-shirt with capped sleeves tucked into a swinging midi skirt and ankle boots. It wasn't the fanciest thing in my closet, but the fundraiser didn't sound like an elegant event. My outfit was safely in the middle ground. I'd applied six layers of mascara, per Blair's instructions, and brushed my teeth.

Gigi had both of my kids, who didn't even give me a backward glance when they took her hands and walked down the street, which had been more freeing than I anticipated. They were safe and happy and didn't feel abandoned.

Which meant I could enjoy—

Ding. The doorbell went off, making my heart hammer in my ears. I checked my breath with a shaky hand. *Okay, calm down, Nova.* Dusty wouldn't be jumping me the moment I opened the door. If I decided to kiss him good night, that was hours away. Besides, he might not even want that, which would mean I was FREAKING OUT for no reason.

But could you blame me? I hadn't had a first kiss in eleven years.

I swung the door open, a smile plastered on my face. Dusty stood there, backlit by the late afternoon sun. When his honey-colored eyes fell on me, comfort swooped through my body at once, driving away my anxiety and doubts. His smile was soft, spreading as he took me in. "You look amazing."

"Thank you." I picked up my purse and shrugged my jacket on, then followed him out to his truck. "Where are we eating?"

"Casa de la Hayes."

"You cooked?" I asked, climbing into the front seat and buckling in. "I could have driven to you."

"Nah, it's all good. I had to drop off some things at the high school, anyway." His smile lingered on me, the silence in the car growing thick. He seemed to shake himself loose and pulled onto the road. "Did you have a good day?"

It was weird how easy our conversation was, like we'd known each other for years. I sank into my seat, comfortable with him, and we talked about the park I'd found that morning with the kids.

When he pulled onto the road that led out of town, I watched the cars passing us.

"Have you gone running yet?" he asked.

"No, but I might try this week. It's warm enough now I don't think I'll freeze before I hit the end of the block." I shot him a sheepish smile. "You're right. It wouldn't hurt to do something for me."

"You can borrow gloves, if you need them."

"Maybe." We waited at a stoplight, and I looked in the car turning onto our road. My stomach lurched at the familiarity of the man in the silver sedan—dark blond hair and a sharp jawline. It couldn't be Carter. There was no way. I lifted from my seat, craning over Dusty to get a better look as the car drove by, but that didn't make me feel any calmer. Even from the back, it had looked like my ex.

That was crazy. Carter wouldn't even take off enough time from work to take the kids to Disney World. There was no way he'd just show up here, after we were divorced, with nothing to gain. That wasn't in his nature.

"What's wrong?" Dusty asked.

For a split second, I debated telling him but thought better of it. It wouldn't do either of us any good if I mentioned Carter. Dusty and I deserved an ex-free evening. Besides, it couldn't have been him. Carter would never drive what he deemed a boring sedan, not even a rental.

"Thought I saw a ghost," I said, flashing him a smile.

When we pulled up to his farmhouse, it was definite love at first sight. A water tower was visible in the distance, but between that and Dusty's two-story farmhouse with its wrap-around porch was a barn and fields of open space. Those feelings I'd had at the Homestead during June's bridal shower came back in full force, like I could picture a happy life here. It scared and strengthened me at the same time, the idea that I could find happiness. Things could be even better here if I let them.

"Most of this isn't our land," Dusty said, like he needed to disabuse me of the idea that he was some farmer baron. "But we have an acre."

His use of the word *we* made my heart flutter, knowing he considered it his family house still. "How is your grandpa doing?"

"He's in and out," Dusty said. "Wait, don't move." He jumped down from the truck and ran around to open my door.

I tried not to love it, but I really, really did.

We walked up to the porch and he took me around it to the back. A table was set up on the deck with a view of the sunset. Lights were strung from the deck to the nearby trees, throwing soft light over us. Pink clouds snaked across the sky in puffy tufts, mixing with pale blue and looking like cotton candy. I wanted to take a mental snapshot of this scene and keep it forever.

A high-pitched buzzing sound came from the grass and Dusty looked at me. "Cicadas."

"Sounds evil."

"They look evil, for sure, but they're harmless. You'll probably get used to them."

"Wait...now I need to see one."

Dusty pointed to where a brown shell of a bug was stuck to the rail of his porch. "That's a husk. The live ones are a little better."

I shuddered. "Gross." Maybe that's what I should change

Carter's picture to. It looked like a bug straight from the devil's garden.

I expected things to be a little awkward between us as we got settled, that period where you try to find a rhythm with someone else, but everything seemed to flow easily. Dusty went inside and brought out plates of roast with carrots and potatoes, sliced bread, and salad. We dished up plates on the patio furniture and ate under the awning, watching the sunset change the sky and talking about everything from what shows we watched to our favorite things to cook.

Dusty glanced at me sideways. "Is it awful that I kind of want to stay here tonight?"

I held his gaze. "No." I wanted to stay here forever, so I understood.

My phone started ringing. I looked to make sure it wasn't Gigi. When I saw Carter's picture, I silenced it.

The moment was broken. "We should head to the school. Your cookies look great, by the way. I might have checked them out when I was setting up. How did you know football moms would pay a lot of money for jerseys and footballs?"

"I like a good theme." I shrugged. My phone started ringing again, but I clicked the button to silence it. There was no way on this green earth I would answer Carter's call while on a date. I stood up, crossing my chilly arms over my chest and moving to the railing to look out over the view. "This is incredible."

"I like it," he said easily, coming to stand at my side. Dusty hesitated before reaching over and taking my hand. I let him hold it. I wanted to stop resisting him. Blair's voice was in my head: *definitely let him kiss you.* Gigi had given her approval. My kids liked him.

What was getting in my way? Myself, obviously.

"You okay?" he asked.

"It's been a long time since I've been on a first date."

Dusty scoffed, his arms wrapping around me. His chin rested

lightly on the top of my head while we looked at the disappearing sun. "This isn't our first date, Nova. We did that ages ago. Furniture moving, lasagna, tornado night. I count all of those."

"When you say it like that, then really we're on like date four."

"Something around there."

My phone buzzed again, but I ignored it. Leaning back, I looked at Dusty. His thumb brushed along my jaw, then beneath my bottom lip, his eyes following the motion. He released a breath and swallowed hard, his Adam's apple bobbing. "I really don't want to mess this up."

"So far, so good," I told him.

A grin split his mouth into the widest smile. I couldn't help returning it. Dusty pulled me closer, wrapping his hands over my back. He pressed a feather light kiss to my temple, then another one on my cheekbone. He moved lower with each kiss, taking his time, until he reached the corner of my lips.

Dusty paused, like he was waiting for permission to continue.

I was frozen still, my body shaking with anticipation and need. I wanted him to finish, to close the distance and take away my concerns. I wanted to feel nothing but Dusty.

His lips hovered over mine. It didn't take a degree in rocket science to realize he would not be the one to close the distance. He had given that to me, a brightly wrapped gift, his awareness of my need to keep things slow between us. If I wasn't ready, he wouldn't force it.

I was ready.

"Nova," he said, after I didn't move.

My heart thrummed, my pulse beating so loudly I could hear it in my ears. Just one moment more, and I would have been brave enough.

He didn't release me. "We should be going."

"Okay." My voice was dry and scratchy—too much mouth breathing going on—and I swallowed. Disappointment cut through me. I wanted to rewind the clock and just do it. Just take the step. My skin burned where his lips had dragged a trail along the side of my face. But he was right. He needed to get to the school. "Can I use your bathroom first?"

Dusty hesitated, then smiled. "Of course."

He showed me inside while he put the food away, and I admired the interior. It was simple and outdated, but comfortable and worn, like the sofa in the living room had been there and loved for his entire life.

When I met him back in the kitchen, I looked at the empty space in front of the bay windows and blinked.

Dusty shot me a sheepish smile. "Ready?"

"Yeah." I followed him out, but my brain wouldn't make the connections that seemed to be obvious.

It wasn't until we had reached the main road that it hit me: Dusty had no kitchen table.

Because it was in my apartment.

CHAPTER THIRTY

DUSTY

HONESTLY, I hadn't thought through the fact that a date night at my house meant the possibility of being *in* my house. Of course Nova would need to use the bathroom. Of course she would notice that my table was missing. Of course she was smart enough to put those things together.

What I didn't expect was that she wouldn't say anything about it. It was worse this way. I would rather know exactly where her head was at than have to guess.

The truck was silent. My mind ran our moment on the deck in a loop. Part of me wished I'd just kissed her, but it was important to communicate I was happy to go as slowly as she needed. I wasn't going anywhere. As impatient as I felt, we really did have all the time in the world.

My hand snaked across the center console and ran down her wrist, taking her hand. Maybe I couldn't kiss her until she was ready, but I could try to hold her hand.

Nova didn't pull her fingers away. "Is this the kind of small town I've seen in all those Hallmark movies, where two people announce they're dating and the next thing you know, the mayor is congratulating them on their engagement?"

"I don't think I've seen that one," I said, shifting her hand so it fit perfectly in mine. "But I'm interested to know if this means we're dating."

Nova started to pull her hand free. She was skittish tonight. Noted.

I held fast. "Okay, no pressure. We don't have to define anything right now."

"I shouldn't have used that word. My kids—you know, I still haven't talked to them. Alice asked me the other day if you were my boyfriend."

My heart was already beating wildly, but those words sent it into overdrive. "What did you tell her?"

"No," she said. "Because you aren't. I should have asked what she thought about it then, but I didn't. Too chicken, I guess."

I was just glad she still let me hold her hand.

She plucked at her skirt with her free fingers. "Maybe we don't have to worry about it yet."

"Can people know that we came together?"

"Is 'people' Gracie Mae?" she asked.

"She's one of them."

"You know, at some point you have to tell her yourself. You call these people your friends, but can you really consider someone a close friend if you can't tell them how you truly feel?"

My pride stung, but she was right. I kept hoping someone else would step in and tell Gracie Mae to back off, that she would read the signs I was putting out to her and make the choice herself to understand I wasn't interested. But it was the coward's way.

"I wondered if I was just another Gracie Mae for a hot second," Nova said, surprising me.

"What does that even mean?"

"You know, you're a flirt. I've seen how you put your arm

around her at the diner. You can't really blame the woman for holding out hope." She looked out the window. "Part of me wondered if I was reading into your teasing the wrong way, too. But that was anxiety talking, and I saw the light."

"You aren't," I said as boldly as I could. "I'm hoping to get that mayoral endorsement soon."

Nova laughed. "Good thing this isn't a Hallmark movie or we'd have ninety minutes to fall in love."

I squeezed her fingers gently. We could take all the time she needed.

Me? I didn't need more time. I knew how I felt about her.

"Are you hoping to keep us a secret for now?" I asked, a little afraid of her answer.

Nova seemed to consider the question. Or maybe she was formulating an answer. "No. I wouldn't have agreed to go out with you if I was afraid of what people would say."

"I have to hand it to you. Most people are afraid of the gossip in this town."

She seemed to think about this. "I guess if I have nothing to hide, I don't really care what people say about me."

That was healthy. Or maybe her dissociation was the healthy part. Either way, I liked that I didn't have to hide.

The high school gymnasium was crawling with people by the time we got there. Tables were set in a U formation, holding all the auction items with clipboards for people to write down their bids. My seniors were behind the food table, helping people purchase drinks and concessions. Roy was right outside the doors setting up a photo-op with his longhorn, Steve. Bounce houses with entrance fees lined the lawn.

It was a family event, and there were many avenues to raise the money we needed to send our boys to camp.

Coach Henry stood near the risers, hands in his pockets. "Brody didn't come with you?" he asked, looking past me. "Oh, howdy, Nova."

"Hello," she said, stepping close to my side. She didn't touch me, but the energy buzzing between us was palpable. Neither of our bodies had forgotten the moment we'd shared on my back deck.

I did a sweep of the gym, but didn't see Brody. Now that I thought about it, I hadn't seen him when we were setting up, either. "Did he come earlier?"

"Not that I saw. I called his grandma an hour ago, but she didn't answer."

Uneasiness settled in my gut. Brody had been my number two guy ever since we'd caught him after he'd snuck into the high school gym. He'd worked hard for this fundraiser, and he was planning to be here.

"I'll try his phone first," I said. "If he doesn't answer, I'll try to reach Patty at Pleasant Gardens. She's there in the evenings pretty often."

"Okay." Henry frowned. "I don't have a good feeling about this."

Neither did I.

"What can I do?" Nova asked, pinching the elbow of my sleeve.

"Right now, just try to enjoy yourself. It could be nothing. I'll check in with his grandma to make sure he's okay, then we can go bid on a sunset tractor drive."

"Someone's offering that up?" she asked, tucking her chin slightly in disbelief.

Teasing Nova was a sport. She was so smart, it was hard to get her sometimes. But her ignorance in our country ways helped. "No, but I can make it happen if you're interested."

Nova laughed, the sound rich and sweet. "I'll go see what they have."

She didn't laugh often enough, in my opinion. Getting to hear that sound was like catching a glimpse of the aurora borealis. Magical. I watched her walk through the crowds of people, greeting Flora, then continuing to mosey on to the long tables. She was walking down the line, reading the placards with concentration.

She would be fine alone for five minutes while I made a phone call, but I still didn't want to leave the room, to leave her sight. I wanted to be around her always, and getting to spend time with her tonight had been a glimpse into what the future could look like, one where I wasn't alone. The sounds of kids running around or Nova baking to fill my house. Of having someone else to cook for. To smell a roast in the crock pot and know I didn't have to portion it into lunches for the entire week. To sit on the back porch watching the sunset while kids jumped on the trampoline, trying to rocket launch each other.

I yearned for it.

"Hey, man," Tucker said, walking my way and holding June's hand. "Dad's already got a line for pictures with Steve."

I clapped him on the back. Steve was always a success. "That alone will bring in enough money to send at least a few of these boys to camp."

June put her arm around Tucker's waist, pressing into his side. "Do you think you'll hit your goal?"

"It'll be tight, but it's possible. A parent donated the bounce houses without rental fees, so I hope that closes the gap." I shrugged. "We won't know until we add up all the bids. Hopefully everyone is feeling mighty generous."

"I'll bet they are," June said. "These folks love their football."

Henry's idea of having the teams wearing uniforms and working all the tables was a great idea. Get the boys in front of their eyes.

"Gracie Mae is coming," June continued. "Maybe when it's all cleaned up, we can go out—"

"I brought someone tonight."

They both blinked at me. Tucker didn't seem as surprised as

June. Time to be blunt with them. What had Nova said? If I can't tell people how I really feel, can I consider them my close friends? Well, I'd already told Tucker multiple times and he understood, but June and I still needed to cross that barrier.

Time to put the past behind us for good and allow myself to consider her a close friend again. "Gracie Mae is a wonderful person, but I don't feel that way about her. I don't know how to be more blunt than I already have been, either."

June held my gaze, standing straighter. "She's been holding onto hope that you'd change your mind, I think. I've tried not to get in the middle."

"I don't want to hurt her, but I have feelings for someone else. I don't know how else to say we'll only be friends."

June gave me a sheepish smile. "I can talk to her."

"It needs to come from me," I said.

She nodded, then tilted her head, her long, curly blonde hair trailing over her arm. She seemed hesitant, tense. We were never this strained before, back in school. "Is it Nova?" she asked.

"Yes." I found her in the crowd again, talking to Desi Partridge. "I hope tonight is the start."

"How do her kids feel about it?" Tucker asked.

"I don't know. But they're pretty rad kids, so I hope they approve." I kept looking, hoping to see Brody mixed in with some of his friends, but he wasn't here. My gaze dropped to June. "Anyway, I…uh…thought that in the spirit of honesty, I would apologize for making things difficult with us since you've gotten back. I'm super happy for you both."

Tucker beamed at me, patting me on the back. "There we are. Only took you six months."

I shoved him off playfully.

"Thanks, Dusty," June said. We shared a look, and I felt the moment peace passed between us, the tension easing. She looked behind me. "Gracie Mae's here."

It was time. "Okay. See y'all." I turned around, walking a few steps from them to meet Gracie Mae on our own.

She smiled widely at me, her blonde hair curled and makeup pristine. She was beautiful. "Hey," she said, her smile growing. "Great crowd tonight."

"You can always count on Arcadia to show up when it matters, right?" I asked. Before she could answer, I powered ahead. "Listen, I...uh...brought a date tonight."

Gracie Mae's face fell slightly before she fixed it again, a slight blip.

"I didn't want you to hear it from someone else," I continued. "But I think things are going well with Nova Walker, and... uh...I wanted you to know."

Her expression looked frozen. "Yeah, cool. She's super nice. That's really great."

I could see her fighting disappointment.

"So, uh...I hope we can stay friends, Gracie Mae. I really value your friendship."

She nodded a little too enthusiastically. "Of course, yeah. I mean, I knew...it's not like you haven't said that before. I just hoped...anyway, thanks for telling me. I do hope you guys have a good time tonight."

"Yeah, I'm sure we'll see you around."

It was palpably uncomfortable between us, but I couldn't help feeling a wash of relief that we'd been honest and talked it out bluntly. She seemed to accept it this time.

I rubbed the back of my neck, anxious because I still couldn't see Brody. "Anyway, I need to run. Gotta check in on a student."

"Okay. See you around."

I slipped outside, the late spring air pleasantly warm in the twilight. Finding Brody's number, I tried that first, but it went to voicemail. Then I called his grandma and got the same thing. The longer the phone rang in my ears, the more nervous I became. By the time I found the number for Pleasant Gardens, I was pacing.

Cindy answered the phone. I could tell by the slight rasp in her tone.

"Hello, Cindy, it's Dusty Hayes."

"Good evening, young man. I just saw your grandpa walk back to his room after dinner. Want me to put you through?"

"No, actually. I'm not calling about him. I was hoping to speak to Patty McAllister."

"Oh, honey, she isn't in tonight."

Shoot. "Did she work earlier today?"

"No, she was supposed to be here, but—well, you know how things are." Cindy lowered her voice. "I don't reckon that boy makes it easy on her to leave."

A sinking feeling filled my gut. Was Brody hurt? He lived a very independent life. "Brody's a good kid, ma'am. I have the pleasure of coaching him, and—"

"Not Brody," she said. "Good heavens. He's an angel."

Well, I wouldn't go *that* far. The kid had a mouth on him during practices.

Cindy lowered her voice further, like a good southern woman with a juicy bit of gossip was apt to do. "I'm talking about that nasty son of hers."

The hair stood up on the back of my neck. "You don't mean Brody's dad." Saints alive, I sure hope she didn't.

"Mmhmm. She won't say anything, but you know he brings trouble."

"I thought he was in jail."

"Got out last month."

Brody's bruises suddenly had a lot more clarity. I'd never understood why such a popular kid was getting in fights. And here I'd been, trying to connect with him. Just a stupid, ignorant adult trying to tell him I understood when, really, I'd *never* gone through what I suspected Brody had suffered.

I thought back to Henry finding him in the school gym, showering with a bloodied lip. If his father was responsible?

I was going to kill that man. No, because then I'd be in jail. I needed to breathe and think through this. Calling the police sometimes made these situations worse for the victims, so I needed to be sure that whatever I did got Brody's dad away for good.

It wouldn't be enough to find a place for Brody to stay, because that left Patty alone with the lowlife.

Think, Dusty.

"It's really a shame. Patty can't turn him away, but I'm not supposed to tell anyone," Cindy continued, unaware of my broiling rage. "You know he'll be in trouble if he's found within one hundred yards of that place."

My entire body stiffened. "Right," I said, pretending I knew exactly what she was talking about. "Don't want the law involved."

"Maybe that would be best. Call in that he's breaking the restraining order and they'll cart him away, won't they?"

I wanted to shout at her. Why hadn't she done so already? That was sure to put him in jail long enough to figure out a safe plan, wasn't it?

"I need to go," I told her, suddenly feeling her release of information had been more calculated than I'd given her credit for. If I took care of it, she wouldn't be breaking her friend's trust. "Thanks, Cindy. You've been very helpful."

I hung up the phone and slid it into my pocket. The event was going strong. Floodlights had come on in the football field while I'd been on the phone, lighting the grassy area swarming with kids and bounce houses. The way back into the gym was crowded, and the tables with auction items were teeming with people.

Maybe getting enough money to send everyone to camp and supply them with uniforms free of charge next year was possible. A surge of affection for this town and their love and care shot through me. Maybe I'd grown up without parents, but I hadn't grown up without love. Arcadia Creek was a community that looked out for each other, that showed up when we needed them.

I found Henry standing beside the table of refreshments chatting with a parent. When he noticed me watching him, he excused himself and came to my side. "You found him?"

"Not really. But I learned that his dad is back."

Henry swore.

"My thoughts exactly, Coach."

Henry ran a hand over his face. "We shouldn't get involved." The look on his face was saying the exact opposite.

"I also learned his dad is breaking a restraining order."

Henry swore again. "We can call that in."

"Right, but I want to make sure it's handled right. We don't want anything blowing back on Brody or Patty."

"I trust you, son. What did you have in mind?"

"This place is crawling with cops." I scanned the crowd, looking for someone I could trust. "I figured I'd start by talking to one of them."

CHAPTER THIRTY-ONE

NOVA

DESI HAD APPROACHED me while I was trying to peek at the auction slip for my cookies. Could you blame me for hoping someone would want them? I was prepared to write a fake name and bid ten bucks myself if it meant they didn't sit on the table all night, unwanted. Instead, I saw Dusty had started the bidding at $100, and the rascal had already been outbid. He must have done it while setting up. These people really had come in clutch to support the team. We all knew that was why the bids were so high, and it warmed my heart.

I scanned the crowd, half-listening while Desi talked about the latest drama with the elementary school's spring carnival. I couldn't see Dusty anymore. He had been talking to Tucker and June a minute ago, but he must have excused himself to make that phone call.

"What do you think?" Desi asked.

Shoot. What had she been talking about? The carnival, right? Gosh, I hope she wasn't asking me to join the committee. "Sorry, I was distracted."

Desi looked like she could see right through me. "A girl's

night. We could throw on an old romcom or go to Beeler for dinner."

Oh. She wanted to friend-date me. The part of me that desired friends of my own wanted to eagerly leap at this opportunity. She embodied the police family I'd left behind in New York, which was obviously a draw. To say nothing about how well Kendall and Alice got along. But it was important to be honest with her. I'd meant what I said to Dusty earlier. If we were going to become friends, I had to tell her how I felt.

"I'll never date Chad," I said, holding her gaze.

Desi looked thrown off, her brows drawing together. She shifted, the motion making her perfectly highlighted blonde hair sway like a shampoo commercial. "That's okay."

"Kendall told me and Alice what you said, that Chad could become my husband and we could all be friends." I put my hand up to stave off her explanations. "I'm not mad, and I totally get it. It's so convenient having couple friends when you get along with both people. But he's just not…" How did I finish that sentence honestly? A good person? Not a good idea. "I'm not interested in him. I don't want to lead you on if that's your end game here."

Desi took my arm and pulled me away from the tables until we were alone near the wall. "I don't blame you. He can be kind of a tool. Please don't let my stupid daydreaming come between us. I'm sorry I said anything around Kendall. I know how kids can talk."

She was so honest and forthright I found myself believing her. Desi had accepted me from the minute we'd met and, despite my disparaging the PTA, she still invited me to her house and offered me friendship. My walls had been up, but had hers? I began to wonder if I'd projected my assumptions onto Desi this entire time. She wasn't Trish. Being well dressed in Arcadia Creek did not make her into all the frustrating moms I'd left behind in New York, either.

"I'd love to do a girls night sometime," I told her, and I meant it.

Desi's face lit up.

"Maybe you can come over one night after all our kids are in bed," I said. It meant I needed to buy a TV if we were going to be watching romcoms, but the kids were tired of watching movies on my laptop anyway. It was worth dipping into savings or trying to sell some cookies.

"That would be great. I'll look at Travis's schedule and text you later to nail down a day."

"Okay." I tried to sound like it wasn't a big deal, but inside, I was glowing. Warmth blossomed in my chest and made me giddy. Coming here hadn't just meant pulling my kids away from everything they'd known; it had meant tearing myself away from the places and communities I'd spent my entire life in. Maybe I hadn't grow up in Manhattan, but I'd built a community there the last ten years. I missed my neighbors and friends. My family home in Brooklyn was only on the other side of the water, which meant I had seen my parents and brother often.

It was nice pulling Blair up on FaceTime every few days and letting the kids chat with their cousins, but that wasn't the same as dropping by their apartment or meeting at the park. We missed them, and it had left a hole in my heart. This invitation seemed to shove Play-doh in that hole, filling it a little with the female companionship I hadn't realized I'd been missing.

Between Desi and Kendall, Pete, Gigi, and now Dusty, and all the people they were introducing me to, I was building a new community here. It wasn't my old familiar group, but it was worn and comfortable still, like my blue couch from the yard sale—comfy and loved and ready to bring me in.

"I talked to Ashley about throwing an end-of-the-season party together for the football team and the cheerleaders," Desi said. "Maybe we can invite her and make this a party planning meeting."

Bonus. Two friends. "We should do that. Ben and Alice would both love it."

"Hey," a warm voice said behind me. Dusty slid an arm around my waist and smiled at Desi. That sense of community and home grew warm and fuzzy, the pressure of his arm anchoring me to Texas. "I need to talk to your husband. Is he around?"

It took a moment to realize he was addressing Desi.

"He took Kendall to the bounce houses," she said, looking as curious as I felt. Her eyes dipped to his arm around my waist and her eyebrows seemed to say she knew exactly why I wasn't interested in Chad.

But my cozy feeling evaporated. Dusty had come here looking for Travis. Seeking out a police officer right after trying to locate one of his students didn't seem like a good sign. I tried to look up and read Dusty's expression, but it was guarded. I could sense strain in the feathered lines around his eyes.

"Come on. Let's go try to find him," Desi said, sensing he needed Travis *now*.

"Is everything okay?" I asked.

"No, but I'm hoping it will be." He looked like he wanted to say more. We wove through the crowds together and funneled outside. The football field was still crawling with people. Desi called Travis's phone, but it still took a while to find him. Once we did, Dusty offered his hand. "How's it going, man?"

Travis shook it. His red hair looked vibrant under the floodlights. "Good."

They seemed a little stiff.

Desi noticed the same thing. She raised her sleek blonde eyebrows. "You in trouble, Dusty?"

"No, not me." He scrubbed a hand over his face and glanced

around, satisfied we were far enough away from other people to talk freely. "One of my boys. I think he's getting knocked around at home."

Travis's face darkened, his mouth tightening. "Do you have proof?"

"Besides bruises? I don't know. I want to know what my options are, mostly. The dad just got out of jail."

"Does the kid live with his mom? The parents divorced?"

"Mom's long gone. Kid lives with the grandma. They put a restraining order on the dad a few years ago. Is that enough to take him in?"

Travis folded his arms over his chest, planting his feet. "It is, if they renewed it. When was it filed?"

Dusty's face fell. "No idea."

"Who's the kid?"

There was only a slight hesitation before Dusty said, "Brody McAllister."

Travis nodded. "They renewed. The dad's out of jail, then? I know Patty was in the courthouse late last year making sure it was still valid."

So she was worried she would need the restraining order, then. That made my stomach sick. I wanted to find that boy, pull him into my arms, and give him the longest hug. "What can we do?" I asked.

Dusty looked sharply at me. "You aren't going near them. The man is violent."

I didn't want to jump into an altercation, but I wasn't going to sit back and do nothing.

"Can you come with me now?" Dusty asked Travis. "If we take him by surprise, you can catch him breaking the restraining order."

"I'd better call Hank. We need someone on duty. But yeah, I'll come." He looked at his wife. "You okay if I take off, babe?"

"Of course," Desi said without hesitation.

Dusty looked at me with the same question.

"I'll stay in the truck," I promised. "But let me come." I cared about Brody too, and I couldn't just sit here and wait.

He hesitated. "Okay. Let's go."

We went straight for Dusty's big black truck, but Travis took a detour and met us there. I climbed in the back seat, and the men took the front, discussing their options. Travis made a phone call and spoke to someone about the situation for a minute. Dusty watched me in the rearview mirror, his eyebrows pulling together.

"We can't go in guns blazing," Travis said, putting his phone away. "The guy just got out, so he won't go back in easily."

I was guessing he meant jail.

"How long can you put him away for this time?" Dusty asked.

"If we can prove abuse, this just became a felony," Travis said. He let out a breath. "Not my favorite part of the job."

"Can Brody stay with his grandma?" I asked.

"That shouldn't be a problem. No one's saying she's endangering him."

She hadn't called the police about her son staying at their house, but I wouldn't mention that right now. The woman was probably scared.

Dusty pulled along a dark road of houses separated by chain link fences. They were similar to most of the houses I'd seen closer to the heart of town, but looked more neglected—overgrown grass and weeds, discarded rusty cars. "It's the blue one," he said, pointing ahead. The lights were on and an older Toyota sedan sat in the driveway. He parked and shut off the engine.

"Let's wait for backup. We can knock first and offer to take Brody to the event so we have a reasonable excuse to be there. Hopefully Patty will answer the door and provide permission to enter. It shouldn't be too hard after that. Our priority is getting both of them out of the house first."

"Got it," Dusty said. "Just tell me what to do."

I looked between the men in the front seat, then at the house, and closed my eyes. There was no way this would go as easily as that. Anxiety roiled in my gut, and the pleas I'd silently repeated the whole way here felt useless against real violence. I pulled out my phone and texted my mom. At least it was late enough here that they were probably having breakfast by now in the Philippines.

> NOVA
>
> If you're praying this morning, will you add my friends to your list? I'm watching a domestic situation unfold that is unsafe, and these guys could use all the help they can get

> MOM
>
> Can I call?

> NOVA
>
> Not right now. I'm safe, don't worry. The kids are with Gigi

> MOM
>
> Okay. We're on it. Be safe and call me later, please.

> NOVA
>
> Of course. Love you both

> MOM
>
> We love you too.

Travis put his phone away. "Hank is pulling up now. He's going to park down the road and turn his lights off. If we can get Brody and Patty into the truck, then I want you to come with them."

"I'm trained—"

"You aren't a police officer. We each have our parts to play."

"Okay. True."

I had the sense Dusty was just grateful Travis wasn't making him wait in the truck, too. I could sense it was important to him this was done right.

"Ready?" Travis asked.

Dusty reached back and squeezed my knee. "Yep."

CHAPTER THIRTY-TWO

DUSTY

WHEN I first started getting to know Nova and fantasized about taking her on a date, breaking up a scary domestic situation in the middle of it wasn't on my radar. Knowing she was waiting safely back in the truck made it possible for me to mount the cement steps to Brody's front door with less anxiety, though.

Travis knocked on the screen a few times.

Minutes went by while we heard movement on the other side of the door. We exchanged a glance before I reached over him and knocked a second time.

The door swung open. Patty stood there in her maroon scrubs, her white, shoulder length hair tucked behind her ears. "Dusty," she said loudly. "What can I do for you?"

I noticed she didn't greet Travis.

"We've got the silent auction going on at the school tonight, ma'am, and we're missing Brody. Any chance he's home?"

She hesitated.

I didn't want to say the wrong thing and alert the dad that we were here with backup, so I hoped she could read the expression in my eyes and trust me. "I'll have him home at a decent time."

"Yes, of course," she said in a rush. "We've had a bit of a day around here, but he was planning on being there. I'm sorry he's late."

"It's not a problem."

"Brody," she called, not moving from the front door. "Coach Hayes is here to take you to the fundraiser."

We waited in silence for another minute, the three of us holding our breath. When Brody stepped from the hallway, he had a hoodie pulled low over his face. "I don't want to go."

Patty stiffened. "You'll do as you're told."

"But—"

"Brody," she snapped.

He made a frustrated sound. "Yes, ma'am," he muttered, but it was easy to see that he didn't want to step past his grandma.

What could I say to put him at ease? The kid didn't need to come to the fundraiser, not really, but he needed to be out of this house so we could remove the real threat. "You need to assist this evening if you want to be allotted your portion of the proceeds, same as everyone else." Even as the words left my mouth, they felt hollow. Brody had put more work into the event than anyone else on the team, and we both knew that.

He glanced up in surprise, and I got a good look at the fresh bruise spreading down his cheekbone.

I saw red.

Travis put a hand on my forearm, sensing my need to charge into the house and lay a fist on that good-for-nothing waste of space parading as a parent. But more violence was never the answer to violence. Never.

"Why don't you walk Brody to the truck so I can speak to Mrs. McAllister?" Travis asked.

"Sure." I flicked my head toward the sidewalk. "Come on."

"Don't dawdle," Travis whispered. "Flash your brights when he's safe."

I didn't need clarification to know he wanted me to signal

Hank. Travis hadn't worn a walkie-talkie. Brody's slow steps were almost painful. By the time we reached my truck, I was ready to throw the kid over my shoulder and bolt. He didn't know it, but he wasn't stepping foot back in that house until it was safe to do so. I didn't care if he and his grandma had to move in with me. If I could help it, his dad would never lay a hand on him again.

"Get in the back," I said quietly, leaning through the door to flash my lights.

Brody looked at me with confusion, then did as he was told.

"Hey, Brody," Nova said from the back row. "You want a fruit snack?"

I couldn't help the smallest of smiles as I climbed into the driver's seat and watched the house. Or the way my smile grew when I heard the crinkling of the wrapper as Brody took it and popped a few in his mouth.

"Why aren't we leaving?" he asked.

"Is your dad in there, Brody?"

He went quiet.

"You aren't in trouble, but I need to know."

"Yeah," he said.

"Then he's breaking an active restraining order right now and Officer Partridge has the authority to take him away." I glanced at Brody through the rearview mirror and my heart tore in half when I clocked the expression of hope flashing across his face. "But your grandma needs to give them some information first. There's a proper way to do these things, so we're going to wait here until the police have done their jobs, then we're going to get you something to eat."

"I had dinner," he muttered.

"So you aren't hungry?"

He didn't refute that. The kid could always eat.

A shout and a thud came from the house, making everyone in the truck go still. Hank ran into the house with someone behind him. We waited with various degrees of breathing difficulties—Brody nearly hyperventilating in the backseat.

"Stay here," Nova said calmly. I didn't turn around, but I figured Brody wanted to run back in after his grandma and she had stopped him.

Minutes passed that felt eternal before the door opened again, pouring yellow light over the porch and along the walkway. Hank was leading a barefoot man in pajamas and handcuffs from the house. He didn't look our way, and we all stayed very quiet until Hank had pushed him into the back seat of the cop car.

Brody let out a long breath. "How long will he be away this time?"

"Officer Partridge mentioned that if we can prove assault, this will be a felony. He'll have questions for you, son," I said, surprising myself. I sounded like Coach Henry. "It won't be easy, but it's best if you're honest. You and your grandma won't get in trouble."

"Okay."

His voice was so small. I could see Nova was moving through the same emotions I was. Pain, heartache, the desire to take away this kid's troubles and give him a safe life.

"Are you willing to go in and talk to them now?" I asked.

"Sure."

"I'll run and get you some food if you're hungry. Has your grandma eaten?" Nova asked while we all got out of the truck.

"No," Brody said. "She hasn't."

"Okay. I'll be back in a minute." Nova looked at me. "Can I take your truck?"

"Definitely." Tenderness swelled within me, and it took a lot of restraint to keep from pulling her in for a kiss right there. The easy way she handled everything. How unflinching she was. The willingness to jump into action in a way she knew how to help. Those were all testaments to her character.

Nova walked around the truck and met me at the front. "I'll call ahead at Gigi's. Dal can whip something up for us real quick."

"Thanks." I squeezed her hand. "Sorry our date took a detour."

"This isn't something you need to apologize for." Nova fisted my shirt and pulled me down, then laid a kiss on my cheek. "I'll be back soon."

She left me standing there, stunned for a hot second.

"Come on, Coach," Brody said, a hint of amusement in his tone. His hood was down and his posture already more relaxed. If only I'd thought to question him more a month ago—but I couldn't think like that. We were here now, and he wouldn't have to deal with his dad anymore after tonight. "Stop drooling. My grandma is waiting."

I shot him a sheepish smile. "You didn't see that."

"See what? That was nothing."

Oh, how very, *very* wrong he was.

I threw my arm around his shoulder and messed up his hair. "You'll understand when you're older."

NOVA

MY PHONE HAD BEEN RINGING nonstop, but I hadn't been notified since I'd put my phone on *do not disturb*. Missed calls from Mom, Blair, and Carter filled my screen. It had been days since I'd talked to Carter, and he clearly didn't like being put on the back burner, but he would have to wait. My mom needed to be informed no one was in great danger anymore. I probably shouldn't have texted her for help because she was apt to worry, but she was religious and I'd been scared.

I clicked her name and put the phone on speaker while I maneuvered through the dark streets toward the diner.

"We're coming home," Mom said firmly the moment she answered the phone. "I've already started talking to the pastor here, and he can arrange—"

"Mom, listen."

"It's not a trial, honey. Your dad and I have considered it more than once in the last few months. We'll rent a place big enough for all of us until the lease is up for the renters in my house, then we can move home."

A spark of hope flared within me before dying swiftly under a bucket of cold water. "Listen, I'm safe. The kids are fine. We were just..." How did I explain this? Why did I ever send that stupid text? I pulled in front of Gigi's Diner and put the truck in park, letting out a breath. "I've been kind of seeing this guy."

"I know," Mom said. "Gigi does talk to me, honey."

"Right." What had my aunt said? It's not gossip when it's family. I should've known she'd report on me to my parents. "Well, he's a high school football coach, and one of the kids on his team had a terrible situation at home." I filled her in on Brody's last few months, culminating tonight.

"It was smart to get the law involved," Dad said, cutting into the conversation. "You did the right thing."

"Maybe, but it was scary for a minute there. I'm relieved it's over."

They were quiet for a minute. "Nova, listen. I don't want you to decide right now. I take it you care a lot for this man, and after everything that happened with Carter, you deserve someone who puts you first. But Dad and I are serious about coming home. It looks like Dad will need hip surgery soon, and it would be better for us to cut our time here short and take care of it in the States. Take some time to think about it, okay? I'd love to have you three come stay with us. You know it won't be a burden."

I did know that. My mother adored my kids, and we could manage to share a place for a while. But it meant leaving Arcadia Creek, which left a bitter taste in my mouth. "I don't know—"

"Think about it," Mom repeated. "Call me later. I don't want you making decisions while you're fresh out of this situation. You need time to let your emotions settle again."

"Okay," I agreed. "I'll think about it."

Mom promised to fill Blair in for me, since she'd gone so far as to call my sister-in-law and ask if she knew what was going on, and we hung up the phone. I sat in the truck, immersed in silence. Dal would need a few more minutes to get the food bagged up anyway, and my parents had given me a lot to think about. My gut reaction was to brush them off because the thought of moving again so soon made me feel hives threatening to break out.

But we *could* move home, live with family. Even if I chose a school in Brooklyn, the kids would be close enough to see their old friends, and we would be near their cousins again. It wasn't an option without merit.

I didn't necessarily want to live that close to Carter, but the kids would be able to see more of him. They could maintain a relationship with their dad.

I shook my head and jumped out of the truck. Mom was right. It wasn't smart to make life decisions while I was riding the wave of adrenaline and coming down from high emotions. Sleep would level me out, and I would talk to my kids, and then I would know what the right thing was for us.

CHAPTER THIRTY-THREE

DUSTY

WE STAYED at the house for another twenty minutes before Brody and Patty got in their car and went to meet Hank at the station to file an official report. The way they carried themselves as they walked to the old Toyota revealed how much relief they felt to have Brody's dad in custody. Some people weren't meant to be in their children's lives, and this guy was one of them. I'd never considered my own situation like that before, but maybe it was similar. Maybe if my parents had stayed, our situation would have only escalated.

My grandpa was a level-headed guy who was very happy spending most of his time alone. If he'd thought he was the better choice for raising me, then my parents had to have been a terrible option. I actively avoided thinking about them, but after almost fifteen years of no contact, sometimes I couldn't help but wonder where they were. I was only human.

I was waiting on the sidewalk with Travis when Nova pulled up in my black truck, and my heart flipped over at the sight. She looked good behind that wheel.

"Where'd they go?" she asked, hopping out and carrying two

brown paper sacks. Her skirt swayed with each step, and she tucked her hair behind her ear.

"Police station," Travis said. "We can put the food inside and lock the door on our way out. Patty left us her spare key."

"Okay." Nova smiled at him. "I think it should reheat well. Dal put together more food than they could eat in one night anyway."

I wondered how much she'd told him about the situation. Honestly, she only had to say that someone needed food and he'd fill bags, no questions asked. People in this town looked after one another, as evidenced by how things went down tonight. My faith in Arcadia Creek was rewarded, and my gratitude that Nova got to experience it made me glow.

Nova carried the bags into the house. We put them in the fridge and met Travis at the truck. "Can you drop me off at home?" he asked. "Desi had to get Kendall to bed, so they left the fundraiser."

"For sure." I glanced at the time, surprised to see how late it was. By the time we'd taken Travis home, the auction was definitely over. We sat in my truck while I sent Henry a text to update him on the situation.

DUSTY

> Brody is good now. His dad was taken back to jail. I'll give you the full update when I see you

COACH GABLE

> Don't worry about coming back. We have enough boys here. Clean up will go fast.

DUSTY

> Did we make enough?

He didn't text back, so I put my phone in the cupholder and pulled onto the road. "The fundraiser is over."

"Okay."

"Should we...do you want to..." How could we continue spending time together without me making it sound unwholesome? It was so important to me that Nova understood I was willing and happy to take things slowly...which was absolutely cramping my game.

"I don't have a TV or I'd invite you to come back and watch a movie," she said.

"I'd ask you to go for a moonlit walk with me, but I'm beat. I think my adrenaline has been on high for the last two hours. Now I'm coming down and I'm feeling it."

Nova looked at me until the stop light turned green. "I have dessert at my apartment and a laptop. We could throw on a miniature movie and eat apple pie."

"You've been holding out on me," I said, eyeing her. "Apple pie?"

"Caramel apple pie, actually."

"Marry me already."

She went silent.

"Bad joke," I muttered.

"No, it's good to know what you value. Caramel apples rank high on that list."

"Incorrect," I said, pulling the truck behind the diner and parking in front of her apartment building. "Caramel apple *pie* does."

"Noted," she said lightly, then cleared her throat. "My mom called."

I shut off the ignition, looking at her. Nova's tone had changed, and I felt the weight of an impending revelation. After the emotional stress of the evening, it put me on high alert. "Is everything okay?"

"My dad needs hip surgery, I guess, so they're coming home early and renting a place until their house is vacant again."

"I bet your brother will be glad to have them back," I said, hoping that was the end of the conversation. The thought of her and the kids leaving sent a rush of fear through me.

"Yeah." She chewed on her bottom lip and looked through the window, staring at something in the distance. "She invited us to come live with them."

The truck was deadly silent. I could hear both of us breathing. I hadn't even kissed this woman yet, but I knew she needed to be in my life. The idea of her going back to New York felt like a swift slice through the gut, opening an old wound and laying it bare.

People left. It was what they did. My parents had done it more than once. I'd always wondered if maybe I hadn't given them enough of a reason to stay, and I would not make that same mistake with Nova.

With her, I would fight.

"I want you to stay."

She looked at me sharply.

"Yeah, I said it. Maybe I should be more stoic, but it's the truth. I don't want you or Ben or Alice to leave. I want all of you to stay."

Nova closed her eyes. When she looked at me again, she seemed tired. "I'm not making any decisions tonight."

Well, that was a good sign.

When she opened her eyes, she looked at me. "Should we go have some pie and pretend I never told you that?"

"Yes to the pie," I said, "but I don't want to pretend anything. I'm glad you could trust me."

Nova's smile was the little shot of adrenaline I needed. We seemed, with mutual understanding, to decide to table the conversation for now, which gave me hope. I had time to convince her to stay.

She hopped out of the truck. My phone buzzed, so I picked it up and read the text while I got out and closed my door behind me.

> **COACH GABLE**
> More than enough. These boys are going to camp.

"We did it," I said, putting my phone in my pocket. "We made enough to cover summer camp."

"Yes!" Nova jumped in the air, then flung her arms around my neck, giving me a good squeeze. "You did it, Dusty."

Words failed me.

My brain stopped computing anything outside of this woman in my arms. I closed my hands over her back, our lungs expanding in sync. The embrace shifted, Nova melting against me while my arms wrapped around her, pulling her closer. I inhaled slowly, my eyes fluttering closed, and breathed in the sweet scent of her shampoo.

I wanted to take her with me to my warm house where we could sit on the porch and look at the stars with hot cups of tea. I wanted her to be there when I got home from my shifts in the morning so we could make breakfast together and get the kids off to school. I wanted to shop for Christmas ornaments and plan a Thanksgiving menu with her. I wanted to walk the aisles of Walmart slowly while the kids chose their lunch boxes at the end of the summer. I wanted an extremely domestic life, and I wanted it with her.

I was already planning our happily ever after. Because, despite how slowly I was willing to take things, I could see a future with Nova, Ben, and Alice. It seemed like it would be rich and full of goodness.

Her hands smoothed up my shoulder blades, and I leaned away to cup the back of her neck, looking her in the eye. "I'm so impressed with the way you handled things tonight."

"I did nothing," she argued, her eyebrows rising in surprise. "Well, I gave Brody a snack, but it would have been better if I'd had protein and not sugar on hand."

"You were a calming presence for us."

Her arms tightened around my waist as she tipped her chin up to look me in the eyes. Nova's height meant I wouldn't have to bend too much to kiss her. She was perfect.

"I will go at whatever pace you need to go, but just know I'm a patient man. I'll wait as long as it takes for you to be comfortable with me."

Nova stiffened. "I have to think about the kids."

"Exactly. If you don't want to tell them we're dating, I'll respect that."

"We're dating now?" she asked, her voice oddly void of emotion. I couldn't tell what she was thinking.

"I hope so. But if you need a few more first dates, that can be arranged."

Her quiet chuckle made some of my nerves melt away.

"Just stay here with me," I said. "Don't go. I have a recipe for happily ever after. Want to hear it?"

"Yes," she whispered, burying her head against my chest.

"Me, you, Alice, and Ben."

"What about Leia?"

"I'm not finished. You have to mix the first four ingredients together, stick them in a house full of furniture, toss in a blue couch, some homemade cookies, and sprinkle a cat on top."

"How about then you have to top it with a cat? It sounds less gruesome."

"Top it with an orange striped cat and enjoy for…hmmmm… maybe forever?"

She grinned up at me. "That's a long time to be stuck with that same blue couch."

My heart soared simply because she didn't run away after I painted a picture of us being happy together. This was a step in the right direction.

"True. And the view from my back deck could get boring after a while."

"No, it won't."

"Yeah, it definitely won't." I brushed loose hair away from her forehead, looking into her eyes. "I really want to kiss you."

Nova didn't rush to respond. She blinked, looking at me, her brown eyes searching mine as if she could look through them and read my entire history. She drew in a shuddering breath. "Okay. Then do it."

My lips broke into a wide grin. I brushed my thumb along her bottom lip, smooth and velvety. I was pretty sure it was the most beautiful thing in the world, and I didn't think I was biased about that.

Sliding my hand along her jaw, I leaned forward, our lips just a breath apart.

"Nova," a man said sharply, making us flinch and knock our foreheads together.

We turned in unison, though I didn't release her. A man stood at the base of her apartment steps, shadowed and dark. He looked put together, his dark blond hair brushed to the side, his suit spotless, but his expression was pure rage.

"Carter?" she asked, peering closer like she couldn't tell if he was real or a terrible hallucination. "What are you doing here?"

He slid one hand into his pocket, his eyes running over her and avoiding me. "I'm here for my kids."

CHAPTER THIRTY-FOUR

NOVA

HELLO, worst nightmare.

No, scratch that. My worst nightmare was anything happening to my children. Having Carter show up in a fit of pique because Ben wasn't worshiping him was a close second, though. There was *no* legal way he could do anything to change where Ben and Alice lived. He'd already signed the form saying they could move to Texas with me, so he had no trump cards here.

At least I didn't think he could. The night was balmy and comfortable, but a chill swept over me when I stepped out of Dusty's arms, and he let me go.

"I think you need to explain yourself," I finally said, when Carter had nothing to add.

His gaze flicked to Dusty before settling back on me with an accusatory glare. His blue eyes were sharp, assessing. "Can we go inside? Alone."

Dusty's hand found mine, his fingers brushing along my palm. It was subtle, but I read the message. He was here. There was no reason he couldn't stay.

On the flip side of the coin, Carter was my children's dad, and I would be dealing with him on some level for the rest of their lives. Better to keep things as neutral as possible.

"It's late, Carter," I said. "Why don't we meet up in the morning? I'll bring the kids, and you can spend the day with them."

He took a step forward, orange light washing over his face from the house's porch lights across the street. "I'm not here for a visit, Noves. I'm here to take them back home."

My stomach split, forming a chasm that threatened to take all my equilibrium away. He couldn't just show up and change the settlement, could he? My teeth hurt from clenching them together while I thought through the situation. Of course, he could have written some clause into the agreement that would give him power I knew nothing about, but my lawyer had combed over it. He would have spotted a loophole.

No, this was classic Carter. He had to be bluffing. If not, then I was about to break the law, because *no one* would take my kids from me.

"I'm not staying," he said, as if I hadn't heard him the first time.

My body went cold. At least he didn't know where Gigi lived. In fact… "How did you get my address?"

"I had to send Alice's birth certificate, remember?"

Then he really couldn't know where Gigi lived. I was afraid I'd left it on a piece of mail somewhere and he'd brought it with him. "It's late. We'll meet you in the morning."

Anger slashed over Carter's face, and he took another step forward. Dusty did the same, coming to stand at my side. I hadn't ever expected to be in this situation, so I hadn't thought about how it would feel. I tended to be so independent that I wouldn't want anyone stepping in to help me fight my battles. It was nice having Dusty's support, knowing he was going to let me manage this on my own. But something about the way he had taken one small step to stand beside me infused me with confidence and security. He was still allowing me to handle it on my own, but now he wasn't just reminding me he was here if I needed him—he was reminding Carter, too.

"Seriously?" Carter asked, glancing from Dusty to me. His frustration was mounting, and I'd been married to him long enough to know how this was going to go. He didn't like not being the hero. He despised having to give even a quarter. This was not going to de-escalate easily. He was never violent, but he could become pretty angry.

"Okay, let's compromise," I said. "We can talk now, but you still won't see the kids until tomorrow, after you've had time to cool off."

"I don't like this, Noves," he said, ignoring Dusty again. There was a shift in his posture, his tone. His voice lowered in that conciliatory way he had, using it the same way he would before to charm me out of my point of view and edge me toward his. He'd done it so much during our marriage, but I had never really seen it for what it was before: manipulation, not true compromise. "You travel across the country, bring my kids to this backwater armpit town, and now they're not speaking to me."

Did he need to be reminded he'd left first? Besides, Alice had never stopped talking to him. He was lumping the kids together, only seeing the negative and magnifying it in his mind.

"The way I see it," he continued, "there are two options. You come home and bring the kids with you, or they come home with me and you can stay here. I'll put them back in school, cover the whole tuition. We can split custody down the middle. It'll be like they never left."

Except they did leave. Our marriage *did* dissolve and fracture and split beyond repair. Carter was asking for parts of his old life back, but he didn't want his old life, not really. He still didn't want me. The lack of control had caught up to him, and he saw us moving on with our lives and being okay, and it threatened his sense of self-worth. I could see it so clearly now, how everything revolved around him.

It was why he was here, late on a Saturday night, in a dramatic move to regain control after I'd stopped answering his calls for the last two days. He must have been out of his mind with frustration.

Standing there and being handed the option to return to my old life—sans husband—made me realize with startling clarity how much I didn't want that. It wasn't even that I didn't want to step backward. I just wanted to stay here.

"No one is leaving Texas," I said coolly. I didn't miss the sharp intake of hope from Dusty. "But you're welcome to come visit the kids tomorrow. They would love to see you."

Carter narrowed his eyes. "You wouldn't prefer to keep them here. I know you. You miss the city and your friends and your family."

That was true.

"Don't tell me you haven't talked to Blair every day, wishing you were close enough to go to her place for lunch," he pressed.

Not *every* day. But, yeah, he was right about that, too.

Carter seemed to sense this, because he kept going. "They have nothing here. No Target, no Met museum, no Carmines or Barney Greengrass."

Yes, I missed those things. Yes, I talked to Blair most days, and when my parents returned home, my homesickness would probably mount in a cataclysmic wave. But Carter was so wrong on a more important fundamental level. Arcadia Creek didn't have *nothing*. It had the same sense of community I'd grown up with on our Brooklyn block. It had stability and consistency and traditions. It had friendship and diner regulars and Gigi and that bone-deep feeling of home when I was standing on a back porch looking at a sunset.

It had Dusty.

I cleared my throat, searching for the patience to remain calm and not shout all of that back at him. "There's a cute inn just down the street. It's right up a little hill, and they might have a vacancy. If you want to stay there, we can meet up in the morning—" I stopped myself before inviting him over for breakfast. He didn't need to step foot in my new home. It was safe and mine, and I didn't want him tainting that. "We can grab coffee—"

"Where are my kids?"

"With Gigi," I said bluntly. "They're having a sleepover, and we aren't going to ruin it."

His jaw ticked. "I deserve—"

"No," I said firmly. "We will not talk about what *we* deserve, or I will start talking about how much more child support I deserve." I hadn't known how he had done it, but he must have hidden funds somewhere in order to get my payments so low, and it wasn't until I'd come out of the post-divorce fog that I realized it. I knew Carter's income. I'd been so stupid before now.

"You wouldn't," he said quietly.

I turned, pointing up at my apartment. "We're good here. The kids have a great room, and we're warm and well fed. You haven't ruined anyone's life. But your kids deserve a lot more than you've given them. Alice should be able to do gymnastics and Ben should be able to join a flag football team without me needing to dip into my savings. If you want to storm in making demands, then I will counter them."

Carter's chest rose and fell rapidly, his anger manifesting in the clenching of his jaw and heavy breathing. "I don't like this."

He wouldn't though, would he? It wasn't going the way he'd

planned. I wanted to ask about Kristen, to find out if she was home waiting for him, if she knew where he was right now. But his life had moved on, and until it became relevant for me to know—like my kids going to visit him in the summer—then I wouldn't ask. Our lives were separate, and it hit me like a wave of relief that he could move on and so could I.

Feeling Dusty's presence beside me, I realized I already had.

It was time to delete that screenshot I'd taken of their moving day. Later, when I was alone. "I'll call you in the morning and we can walk over to Gigi's together."

Carter's gaze flicked to Dusty before falling back on me again. "You've changed."

I disagreed. He was just seeing me differently now that I wasn't diminishing my thoughts and shaping myself to fit him better. "Good night, Carter."

He shook his head softly before walking down the road and climbing into a silver sedan.

"Do you want me to call Jack and see if he has vacancies?" Dusty asked softly, once Carter had closed his door.

"No." I drew in a shaky breath and let it out. "I have a feeling he won't be staying tonight."

Dusty turned to face me sharply. "You think he'd leave? He hasn't even seen the kids yet."

"He didn't really come for them," I said. "I mean, that's what he said, but it was just a stupid power move. He wanted me to agree to move the kids back to New York, but for what? So he could have us under his nose. I hope I'm wrong, but until we know for sure, it would be best if no one knows he was here."

"So it doesn't get back to Ben and Alice," he said. "I get it."

"They're so little. They won't understand."

"Disinterested parents are hard to deal with, no matter what age you are," Dusty said quietly, his eyes raking over my face with concern and breaking my heart for the pain he'd gone through as a kid. "For what it's worth, I think you're making the right call."

"In refusing to take him to them tonight?"

"That, yeah, but also in staying. That's what you meant when you said no one was leaving Texas, right?"

"Yes," I whispered.

He took my hand, his fingers holding mine in a loose grip, and tugged me away from the sidewalk and down to the end of his truck. He put down the tailgate and lifted his eyebrows. "You look like you need to sit down."

"My adrenaline rush is fading."

He put his hands on my waist and guided me up to sit on the edge of his truck bed, the cool metal seeping immediately through my skirt. The truck dipped when he lifted himself to sit beside me. "Should we go ask Mr. Roberts to turn off his insanely bright porch light so we can see more stars?"

I stared at him. "Do you know *everyone* in town?"

He gave me a sheepish smile. "Most people, yeah. I've spent my entire life here. Well, almost all of it."

"It looks good on you."

"The town?" he asked, his brow bent in confusion.

"The small-town Texas thing. The Arcadia Creek community. The Wranglers."

Dusty's face brightened in a grin. "You like my jeans."

"Everyone likes your jeans," I shot back. He couldn't be entirely blind to how women looked at him.

"I only care if you do."

"Well, I do. They're very nice."

Dusty laughed, the sound breaking through the cool night and my residual restlessness. It was like a comfort blanket, or a hug from Peaches after a long day.

"You didn't meet my grandpa at the Battle of the Badges," he said carefully, meeting my gaze, "and I assumed it was a message."

"It was." I slid my hands under my thighs to warm them. "I was nervous. It felt like a big step, but I know that was mostly in my head. I'd just—Alice had asked if you were my boyfriend, remember? It made me think we needed to keep our distance until we knew where we stood and how my kids felt about it."

"Where do we stand now?"

"Honestly, I don't know." Inhaling fresh air, I let it out in a rush. "I like you."

"I like you, too."

"I wouldn't say no to another date."

"Me either," he agreed.

"But I have to ask Ben and Alice what they think."

"I'm a patient man."

"You'd have to be. You're a Longhorns fan."

"What?" Dusty asked, his grin crinkling the lines next to his eyes. "What kind of burn was that?"

"I don't know." I grinned back. "I know nothing about the team except that Gigi hates them."

"Apparently. This town is divided, but facts don't lie, and our win-loss percentage—"

"I don't really care about football right now."

He seemed to sense the shift in my mood. "Me either."

We looked at each other, listening to the distant buzz of cicadas in the otherwise quiet town. So much had happened tonight, but the one constant in all of it was Dusty and his purity. He was a good man. He slid down from the tailgate and faced me in a fluid motion, stopping my legs from swinging by standing in front of them. "In fact," he said, cupping my face with both hands, "I don't think I've ever cared about football less."

Clutching his shirt, I tugged him closer until he was flush with the tailgate, my legs wrapping around his waist. "Yeah? Well, I can one-up you. I've never cared about football at all."

He cringed. "Oh, straight to the heart."

"But I'm growing to appreciate flag football. My kid's coach is kind of hot."

He leaned so close, his breath tickled my skin while he talked. "Do I need to fight Jake now?"

"Assistant coach, then? What are you?"

"Something like that." His hand slid to my waist, pulling me closer, while his lips brushed the edge of my jaw. "But, again, I don't care about sports right now."

"You care about me," I said quietly, the words heavy. He grew still. "I noticed your missing kitchen table."

Dusty straightened. He didn't remove his hands, but his face leveled me with a look so full of longing it struck me. "I care about you a lot, Nova. Probably more than I have a right to, honestly. You, Ben, and Alice are important. I'm sure it's been obvious for a while now, but I've been drawn to you since the moment I saw you in the ice cream aisle. What really clinched it for me was watching you with your kids and the Hot Wheels mess. You are incredible. Ben and Alice are incredible. I'm a lucky man since you're even willing to give me a shot."

My eyes grew misty, my chest warm and fuzzy. Everything disappeared around us except for me and this man. "You're not real."

"I can show you exactly how real I am." Dusty didn't hesitate. He pulled me close, his lips crashing over mine with a wave of heat that could melt Alaska. Time stopped, the world ringing in silence. I felt nothing but his hands roaming my back and my waist, his heart thundering under my palm, the warm, rough skin of his neck as I slid a hand up his jaw.

Dusty's kiss brought a rush of butterflies swarming through my body, giving me a deep need to be closer to him.

Maybe I didn't know what the future had in store for me, but I did know with a sudden clarity that it would be in Arcadia Creek, and it would probably be with this man.

His hands cupped my cheeks, his lips layering tender kisses on mine that made my breath catch.

"We don't have to define anything yet," he said breathlessly, "but you know you're probably going to marry me someday, right?"

My lips curved into a smile I felt him mirror. I didn't bother answering with words. I just showed him exactly how in sync we were.

CHAPTER THIRTY-FIVE

NOVA

LIKE I'D PREDICTED, when I called Carter the next morning to plan a time to meet up, he was already back in New York. The self-centered coward had driven straight back to Dallas and taken the first flight home. He didn't get what he'd come for, and I thought I'd probably frightened him away by letting on that I suspected he'd swindled me in the divorce settlement.

It was bittersweet, but I didn't need his money to give my kids a satisfying life. We still didn't have a TV, and we were doing just fine.

The reality that he prioritized himself over his children still hit me like a slap in the face. It wasn't new information, but the fresh reminder stung. It also made it easy for me to delete the screenshot of his Instagram story and remove the photo from his contact information. I didn't replace it with something nasty like cicadas or a devil emoji, despite how badly I wanted to. My kids would be answering his calls and seeing that photo, and I wanted to remain neutral when it came to their relationship with him. If things went well with Dusty, they'd be forging healthy father-figure relationships anyway.

Hopefully, someday, Carter would learn to step up for their sakes and not his own selfish gain.

I shoved my hands into the pockets of my sherpa pullover as I walked to Gigi's house to pick up my kids. The slight chill in the air would burn off the second the sun reached a prime spot, and I was coming to like springtime in Texas. It wasn't nearly as cold as we were used to.

My phone rang, and my heart gave a leap when I saw Dusty's name cross the screen. "Hello?"

"Hey, there," he said easily. "Just checking in."

His voice flowed through me like a shot of caffeine and lavender, invigorating and soothing at the same time. I filled him in on Carter's disappearing act and received his curse-laced agitation in return. "Yeah, but the kids won't ever know."

"True," he said. "Protect them at all costs."

My stomach tightened with butterflies. We talked until I reached the house. "I need to go inside and get them, but thanks for calling."

"Of course. Talk to you later, Nova."

I could hear Gigi and the kids singing the days of the week song to the tune of *The Addams Family* theme song when I reached the porch. I paused with my fist poised above the door to knock and soaked in the happy sounds of my babies, wholly unaware that their father had been across the street last night and had chosen not to remain for twelve hours in order to see them. Anger pooled hot in my belly. It was better if they didn't know.

Pasting a smile on, I knocked twice and opened the door to let myself in. "Good morning!" I called.

"Mom!"

"Mommy!"

The kids ran out of the kitchen and barreled into me like I'd left them for a year and not one night. Their little arms went around my legs and my waist, squeezing. My eyes misted against my better judgment. I looked at the ceiling, willing the emotion to return to wherever it came from. Honestly, how could anyone *not* want these precious babies in their life?

Carter was an idiot.

"Okay," Gigi said, clapping her hands together. "We have French toast and bacon waiting on those plates. Get to the table, buckaroos."

"Yes, ma'am!" Ben said, then ran to the dining room.

Alice somersaulted her way behind him. So, that was still a thing.

Gigi leaned against the wall, fiddling with a dishtowel in her hands and watching me. "Do you want to talk about it?"

So much had happened, I didn't even know what she was referring to. I took a step back and sank onto the arm of the upholstered chair. "Carter showed up last night," I whispered so the kids wouldn't hear me. They were arguing over syrup, so I figured I was safe.

Gigi froze. "Is he coming over?"

"No, he left." I shook my head, laughing incredulously. "He *actually* left. It was late and I didn't want to bother the kids until this morning, but really it was a power play that backfired on him. He's back in New York now. His plane landed like a half-hour ago."

Her face hardened. "Self-serving—"

"Yeah," I agreed, before she started swearing and the kids heard. Somehow, they could ignore everything until one wretched curse word slipped through. They tuned in every time, no matter how far away they were. "I don't know how to protect my babies, Gigi. Legally, I have to abide by our settlement, but he doesn't prioritize them. I never want them to feel anything but wholly loved."

She crossed the room and sat on the edge of her coffee table so she faced me. Her mouth was pinched into a line, her white hair styled in the perfect Q-tip she always wore. Not a hair out of place. "They are wholly loved. You can't control anyone else's actions, and you certainly can't protect them from pain. The only thing you can do is be a safe place. You can love them with all your heart so they never have to question their worth. No matter what life throws at them at any age, they will know they are loved because of you. The rest is out of your hands."

Tears streamed down my face in earnest now. I dashed them away, but I knew she was right. "Part of me wishes he was out of the picture entirely, but the other part recognizes that having him in their lives is healthier."

"You handle it well, Nova. You can only be the liaison between him and the kids."

"Even then, his calling is sporadic. Ben won't even get on the phone now, which is what sparked Carter's trip to Texas in the first place."

"Set boundaries. You have to be the liaison, but you don't have to live by his schedule. You have the kids, you set the boundaries. If he calls outside of the times you provide, then you don't have to answer the phone. That's healthy."

It sounded amazing. "I can do boundaries."

"You should probably talk to Ben, too. He's been angry, I think."

"Did he speak to you about it?"

"He might have mentioned that his dad was going to have a new family and didn't need him anymore."

My stomach went cold. "Why would he say that?"

"I didn't push it," she said, squeezing my knee. "You could."

"Yeah." I closed my eyes and let out a breath.

"He also mentioned he heard you telling someone on the phone that you don't love cooking at the diner."

My eyes shot open, heat rising in my cheeks. "Everyone complains about their job."

"Maybe," Gigi said, watching me.

"It isn't the diner I don't love. It's that baking is where my heart is, not cooking. They're different, you know?"

"I do know. I also heard your parents might be coming home early."

We stared at one another, all the unspoken things floating between us. Possibilities of the kids and me moving back to the city, leaving Texas. "I'm really happy with our arrangement here, Gigi."

"I'm glad, sugar. I just want you to know I don't intend on holding you to anything. If you want to go back to New York when your parents move home, I won't hold it against you. If you choose to stay here and find a different job, that's okay, too."

"I've decided to stay."

Her white eyebrows shot up. "Did you tell your parents that?"

"Yes, but they want me to think about it a little longer, so I'll tell them again in a few days. We miss home a lot, but Arcadia Creek has become a new home for us in the last few months. I'm ready to settle here."

"Have you considered starting your cookie company again?"

"My quaint cookies?" I joked, seeing Carter's judgmental sneer edge into my memory. I immediately banished it, free and clear of his opinion. It was nice and calming to know his opinion didn't matter anymore. I cleared my mind, bringing my attention back to the matter at hand. "It wasn't ever a real business. It wouldn't pay the rent."

"Maybe not, but alimony should. You could stay part time at the diner to keep our arrangement while you build it up. Test it out and see." She narrowed her eyes. "Do you prefer waitressing?"

"I like interacting with the customers," I told her honestly. It was part of the reason Arcadia had come to feel like a community so quickly.

"Well, Dal and Bonnie aren't going away anytime soon. We'll move you to the waitressing rotation part time while you figure out what you want to do. I can get a list of farmers' markets together if you want to look into booth rentals."

"Okay," I said, warming to the idea, but simultaneously stressing about the finances of it. I did have some of Carter's settlement tucked away in the bank for startup costs, but it was a little hard to believe I could sustain a living on cookies. I would need to think on this. "I'll look into it. If you're sure? I don't want to leave the cooks hanging."

She chewed on her lip, debating something. "Want the truth?"

"I won't like it, will I?"

"It's not charity," she said in defense. "But I didn't need a cook. I just wanted you to feel like you were earning your keep. I assumed you'd prefer to stay in the back and not be on display for the entire town, so I had Dal make room for you in the kitchen during the daytime shifts."

"That was thoughtful, Gigi." I stood, pulling her in for a hug and trying to suppress the shame of accepting charity. She had done what she'd done out of love. "I don't know how I would have gotten through any of this without you."

Gigi blew a little raspberry. "You're equipped to heal on your own. I just gave you a place to do it."

I squeezed her again before letting go. "Right. Well. Did I hear you made French toast? Because I could steal a slice."

She grinned. "Right this way."

GIGI'S OFFER TO help me focus on my baking lit a fire under my determination, and I spent the next few days working the numbers and figuring out how many cookies I'd need to sell in order to turn a profit. It seemed next to impossible to turn this into a full career, but I was going to give it a chance.

I'd also begun running in the mornings after dropping the kids off at school. It was harder to get back into than I'd remembered, but the fresh air and personal time were doing wonders for my mental health, and I was only three days in.

On Wednesday night, I was getting ready to have Desi and Ashley over to plan the end of season joint football/cheerleader party. I'd made fresh strawberry sauce to put over ice cream and had gotten the kids out of the bath and into their pajamas with twenty minutes to spare.

"Do we *have* to go to sleep?" Alice asked, hugging Peaches to her side. "I want ice cream too."

"You can have some after school tomorrow. It's too late for sugar now, or you'll never go to sleep."

"Unfair," Ben said from where he scowled on the top bunk.

"Totally fair. You aren't an adult yet, so I get to make your eating decisions."

His scowl deepened. "Dad would let us have ice cream."

Dad also wouldn't have to deal with the repercussions of that choice, I thought. I was pretty sure Ben was remembering a different, less health-conscious version of his father. "Well, you're stuck with me."

"Forever," Ben muttered.

Alice went quiet, looking up at her brother.

"Hop in bed," I said to her, then climbed up on the bottom rung of the ladder to be eye-level with Ben. "What's wrong?"

"Nothing." He rolled over to face the wall.

My stomach clenched. "Is this about why you don't want to talk to your dad on the phone?"

"Maybe."

I clutched the edge of the bed rail, then inhaled. "Ben, what happened?"

He was silent. I waited until he was ready to talk, because I knew the power of silence. Finally, after so long I'd convinced myself he wasn't going to tell me, he sighed. "Dad's new baby is going to be a boy, and he won't need me anymore."

My entire body went cold. "What new baby?"

"Kristen's baby."

Oh. My. Gosh. I tried to keep calm, to pretend this wasn't filling me with all sorts of weird feelings. The blasé way he'd said Kristen's name, like he expected me to know who she was, belied a level of intimacy between Carter's new girlfriend and my kids that I didn't like. "When did you learn about this?"

Stupid question. Probably weeks ago when he'd stopped talking to his dad. Everything was clicking into place. Why she'd moved in with him so quickly. Why Carter had been so cagey lately. Why he would have been able to take them back to New York if I chose to stay here, because now he had built-in babysitting. Suddenly, the possibility that he could have dragged them away that night hit me with a fresh wave of terror. If he was starting a new family and wanted these two to be part of it, how could I stop him?

With a veiled threat of legal action and my knowledge that he made way more money than he was somehow able to report. That had been what saved us.

But right now, my little boy needed reassurance. I swallowed my anger and brushed his messy blond hair from his face. "Love doesn't divide, Ben. It grows. Someday, I hope to get married again, and when we welcome another little baby to this family, do you think it will mean I have to give all of my love to him or her?"

He sat up, his little brow furrowed, blond hair messy. "No, but you and Dad are different."

Of course we were, and because children are little emotional geniuses, he could sense that even if he couldn't understand it. "He shows it in different ways, but he doesn't love you any less.

A new baby won't change how he feels about you, okay?" At least that much was true. Carter wasn't a very attentive dad, but he wasn't a monster. He would probably always have this level of disconnect, new baby or not.

"Who are you going to marry, Mommy?" Alice asked, making me flinch.

I leaned down to see her lying in bed, Peaches under the covers beside her. "I don't know yet."

"But it won't be Chad," Alice said with conviction.

"No, it won't be Chad." I fought a smile. "I think I might like to try dating Dusty, though, if you both think that's okay."

"Yes!" Alice squealed. "Then we'll have a kitty."

Priorities.

I nodded and turned my attention back to Ben. "What do you think?"

"It would be okay with me," Ben said, peering at me through narrowed eyes. "But if you have any more babies, do I have to share a room with them, too?"

"Babies always sleep with the parents in the beginning," I told him. "Then I'll probably have to put him or her in bed with you. We don't have any other space. You could share your blankets, though, right?"

Ben gave me a wry smile. "You can't trick me, Mom. Dusty would build the baby its own bed."

His quiet confidence smashed into me, stealing my breath. How easily he *knew* how Dusty would handle that dilemma made my heart soar to the moon and back. The difference between the men, and the difference in Ben's perception of them, boiled down to their actions—what they'd proven to us time and again. Carter couldn't be relied on; Dusty could.

"Get to sleep now, you hooligans. I have a meeting out there soon to plan a party." I leaned over and squeezed Ben, kissing him all over his face against his squeals, then repeated the process with Alice. "Love you both."

Their echoing chorus of good nights went on for quite a while, but I left them and closed the door, leaning against it for a moment in quiet gratitude—thankful I felt settled, that the future had a plan, that my kids would be okay, that good people loved me.

I pulled out my phone and texted Dusty.

NOVA

The kids approve

DUSTY

Yeehaw!

I had to smile at him knowing exactly what I meant.

NOVA

Oh, no. I think they just rescinded their approval. Shoot.

DUSTY

Well, like you once told me, it's been a good run

NOVA

Nice to know you, of course

DUSTY

Good luck with your future endeavors

NOVA

Can I see you tomorrow?

DUSTY

Not unless you need me to put out a fire. Which I really hope you don't

I'll plan something for this weekend if you're interested

NOVA

I'm interested

Kids or no kids?

DUSTY
Kids. Always kids.

My heart melted into a puddle and pooled near my feet. It was a wonder I could walk to the door when the party planners arrived.

Finally—happiness.

CHAPTER THIRTY-SIX

DUSTY

FRIDAY DAWNED NICE AND SUNNY. I got off shift early that morning and went home to shower. Thanks to a pretty boring night at the station, I felt nice and rested, too. I had the entire day to plan a date worthy of Nova, Ben, and Alice. I was trying to get three people to fall in love with me, which changed the stakes, but I thought I'd probably made good inroads already. Or Leia had.

Toweling off my hair, I tapped my phone to read the text waiting for me.

TUCKER
What do you know about Costa Rica?

DUSTY
Literally nothing. Is that where June wants to go on your honeymoon?

TUCKER
No, but she's stressed and planning our trip is something I can take off her plate. She said she doesn't care where we go as long as there's a beach

> **DUSTY**
> What did Jack say? Didn't he and Lauren go to the Bahamas on a cruise? They might have a good recommendation

> **TUCKER**
> Good point. Lauren would know where we should go. Lauren knows everything

> **DUSTY**
> I'd take her word, for sure

> How are the other plans coming along? You haven't asked me to a meeting all week

> **TUCKER**
> June is doing those with my mom and Gracie Mae now. I'm so glad you said something to her at the fundraiser so she would stop making us attend. June feels bad she made everything drag out as long as it did

> **DUSTY**
> It's not her fault. I should have said something sooner

I did, in my defense, but I hadn't been clear enough.

> **TUCKER**
> You want to come over for dinner later? Invite Nova and her kids? We could throw burgers on the grill

That sounded like a great way to spend Friday evening. Nova and June got along, too. And I knew the kids would love Sadie, Tucker's dog.

> **DUSTY**
> Probably. I'll talk to her and let you know

Tucker thumbs-upped my text. I finished getting dressed and sat on the edge of my bed to pull my socks on. Leia jumped onto my lap, getting in the way, her tail curling under my jaw in a desperate cry for attention. I stroked her soft back. "I know, I know. I miss you when I'm at work, too. Just think, Leia. If Nova and the kids move in, you'll *never* be alone again."

She turned her little orange head to look at me, blinking as though to say, *don't go too far, Dad.*

"Okay, fine. We'll take this one step at a time. But get used to the idea. You're going to have siblings soon."

She meowed, then jumped to the floor and walked away. The girl was a tease, but she'd loved all the attention Ben and Alice had given her when they met. I wasn't too worried.

Grandpa and I had finished the United States puzzle Wednesday, so I'd ordered a new one online that night, and it had arrived while I was at work yesterday. I went downstairs to snap a picture of the New York skyline with a thousand little orange-lit windows and various shades of blue and black shadows, then sent it to Nova.

DUSTY

> Puzzle level 100. This might be worse than the ocean around America

NOVA

> Nothing is worse than the ocean. We deserved to have a pattern, at least

DUSTY

> Agreed

She didn't text me again, so I hopped in my truck to head to Pleasant Gardens. The late spring air was warm and fresh through my open window. We'd had a few rain showers over the week that had given the countryside a dewy freshness. Trees were green and the grassy fields didn't seem too far behind. Bluebonnets lined the sides of the roads in rich blue pops of color. It was well into Texas spring, and I was here for it.

A woman jogging on the side of the road moved over further

as I approached, her brown ponytail swinging with each step. I knew that ponytail. I slowed my truck until I was crawling just behind her and rolled my window down. She glanced over her shoulder and my face broke out in a grin.

Nova.

She slowed.

"Don't stop," I said. "I don't want to mess with your times."

"My times…are…crap," she said between breaths. "How was this…so much…easier…in high school?"

"You probably hadn't taken a ten-year hiatus."

She shot me a wry look, then moved to a walk.

I had to stop the truck entirely and wait for her to catch up. "Want a ride back into town?"

Nova reached my passenger window and stopped, her chest heaving, hands on her hips. "And be all smelly in your truck? No."

I rolled my eyes, shaking my head. "It doesn't bother me. We can leave the windows down, though, if that makes you feel better."

She looked from me to the road again. We really weren't that far from Main Street. "Okay, thanks." She climbed in, buckled her seatbelt, and shot me a tired smile.

"Did Gigi give you the morning off?" I asked.

"She gave me the day, actually. You know Ashley Hart, Jake's wife?"

"Yes." I'd known her since high school.

"Did you know she sells sourdough bread?"

"Yeah, it's really good." I drove slowly, but we'd made it to town. I pulled up in front of her apartment and parked the truck, then leaned back and looked at her.

"She came to my house Wednesday night to plan our end of season party, and we got talking about my potential cookie business plans. She was really on board. She has a booth at a spring market in Beeler tomorrow, and she offered to share the space with me since her other partner bailed. If it works out, we might be able to do it all summer." She shook her head. "I'm not going to get ahead of myself. I just hope to break even tomorrow."

"Nova, that's amazing."

Her smile widened. "I'm kind of excited. I baked nonstop yesterday, and I have a lot to do today to finish up."

"I won't keep you then."

She leaned her head back on the headrest. "I don't mind if you keep me for a bit. You heading to Beeler now?"

"Yeah. Do you want to come?"

She chewed on her bottom lip. "Are you going to see your grandpa?"

"He's dying to meet you."

Nova's phone started ringing, and she looked down. "Shoot. It's Carter. I kind of need to talk to him."

"Go ahead."

She gave me a grateful smile and, to my surprise, answered it right there. "Hey, thanks for calling me back."

The phone was so loud I could hear Carter talking. I tried not to listen, but he made it hard not to. "We need to go over a few things."

"Agreed," Nova said. "Like Kristen. Ben has been worried your new baby will replace him, and I need to know it won't."

Woah. New baby?

"That's ridiculous," Carter said, but even then, the man wasn't an idiot. Surely he could see why his kid was concerned.

"If you proceed with a wedding, I need to be consulted before you tell the kids."

"You'll do the same for me?" he asked.

She hesitated. "They live with me, Carter. They'll know if I'm getting married, and I would obviously plan a wedding around their schedule. You can't really pretend it's the same thing."

He sighed. "What else?"

"We'll do calls on Sundays. Standing appointment. We need structure and order if this is going to work long term"

"Fine."

She exhaled silently, like a weight had been lifted from her chest. I reached across the console and took her hand. "That's it."

"Okay." He cleared his throat. "I've given it some thought, and I will…uh…raise your child support payments by five hundred a month, okay? I think we've always been good at negotiating terms and coming to an understanding. We don't need to get the law involved."

She looked out the window, eyes hard, and clutched my hand. "That makes me think it should probably be much higher."

"You live in Texas, Noves. You can't really expect to need the same amount of money you'd need here."

"We can revisit this later—"

"Fine. Eight hundred."

She smiled. "Okay. Eight hundred."

"And you won't go to the cops."

"No, I won't."

Did he not know her? She wouldn't drag him through the mud for the sake of her children alone. Carter never knew what he'd had.

"I need to go," she said. "We can nail down a time for Sunday calls later."

"Okay. Bye, Nova."

"Bye." She hung up and released a breath. "I didn't expect that."

"The money?"

"I'm pretty sure he hid a lot of his money offshore somewhere during our settlement. I don't know. It was all a blur." She looked at me. "But he used the same excuse then. *We're good at compromise, so we should just handle it on our own.*"

"Should you take it to the police?"

"Maybe? But now we'll have what we need. I can pay some rent to Gigi and Alice can join gymnastics. He can afford it."

Did Nova realize how strong she was? I tugged on her hand until she was leaning over the console.

"Eww," she said, pulling away. "I'm so gross right now."

"You're never gross." I leaned in, kissing her until her tense posture slipped away and she relaxed against me. Her lips were salty and her hands warm.

"I need to shower."

"I'll wait."

She eyed me. "Okay. Might as well come up. I'll be quick."

I followed her. "Take your time."

PLEASANT GARDENS WAS BUSTLING with activity when we arrived, thanks to the Friday Jeopardy game they had going. We found Grandpa at our puzzle table, waiting patiently. He rose when we approached, his eyes running over Nova. "This is your special lady?" he asked, eyebrows up. "How'd you convince her to go for a Hayes man? Think I have a shot?"

"Oh, so this is where he gets the charm," Nova said, leaning in to kiss Grandpa's cheek. "It's so lovely to meet you."

"Kissing on the first date," Grandpa said with a wink. "I'm already winning."

"Settle down." I plopped the puzzle on the table. "You won't like her as much when she schools you at the puzzle edges."

"I welcome the challenge," he said, his eyes glinting.

The following hour passed in a similar way, with Grandpa and Nova bantering back and forth. Turned out he'd been to New York City before I was born, and they had a few things to talk about.

"I like this one," Grandpa said when we stood to walk him to his room. He was tired and wanted to nap before lunch.

"Me, too," I told him.

We reached the door, and Nova gave him a hug.

"I'll see you tomorrow, son," Grandpa said, opening the door to his room. "Oh, have you gotten a call back from Dave yet? I left him all those messages."

My body went rigid. Why had he been trying to call my dad? No, better question: how did he know how to contact him? "No, not yet. Did he, uh, say what he'd be calling about?"

"I called him," Grandpa repeated. "He should have called by now. Your graduation is next week."

My graduation. "Which school is it at again?"

Grandpa laughed, shaking his head to Nova like, *can you believe this guy?* "Arcadia High. You're really on one today, aren't you?"

He went into his room, but my heart was hammering hard. This weird time-warp had something to do with my dad and my high school graduation, but I couldn't push him or he would get confused.

Nova seemed to sense something was going on, because she backed off and waited against the wall.

I followed Grandpa into his room. "Dave left me a message," I said. "But it didn't make much sense."

"It never does," Grandpa said. "Probably high as a kite. That's why I told him to stay away. It's not good for you to have them around, not when you're doing so well."

My chest thudded like a hammer to an anvil. "Right. So he wanted to come to my graduation and you told him not to?"

"He'd just lost his wife, son. You can't expect him to show up in a good state. I don't want your big day to be ruined."

Lost his wife. My breath stopped completely. "How did she die? His wife." *My mother.* But I needed to use his language so I could keep getting information.

"Overdose. Can't tell the boy, though. Really don't want to ruin his big day. He's worked so hard for it."

He's worked so hard. Who did Grandpa think he was talking to now? It hardly mattered. I nodded, reeling. "Okay, well, have a good nap."

He lowered himself onto his bed and pointed at me. "I like that one. Always choose a woman who can best you at games. You've got a smart one, here."

A smile bent my lips. "I do."

When I got back to the hallway, Nova was watching me with concern. Smart one, indeed. I'd left the door open, and she must have understood enough of the madness that had transpired in there to know it was a big deal. "How are you?" she asked, like she would burn the place down if I needed her to.

"Confused. If he had a way to contact them, why didn't..." That question answered itself. He had been faced with the same dilemma Nova had: subject the kids to a crappy parent or protect them from the pain of repeated rejection? In this case, my grandpa had chosen to protect me in the way he thought was best. I didn't have to agree with his choice to appreciate that he'd made it out of love for me.

Then again, Carter wasn't a deadbeat drug addict, so it wasn't entirely the same. But it was enough.

She crossed the hallway and pulled me in for a hug. "I'm sorry."

"I've always pictured them living in a tent in North Carolina, but I've also wondered if they were dead. Fifteen years is a long time to go with no contact. Is my dad alone out there somewhere?"

"Give it time and question him again. You can have the answers you need if you want them."

I nodded, pulling her closer. "I'm pretty sure I love you."

"You should. I'm very smart."

I chuckled, taking her hand and pulling her away. "Let's go home. I want to watch you decorate cookies."

"Okay, weirdo. But you aren't eating any."

"Not even one?"

"You can have the rejects."

I pulled her to my side and kissed the top of her head. "How about we take the rejects to dinner at Tucker's tonight? He and June invited us."

She smiled at me. "Sounds good. But first, if you're coming over, I need your help with something."

"Anything."

"We ran out of jam this morning when I was making the kids' lunches. I've got another jar in the fridge—"

I flexed for her, making her laugh. "Say no more."

CHAPTER THIRTY-SEVEN

NOVA

NINE MONTHS LATER

HOW DID I get roped into making cookies for another elementary school science fair? Trish hadn't talked to me since the last time she'd tried to weasel information about my divorce, yet here I was, willingly offering cookies to a school event. Though since the PTA president came over almost weekly now to watch *The Bachelor* and taste whatever new thing I'd baked, it wasn't a surprise I'd get roped into this.

It was February now and frigid outside. My breath clouded before me as I carried my rockets, planets, and astronauts into the school, passing a police officer on his way out.

"Thanks, Chad," I said, offering him a smile as he held the door.

He gave me a nod and continued on. I didn't know if he felt like I was another thing he'd lost against Dusty, but ever since the Battle of the Badges last year, he hadn't been as friendly.

His loss.

"Good afternoon, Ms. Walker," Ms. Corbin said from the front desk, her hair not shifting even the slightest as she moved.

"I'm here to help set up for the fair."

"Go right in," she said. "I won't make you dig out your license with those trays in your arms."

"Thank you, Ms. Corbin."

She held the door for me and I walked down the hallway, the smell of glue and rubber filling my nose. The door to the gym was propped open, and my heart leapt when I noticed Dusty standing off to the side, looking at his phone.

I put the tray of cookies on a table and went to him, my feet slowing when I noticed the despair on his face. It had taken a series of conversations with his grandpa, some more lucid than others, to piece together the story of his parents. They had made contact a few times, but since they'd usually only wanted money, Dusty's grandpa had cut them off. When they'd stolen the Darth Vader bank, that had been the final straw. He'd forbidden them from contacting again.

It hadn't stopped them entirely, but Dusty's grandpa did his best to protect him. Both of his parents had died within a few years of each other, before Dusty finished college. His grandpa kept the secret because he didn't want anything to derail Dusty. Now that he knew, though, he'd been free of that nagging curiosity, wondering if they were out there somewhere.

Given the expression on his face, I was worried something had happened with his grandpa, leaving him entirely without blood relatives.

"What happened?" I asked.

He looked up sharply, noticing me for the first time. "It's Brody."

I clutched his arm. "He's hurt?"

Dusty's brows drew together. "What? No. He's fine. Well,

he's *mostly* fine. You know how he got into both UT Austin and Texas A&M?"

My concern immediately vanished. "Let me guess—he chose A&M?"

Dusty's face was a picture of sorrow. "*Yes*."

I started walking away. Tables needed to be set up and we had planets to hang from the ceiling.

"You don't understand," he complained. "I don't know how to support A&M."

"But you know how to support Brody," I shot back.

"Yeah." He closed his eyes and breathed. "This will be hard for me."

I rolled my eyes. "I thought someone *died*."

He looked wounded. "My pride has, a little."

I picked up the paper planets Desi had ordered and crossed the gym to slap them against his chest. "Go ahead and assemble these. They'll take your mind off it."

He closed his hand over mine and tugged, leaning in. "You haven't kissed me yet."

"After that whole display?"

"I need it more now. You know how hard this is for me."

It was true. This man and his football. I leaned against him, squishing the paper planets between us, and kissed him. "Hello."

"Hello," he repeated against my lips.

"Keep it rated G, please," Desi said, coming into the gym with her arms full of decorations. She was laughing, though, so I kissed him once more.

"You'll survive, I think," I said, taking one planet back to start assembling it.

"Maybe," Dusty said noncommittally. "Brody is meeting us at Gigi's for a celebration dinner tonight. Can you make it?"

"After the science fair? Yes."

"Perfect."

He'd be fine. I knew it, and he knew it. And he proved it that night when he showed up at Gigi's Diner wearing a Texas A&M shirt he'd pilfered from Tucker's closet, then proudly hugged Brody.

My man was the best.

EPILOGUE
NOVA

ONE YEAR LATER

THE LINE TO ride Star Wars: Rise of the Resistance at Hollywood Studios was over an hour long, but that didn't stop Ben or Dusty from wanting to ride it again as soon as we stepped off. Don't get me wrong, the ride was fun, but these two were a different level of nerd. I kind of loved that about them, though. Now that we were married and Dusty joined all our family movie nights, I was outvoted more frequently. We'd watched all nine *Star Wars* movies just to prep for this family vacation.

Clearly, I loved my husband.

I drew the line at the offshoot cartoons. He and Ben could have their own movie nights for those.

"What if you two get in line, and I take Alice on something else?" I offered.

"I want to stay with Dusty," she said. Peaches was fastened around her neck, its legs around her back so it would hold on tight. She'd insisted on bringing it to Disney World, and I said she only could if it stayed velcroed to her. I didn't want to face the trauma of it falling off and being lost forever.

"I thought you wanted to find Leia a costume," Dusty asked.

Alice's face lit up. "Yes!"

Dusty raised his eyebrows. "You can always join us in line again later."

"Okay, maybe." I gave him a noncommittal smile that made him laugh. "I'll call you once we're finished cat-costume shopping."

He leaned over and kissed me. "You know where to find us."

I took Alice's hand and watched the boys jog back toward the ride's entrance, my heart in my throat. Marrying Dusty had been the easiest decision I'd ever made. Waiting long enough so the kids had eased into it had been the hard part. But, like I'd expected, they were thrilled when we told them we were getting married.

They were resilient little sprites. Our wedding was small but full of love. My parents came out to stay for a month during the summer, spending time with us and getting to know Dusty—whom they heartily approved of—and helping plan the wedding. Everyone had traveled to Arcadia Creek in the fall for the wedding, and by the end of the trip even Blair could understand why I'd want to stay in Texas. She helped me move my things over to Dusty's house and fell in love with the view from the back porch, too.

Life wasn't without its challenges, but together, Dusty and I had weathered all the storms—both literally and figuratively.

The first shop we stepped in was *Star Wars* themed—thanks to the proximity to the ride—but we couldn't find cat costumes. I asked an attendant and she told me which shop to check out to find one, but it wasn't in this park. I followed Alice as she looked through the Mandalorian helmets and lightsabers, when her gaze landed on a Chewbacca figurine.

"Mom," she said, reaching for it.

I helped her pull it from the shelf. "It looks like Ben's old one."

She nodded, staring at it.

"He has Dusty's old toy now, remember?"

"Yeah." She still held it, looking at the figurine. "Can I get this for Ben?"

One could never have too many Chewie toys, I supposed. The boys would believe that, at least. "Are you sure?"

"It's my fault his died," she said quietly, looking up at me. Her round blue eyes were sorrowful, and it occurred to me this was just as much to heal her as it was to replace what Ben had lost.

"Okay, we can get it for him."

Her little shoulders relaxed. Then she spotted the baby onesies with Grogu on them, and I steered her toward the register before she tried to buy something for everyone we knew. Things between the kids and Carter had been better recently. We had taken a family trip out to New York after Kristen had the baby so the kids could meet him, which was good for Ben. He liked being a big brother again. Hopefully Dusty and I would give them another little one soon.

"Should we go find the Toy Story rides?" I asked, putting the bagged toy into my backpack once we got outside.

"I want to ride the *Star Wars* one again," she said.

"The drop didn't scare you?"

Alice vehemently shook her head, even though I'd felt the squeeze of her hand and heard her scream during the ride. "Please?"

"Okay." It took a minute to locate Dusty and Ben and reach them in the line. When I saw them, my heart did a little leap.

"Any luck?" Dusty murmured, taking my hand and pulling me to his side.

My arms went lightly around his waist. "No cat costumes,

but I found out where we can look later. Alice got something else, instead."

"I want to do it!" Alice said, bouncing on her toes.

I stepped back, sliding my backpack around and opening the zipper. I pulled out the bagged toy and gave it to her, which she promptly stuck behind her back. The bag showed easily, but Ben was too distracted by the animatronic BB-8 up on the platform to notice.

"Ben," she said. "Ben!"

He turned. "What?"

"I got something for you." She bounced on her toes.

Dusty took the backpack from my hands and slung it over his shoulder, then his arm went around my waist.

"What?" Ben asked again.

Alice took the bag from behind her back and thrust it at him. He took it, pulling the Chewbacca figurine out and gasping. His eyes went straight to me. "It's just like my old one!"

"What do you say?" I prompted him.

"Thanks, Alice," he said, but he was already trying to get it from the packaging.

She beamed.

"That was sweet," Dusty said.

"It was all her idea."

"Now I have *two*!" Ben shouted.

We nudged him to keep walking, since the line had started to move again. At least Alice knew better than to somersault here.

Dusty helped Ben get all the packaging off the toy and put it in the backpack to throw away later. Ben and Alice found a way to entertain themselves with Peaches and Chewie, so I leaned my head against Dusty's shoulder and watched.

"I just thought up a new recipe," I said.

"Oh, yeah? What's that?"

"Happiness: take one family, tie them together with love and vows, and send them on a trip to geek out to science fiction and princesses."

Dusty pressed a kiss to my forehead. "You forgot Peaches. She's utterly essential."

"Oh right. Don't forget to mix in a little stuffed monkey, a plastic Chewbacca, a cat, a half-brother and, someday soon, another little baby."

He grinned. "Very soon, I hope."

"We can only hope," I agreed.

"Alice needs someone to teach all those new gymnastics moves to," Dusty said. "I tried to do the back walkover with her last week and thought I was going to put my back out."

"Better leave those to the seven-year-olds." I leaned up and kissed him, but I knew my words would go in one ear and out the other. Dusty would do anything for Alice. She had well and truly taken his heart. He was a prime example of what I'd tried to explain to Ben all those months ago—love doesn't divide, it grows.

Our little family was proof of that.

"Love you," I whispered, moving ahead with him in the line again.

We stopped with the crowd.

"Love you too," he said, pressing a sweet kiss to my lips, which was promptly interrupted by Ben and Alice bickering over who got to stand in the front for our family.

Like all things, it had a way of working itself out.

And, because I love my husband, after a break to check out the *Toy Story* rides, we got in line for Rise of the Resistance a third time that day.

WHAT TO READ NEXT

Beachy Keen

He has it all, except the one thing money can't buy: her heart.

ACKNOWLEDGMENTS

I think, for me, Nova will always rank among the top most relatable heroines I've written because she's a mom, which is also a large part of my identity. So Nova and me? We get each other. She faced trials I haven't faced, but kids will somersault their way to dinner no matter what, and a lot of her putting her babies first is relatable to moms everywhere. Dusty and Nova's journey to love means a lot to me, and writing the process of them finding a person who treats them well was rewarding and satisfying.

And it wouldn't be a proper thank you without including my cousins, Connor and Brock, who gave me cowboy ideas when I was plotting—thank them for the way Tucker roped in June in their book, and Dusty's approach to money and women. I come from cowboys on both sides, and my parents, grandparents, and uncles have influenced quite a few of my Arcadia Creek characters, as well as the town itself.

Thank you, Grandpa Shorty, for giving me so much great content for Dusty's grandfather. You keep us laughing, and I love you.

Thank you to all the readers who went through this book and gave me feedback about the characters and their relationships. To my beta readers and sensitivity readers: Brooke Losee, Justena White, Emily Flynn, Maren Sommer, and Jacque Stevens. Huge thank you Mandy Biesinger for your sensitivity read, for giving me confidence and loving Dusty.

Thank you to my editor, Karie Crawford, for cleaning up my

words on a technical level. You are so important to me and your comments make me laugh. I love that I get to keep my Texas card.

Thanks to my critique group, Deborah Hathaway, Jess Heileman, and Martha Keyes. Thank you to all the ARC readers, bookstagrammers, and readers who leave reviews, post about the book, or tell your friends to pick it up. You are the reason I can keep writing these, and my gratitude knows no bounds.

Thanks to Melody Jeffries for the perfect cover. I love love love it. The characters are spot on, as always.

Thank you Jon for being everything to me. Our kids are pretty rad too, and I love our little family. Thank you to my Father in Heaven for all of the books in my life, for blessing me with the skill to write and the stamina to keep publishing.

Have a blessed day, y'all.

ABOUT THE AUTHOR

Kasey Stockton is a staunch lover of all things romantic. She doesn't discriminate between genres and enjoys a wide variety of happily ever afters. She publishes both contemporary and historical novels, and all of her titles fall under clean romance. She loves reading, chocolate, and period dramas, but nothing tops her very own prince charming, their three children, and their sweet goldendoodle.

Made in the USA
Coppell, TX
30 January 2025

45190941R00215